MORTIMER

SEASON *of* SECRETS

Carole
MORTIMER
SEASON of
SECRETS

MILLS
BOON

Published in Great Britain 2017
By Mills & Boon, an imprint of HarperCollins*Publishers*
1 London Bridge Street, London, SE1 9GF

SEASON OF SECRETS
© 2017 Harlequin Books S.A.

Not Just a Seduction © 2013 Carole Mortimer
Not Just a Governess © 2013 Carole Mortimer
Not Just a Wallflower © 2013 Carole Mortimer

ISBN: 978-0-263-93063-4

09-0417

Printed and bound
by CPI Group (UK) Ltd, Croydon, CRO 4YY

NOT JUST A SEDUCTION

CAROLE MORTIMER

Carole Mortimer was born and lives in the UK. She is married to Peter and they have six sons. She has been writing for Mills & Boon since 1978 and is the author of almost 200 books. She writes for both the Mills & Boon Historical and Modern lines. Carole is a *USA Today* bestselling author and in 2012 was recognised by Queen Elizabeth II for her 'outstanding contribution to literature'.

Visit Carole at carolemortimer.co.uk or on Facebook.

Chapter One

April, 1817
The London home of Lady Cicely Hawthorne.

"I trust, ladies, that you have not begun to discuss the matter of our grandsons' future wives without me...?" Edith St. Just, Dowager Duchess of Royston, frowned down the length of her aristocratic nose as she entered the salon where her two closest friends sat on the sofa in cozy conversation together.

"We would not think of doing such a thing, Edith." Her hostess stood up to cross the room and greet her with a warm kiss on both of her powdered cheeks.

"Of course we would not." A smiling Lady Jocelyn Ambrose, Dowager Countess of Chambourne, also rose to her feet.

The three women had been firm friends since some fifty years ago when, at the age of eighteen, they had shared a coming-out Season, their friendship continuing after they had all married. After becoming mothers and then grandmothers in the same years, the ladies continued to meet at least once a week while their respective husbands were still alive and sometimes two or three times a week since being widowed.

The dowager duchess nodded her satisfaction with her friends' replies before turning to the young lady who had accompanied her into the salon. "You may join Miss Thompson and Mrs. Spencer at their sewing, Ellie."

Eleanor Rosewood gave a brief curtsy to the lady who was not only her step-great-aunt by marriage but also her benefactress before stepping lightly across the room to join the other companions quietly sewing in the window alcove. The ladies, much older than her nineteen years, nevertheless smiled at her in welcome. As they had for this past year.

If not for the dowager duchess's kindness, Ellie feared that she might have been forced to offer herself up to the tender mercies of becoming one of the demimonde after the death of her mother and stepfather had revealed she had not only been left penniless but seriously in debt. Edith St. Just, hearing of her nephew's profligacy, had wasted no time in sweeping into his stepdaughter's heavily mortgaged home and paying off those debts before gathering Ellie up to her ample bosom and making a place for her in her own household as her companion. This past year in that lady's employ had revealed to Ellie that Edith St. Just's outward appearance of stern severity hid a heart of gold.

Unfortunately the same could not be said of her grandson, the arrogant and ruthless Justin St. Just, Duke of Royston, the haughtiness of his own demeanor a reflection of the steel within…

"Are you sure this is altogether wise?" Lady Cicely ventured uncertainly. "Thorne is sure to be most displeased with me if he should discover I have plotted behind his back to secure him a wife."

"Humph." The dowager duchess snorted down the length of her aristocratic nose as she took a seat beside the unlit fireplace. "We may plot all we like, Cicely, but it will be our grandsons' decisions as to whether or not they are equally as enamored of our choices of brides for them. Besides, our grandsons are all past the age of eight and twenty, two of them never having married, the third long a widower, and none of them giving so much as a glance in the direction of the sweet young things paraded before them with the advent of each new Season."

"And can you blame them?" Lady Cicely frowned. "When those young girls seem to get sillier and sillier each year?"

"That silliness is not exclusive to the present." The dowager duchess frowned. "My own daughter-in-law, but eighteen when Robert married her, was herself evidence of that very silliness when a year later she chose to name my only grandson Justin—to be coupled with St. Just! Which is why it is our duty to seek out more sensible women to be the future brides of our respective grandsons, and mothers of the future heirs."

Lady Cicely did not look convinced. "It is only that Thorne has such an icy demeanor when angry…"

Lady Jocelyn gave her friend a consoling grimace. "I am afraid Edith is, as usual, perfectly correct. If we are to see our grandsons suitably married, then I fear we shall have to be the ones to arrange matters. No doubts they will all thank us for it one day. Besides," she added coyly, "with the advent of my ball tomorrow evening, I do believe that I have already set things in motion regarding Christian's future."

"Indeed?" The dowager duchess raised steely brows.

"Oh, do tell!" Lady Cicely encouraged excitedly.

Ellie, listening attentively to the conversation while giving the outward appearance of concentrating upon her own sewing, was also curious to hear how Lady Jocelyn believed she had managed to arrange the securing of a wife for her grandson, the cynical and jaded—frighteningly so, in Ellie's opinion!—Lord Christian Ambrose, Earl of Chambourne…

Chapter Two

"Tell me, how did you explain your…loss of innocence to your elderly husband on your wedding night?"

Sylvie's spine stiffened upon hearing that soft and cruelly mocking voice just behind her as she stood alone in the candlelit ballroom in the Dowager Countess of Chambourne's London home. A voice, and man, standing so near to her that the warmth of his breath slightly ruffled the loose curls at her temple and beside her pearl-adorned earlobe. So near that she could feel the heat of that gentleman's body through the silk of her gown…

She would have been foolish not to have expected some response from Lord Christian Ambrose, Earl of Chambourne, after arriving at his grandmother's ball some half an hour earlier and finding the countess's coldly arrogant grandson at that lady's side as he acted as host to her hostess.

Yes, Sylvie had known, and expected, when she had accepted the invitation to this ball, some sort of acknowledgment of their previous acquaintance from Christian, but she had not expected it to be quite so cruelly pointed in nature!

She stiffened her spine and drew in a slow and controlled

breath before turning to face him, her outward expression one of calm disdain. At the same time, her pulse gave an alarmed leap as she had to look up at least a foot in order to meet familiar moss-green eyes set in a face of such stark male beauty it might have been carved by Michelangelo. Arrogant dark brows above those moss-green eyes, high cheekbones either side of a long and aristocratic nose, chiseled lips above a square and determined jaw, raven-dark locks falling rakishly across the wide and intelligent brow.

She did not need to lower her gaze to know that Christian's black evening jacket had been tailored to fit like a glove over the wide expanse of his shoulders and muscled chest. His linen snowy white beneath a pale-silver waistcoat, black satin breeches encasing the long and muscled length of his thighs.

No, Sylvie did not need to look to know all of those things, having taken in Christian Ambrose's appearance fully upon her arrival earlier. And cursed herself for noticing that Christian had only grown more handsome—disturbingly so—rather than less, in the years since she had last seen him.

Four years, to be precise. Years that had seen Sylvie change to the coolly composed woman she presented to Society this evening, rather than that young girl of eighteen summers who had been totally besotted with this gentleman's rakish good looks.

That same young girl who had so trustingly given this man the innocence which he now dismissed so contemptuously...

To say that Christian had been disarmed to discover that Lady Sylviana Moorland, widowed Countess of Ampthill, was one of the guests at his grandmother's ball this evening would have been deeply understating the matter. He could not have been more surprised if that upstart Napoleon, presently and hopefully forever incarcerated on St. Helena, had arrived on his grandmother's doorstep brandishing an invitation!

Not that he had not been fully aware of Sylviana Moorland's

return to Society, now that her year of mourning her husband was well and truly over—indeed, it was closer to two years since Colonel Lord Gerald Moorland had been struck down at the battle of Waterloo. And having heard that gentleman's widow had returned to town at the start of the Season, Christian had taken the steps necessary to ensure that they were never in attendance at the same social function.

Steps that had been shattered this evening by his own grandmother, of all people!

Unintentionally, of course, for surely his grandmother was as much in ignorance of Christian's previous acquaintance with Sylviana as was the rest of Society.

If anything Sylvie was more beautiful than Christian remembered, no longer that young girl on the brink of womanhood but now fully matured into a beautiful woman. The gold of her hair was arranged in artful curls upon her crown, with several loose tendrils at her temples and nape. Brown eyes surrounded by long dark lashes, and as deep and impenetrable as the golden molasses they resembled in her heart-shaped face; a small and delicate nose, with full and pouting lips above a small and determined chin. Her body was no longer coltishly slender, either, but lush and sensual, the fullness of her creamy breasts spilling over the low neckline of her green silk gown.

A gown of the same moss-green color as Christian's eyes…Deliberately so?

The challenge in her dark gaze as she gazed up at him so disdainfully would seem to imply so. "How unfortunate, my lord, that the passing of the years appears to have done nothing to improve your manners!"

Christian gave a hard and derisive smile. "Did you expect them to have done so?"

She eyed him coolly. "One might have hoped so, yes…"

"Why did you come here this evening, Sylvie?" He snapped his impatience with that coolness. "Or perhaps you prefer the grander Sylviana now that you are become a countess?" he added contemptuously as he saw the way she stiffened at his familiarity.

"I believe 'my lady' and 'my lord' are a more fitting address between two people of equal rank." She had drawn herself up to her full height of just over five feet. "And I am here this evening because your grandmother invited me."

Christian gave a derisive snort. "And are your invitations into Society so few and far between that you must needs accept this one?"

"On the contrary." That golden gaze raked over him contemptuously. "Perhaps you have not heard, my lord, but I believe I am considered to be something of a matrimonial catch this Season, and as such in receipt of more invitations than I could ever hope to accept."

His mouth twisted with disgust. "I had heard that your elderly husband left you a rich widow, yes. Which, no doubt, was your intention when you married a man so much older than yourself."

Her eyes widened. "How dare you—"

"Oh, I believe, Sylvie, that you will find I dare much

where you are concerned!" His eyes glittered dangerously. "A first lover's privilege, shall we say?"

"No, we will not say!" All the color had now faded from her cheeks.

Christian gave a humorless smile. "What reason *did* you give your ancient husband when he discovered that there was no maidenhead for him to breach on your wedding night?"

It took every effort of will on Sylvie's part not to flinch at the

unmistakable disdain in Christian Ambrose's tone, and the hard censor of his moss-green gaze as it raked over her with slow contempt, from her blond curls down to her green-slippered feet, before shifting, deliberately lingering, on the firm swell of her breasts.

As if she were nothing more than a slab of meat on a butcher's block that he was considering the merits of purchasing!

As if this man had no recollection of once upon a time slowly removing every article of clothing from her body—much more than once!—before making love to her as if she were the most delicate, precious thing upon this earth…

Once upon a time?

For Sylvie it was a different lifetime!

Certainly she was no longer that innocent young miss who had believed, in her naïveté, that Christian Ambrose, a gentleman six years her senior—in experience as well as years—returned the deep love she had felt for him. That trusting young girl had disappeared long, long ago, upon the realization that she had been nothing more than yet another female conquest to the rakish Christian Ambrose.

In her place was Sylviana Moorland, wealthy widow of

Colonel Lord Gerald Moorland, a coolly composed woman of two and twenty, who felt as cynical toward love as the gentleman now standing before her gazing down at her so disdainfully.

Sylvie drew in a deep, controlling breath. "I—"

"I believe it would be best if we were to finish this conversation outside on the terrace," Christian Ambrose grated harshly even as he grasped Sylvie's arm and pulled her toward one of the sets of open French doors.

She resisted that painful hold upon her arm. "Unhand me at once, sir—" She broke off her protest abruptly as Christian turned to focus the full fierceness of his icy-cold moss-green eyes upon her, eyes that had once caused her to melt with passion but which she now knew only too well to be wary of. "People are staring at us…" she substituted lamely.

"Let them," he grated unconcernedly as he continued to pull her effortlessly across the candlelit room, through the open doorway and out onto the dark seclusion of the terrace.

Chapter Three

No sooner had they stepped outside into that shadowed darkness than Sylvie felt the steely strength of Christian's arms as he pulled her hard against him, the lowering of his head blocking out the brightness of the moon overhead as his lips claimed hers.

Not a gentle or exploratory kiss, but that of an experienced lover, demanding she return that same heat of passion. An experienced lover who knew exactly how to kiss and caress the woman in his arms until she was weak with arousal…

Try as Sylvie might to resist that seduction, and her determination never to fall for this man's rakish charms ever again, she found she had no defenses against the onslaught. Christian's tongue parted her lips before plunging possessively inside, his hands moving in a restless caress down the length of her spine before cupping beneath her bottom to pull her in so tight against him Sylvie could feel the hard ridge of his arousal.

Betraying heat flooded between her thighs, her nipples

aching beneath the bodice of her gown as Christian deliberately rubbed his chest rhythmically against them, eliciting
a want, an unwanted hunger deep inside her—

Christian wrenched his mouth from hers to lower his
lips to the swell of her breasts, his tongue rasping, lapping,
across that sensitized flesh before he tugged down on the
bodice of her gown. One of those swollen orbs spilled out
of its confinement to allow him to place his lips about her
nipple.

Arousing a heat that none of Sylvie's late-night imag-
inings had even come close to replicating as she stroked
the nubbin between her thighs, faster and harder until she
reached a shuddering climax.

Sylvie felt that same climax rapidly building within her
now as Christian continued to caress her nipple, harder,
deeper, teeth biting, tongue laving as her back arched to
press her breast deeper into that sensual delight.

She had no intention of ever falling in love with this man
again, but that was no reason why she should not take the
sexual gratification he now offered, in the same way he had
once taken sexual gratification from her.

Sylvie parted her thighs and moved up on her toes so that
she might rub herself against the hard ridge of Christian's
arousal, perfectly positioning that hardness against herself
as she stroked herself against him in a rapidly increasing
rhythm—

She gave a groan of protest as Christian wrenched his
mouth away from her breast even as he grasped her shoulders to steady her before he stepped back and away from
her, his eyes a hard and glittering green. "I do not in the
least mind paying for a woman's...services, but I prefer to
know the price of those services *before* I bed her rather than

be apprised of it afterward," he drawled contemptuously as he straightened the lace at his cuffs.

"Price…?" she repeated sharply.

He gave a mocking inclination of his head. "I have no doubts that a man of Ampthill's advanced years thought himself truly blessed when he took such a young beauty as his wife. I, however, am in no hurry to contemplate marriage," Christian drawled contemptuously, at the same time feeling a moment's regret as Sylvie set the front of her gown to rights. "Especially when I have already sampled your goods—"

He got no further in his insult as the palm of Sylvie's left hand made loud and painful contact with his right cheek. "I will allow you that one small lapse," he bit out harshly, a nerve now pulsing in that no doubt rapidly reddening cheek. "But be warned, Sylvie, that the next time I will retaliate in kind."

"You are as much a bastard as you ever were, I see!" Her eyes flashed.

Christian raised mocking brows. "Because I gladly took what you offered four years ago?"

Her eyes glittered darkly. "Because you took what you wanted before departing to enjoy the licentiousness of London and then returning to your regiment with not a thought for what might become of me!"

Christian studied her flushed face between narrowed lids. "Unless I am mistaken, you became the Countess of Moorland."

Her hands had clenched into fists at her sides, her breasts quickly rising and falling as she breathed deeply. "And you returned to your life of debauchery with not a thought to the fact that I was ruined. Used goods."

"Not so 'used' you did not marry within months of our parting. And to another earl, no less," he added. "Although well beyond the flush of youth." Christian's mouth twisted derisively at the thought of the gentleman who had been old enough to be Sylvie's grandfather rather than her husband. "But perhaps he was so grateful to have you in his bed that he chose not to question your lack of virginity?"

There appeared a look of such chilly contempt upon Sylvie's face that it took every effort on Christian's part not to flinch from that coldness. "You may insult me all you wish," she bit out. "But you will never talk of Gerald again in that tone. He was a gentleman. A man of honor. Of integrity. And you—you are not even fit to so much as lick one of his boots!"

Christian scowled his displeasure. Not because Sylvie had just roundly insulted him, but because her words made it very clear that even if she had not loved her aged husband, she had deeply respected and liked him. A respect and liking she made it equally clear she did not feel for Christian...

Did he want Sylvie's liking and respect?

Before this evening his answer would have been a resounding no. Before he had kissed her again, caressed her, suckled the fullness of her breast and felt the heat of her response to him, he would have said no. But now? How did Christian feel now that he had done all of those things?

Four years ago Sylvie had been the only daughter of the family living on the small estate neighboring his own in Berkshire. A young girl he had seen about the village for most of his life, even if his years away at school, university and latterly the army had meant he had never known her well.

But he had come home on leave from his regiment the

summer of 1813, battle-worn and inwardly scarred and sickened from seeing too much blood and the death of many of
his friends. And the young and beautiful Sylvie Buchanan,
with her ready smile and innocently eager body, had been
exactly the distraction Christian had needed to help him
forget, if only for a few weeks, that he must soon return to
that bloodbath.

Their first meeting had been completely accidental.
Christian, strolling about the countryside several days after
his arrival, had come upon Sylvie swimming in a curve of
the local river.

Even now Christian could remember the warmth of that
day and how the sun had turned Sylvie's long hair to rip-
pling gold as it flowed out to float loosely in the water behind her after she had given a surprised shriek at espying
him on the grassy riverbank and dipped below the water to
just below her chin.

Far from leaving, as she had begged him to do, Christian
had instead made himself comfortable on that grassy riverbank and laughingly dared her to come out of the water. A
dare Sylvie had protested, her beautiful face burning hotly
with embarrassment. Christian had persisted in his request
at the same time as he informed her he was in no hurry to
leave, his breath catching in his throat when, almost an hour
later, she finally stood up in the water to reveal she wore
only a wet and clinging chemise.

The water had rendered that chemise almost completely
see-through, revealing all of her charms as she stepped fully
from the water—pale and satiny skin, those high and tilting
breasts tipped by rosy nipples, the slightly darker-blond curls
nestled between her thighs, her legs long and slender—and
all causing Christian's manhood to harden in a way it had

not done in the last months of bloody battle, and which he had secretly feared it might never do again.

The relief of knowing that his lack of desire had only been a temporary aberration had allowed Christian to rein in his own needs and only kiss Sylvie lightly that first day, not wanting to frighten her with the depth of the desire he felt for her.

He had so enjoyed her company, her innocence of passion, that he had arranged to meet her at the same place the following day. And the day following that one. And the one after that. And as each day passed, their kisses deepened, became more passionate, needy, quickly advancing to caresses, and then finally the two of them had made love on that grassy knoll beside the river, the sunshine continuing to shine down on them as Christian made love to Sylvie a second time, and then a third, his hunger to possess her, to claim her, seeming never ending.

A hunger that Christian's response to kissing Sylvie again this evening had now shown him, no matter how he might wish it otherwise, had never completely gone away…

Chapter Four

His mouth twisted disdainfully. "I believe I would far rather lick the honey from between your silken thighs than I would your husband's boots," he drawled suggestively. "Something, if my memory serves me correctly, that you would also enjoy?" He quirked one mocking brow.

Her breath caught in her throat. "You are disgusting!"

"Have a care, Sylvie." His eyes narrowed dangerously.

"And if I choose not to do so?" she dared.

Christian gave an unconcerned shrug. "Then you will suffer the consequences of deliberately challenging me."

Sylvie gave an involuntary shiver as she heard the steely edge beneath Christian's tone, knowing she should not have attended the Dowager Countess of Chambourne's ball this evening.

Recently returned to Society, and having only seen Christian Ambrose occasionally from a great distance, Sylvie had known that it was only a matter of time before the two of them were introduced by a hostesses at one function or another. That being so, Sylvie had decided that she would prefer to be in control of when and how that meeting took place, her years of being married to the gentlemanly Gerald having led her to believe she was now immune to Christian Ambrose's dangerous brand of sensuality.

Instead she had found herself in his arms within minutes of their having met again, telling her that if anything, her response to Christian's lovemaking was even more intense, more immediate, than it had been four years ago.

Because *she* was also four years older? And as such her physical desires had become that much more mature too?

Whatever the reason, Sylvie knew she should not have come here this evening. Should never have risked drawing Christian's attention to her. And she most certainly should never have allowed herself to respond to him on even a physical level! He—

"Why did you not wait for me, as I asked you to?"

Sylvie blinked up at him. "I beg your pardon?"

Christian's jaw tightened. "Four years ago. I told you I loved you and asked you to wait for me." And only thoughts of this woman waiting for him in England had kept him alive.

Her chin rose defensively as she recalled how his own household in the country, unaware of Sylvie's previous involvement with Christian, had been indulgently abuzz with the rumors of his return to his rakish behavior during his week's stay in London prior to returning to his regiment. Rumors that had put Sylvie's own importance in his life in its proper context.

She lifted her chin. "And when, after two months, you had not so much as written me a single letter, I had no choice but to accept that our affair was over."

He scowled. "There was a reason I did not write to you—"

"None that are acceptable to me, I assure you." Sylvie gave him a contemptuous smile.

Christian's jaw tightened as he remembered those weeks he lay suffering, when only thoughts of Sylvie, waiting for him at home, had prevented him from succumbing to the fatality of his infected wound. "And how long after I left did you wait before accepting Ampthill's offer of marriage?" His top lip curled back in disgust. "A week? Two? On the basis, no doubt, that an earl 'in the hand' was better than the uncertainty of the return of the one who had so recently gone back to the war!"

Sylvie gave a rueful shake of her head. "How dare you stand there and accuse me of inconstancy when you were the one who left without so much as a single glance back at the girl you had used to fill your hours of boredom whilst in the country!"

"I told you I loved you and asked you to wait for me, damn it!" His eyes glittered.

Sylvie forced herself not to wilt under the barrage of Christian's accusing tone, distrustful of that anger as she had good reason to be distrustful of the man himself. "I was eighteen years old, Christian, with all of the impatience of youth."

"So impatient you could not even have waited a few months?" Christian frowned as he recalled finally returning to England three months after he and Sylvie had last seen each other, only to be informed by her proud parents, when he rode over to their estate to pay his respects, that Sylviana no longer lived on their estate with them, but was now residing in Bedfordshire with her husband, Colonel Lord Gerald Moorland, Earl of Ampthill.

Christian had no recollection of the rest of his conversation that day with Henry and Jessica Buchanan, or of taking his leave some half an hour or so later. He had felt as if someone had punched him in the chest, rendering him both speechless and numb. He'd had no choice but to accept that Sylvie was now another man's wife, and as such, was far beyond his reach.

That numbness had lasted for several days, only to be replaced by anger and disillusionment. He had believed Sylvie was different from all those other marriage-minded chits he so frequently met in Society, that she actually cared about him, Christian the man, rather than his title. The fact that she had married an ancient earl in the few months of his absence showed Christian that had not been the case, that the title was everything to her.

And so had begun the months and years of debauchery he had embarked upon following his disillusionment. Those same years that had quickly earned him the reputation for being a rake and a dissolute, a man who cared naught for the softer emotions and everything for the pleasure of the moment.

"Obviously you could not," Christian answered his own question contemptuously. "And as luck would have it, you only had to suffer an old man's pawing for a year or two before you were conveniently left his widow and in possession of all his fortune."

Sylvie felt the color leech from her cheeks at Christian's deliberately insulting tone. An insult she did not deserve from this particular man. Not now, and certainly not four years ago.

She had been deeply in love with Christian. Even when she had been told of his behavior in London after he left her, she had tried to dismiss it as just rumors, malicious gossip that could not possibly be true. The months of silence that had followed those rumors had left her with no choice but to accept she had merely been a diversion for him during the weeks he spent in the country attending to estate matters.

"You know absolutely nothing of my marriage to Gerald—"

"I know enough to realize that an old man of sixty could not possibly have hoped to satisfy the physical demands of a young girl of eighteen!" His top lip curled back with distaste. "I know *you*, Sylvie," he added softly. "How to touch and arouse every silken inch of your body." He reached out to run his fingers lightly across the firm swell of her breasts revealed by the low neckline of her gown. "I have watched you, enjoyed you, time and time again, as you experienced climax after shattering climax. Did Moorland do that for you, Sylvie? Did he touch you in all the intimate places that I know give you such pleasure—"

"Stop it!" she protested, knowing and regretting that the heated flush to her cheeks and breasts revealed how much Christian's words had aroused her. Aroused her, but never again would she allow her heart to be broken by this man. "All this talk of the past achieves nothing—"

"And if it does not have to be the past?" Those long and caressing fingers dipped beneath the bodice of her gown to pluck unerringly at one roused nipple. "It so happens I am currently without a mistress—"

"And I am not so desperate for a man's intimate touch that I would ever consider accepting such an offer from you!" Sylvie glared up at him. Not on his terms, at least. Not on any terms that would endanger her heart or the independent life she now lived.

Those sculpted lips curved into a humorless smile. "All

evidence to the contrary, my dear." He squeezed that roused nipple between thumb and finger, looking down at her dispassionately as she drew her breath in sharply. "Are you damp and ready for me between your thighs, Sylvie? Perhaps I should touch you there too and see for myself—"

"Leave me be!" Sylvie could stand it no more, slapping his hand away before stepping back.

"You are," Christian murmured with quiet satisfaction as he continued to regard her flushed cheeks dispassionately. "You will give me the name of the gentleman—or gentlemen?—currently sharing the pleasure of your body and your bed," he said.

"And why would I wish to do that…?" She eyed him contemptuously.

"So that I may dispense with his, or their, services, of course." He shrugged those broad shoulders. "I may be considered an out-and-out rake by all of Society, but I draw the line at sharing my woman with another man!"

Sylvie gave an indignant gasp. "I have no intention of ever becoming *your woman*!"

"Oh, but you will, Sylvie," Christian assured her confidently. "In fact, I intend calling upon you tomorrow so that we might…discuss the terms of that agreement."

Sylvie stared up at him for several long moments, knowing by the cold implacability of Christian's pale-green gaze that he meant exactly what he said. "I do believe that your arrogance has now become as large as your overinflated ego!" she finally snapped dismissively. "Now, if you will excuse me, I have a headache, and wish to go and make my excuses to your grandmother before taking my leave." She turned briskly on one satin slipper before marching away.

Christian watched between narrowed lids as Sylvie

walked the length of the terrace before stepping lightly back into the ballroom, knowing he needed to delay his own return several more minutes if he was not to appear before his grandmother with an indecent erection tenting the front of his silk breeches.

And despite her protests to the contrary, he had every intention of having Sylvie satisfied on the morrow…

Once safely returned to her home in Berkeley Square, Sylvie went straight up the stairs, moving quietly into the candlelit bedchamber before nodding dismissal of the nurse and taking that lady's place in the chair beside the small bed, the tension leaving her expression as she gazed down at her sleeping daughter.

Sylvie felt a deep outpouring of love as she reached out to gently touch the abundance of dark curls framing those baby cheeks and small rosebud of a mouth, and knowing that if Christianna's eyes were open, they would be a beautiful, warm, moss green.

The exact same shade as her father's…

Chapter Five

"What are you doing here?" Christian scowled darkly at Sylvie when he entered the drawing room of his London home the morning following his grandmother's ball, accepting that he owed his butler an apology for disbelieving him when that gentleman had entered Christian's darkened bedchamber a few minutes ago and informed him that Lady Sylviana Moorland, Countess of Ampthill, was waiting downstairs to speak with him.

Christian's mood was taciturn at best this morning, after the hours he had necessarily spent at his grandmother's ball following Sylvie's early departure, most of that time spent in fending off his grandmother's less-than-subtle determination to see him in the company of Lady Vanessa Styles, a young lady of one and twenty whom his grandmother had obviously decided would make him a suitable countess.

Having finally managed to escape those machinations shortly after midnight, Christian had spent the hours until daybreak at one of the more disreputable clubs, rebuffing the obvious attentions of the willing ladies there in favor of drinking copious amounts of brandy and winning at the gaming tables.

As a consequence he had not been best pleased to be awakened, only hours after falling fully clothed into his bed, and informed by his butler of Sylvie's presence downstairs in his drawing room. So certain had Christian been of the butler's error that he had not even bothered to tidy his appearance before coming downstairs, let alone change his clothes.

An oversight he deeply regretted as he saw the way Sylvie's tiny nose wrinkled with distaste as she took in his disreputable appearance—the crumpled clothes he had been wearing the evening before, the darkness of his curls in disarray, a growth of beard darkening his jaw. That jaw now tightened. "I asked—"

"I heard you," Sylvie spoke quietly, her own appearance immaculate as she perched, ladylike, upon the edge of her chair, several loose gold curls peeking out from beneath the yellow silk bonnet that was an exact match in color for her gown, her hands and arms covered by cream lace gloves.

Christian gave a wince as the brightness of those colors hurt his eyes. "And yet you did not answer," he bit out.

In truth, Sylvie regretted the need for her having to come here at all, let alone finding herself faced with Christian's disreputable appearance. His evening clothes were crumpled, as if he had slept in them. At the same time, the dark shadows below his eyes and the stubble on his arrogant chin gave the impression he had not been to bed at all. To sleep, at least…

She stiffened her spine. "Perhaps you would like to return upstairs and…see to your appearance before we commence our conversation…?"

He raised mocking brows as he threw himself down in the chair facing her own. "I am perfectly comfortable as I am, thank you," he drawled dismissively as he leaned his elbows on the arms of the chair and steepled his fingers in front of him. "And I believe we are already in conversation...?"

Sylvie drew her breath in sharply, having known the moment she saw Christian's rumpled appearance that she should not have come here today without first making an appointment. She had thought to put Christian at a disadvantage by doing so, and instead she once again found herself the one who was wrong-footed. "You put forward a suggestion to me yesterday evening—"

"If you are referring to becoming my mistress, that was not a suggestion but a statement of intent," he cut in, eyes gleaming through narrowed lids as he looked at her above those long, steepled fingers.

Sylvie was well aware of that. Just as she knew she had no intention of allowing this man to call at her home. The home where Christianna also resided...

"Perhaps your...other activities last night have now rendered that conversation obsolete?"

Those chiseled lips tilted in a humorless smile. "If you wish to know if I bedded another woman last night then just ask, Sylvie," he mocked. "I promise I will not lie to you."

"That will certainly be a novelty!"

Christian's eyes narrowed in warning. "To my knowledge I have never lied to you. Nor will I lie to you now."

Sylvie's cheeks warmed even as she berated herself for caring one way or the other whether or not Christian had gone to another woman's bed last night. In truth, it would be preferable if he had done so, would give her the perfect excuse to turn down his scandalous offer to her the previous evening. "Very well. Did you bed another woman last night?"

"No."

"Oh."

"Do not look so disappointed, Sylvie." He gave a hard laugh. "Why would I even consider the idea of bedding another woman after making love to you earlier in the evening?"

Her mouth firmed at his mockery. "You must know that you are not known for your constancy in regard to any particular woman."

He raised dark brows. "And is that to be a condition of our own arrangement? That, for the time of our…affair, I will occupy only your bed?"

"We do not have an arrangement—"

"As yet," Christian bit out decisively. "But that is your reason for being here today, is it not? So that we might thrash out the terms and conditions of such a relationship between the two of us?" The alcoholic fog and lack of sleep had now cleared enough from Christian's head for him to have considered all of the reasons Sylvie had chosen to call on him this morning.

She wished to reiterate that there would be no affair between them, now, or in the future? Something she could far more easily have told him in a note, or when he called upon her later in the day.

That she had decided to take another man as her lover? He was sure Sylvie knew him well enough to know that he would never accept such a decision.

Which only left the more obvious reason: that Sylvie had decided to accept his offer after all, but on her own terms.

And Christian was very interested in knowing what those terms might be.

"Well?" he prompted at her continued silence. "Is that not the reason you are here, Sylvie?"

Chapter Six

Damn him!

Damn, damn, damn Lord Christian Matthew Faulkner Ambrose, the Earl of Chambourne, to the hell he deserved!

Because, having considered all of the options during the long and sleepless night, and out of a need to protect Christianna, that was precisely the reason Sylvie had called upon him this morning.

Christian had made it abundantly clear the evening before that, the two of them now having met again, he had no intention of quietly absenting himself from her life a second time. Not, at least, until he had taken what he wanted from her. As clear as he had made it that what he wanted was *her*, in his bed, for as long as it took him to tire of her again. None of which would have—should have—mattered in the least to Sylvie after Christian's despicable treatment of her four years ago.

And it would not have done.

If not for Christianna.

The man Sylvie had met yesterday evening was even less the man she had thought him to be four years ago, the

Christian from the past having at least given the appearance of warmth and caring. Last night he had been every inch the cold and arrogant Lord Christian Ambrose, the Earl of Chambourne, a known rake and a man who cared for no one—except a possible affection for his grandmother?—and neither expected nor wanted anyone to care for him. Even so, Sylvie had no doubts that he would care about his daughter if he ever learned of her existence. As he must surely do, if he were ever to actually see Christianna.

Which was precisely the reason Sylvie had decided to accept, and put her own limitations—some control—on the... relationship, Christian stated, no, demanded, there now be between the two of them.

That, and the fact that—despite everything that had once passed between them—Sylvie still responded physically to this man. Her heart, she was sure, was in no further danger from this man; how could it be when he had used her so shamefully in the past?

She rose briskly to her feet. "Being a young and wealthy widow, I have received several such offers as yours these past few months—"

"A young, wealthy and beautiful widow," Christian corrected softly.

Sylvie refused to allow herself to be moved by his compliment; Christian Ambrose was a silver-tongued devil bent on seduction, nothing more. A seduction that would take place under Sylvie's rules or not at all. "I obviously cannot vouch as to that—"

"I can," he bit out tersely. "If anything, Sylvie, you are more beautiful now than you were four years ago." And it was true, Christian acknowledged with a frown. There was a confidence to Sylvie now that had not been present four years earlier, an elegance in her carriage and demeanor that implied a coolness to her nature that Christian knew to be only skin deep; her responses to him yesterday evening had been every bit as fiery as he remembered from the past.

"Yes. Well." She gave him a scathing glance. "Several of these gentleman have been…pressing, in their attentions—"

Christian's eyes were narrowed. "Tell me the names of these other gentlemen and I will consign them to the devil."

She gave a shake of her head. "I only mentioned them at all in order to explain why I have decided to accept an offer of…protection, from one gentleman, a gentleman of my own choice, rather than continue to be plagued by many."

"And I am to be that gentleman…?"

Sylvie looked at him coolly. "Only if you are willing to accept the relationship under my terms."

His eyes narrowed. "And those terms are…?"

She drew in a deep breath. "One—there will be no other lovers in your life for as long as this…arrangement between us lasts, the arrangement becoming null and void if that should ever be the case."

"I believe I have already stated there will be no other women."

"No, you stated I should not be allowed other lovers but you," she recalled dryly.

He frowned grimly. "I give you my word there will be no other women for me, either, for the time of our own affair."

Her mouth thinned. "Two—we will meet a maximum of two nights a week—"

"Two?" Christian repeated, astounded. "I had it more in mind to spend every night together until we had sated our desire for each other."

"A maximum of two," Sylvie repeated firmly.

"Three," he stated stubbornly. "And let us hope that you will succeed in so satiating my appetite during those times that I have no strength left to so much as think of bedding another woman the other four nights of the week!"

Sylvie looked at him searchingly for several long minutes before nodding slowly. "Very well, three."

"Beginning with this one," he added softly.

Sylvie's eyes widened in alarm. Tonight? Christian wished to start bedding her this very night?

Somehow, in all her thinking the evening before, Sylvie had avoided actually dwelling on *when* Christian would require her to start sharing his bed. Just the thought of it being this night, in several hours' time, was enough to make her tremble. In trepidation, she hoped…

"Very well," she agreed. "Three—our times together will be spent here rather than in my own home—"

"Why?"

Sylvie avoided directly meeting that piercing green gaze. "It is enough that I prefer it should be so."

Christian's lids narrowed as he looked at her searchingly for several long seconds before murmuring. "It is not the usual way of things…"

"I am aware of that."

"The fact that you are here this morning, calling at the home of a single gentleman without so much as your maid in attendance, would be cause for gossip among the ton if any were to learn of it, let alone the knowledge that you are spending three nights a week here in my bed."

"Then we will have to endeavor to ensure that none of the ton learn the terms of our arrangement," Sylvie dismissed. "And I will not be spending the whole night here, merely a few hours."

His brow rose. "You intend sneaking out of my house like a thief in the middle of the night?"

Her jaw tensed. "Gentlemen do it all the time, so why should I not do the same!"

"Why would you even risk such a thing?" Christian pondered.

Sylvie's eyes flashed darkly as she looked at him with contempt. "Perhaps because I have no intention of sharing a bed with you in the home I shared with my husband until his death?"

Christian felt a harsh shard of jealousy rip through him at the thought of Sylvie sharing the home—and the bed—of another man. Especially that of the husband she had thrown him over for four years ago.

He rose slowly to his feet, his mouth curving into a hard smile as he saw the way Sylvie instantly took a step back and away from him. "Did you love him after all, then?"

She looked startled for a moment, and then that coolness settled on her face once more. "As I told you yesterday evening, Gerald was a man it was all too easy to respect and admire."

"I asked if you loved him!" Christian reached out to grasp the tops of her arms, his glittering gaze easily holding her own captive.

She moistened her lips with the tip of her tongue. "I have already told you—"

"That you respected and admired Gerald Moorland." A nerve pulsed in Christian's clenched jaw as he continued to glare down at her. "They are the emotions one feels for a favorite uncle, not a husband!"

Possibly because that was how Sylvie had always regarded Gerald, who had been a friend of her father's. That affection had grown exponentially when Gerald, finding her alone and sobbing in the garden during one of his visits, had demanded she tell him what ailed her, only to then offer her the respectability of marriage to him and legitimacy for her unborn babe rather than scandal for her whole family.

Sylvie had initially refused Gerald's offer, of course, claiming that a marriage between the two of them would be unfair to him, when she was still in love with the father of her baby, when a part of her had still hoped—prayed— that the rumors she had heard about Christian were untrue, and that he would either write to her or appear in person and that the two of them would then marry.

But Gerald had been tenacious, repeating his offer several more times during the next few weeks until, tired and heartsick at Christian's continued silence, Sylvie knew she had no choice but to acknowledge she had merely been a passing fancy for him, someone for him to make love to and with during the weeks of his leave from the army.

She looked up to meet Christian's gaze unflinchingly. "Any discussion of my feelings for my husband will not be a part of our arrangement."

Christian frowned down at her in frustration for several minutes, annoyed with Sylvie's stubbornness, but even more annoyed with himself for still desiring her so much he was willing to allow her to dictate the terms of their future relationship. Up to a point!

"I believe it is usual for gentlemen to shake hands at the successful conclusion of a deal," he murmured gruffly. "And for men and women to kiss," he added before his head swooped down and he claimed her lips with his own.

She tasted of honey, and smelt of violets, the fullness of her curves fitting perfectly against Christian as his arms tightened about her and he deepened the kiss, his erection rising to press against her as his tongue swept between the parted softness of her lips—

Sylvie wrenched her mouth from his, her cheeks flushed as she pushed away from him, her eyes bright as she looked up at him, her nose wrinkling with distaste. "You smell of cheap liquor and even cheaper perfume!"

Christian scowled his frustration. At eighteen Sylvie had seemed like an open book to him, her brightness and enthusiasm for life attracting him as nothing else could have done after so many months of battle and death. A brightness and innocence that had been deliberately designed to entice, Christian had realized after he returned to England and learned that she had married another man, another *earl*, in the three short months of his absence.

He found the confident woman who now stood before him, her every thought a mystery to him, totally frustrating and yet no less intriguing.

His mouth firmed. "What time will you come to me tonight?"

Her throat moved as she swallowed before answering. "Does eleven o'clock suit?"

Christian's brows rose. "You do not intend to join me for dinner first?"

She eyed him coolly. "For what purpose?"

He scowled. "So that we might engage in conversation before the bedding."

"Again, for what purpose?" She eyed him disdainfully. "The rakish life you have led these past four years holds no more interest for me than I am sure my own more sedate one does for you."

"Very well." Christian breathed his irritation with her

coolness. "I will expect you here at eleven o'clock this evening. And I will endeavor to ensure there is no lingering odor of 'cheap liquor or even cheaper perfume'!" he taunted as she straightened her appearance in preparation for leaving.

Christian remained where he was for several more minutes after Sylvie's departure, knowing there was something about her acquiescence to becoming his mistress that was... not quite right. Oh, there was no denying her physical response to him the previous evening, or his own determination that Sylvie would become his mistress. But she had fought her own attraction to him last night, been determined that she would not give in to him, that she had no intention of ever becoming 'his woman'. Even under her own terms.

Something had happened to change her mind in those intervening hours, and despite what Sylvie said to the contrary, Christian did not believe for one moment that it had anything to do with those other gentlemen 'pressing' for her attention.

Chapter Seven

"**W**ould you care to join me in a glass of port?" Christian indicated the decanter on the table beside him as he remained seated in an armchair beside the unlit fireplace, looking across the room to where Sylvie stood hesitantly beside the door Smith had recently closed behind her, and looking ethereally beautiful in a gown of deep gold. "Or perhaps you would prefer a glass of wine?"

Sylvie was more than a little disconcerted to find herself in a room that was so obviously Christian Ambrose's private domain, serving as both a library and his study, if the book-lined walls and the cluttered desk in front of the window were any indication.

She was even more disturbed by Christian, his appearance impeccable and stylish this evening, in a dark-green superfine worn over a paler-green waistcoat and snowy-white linen, buff pantaloons outlining the muscled strength of his legs above shiny black Hessians. His dark curls looked slightly damp, as if he had recently bathed, the squareness of his jaw showing no evidence of this morning's stubble.

A pity his manners did not match that gentlemanly

appearance. But no doubt his neglecting to stand up when she had entered the room was an indication of their arrangement.

"Sylvie?" he prompted softly at her continued silence.

Her spine stiffened. "Thank you, but no, I do not require any refreshment. I would much prefer that we just retire to your bedchamber and get this business over and done with."

Christian's eyes widened before narrowing. "You earlier refused conversation, and now you are also refusing to share a glass of wine with me?"

She nodded. "Because I do not believe either of those things to be a requirement of our arrangement."

Christian frowned. "You would prefer, perhaps, that I dispense with the niceties altogether and simply toss your skirts up now and take you where you stand?"

She gasped. "There is no need for crudeness!"

Christian sighed as he placed his glass of port down on the table beside him. "I freely admit I do not quite know what to make of the woman you are now, Sylvie…"

He had been angry with Sylvie four years ago for not waiting for him as he had asked her to do, but he'd had every intention of her enjoying their lovemaking tonight. Of perhaps realizing all she had given up in her youthful eagerness to become Gerald Moorland's countess…But he found her continued coolness, despite having agreed to become his mistress, completely baffling.

"There is nothing to know," she dismissed flatly. "We have an arrangement, I am simply making it clear that I am…willing to begin that arrangement."

Christian looked at her through narrowed lids for several moments before giving a rueful shake of his head. "I am used to receiving a little more enthusiasm from my lovers."

"No doubt. But I should perhaps tell you—warn you—that there have only been two men in my life, Christian." Her cheeks were flushed. "You. And my husband. I am not—I ask that you not expect me to have the physical expertise of your previous mistresses."

Christian drew his breath in sharply at her hesitant admission. "I do not believe I found you in the least wanting four years ago, Sylvie." The opposite, in fact—Sylvie's enthusiasm for enjoying all things physical had been its own aphrodisiac to his battle-numbed senses. "And it pleases me to know you have taken no other lovers since your husband died," he added.

She blinked. "It does?"

"Yes." Christian nodded. "Whatever thoughts you may have of this arrangement, Sylvie, I assure you it is not my intention to ever hurt you. On the contrary, it is my hope that we both enjoy our times together."

Sylvie's fear was that she might enjoy Christian's lovemaking too much, that she might fall in love with him all over again.

If she had ever stopped loving him…

She might only have been eighteen when the two of them were last together, but her love for Christian had been that of a woman, deep and true. Much as she had liked and respected Gerald, she had never felt a romantic love for him. Or for any other man. Mere hours after meeting Christian again, being in his company, she found herself here in his home, having agreed to become his mistress.

Oh, she had told herself earlier today that she acted out of a need to protect Christianna, to ensure that Christian never learned of the existence of his daughter, with all the accompanying complications that knowledge was sure to create.

But that excuse did not explain the excitement that had thrummed through Sylvie's veins earlier this evening—that still thrummed through her veins!—as she had dressed to meet her lover, deliberately choosing a gold gown that she knew flattered her fair coloring, its low neckline revealing the full swell of her breasts. Breasts which Christian had caressed and suckled the evening before...

And which Sylvie knew she had longed, ached, for him to caress again ever since.

"Will you join me here, Sylvie?" Christian held his hand out to her invitingly.

Her cheeks felt flushed, her heart beating wildly in her chest as she took a step toward him, and then another, and another, until she placed her gloved hand in his as she now stood beside his chair. "I— Should we not go upstairs to your bedchamber...?" Her heart skipped a beat as Christian instead pulled her in to stand between his thighs, holding her gaze with his as he slowly began to peel her lace glove down the length of her arm.

He smiled slightly as he glanced up at her. "There is no need for us to rush, Sylvie." He slowly, leisurely, pulled the lace from each of her fingers before pulling the glove off completely and allowing it to drift softly to the carpeted floor as he raised her hand to his lips, his gaze holding hers captive as his tongue became a silky-soft caress against her fingertips before he sucked the length of one of those fingers into the heat of his mouth.

Sylvie's breath caught in her throat as she watched that steady and erotic in and out pull on the dampness of her finger, her breasts full and aching beneath her gown, her body aching.

"I have waited too long for this to be in any hurry," Christian murmured softly as he reached back and unfastened the buttons at the back of her gown before allowing it to fall down the slender length of her arms to the carpeted floor, revealing that she wore only a thin chemise beneath, golden curls visible between her thighs, swollen nipples tipping the fullness of her breasts. Christian slipped the ribbon strap of her chemise down her arms and allowed that to fall too.

"Christian…!"

"Let me look, love," he groaned as he caught both her hands in one of his as she would have covered those bared breasts. "You are bigger here than I remember, Sylvie." He watched as his fingertips skimmed her rounded breasts. "And your nipples are darker." He ran the soft pad of his thumb across her before lowering his head to suck first one, and then the other, into the moistness of his mouth, laving those tight buds with his tongue, gently biting with his teeth as he continued to caress, causing her nipples to swell and elongate in the heat of his mouth.

He ran his hand along the silky length of Sylvie's thigh, feeling the throb of her hidden nubbin against his palm as he cupped those silky gold curls to stroke her before entering her with first one finger and then two. He heard the catch in Sylvie's ragged breathing. She cried out in pleasure as she exploded in climax before collapsing against him weakly.

Christian rested his head against the fullness of Sylvie's breasts, feeling completely at peace as he enjoyed the feel of her fingers lightly caressing his hair. She continued to tremble and cling to him in the aftershocks of that climax.

A peace and completion he had not felt since last making love to Sylvie four years ago…

Chapter Eight

"Where are you taking me?" Sylvie gasped as Christian stood up and swung her up into his arms to carry her over to the door, the darkness of his hair tousled from her caressing fingers.

"Upstairs to my bedchamber—"

"But my clothes…? The servants…?" she protested weakly.

"We can collect your clothes later, and I instructed Smith to dismiss the household for the rest of the night once you arrived," Christian assured her with satisfaction. "Open the door, Sylvie," he encouraged.

Sylvie knew that Christian did not love her, that he had never loved her, but she appreciated that he had made love to her just now with tenderness as well as passion rather than the disrespect she had expected. A tenderness and passion that were irresistible to her…

"Good girl." He murmured his approval as she bent to open the door to allow him to step out into the deserted, candlelit hallway before striding purposefully toward the stairs, carrying her in his arms as if she weighed nothing at all.

A single candle burned in his bedchamber, the green-and-cream brocade curtains at the windows and about the four-poster bed suiting him perfectly, as did the heavy oak furniture.

Not that Sylvie spared too much time in appreciation of her surroundings once Christian had placed her in the middle of the bed, a mute shaking of his head halting her as she would have pulled the bedcovers over her nakedness, the steadiness of his gaze holding hers as he straightened to begin removing his own clothes.

Sylvie forgot her own nakedness as he peeled off his fashionably tight jacket and waistcoat. Followed by his neck cloth, and then he unfastened the four buttons at his throat before pulling his shirt over his head, leaving the darkness of his hair even more tousled as he sat facing her on the stool before the dressing table in order to remove his boots.

Sylvie's breath caught in her throat as his hands moved to his pantaloons, the unfastening of those six buttons revealing that he wore no undergarments. Christian removed his pantaloons completely to stand before her completely naked.

Sylvie's fingers curled into the bedcovers beneath her, her throat moving convulsively as she swallowed. She had forgotten just how beautiful he was, shoulders and chest wide and muscled, waist tapered above that proudly thrusting erection, his legs all long and muscled elegance.

"Do I still meet with your approval, Sylvie?" he prompted.

"Oh, yes," she breathed as she finally managed to uncurl her fingers from the bedcovers before moving up onto her knees and moving to the side of the bed where he stood, gaze heated as she gazed down at his proudly jutting manhood before reaching out to curl her fingers about that hardness encased in velvet. "Oh, yes," she repeated achingly.

Christian groaned low in his throat as he thrust slowly into her caresses. "Sylvie…!" he gasped achingly, his hands moving up to cradle each side of her face as her head lowered and her little pink tongue darted out to continue the seduction.

Satisfaction gleamed in her eyes as she glanced up at him briefly before parting her lips wide and taking him fully into the heat of her mouth. Christian caressed and plucked at her breasts even as he thrust into that moist heat, until he knew he was about to explode as the pleasure became too much even for his rigid self-control.

"No more!" he groaned before reluctantly pulling free of her, his cock a throbbing ache. "I want to be inside you when I come, Sylvie," he breathed raggedly. "But not quite yet," he murmured as he laid her back against the bedcovers before kneeling between her parted her thighs to gaze down in appreciation at those moist and swollen lips. He lowered his head, fingers lightly caressing her opening as his tongue rasped moistly around that pulsing nubbin without ever quite touching it.

"Christian!" Sylvie cried out, back arching restlessly even as her hands moved up to grip his shoulders tightly.

"Tell me, Sylvie. Tell me what you want." His hands cupped beneath the globes of her bottom as he breathed lightly on that throbbing nubbin, eyes gleaming with satisfaction as her nether lips pulsed and parted against the caress of his fingers.

"I need you to touch me there—" She broke off with a gasp as Christian gave her the lightest of caresses with his tongue. "More, Christian. Oh please, more…!" She raised her hips in restless invitation.

His hands tightened on her bottom as he lifted her into

the rasping stroke of his tongue, holding her captive as he stroked time and time again until he felt her exploding beneath him in a trembling, shuddering climax.

Christian reared up onto his knees, taking his weight onto his elbows as he positioned his erection at her entrance before thrusting deeply into that hot and welcoming channel, paying great attention to one nipple to prolong Sylvie's orgasm even as the rhythmic convulsing of her inner muscles took him crashing over the edge of his own pleasure and he released, long and satisfying, inside her.

"Christian…?"

"Am I too heavy for you?" he murmured against the warmth of her throat, his body stretched out above hers.

He was a little heavy, but Sylvie was loath to relinquish their closeness just yet. "No," she denied even as she reached up to caress the heat of his shoulders, fingers lightly caressing down his muscled back. "I merely wondered—Christian?" Her voice sharpened in alarm as she felt and then traced the hard ridge of a scar running from his left shoulder across his back and down to his right side. "What happened to your back…?" she gasped as she attempted to sit up so that she might see his back for herself, only to find that Christian's weight pressing down on her made that impossible. "Christian?"

"It is an old scar," he dismissed lightly as his lips skimmed across her collarbone.

"But—" She stilled suddenly, eyes wide. "How old…?"

"Do we have to discuss this now, Sylvie?" he murmured indulgently as his lips continued that caressing assault on the creaminess of her throat. "I do not recall your having this need for conversation after our lovemaking in the past," he added teasingly.

"Christian, please…!" she pressed, needing to know— exactly—when he had received the wound that had left such a terrible and lasting scar upon his back.

A scar that she knew had not been there four years ago…

Chapter Nine

Christian moved up onto his elbow to withdraw gently from Sylvie before moving to lie down beside her, satiated and satisfied in a way he had not been since they had last made love together. "Does the thought of my scar repulse you?"

"Of course it does not," she dismissed impatiently, her face pale as she sat up and turned him slightly so that she might look at the scar for herself. "How—how did this happen?"

Christian shrugged. "A French saber."

Her face became paler. "When?"

Christian fell back onto the pillows. "What does it matter—"

"It matters to me!" she assured him fiercely. "Tell me, Christian. Please!"

He frowned. "It happened four years ago, two weeks after I left you and two days after I returned to my regiment." He smiled bitterly. "The wound incapacitated me, became infected, and I was out of my head with a fever for almost a week, and then weakened for many more." He shrugged.

"It is the reason I was unable to write to you. The reason for my delay in returning to you."

That is what Sylvie had thought he might say. What she had dreaded hearing. "You were coming back to me?"

"Of course I was coming back to you!" He frowned. "How many times do I have to tell you that before you believe me? I had told you that I loved you and that I would come back to you as soon as I was able!"

Yes, he had. And, despite the rumors of his behavior in London after he had left her, Sylvie had waited and waited for his return, until the babe she carried meant she could wait no longer and she had accepted the offer of marriage made to her by another man.

And all the time she waited, Christian had been ill and fevered, cut down by a French saber. It was the reason he had not returned to England until it was too late; Sylvie had already been another man's wife, and the babe she carried accepted as a child of that marriage.

What had she done?

Christian frowned as Sylvie moved abruptly away to sit on the side of the bed, before standing up to cross the room and pull on his black brocade bathrobe he had draped across the chair beside the window.

"Are you leaving already?" He kept his tone deliberately neutral as he sat up, knowing he had agreed, accepted, Sylvie's decree that she would only stay with him for a few hours, but he had hoped, after the enjoyment of their lovemaking— Whatever he might have hoped, it was obviously not to be. "When will I see you again?"

She finished fastening the belt of the robe before looking up at him with dark and guarded eyes. "I—I will send you a note tomorrow."

His brows rose. "A note…?"

"Yes." She turned away. "I will leave your robe downstairs in the library after I have dressed, and then let myself out—"

"Give me a minute and I will come down with you." Christian swung his legs to the side of the bed.

"No! No," she repeated more calmly, the dullness of her eyes appearing like dark bruises in the pallor of her face as she refused to so much as look at him. "I— We will talk again tomorrow."

"Talk?" he repeated sharply.

"Yes," she sighed. "We will talk. I— There is something— I must

go!" She hurried to the door, wrenching it open before turning back to him briefly, her expression anguished. "Please believe that I—that I am sorry."

Christian tensed, stomach churning. "You are not ending our association already?"

"No! I— " She gave a shake of her head, tears now glistening in the darkness of her eyes.

Relief flooded him. "Then what are you sorry for?"

"For everything!" she choked. "I am sorry for everything," she repeated shakily.

"I do not understand, Sylvie…" He gave a pained frown. "You are not ending our association and yet you are sorry. What—"

"Tomorrow, Christian. I will explain all tomorrow," she assured him dully. "Do not follow me now. I— It is for the best— Tomorrow," she repeated before stepping out into the hallway, the door to the bedchamber closing quietly behind her.

Christian had no idea what had just happened. One minute he and Sylvie had been lying satiated in each other's arms after the most satisfying lovemaking Christian had ever known, and the next she had run from him as if the hounds of hell were at her heels.

Tomorrow.

Sylvie had said she would explain all tomorrow.

And he hoped that explanation did not include the ending of their relationship, because having now made love with Sylvie again, that possibility was even less acceptable to Christian than it had been four years ago...

"The Earl of Chambourne to see you, my lady," Sylvie's butler announced from the doorway of her private parlor.

Sylvie ceased her restless pacing as she turned to him, the deep-brown gown she wore only emphasizing the pallor of her face. "Please show him in, Bellows."

After a sleepless and troubled night, Sylvie had written a note and had it delivered to Christian only an hour ago, requesting that he call upon her at his earliest convenience. She should have known, after the manner in which she had fled his home the night before, that Christian's 'earliest convenience' would be almost immediately.

Quite what she was to say to him, how to explain, was still not exactly clear to her. She only knew that she owed Christian an explanation. For her behavior both the previous night and four years ago...

Christian gave the standing and unsmiling Sylvie a searching glance after the butler left the two of them alone. Her golden curls were fashionably styled, her brown silk gown also the height of fashion, and yet—and yet there was an air of fragility about her, a translucence to the creaminess of her skin, and a haunted look in the dark depths of her eyes. "Tell me," he demanded without preamble.

She gave a shake of her head, not of denial, but as if she was at a loss to know quite how to proceed. She closed her lids briefly before opening them again, her chin rising as if for a blow. "There is something that I wish—no, something I *must* tell you." She moistened her rosy-pink lips. "I have thought about this for most of the night, have considered all the consequences of—of my admission, but I can see no other way. No other honorable way," she added huskily.

Christian frowned darkly. "You are making me nervous, Sylvie."

She swallowed. "I assure you, that is not my intention. I— You see—"

"Mama? Mama, Nurse says I may not visit with you just yet, that you are too busy this morning!"

Christian had turned at the first sound of that trilling little voice as it preceded the opening of the door and the entrance of a little green whirlwind that launched itself into Sylvie's arms before turning to look at him curiously.

His eyes narrowed as he found himself looking down at a beautiful little girl of possibly three years old, dressed in a green gown, with dark curls and—and moss-green eyes...

His own dark curls and moss-green eyes?

Chapter Ten

"Please say something, Christian," Sylvie choked, having just returned from taking a reluctant Christianna back to the nursery and her flustered and scolding nurse. The tears streamed unchecked down Sylvie's cheeks as she saw that Christian's face still bore an expression of shocked disbelief. "Anything!"

His throat moved convulsively as he swallowed. "What do you call her…?"

Sylvie gave a pained frown. "I— Her name is Christianna."

His breath left him in a hiss. "You named her for me?"

"Yes. Christian—"

"Dear God, Sylvie, she is so beautiful!" The tension leached from his body and he dropped down into one of the armchairs, his face pale, his expression tortured as he stared up at her. "Is she— Can she be the reason you accepted Gerald Moorland's offer of marriage four years ago?"

"Yes."

Christian gave a pained wince. "And did he know—"

"Yes, he knew. Oh, not who the father of my babe was,

but I never tried to deceive him into believing the child was his," Sylvie assured huskily. "Please believe—I did not know what to do when I realized I carried your child, and although Gerald's life had been dedicated to the army, and he had never shown any inclination to marry, he nevertheless offered—Gerald was a friend of my father's—"

Christian looked at her sharply. "Your parents know—"

"No." She gave a sad shake of her head. "They have always believed that Christianna was a seven-month babe." Sylvie twisted her fingers together in her agitation. "Only Gerald knew she was not. And he was too much of a gentleman to ever reveal the truth to anyone."

"And—and did you grow to love him…?"

She gave a slow shake of her head. "Not in a romantic way. But he became my closest friend."

"You were not— It was not a physical marriage?" Christian prompted sharply.

Sylvie smiled slightly. "Gerald did not think of me in that way. He did not think of anyone in that way," she added softly as she saw Christian's incredulous expression. "He really was married to the army. Although I never had any doubts that he cared for both Christianna and me. For the short time he was alive after Christianna's birth, he was a wonderful father to her."

"I am glad of it." Christian nodded.

"You do not really mean that!" Sylvie groaned.

"Of course I do."

"How could you? Because of my lack of faith in you, in myself, I have denied you the first three years of your daughter's life!" Her eyes glistened with unshed tears. "And I am so sorry for that, Christian."

"Why did you not write to me?"

Sylvie closed her eyes briefly. "After you left me, there were rumors on your estate of the women you had been seen with in London before you rejoined your regiment—"

"They were untrue." He looked at her bleakly. "I did not so much as look at another woman. Why would I, when it was you I wanted? You I intended to return to? You whom I loved?"

Sylvie looked at him searchingly, seeing the truth in the bleakness of his expression. As she heard the past tense in his last statement. "I am so sorry, Christian. So very sorry that I ever doubted you." She turned away to stare sightlessly out of the window overlooking the garden. "I cannot bear to think of how much you must now hate and despise me!"

Christian rose abruptly to his feet to cross the room in three long strides before grasping Sylvie's shoulders and turning her to face him. "I could never hate or despise you, Sylvie," he assured her gruffly as he cupped either side of her face to brush his thumbs across her cheek and erase the tears. "How could I when I fell in love with you the moment I saw you swimming half-naked in that river four years ago? And it is a love that never died, Sylvie. Never," he assured her fiercely as her eyes widened incredulously, hopefully. "Yes, I felt angry and betrayed when I returned to England and found you had married another man. And I behaved abominably for the next four years—"

"So I believe." She smiled sadly.

"I am not proud of those years, Sylvie," he acknowledged. "How could I be? But I did not know how else to get through the pain of loving you and knowing you were so far out of my reach, that you belonged with another man. And all this time!" He gave a self-disgusted shake of his head. "Was the reason you agreed to become my mistress, but with that proviso that we meet in my home and not yours, because you wished to protect Christianna from me?"

"Partly," she acknowledged.

Christian looked at her closely. "And the other part?"

Sylvie released her breath in a sigh. "The other part was that I only had to see you again, to be with you again, to know, despite denying it to myself, wishing it to be the contrary, that I still had feelings for you."

He stilled. "As I only had to see you again the night of my grandmother's ball to know that I have never stopped loving you."

She gasped. "You believed I had married Gerald for his money and title—"

"And it made no difference to the love I still feel for you!" he admitted fiercely. "I knew that night that I wanted you back in my life—that I *had* to have you back in my life, in any way that you would allow!" He drew in a ragged breath. "How you must now hate and despise me because I tried to force you into my bed!"

Sylvie huskily gave a self-derisive laugh. "Did it seem last night as if I felt forced into responding to your lovemaking?"

"No…" Christian looked down at her searchingly. "And it was lovemaking, Sylvie. No matter how I might have behaved the night of my grandmother's ball, how much I tried to continue to despise you for believing you had married an old man for his title and fortune, once I held you in my arms again, kissed you, I could never do less than make love with you."

Yes, for all of those things, Sylvie knew that Christian's lovemaking the previous night had been every bit as tender and caring for her own needs as it had ever been in the past. "You did not know of Christianna's existence then…"

His hands moved to tightly grip her shoulders. "If anything, that only makes me love you more," he assured her fiercely. "You did what you believed you had to do to in order to protect our daughter when you accepted Ampthill's offer, what was necessary to protect both Christianna and yourself!"

"And by my doing so, you have missed the first three years of your daughter's life," she repeated sadly.

"But God willing I will not miss any more. Or that of any other children we might be blessed with?" He looked down at her uncertainly.

Sylvie gazed up at him searchingly, seeing only love burning in Christian's beautiful moss-green eyes. "What are you saying?"

"Asking," he corrected huskily. "I am asking what I should have asked you before I left four years ago. What, in my arrogance, I believed could wait until the next time I returned to England." He gave a self-disgusted shake of his head.

Sylvie swallowed. "And what is that?"

"That you do me the honor of marrying me," Christian pressed softly. "I had never loved until I met you that summer, Sylvie. Nor have I loved again since. I loved you then, and I love you still, and if you will consent to become my wife, I swear to you that I will tell you, show you, every day for the rest of our lives together how very much I love and cherish you!"

Tears welled in her eyes once more, but this time they were tears of happiness. "I realized last night that I have never stopped loving you either, Christian. I loved you then, I love you now. I will always love and cherish you."

He looked down at her searchingly for several long, disbelieving seconds, his expression turning to one of wonder as he saw that love shining in the darkness of her eyes. He fell to his knees in front of her. "Sylviana Moorland, will you do me the honor of becoming my wife? Allow me to love and cherish you for the rest of your life?"

"Oh, yes, Christian!" She threw herself into his arms. "Oh, yes, yes, and a thousand times yes!"

"You have made me the happiest of men," Christian choked as he stood up to take her gently in his arms and kiss her with all of the tenderness of a man deeply in and forever in love.

And ensuring that Sylvie became the happiest of women. At last…

Chapter Eleven

The London home of Lady Jocelyn Ambrose,
Dowager Countess of Chambourne.

"——and the wedding is to be next month," Lady Jocelyn concluded gleefully to her two closest friends.

"But Chambourne is not marrying the woman you had chosen to become his future wife?" Lady Cicely Hawthorne said doubtfully.

"Well. No." Some of Lady Jocelyn's glee abated. "He did not care for Lady Vanessa at all. But he is to marry. Which, after all, is what we had all decided upon, is it not?" Both ladies turned to the silent Dowager Duchess of Royston for confirmation.

"Yes. Yes," Edith St. Just acknowledged briskly. "Although I agree with Cicely, in that it would be more of a triumph if Chambourne had decided upon the lady you had chosen for him."

Lady Jocelyn looked suitably deflated. "Perhaps one of you will be more success in that regard than I."

"I am not at all sure of any degree of success in regard

to Thorne," Lady Cicely admitted heavily. "Since his first wife died four years ago, he has shown a decided aversion to the very idea of remarrying."

"And yet he must, for he is in need of an heir, the same as our own two grandsons," the dowager duchess dismissed briskly.

Lady Jocelyn looked at her curiously. "How go your own efforts in regard to Royston?"

"Nicely, thank you." Edith St. Just nodded regally.

"You believe he will marry the woman of your choice?" Lady Cicely looked suitably impressed.

"I am sure of it, yes."

"How confident are you of that?" Lady Jocelyn challenged daringly, still feeling slightly stung in regard to her friends' reaction to her news of Chambourne's forthcoming marriage to Lady Sylviana Moorland, the Countess of Ampthill.

"So confident," the dowager duchess assured haughtily, "that I am willing to write that lady's name on a piece of paper this very minute and leave it in the safekeeping of your butler, only to be returned and read by all of us when Royston announces his intention of marrying."

"Is that not rather presumptuous of you, Edith?" Lady Cicely raised skeptical brows.

"Not in the least," the dowager duchess dismissed briskly. "In fact, call for Edwards and we shall do it now. This very minute."

Ellie, sitting in her usual place in the window beside Miss Thompson and Mrs. Spencer, could only watch with a sinking heart as Edith St. Just did exactly as she had said she would.

Could only wonder as to the name of the lady—and secretly envy her—written on that innocuous piece of paper, which was taken away by Lady Jocelyn's butler some minutes later…

As she knew beyond a doubt that it would not be her own name.

Despite the fact she had fallen in love with the arrogantly disdainful Justin St. Just several months ago…

* * * * *

NOT JUST A GOVERNESS

CAROLE MORTIMER

To my very special Dad, Eric Haworth Faulkner, 6/2/1923–
6/12/2012. A true and everlasting hero!

The dedication of this book says it all for me.
My Dad was a man who was and always will be a true hero
to me, in every sense of the word. He was always very proud
of my writing,
but I am even prouder to have enjoyed
the absolute privilege of being his daughter.
I hope you will all continue to enjoy reading my books
as much as I enjoy writing them!

Chapter One

*Late April, 1817—the London home of
Lady Cicely Hawthorne*

'I, for one, am disappointed that you do not seem to be any further along with finding a bride for Hawthorne, Cicely,' Edith St Just, Dowager Duchess of Royston, gave her friend a reproving frown.

'Perhaps we were all being a trifle ambitious, at the start of the Season, in deciding to acquire suitable wives for our three grandsons?' Lady Jocelyn Ambrose put in softly.

The three ladies talking now had been aged only eighteen when they had shared a coming-out Season fifty years ago and had become fast friends, a state of affairs that had seen them all through marriage and their children's marriages. They now had their sights firmly set on the nuptials of their errant grandchildren.

'Nonsense,' the dowager duchess dismissed that claim firmly. 'You had no trouble whatsoever in seeing Chambourne settled—'

'But not to the bride I had chosen for him,' Lady Jocelyn pointed out fairly.

'Nevertheless, he is to marry,' the dowager duchess dismissed airily. 'And if we do not see to the marriage of our respective grandsons, then who will? My own daughter-in-law is of absolutely no help whatsoever in that enterprise, since she retired to the country following my son Robert's demise three years ago. And Royston certainly shows no inclination himself to give up his habit of acquiring a mistress for several weeks before swiftly growing bored with her and moving on to the next.' She gave loud sniff.

Miss Eleanor Rosewood—Ellie—step-niece and companion to the dowager duchess, glanced across from where she sat quietly by the window with the two companions of Lady Cicely and Lady Jocelyn, knowing that sniff only too well: it conveyed the dowager duchess's disapproval on every occasion.

But Ellie could not help but feel a certain amount of sympathy towards Lady Cicely's dilemma; Lord Adam Hawthorne was known by all, including the numerous servants employed on his many estates, for being both cold and haughty, as well as totally unapproachable.

So much so that it must be far from easy for Lady Cicely to even broach the subject of her grandson remarrying, despite his first marriage having only produced a daughter and no heir, let alone finding a woman who was agreeable to becoming the second wife of such an icily sarcastic gentleman.

Oh, it would have its compensations, no doubt; his lordship was a wealthy gentleman—very wealthy indeed—and more handsome than any single gentleman had a right to be, with glossy black hair and eyes of deep impenetrable grey set in a hard and arrogantly aristocratic face, his shoulders and chest muscled, waist tapered, legs long and strong.

Unfortunately, his character was also icy enough to chill the blood in any woman's veins, hence the reason he was known amongst the *ton* as simply Thorne!

Hawthorne's cold nature aside, Ellie was far more interested in the dowager duchess's efforts to find a bride for her own grandson, Justin St Just, Duke of Royston...

'Adam is proving most unhelpful, I am afraid.' Lady Cicely sighed. 'He has refused each and every one of my invitations for him to dine here with me one evening.'

The dowager duchess raised iron-grey brows. 'On what basis?'

Lady Cicely grimaced. 'He claims he is too busy...'

Edith St Just snorted. 'The man has to eat like other mortals, does he not?'

'One would presume so, yes...' Lady Cicely gave another sigh.

'Well, you must not give up trying, Cicely,' the dowager duchess advised most strongly. 'If Hawthorne will not come to you, then you must go to him.'

Lady Cicely looked alarmed. 'Go to him?'

'Call upon him at Hawthorne House.' The dowager duchess urged. 'And insist that he join you here for dinner that same evening.'

'I will try, Edith.' Lady Cicely looked far from convinced of her likely success. 'But do tell us, how goes your own efforts in regard to Royston's future bride? Well, I hope?' She brightened. 'Let us not forget that a week ago you wrote that lady's name down on a piece of paper and gave it to Jocelyn's butler for safekeeping!'

The dowager duchess gave a haughty inclination of her head. 'And, as you will see, that is the young lady he will marry, when the time comes.'

'I do so envy you, when I have to deal with Adam's complete lack of co-operation in that regard...' Lady Cicely looked totally miserable.

'Hawthorne will come around, you will see.' Lady Jocelyn gave her friend's hand a reassuring squeeze.

Ellie, easily recalling the forbidding countenance of the man, remained as unconvinced of that as did the poor, obviously beleaguered Lady Cicely...

'Oh, do let's talk of other things!' Lady Jocelyn encouraged brightly. 'For instance, have either of you heard the latest rumour concerning the Duke of Sheffield's missing granddaughter?'

'Oh, do tell!' Lady Cicely encouraged avidly.

Ellie added her own, silent, urging to Lady Cicely's; the tale of the missing granddaughter of the recently deceased Duke of Sheffield had been the talk both below and above stairs for most of the Season, the duke having died very suddenly two months ago, to be succeeded by his nephew. The previous duke's granddaughter and ward had disappeared on the day following his funeral, at the same time as the Sheffield family jewels and several thousand pounds had also gone missing.

'I try never to listen to idle gossip.' The dowager duchess gave another of her famous sniffs.

'Oh, but this is not in the least idle, Edith,' Lady Jocelyn assured. 'Miss Matthews has been seen on the Continent, in the company of a gentleman, and living a life of luxury. Further igniting the rumour that she may have had something to do with the Duke's untimely death, as well as the theft of the Sheffield jewels and money.'

'I cannot believe that any granddaughter of Jane Matthews would ever behave so reprehensively,' Edith St Just stated firmly.

'But the gel's mother was Spanish, remember.' Lady Cicely gave her two friends a pointed glance.

'Hmm, there is that to consider, Edith.' Lady Jocelyn mused.

'Stuff and nonsense,' the dowager duchess dismissed briskly. 'Maria Matthews was the daughter of a grandee and I refuse to believe her daughter guilty of anything unless proven otherwise.'

Which, as Ellie knew only too well, was now the end of that particular subject.

Although she knew that many in society, and below stairs, speculated as to why, if she truly *were* innocent, Miss Magdelena Matthews had disappeared, along with the Sheffield jewels and money, the day of her grandfather's funeral…

Chapter Two

One day later—Hawthorne House, Mayfair, London

'Do not scowl so, Adam, else I will think you are not at all pleased to see me!'

That displeasure glinted in Lord Hawthorne's narrowed grey eyes and showed in his harshly patrician face, as he heard the rebuke in his grandmother's quiet tone. Nor was she wrong about his current displeasure being caused by her unexpected arrival; he had neither the time nor the patience for the twittering of Lady Cicely this afternoon. Or any afternoon, come to that! 'I am only surprised you are visiting me now, Grandmother, when I know you are fully aware this is the time of day that I retire to the nursery in order to spend half an hour with Amanda.'

His grandmother arched silver brows beneath her pale-green bonnet as the two faced each across the blue salon of Adam's Mayfair home. 'And may I not also wish to visit with my great-granddaughter?'

'Well, yes, of course you may.' Adam belatedly strode across the room to bestow a kiss upon one of his grandmother's powdered cheeks. 'It is only that I would have appreciated prior notice of your visit.'

'Why?'

He scowled darkly. 'My time is at a premium, Grandmother, nor do I care to have my routine interrupted.'

'And I have just stated that I have no wish to interrupt anything,' she reminded him quietly.

'Nevertheless, you are—' Adam broke off his impatient outburst, aware that his grandmother's unexpected arrival had already made him four minutes late arriving at the nursery. 'Well, you are here now, so by all means accompany me, if you wish to.' He nodded abruptly as he wrenched open the salon door—much to Barnes's surprise, as the butler stood attentively on the other side of that door—for his grandmother to precede him from the room.

'You really are the most impatient of men, Adam.' Lady Cicely swept past him into the grand hallway, indicating with a nod that her paid companion should wait there for her return. 'I do not believe even your grandfather and father were ever as irritable as you.'

Adam placed a gentlemanly hand beneath his grandmother's elbow as he escorted her up the wide staircase, in the full knowledge that Lady Cicely's overly fussy nature—to put it kindly!—had irked his grandfather and father as much, if not more, as it now did him. Nevertheless, his grandfather and father were no longer with them, leaving Lady Cicely alone in the world but for himself and Amanda, and so it fell to Adam, as the patriarch of the family, to at least attempt kindness towards his elderly relative. 'I apologise if my abruptness of manner has offended you,' he said.

His grandmother released her elbow from his grasp to

instead tuck her hand more cosily into the crook of his arm. 'Perhaps as recompense you might consider dining with me this evening…?'

Adam stiffened as he easily recognised Lady Cicely's less-than-subtle attempt at coercion; he hesitated to call it actual blackmail, although he could not help but be aware of his grandmother's recent attempts to introduce him to suitably marriageable ladies—suitable according to Lady Cicely, that was. Adam was having none of it. The ladies. Or the marriage. 'I have to attend a vote in the House to-night, Grandmother.' After which he fully intended to re-tire to his club for the rest of the evening, where he hoped to enjoy a few quiet games of cards and several glasses of fine brandy.

'Then perhaps tomorrow evening?' Lady Cicely pressed. 'It is so long since the two of us spent any time together…'

Deliberately so, on Adam's part, since he had realised what his grandmother was about. He had absolutely no in-terest in marrying again and his life really was now such that he had little time for anything other than his respon-sibilities to the House of Lords and his many estates. The dinners and balls, and all the other nonsense of the Season, held no interest for him whatsoever.

'We are together now, Grandmother,' he pointed out prac-tically.

'But not in any way that—never mind.' Lady Cicely sighed her impatience. 'It is obvious to me that you have become even more intransigent than you ever were!'

Adam's mouth tightened at the criticism. Well-deserved criticism. But his grandmother knew the reason for his in-transigence as well as he did; having been married for over two years, and so been dragged along as his adulterous wife's escort to every ball, dinner, and other society function during the Season, and to summer house parties when it was not, Adam now chose, as a widower these past four years, not to attend any of them. There was no reason for him to do so. Most, if not all, of society bored him, so why would he ever choose to voluntarily put himself through those days and evenings of irritation and boredom?

Even so, he instantly felt a guilty need to make amends for the tears he now saw glistening in his grandmother's faded grey eyes. 'I may be able to spare an hour or two to join you for dinner tomorrow evening—'

'Oh, that is wonderful, Adam!' His grandmother's tears disappeared as if they had never been as she now beamed up at him. 'I shall make sure to serve all of your favourite dishes.'

'I said an hour or two, Grandmother,' Adam repeated sternly.

'Yes, yes,' she acknowledged distractedly, obviously already mentally planning her menu for tomorrow evening. And her guest list. Some of which would no doubt be several of those eligible females Adam wished to avoid! 'How is the new girl working out?'

'New girl?' Adam's mind had gone a complete blank at this sudden change of subject, not altogether sure he understood the meaning of his grandmother's question; surely Lady Cicely could not be referring to the woman he had briefly taken an interest in the previous month, before deciding that she bored him in bed as well as out of it?

'Amanda's nursemaid.' Lady Cicely clarified.

Adam's brow cleared at this explanation. 'Mrs Leighton

is not a girl, Grandmother. Nor is she Amanda's nursemaid, but her governess.'

'Is Amanda not a little young as yet for a governess? Especially when you know as well as I that society does not appreciate a blue-stocking—'

'I will not have Amanda growing up to be an ignoramus, with nothing in her head other than balls and parties and the latest fashions.' Like her mother before her, Adam could have stated, but chose not to do so; the less thought he gave to Fanny, and her adulterous ways, the better as far as he was concerned!

'—and you never did explain fully why it was that you felt the need to dispense with Dorkins's services after all these years?'

Lady Cicely was slightly out of breath as they ascended the stairs to the third floor of the house where the nursery was situated.

Nor did Adam intend explaining himself now. Having the nursemaid of his six-year-old daughter make it obvious to him that she was available to share his bed, if he so wished, had not only been unpleasant but beyond acceptable. Especially as he had never, by word or deed, ever expressed a carnal interest in the pretty but overly plump Clara Dorkins.

Now, if it had been Elena Leighton, Amanda's new governess, then he might not have found the notion of sharing her bed for a night or two quite so unpalatable—

And where, pray, had that particular thought come from?

Since the death of his wife Adam had kept the satisfying of his carnal desires to a minimum, considering them a weakness he could ill afford. And, whenever those desires did become too demanding, even for his now legendary self-control, he only ever indulged with those ladies of the *demi-monde* whose company he considered he could stand for longer than an hour, possibly two. Less-than-respectable ladies, who expected nothing more than to be handsomely paid for the parting of their thighs.

Adam had certainly never so much as thought of forming an alliance with one of his own employees, hence his hasty dismissal of Clara Dorkins two weeks ago.

Admittedly Elena Leighton, Dorkins' replacement, was quite beautiful in an austere way; she always wore her silky black hair secured in a neat bun at the slenderness of her nape, the severity of her black widow's weeds emphasising the pale beauty of her face rather than detracting from it. Her eyes were a strange light colour, somewhere between blue and green in her heart-shaped face, and surrounded by thick dark lashes, her tiny nose perfectly straight above bow-shaped lips, her jaw delicately lovely, neck and throat slender. Nor did those severe black gowns in the least detract from the willowy attractiveness of her figure: firm breasts above a slender waist and gently swaying hips—

Dear God, he thought, appalled with himself. When had he noticed so much about the looks and attraction of the widow he had recently employed to tutor his *young daughter*?

'*Mrs* Leighton…?' his grandmother prompted curiously.

'I believe she was widowed at Waterloo,' Adam said distractedly, still slightly nonplussed by the realisation he had actually noted Elena Leighton's physical attributes. The woman was his employee, for heaven's sake, not some light-skirt he could take to his bed for a night and then dismiss.

Moreover, she was a widow, her husband having died a hero's death during that last bloody battle with Napoleon.

'Old or young…?'

Adam raised dark brows. 'I have no information whatsoever on the deceased Mr Leighton—'

'I was referring to his widow,' Lady Cicely chided with a small sigh.

Until this moment Adam had given no particular thought to Mrs Leighton's age, but had assumed her to be in her late twenties or early thirties.

He scowled now as he realised, when he thought about it carefully, that it was the lady's widow's weeds which gave her the impression of age and maturity, that, in fact, she was probably considerably much younger than that… 'As long as Mrs Leighton carries out her employment to my satisfaction then I consider her age to be completely immaterial,' he dismissed as he stepped forwards to push open the door to the nursery before indicating that his grandmother should precede him into the room.

Elena looked up from where she had been studying a book of simple poetry with her small charge, her expression one of cool politeness at the entrance of her employer and his paternal grandmother.

A cool politeness, which she hoped masked the fact that she had heard herself become the subject under discussion by grandson and grandmother before they entered the nursery. And that she had tensed warily at that knowledge…

She had hoped the fact that she was the widowed Mrs Elena Leighton, employed by the cold and unapproachable Lord Adam Hawthorne as governess to his young daughter, would be enough to ensure that she escaped such curiosities. But she could see by the assessing way in which Lady Cicely now viewed her that, in that lady's regard at least, this was not to be the case.

Elena resisted the instinct to straighten the severity of her bun, or check the fall of her black gown, instead straightening to her just over five feet in height as she stood up to make a curtsy. 'My lord.'

'Mrs Leighton.' Lady Cicely was the one to smoothly respond to her greeting, his lordship's expression remaining coldly unapproachable as he stood remotely at his grandmother's side.

Elena had already ascertained, before deciding to accept her current employment, that the chillingly austere aristocrat was a man who chose not to involve himself, or his young daughter, in London society, preferring instead to utilise his time in politics or in the running of his country estates. An arrangement that suited Elena's desire—need—for anonymity perfectly.

She had to admit to having been a little startled by this gentleman's dark, almost satanic handsomeness at their initial interview, having had no idea until that moment that Adam Hawthorne bore the dark good looks and muscled physique of a Greek god: fashionably styled dark hair, equally black brows over those dark-grey eyes, high cheekbones either side of a long patrician nose, sculptured and sensual lips, his jaw square and uncompromising, with not an ounce of excess flesh on his tall and muscular frame—as evidence, surely, that he did not spend all of his time seated in the House of Lords or behind the mahogany desk in his study...

But after only five minutes in his company that day Elena had also realised—thankfully!—that not only was he the most haughtily cold and unapproachable man she had ever met, but that he did not even see her as being female, let alone have any of the lewder thoughts and intentions towards her that another male employer might have shown to the woman he was to employ as his young daughter's governess.

Elena now clasped her trembling hands tightly together in front of her, as the warmth currently engulfing her body forced her to realise that was no longer the case, as Lord Hawthorne's narrowed grey gaze slowly perused her from head to toe in what was obviously a totally male assessment. 'Lady Cicely.' She nodded a polite greeting to the elderly lady. 'Stand up and greet your great-grandmother, Amanda,' she instructed as she realised her young charge was still seated at her desk.

Elena had found it strange at first to realise that there was none of the spontaneity of affection in this household that she had been used to during her own childhood, Lord Hawthorne spending only half an hour of each day with his daughter, and even that was usually spent in discussing and questioning what Amanda had learnt during her lessons.

Consequently, Amanda became a quietly reserved child whenever she was in her father's company, the perfect curtsy she now bestowed upon Lady Cicely also reflective of that reserve.

'Great-Grandmama.'

Which was not to say that Elena did not see a different side of Amanda when the two of them were alone together in the nursery, Amanda as full of fun then as any other six-year-old.

Tall for her age, Amanda's face already showed the signs of the great beauty she would become in later years, her eyes a deep blue, her cheeks creamy pink, her little mouth as perfect as a rose in bud, her hair the colour and softness of spun gold. Amanda looked especially enchanting today in a deep-pink gown that perfectly complemented the fairness of her colouring.

A look of enchantment totally wasted upon her father as he stood across the room, his attention focused on Elena rather than his daughter. The same gentleman whom Elena, after only a week spent in his employment, considered to be utterly without any of the softer emotions.

Which was why she now found the intensity of his regard more than slightly unnerving, as if those deep-grey eyes were seeing her as a woman for the first time...

And Elena had no wish for any man, least of all Adam Hawthorne, to see her as anything other than his mousy and widowed employee. Any more than she wished to acknowledge him as being anything more than her employer, even if he was devilishly handsome...

She straightened determinedly. 'I will leave the three of you alone to talk whilst I go and tidy Amanda's bedchamber. If you will all excuse me...' She did not wait for a response before hurrying from the schoolroom.

Only to find that she was shaking so much by the time she had reached the safety of Amanda's bedchamber that she had necessarily to sit down for a moment in order to attempt to regain her senses, pressing a trembling hand against her rapidly beating heart as she fought the rising panic at the thought of Hawthorne seeing her as a woman rather than an employee.

Circumstances had conspired to leave Elena completely alone in the world, and necessitating that she go out to work in order to support herself, and so surely making her life already desperate enough, precarious enough, without the added burden of the sudden interest of the forbidding and forbidden Lord Adam Hawthorne?

Elena was only too well aware that many gentlemen took advantage of the charms of the unprotected females in their household. Indeed, her own cousin—

She would not...could not think about it. Even to think of what that worm—for she could never think of *him* as a gentleman!—had done to her was enough to make her feel ill, the nausea rising even now inside her—

'Are you quite well, Mrs Leighton...?'

Elena stood up so swiftly at the unexpected sound of Hawthorne's voice that all of the blood seemed to rush from her head, rendering her slightly dizzy and causing her to sway precariously on her ankle-booted feet as she reached out blindly for the back of the chair in order to stop herself from falling.

But not quickly enough, it seemed, as he crossed the room in three long strides to take a firm grasp of her arm, allowing her to feel the warmth of his long and elegant hand through the thin silk of her black gown. 'My lord?' Elena looked up at him warily, her breath catching in the back of her throat as she realised how close he was standing to her. A closeness she had not thought she would be able to tolerate from any man. So close that Elena was aware of, and yet not overwhelmed by, how much larger and taller he was than she. So close she could see the circle of black rimming the deep grey of his eyes...

They were, Elena acknowledged as she found herself unable to do any other than continue to stare up at him, the most beautiful eyes she had ever beheld: a deep-smoky grey, with that black rim about the iris, his lashes dark, long and silky.

'Mrs Leighton?' Adam returned softly, frowning slightly as he realised he could smell the citrusy perfume of lemons in her silky dark hair.

Just as he had become aware, having studied her closely in the nursery a few minutes ago, that she was far from being in her late twenties or early thirties, as he had originally assumed her to be. Indeed, she looked possibly one and twenty at most now that he was standing so close to her and really looking at her intently; the alabaster skin of her face and throat was absolutely smooth and flawless, those wide blue-green eyes seeming to possess an innocence as she gazed up at him warily, her slender figure also seeming that of a young girl rather than a mature woman.

His mouth tightened along with the hold he had upon her arm.

'Exactly how old are you?'

She blinked long dark lashes. 'How old am I?'

Adam's jaw tensed as he nodded. 'A simple enough question, I would have thought.'

She moistened rose-coloured lips with the tip of her tongue before answering him. 'Simple enough, yes,' she confirmed huskily. 'But is it not impolite to ask a woman her age? I also fail to see the relevance...?'

Adam's mouth thinned at her continued delay. 'You will allow me to be the best judge of that and please answer the question!' He had little patience at the best of times—and this was far from the best of times; he disliked, above all things, being lied to, and he was very much afraid, that if Elena Leighton had not lied to him outright, that she had at least been economical with the truth.

'I— Why, I am—I am…' Elena paused to flex her nape where it ached from staring up at him for so long, as she weighed up the possibility of this man believing her if she were to lie and claim to be five and twenty, an age that surely even he would consider to be sensible. If untrue. 'I am one and twenty.' Almost. Well…in eight months' time, her birthday falling on Christmas Day, her family having always ensured in the past that they were treated as two separate occasions. Not that there would be any celebration of that event this year, for the simple reason Elena had no family left with whom she wished to celebrate…

'One and twenty,' he repeated evenly, his long and elegant fingers slipping down her arm until they firmly encircled her wrist. 'That would place you as being a mere nineteen when you were widowed and began your employment as tutor and companion to the Bambury chit, is that correct?'

Elena gave an inward wince at this reminder of the reference she had presented to the employment agency some weeks ago, when she had gone to them seeking a placement in a respectable household. A reference, having had no previous experience in employment of any kind, Elena had necessarily to write herself…

She met Adam Hawthorne's scathing gaze unflinchingly. 'That is correct, yes. If you are not satisfied with my work, then I am sure that—'

'Have I said that I am not?'

Her chin rose slightly. 'You implied it.'

Those chiselled lips curled slightly, into what could have been a smile, but was more likely, in this gentleman's case, to be a sneer. 'No, my dear Mrs Leighton, I implied nothing of the sort,' he drawled. 'Perhaps it is a guilty conscience which now makes you assume so?'

Elena's heart skipped several of those guilty beats as she looked searchingly up into Lord Hawthorne's hard and un-yielding face; those grey eyes were narrowed to icy slits, the skin stretched tautly over high cheekbones, deep grooves having appeared beside his nose and chiselled lips. It was the face, Elena acknowledged warily, of a gentleman one did not cross. Not unless one wished to experience the full onslaught of what she believed would be his considerable wrath.

She had, she realised with a sinking heart, been lulled into a false sense of security these past twelve days of only seeing her employer for the half an hour or so he spent in the nursery with Amanda each day, occasions when Elena more often than not excused herself and left father and daughter to their privacy. Consequently, to date he had been a re-mote figure, a haughtily autocratic gentleman who appeared to have more than a little difficulty relating to his young daughter, and as such did not impinge greatly on her own routine and life in the schoolroom.

The gentleman who now regarded her so intently did not appear in the least remote, in regard to her at least. Indeed both he, and his questions, were far too close for comfort. To the point that she felt decidedly overwhelmed by the proxim-ity of that deceptively hard and muscled body. Standing so close to her own as he was, she was able to feel his warmth and smell his deliciously spicy cologne…

She straightened to her own full height, ignoring the fact that she barely reached his broad shoulders as she met that piercing grey gaze unflinchingly. 'I am sure that if you care to check the reference I supplied from the Bamburys you will find it all completely in order.'

And it would be; Elena may be newly cast out upon on the world, but she knew for a fact that a young and widowed Mrs Leighton had acted as tutor and companion to Fiona Bambury before the family had departed for warmer climes at the start of the year, the doctor having recommended as much for the benefit of Lady Bambury's weak chest, from which she had suffered greatly during the harsh English winter. Mrs Leighton, having had no wish to move to the Continent with the Bambury family, had chosen to leave their employment and remain in England.

Except Elena was not, in fact, the aforementioned Mrs Leighton…

'Indeed?' Adam murmured softly.

'If you would care to release me…?'

'Certainly.' The grip he had maintained about her wrist had not been in the least incidental, or an act of intimacy. Rather, it had allowed him to feel the leap in her pulse when he had questioned her as to whether or not she suffered from a guilty conscience.

Adam was now even further convinced that this woman was indeed hiding something. Quite what that something was, he had no idea as yet. But he had every intention of finding out. At the earliest opportunity. After all, he had entrusted this woman with the day-to-day care of his young and impressionable daughter.

Adam looked at her down the length of his nose. 'I must

return to the schoolroom now, but be aware I do not consider this conversation over.'

She gave a slight nod in acknowledgement. 'As your employee, I of course await your further instruction.'

Now there was something to contemplate. Having Elena Leighton—the young and extremely beautiful Elena Leighton, the *widowed* Elena Leighton—awaiting his further instruction…

Adam pondered the dilemma of what he might choose to instruct her to do first. That she take the pins from that unbecoming bun and release that abundance of silky black hair, perhaps? Or that she unfasten those widow's weeds and reveal the fullness of her breasts to him? Or perhaps he would enjoy something more personal to himself?

His gaze moved to the fullness of her lips. What, he wondered, would it feel like to have Elena Leighton on her knees before him and those lips skilfully wrapped about his engorged length? Teasing him, testing him, satisfying him?

Damn it all! What was he thinking?

He was not a man to be led about by that part of his anatomy. If his ill-fated marriage to Fanny had succeeded in nothing else, then it had served to cure him of that particular folly!

Adam stepped away abruptly, a nerve pulsing in his tightly clenched jaw. 'We will talk of this further tomorrow.' He gaze swept over her coldly before he turned on his heel and strode from the room, closing the door forcefully behind him.

Elena staggered back to collapse down on to the chair once more, her breathing fast and shallow, her heart beating erratically in her chest as she endeavoured to calm herself and the panic which had engulfed her, and which she had tried her best to hide, when he had touched her.

She had no idea what had happened to bring about that sudden conversation with him, or the subject of it. Why he had chosen to follow her to Amanda's bedchamber at all even, let alone take hold of her wrist, albeit gently?

What she did know, from the tenor of his questions, and the merciless coldness in his eyes before he left so abruptly, was that he was not a gentleman who would easily forgive being deceived. As Elena had deceived him from the first…

For not only was her name not Elena Leighton, but she was not a widow either—indeed, she had never been married.

Nor had she ever been tutor and companion to Fiona Bambury, the real Mrs Leighton, after leaving the Bamburys' employment, having decided to move to Scotland to care for the elderly parents of her deceased husband.

All of which Elena knew because she had been acquainted with the Bamburys, their country estate some twenty miles distant from her own grandfather's home, the couple occasional guests at his dinner table, as Elena and her grandfather had been occasional dinner guests at theirs'.

Because her name—her true name—was not Elena Leighton, but Miss Magdelena Matthews.

And she was the granddaughter of George Matthews, the previous Duke of Sheffield, and the young woman whose disappearance, so quickly following her grandfather's funeral, still had all of society agog with speculation…

Chapter Three

'Thorne? Damn it, Hawthorne, wait up there, man!'

Adam came to a halt in the hollow-sounding hallways of the House of Lords before turning to see who hailed him. A frown appeared between his eyes as he recognised Justin St Just, Duke of Royston, striding purposefully towards him, several other members moving hastily aside to allow him to pass.

A tall, blond-haired Adonis, with eyes of periwinkle blue set in an arrogantly handsome face, and a powerful build that the ladies all swooned over, Royston was also one of the more charismatic members of the House. Although the two men were of a similar age and regularly attended sessions, and their respective grandmothers had been lifelong friends, the two men had never been particularly close. Their views and lifestyles were too different for that, especially so in recent years, when Adam had avoided most of society events, and Royston was known to have the devil's own luck with the ladies and at the card tables.

Also, Adam had never been sure whether or not Royston had been one of Fanny's legion of lovers…

'Royston,' he greeted the other man coolly.

The duke eyed him with shrewd speculation. 'You seem in somewhat of a hurry to get away tonight, Hawthorne. Off to see a lady friend?' He quirked a mocking brow.

Adam drew himself up stiffly, the two men of similar height. 'I trust that, as a gentleman, you do not expect me to confirm or deny that question?'

'Absolutely not,' Royston drawled unapologetically. 'You appear to have become something of a…recluse in recent years, Hawthorne.'

Adam's gaze became glacial. 'Did you have something specific you wished to discuss with me, or may I now be on my way?'

'Damn, but you have become a prickly bastard!' The duke's expression turned to one of deep irritation. 'Join me in a drink at one of the clubs so that we might talk in a less public arena?' he added impatiently as several people jostled them in their haste to leave and received a legendary St Just scowl for their trouble.

Adam's demeanour lightened slightly. 'As it happens I was on my way to White's.'

The other man grimaced. 'I had a less…respectable club in mind, but certainly, White's will do as a start to the evening. I have my carriage outside.'

'As I have mine.'

The duke regarded him enigmatically for several long seconds before acquiescing. 'Very well. We shall both travel in your coach and mine will follow. Unless you have it in mind to join me in visiting the other clubs later?'

'No.' Adam's tone was uncompromising.

'As you wish.' Royston shrugged.

* * *

They did not speak again until they were safely ensconced at a secluded table at White's and both nursing a large glass of brandy, the duke slumped comfortably in his chair, Adam sitting upright across from him.

The two men had met often in past years at one *ton* function or another. In truth, Adam had always liked the man's arrogant disregard for society's strictures. Indeed, his own reserve towards the man this past few years was caused by his doubts regarding any past involvement between Royston and Fanny; Fanny's affairs had been so numerous during their marriage that Adam was sure even she had forgotten half her lovers' names.

That Adam and Fanny had occupied separate bedchambers after the first month of their marriage had not been generally known and made Fanny's adulterous behaviour, after Amanda was born, all the more of a humiliation. It would have been easier by far if they had occupied separate households, but that Fanny had refused to allow, preferring the shield of the two of them living together to hide her numerous affairs. Unfortunately, she had held the trump card, and had used the excuse of their baby daughter to enforce that decision. For, despite the awkwardness he often felt in being able to relax his emotions and draw close to Amanda as she grew older, Adam loved his young daughter deeply.

'How does your grandmama seem to you nowadays?'

Adam's eyes widened at the subject of Royston's question; Lady Cicely had been the last thing he expected to be discussing this evening, with Royston or anyone else. 'What do you mean?'

Royston stared down morosely into his brandy glass.

'Mine's acting deuced odd and I thought, as the two of them have always been in such cahoots, that I would see if yours was behaving oddly, too?' He grimaced. 'I hope to God it has nothing to do with this Sheffield business, because I am heartily sick of the subject! I liked Sheffield well enough, but all these weeks of speculation as to whether his grand-daughter bumped him off, then stole the family jewels, has become an utter bore.'

The tension left Adam's shoulders. 'No, I do not believe Lady Cicely and the dowager duchess's…current distraction have anything to do with the Sheffield affair.'

St Just perked up slightly. 'No?'

'No.' Adam found himself smiling tightly. 'I believe— and I only know this because Lady Cicely is obviously far less subtle in her intentions than the dowager duchess— that they have it in mind to somehow secure our future wives for us!'

The duke sat forwards abruptly. 'You cannot be serious?'

Adam gave a mocking inclination of his head, enjoying the other's man's consternation. 'They appear to be very serious, yes. Think about it, Royston—they are thick as thieves with the Dowager Countess of Chambourne, whose own grandson has just announced his wedding is to be next month.'

'And you are saying our grandmothers are now plotting our own downfall?'

Adam could not help but let out a brief bark of laughter at Royston's horrified expression. 'The three ladies have always done things together. Their coming-out Season. Marriage. Motherhood. Even widowhood.' He shrugged. 'My own grandmother's less-than-subtle attempts at matchmaking these past few months leads me to believe it is now their intention that their three grandsons shall be married in the same Season.'

'Is it, by God?' The duke slowly sank back in his chair. 'And have you made any decision as to how you intend fending off this attack upon our bachelor state?'

'I see no need to fend it off when my uninterest is so clear.' Adam frowned.

Royston eyed him pityingly. 'You are obviously not as well acquainted with my own grandmama as I!'

'No,' Adam stated, 'but I am well acquainted with my own!'

'And you agree that marriage for either of us is out of the question?'

His mouth tightened. 'I can only speak for myself—but, yes, totally out of the question.' His nostrils flared. 'I have no intention of ever remarrying.'

'And I have no intention of marrying at all—or, at least, not for years and years.' Royston looked at Adam searchingly. 'Even so, I cannot believe that even the dowager duchess would dare—yes, I can, damn it.' He scowled darkly. 'My grandmother would dare anything to ensure the succession of the line!'

Adam gave a slight inclination of his head. 'My own grandmother has also expressed her concerns as to the fact that I have only a daughter and no son.' Not that he had taken any heed of those concerns; Adam felt no qualms whatsoever about his third cousin Wilfred inheriting the title once he had shuffled off his own mortal coil.

'But I take it you do not intend to just sit about waiting for the parson's mousetrap to snap tight about your ankles?'

'Certainly not!' Adam gave a shiver of revulsion.

Royston tapped his chin distractedly. 'There's not much happening in the House for the next week, so now would seem to be as good a time as any for me to absent myself from town and go to the country for a while. I have it in mind to view a hunter Sedgewicke has put my way. With any luck the grandmothers will have lost the scent by the time I return.'

'Highly unlikely,' Adam drawled derisively.

'But, as I am genuinely fond of the dowager duchess, and as such have no wish to be at loggerheads with her over this, it is definitely worth pursuing.' Royston stood up decisively. 'I advise you to do something similar, for I assure you, once my grandmama gets the bit between her teeth there's no stopping her. Oh, and, Hawthorne...?' He paused beside Adam's chair.

'Yes?'

'I make it a point of principle never to dally with married ladies,' Royston declared.

His meaning was not lost on Adam as he answered cautiously. 'That is a very good principle to have.'

'I believe so, yes.' The other man met Adam's gaze briefly, meaningfully, before nodding to him in farewell, pausing only to briefly greet several acquaintances as he made his way out of the club.

Leaving Adam to mull over the predicament of how best to avoid his own grandmother's machinations and to consider his unexpected, and totally inappropriate fantasy earlier regarding Elena Leighton's sensuously plump lips and the uses they might be put to!

Elena assured herself of the neatness of her appearance one last time before knocking briskly on the door of her employer's private study, having received the summons in the nursery a short time ago, delivered by Barnes, requesting she join Lord Hawthorne downstairs immediately.

'Come.'

To say Elena was nervous about the reason for Lord Hawthorne's summons would be putting it mildly—the sudden tension that had sprung up between them yesterday, and their unfinished conversation, were both still very much in her mind. She had no idea what she would say to him if, as she had suggested, he had decided to check her fake references and somehow found them wanting.

She did not see how he could have done so, when she had been so careful in her choice of an alias, her acquaintance with the Bambury family allowing her to write as accurate a reference as possible, considering she was not really Mrs Leighton. But that did not stop Elena from now chewing worriedly on her bottom lip. If Hawthorne chose to dismiss her—

'I said come, damn it.' There was no mistaking the impatient irritation in his lordship's voice.

Elena's cheeks felt flushed as she opened the door and stepped gingerly into a room lined with bookcases halfway up the mahogany-panelled walls, with several original paintings above them, and a huge mahogany desk dominating the room.

At least…it would have been the dominating feature of the study if the gentleman seated behind that desk had not so easily taken that honour for himself!

Tall and broad-shouldered in a superfine of the same dark grey as his eyes over a paler-grey waistcoat, his linen snowy white, the neckcloth at his throat arranged meticulously, his stylish hair dark as a raven's wing above that austerely handsome face, Lord Adam Hawthorne effortlessly filled the room with his overwhelming presence.

But it was a presence that Elena did not find in the least frightening, as she did so many other men following her cousin Neville's cruelty to her. Indeed, Adam Hawthorne, despite—or because of?—his air of detachment, was a man who inspired trust rather than fear...

His mouth thinned disapprovingly as he leant back his chair. 'Did you have some difficulty just now in understanding my invitation to enter?'

'No. I—' She breathed out softly through her teeth before straightening her shoulders determinedly. 'No, of course I did not,' she answered more strongly. 'I merely paused before entering in order to...to adjust my appearance.' It took all of her considerable self-will to withstand that critical gaze as it swept over her slowly, from the neat and smoothly styled bun at her nape, the pallor of her face, down over the black of her gown, to the toes of her black ankle boots peeking out from beneath the hem of that gown, before once again returning to her now-flushed and discomforted face.

He observed her coolly. 'Might I enquire why it is you still choose to wear your widow's weeds when your husband died almost two years ago?'

Elena was visibly taken aback by the directness of his question. Nor did she intend—or, in the circumstances, was able—to explain that she chose to wear black out of respect for the death two months ago of her beloved grandfather, George Matthews, the previous Duke of Sheffield!

He raised a dark brow. 'Perhaps it is that you loved your husband so much that you still mourn his loss?'

'Or perhaps it is that I am simply too poor to be able to

replace my mourning gowns with something more frivolous?' Elena felt stung into replying as she easily heard the underlying scepticism in his derisive tone.

Adam eyed her thoughtfully. 'If that should indeed be the situation, would it not have been prudent to ask me for an advance on your wages?'

Elena's eyes widened. 'I trust you are not about to insult me further by suggesting I might use your money with which to purchase new gowns, my lord?'

Adam frowned his irritation with this young woman's prickliness. He tried to not remember Royston had accused him of having the very same fault only yesterday evening…

Adam owed his own withdrawal from society to the adulterous behaviour of his deceased wife. His fierce pride would not allow him to relax his guard when in the company of the *ton*. Elena Leighton's surliness also appeared to be a matter of pride, but in her case, it was pride over her lack of finances. 'It would be money you have earned in taking care of Amanda,' he pointed out calmly.

'Except, as I suggested might be the case yesterday, I believe you may be dissatisfied with my services…?'

Damn it, Adam wished she would not use such words as that!

The word 'service' once again conjured up images of this woman performing all manner of intimacies he would rather not be allowed to distract him at this moment…

Adam found had already been distracted—and aroused— enough already by the pretty pout of her reddened lips when she entered his study a few minutes ago. So much so that the material of his pantaloons was now stretched uncomfortably tight across the throb of his swollen shaft beneath his desk.

He stood up to try to ease that discomfort before realising what he had done and turning away to hide the evidence of his arousal, gazing out of the window into the garden at the back of his London home. 'I do not recall making any such remark.'

'You implied it when you questioned my lack of years—'

'Mrs Leighton!' Adam turned back sharply, linking his hands in front of him to hide that telltale bulge as he observed her through narrowed lids. 'I believe we have already discussed my views regarding you making assumptions about any of my comments or actions. If I have something to say, then be assured I will not hesitate to say it. How long will it take you to make ready to leave Hawthorne House?'

Elena stepped back with a gasp, her face paling as she raised her hand in an effort to calm her rapidly beating heart at the mere thought of being cast out alone into the world once again. 'You are dismissing me…?'

'For heaven's sake, woman, will you stop reading meanings into my every word, meanings that are simply not there!' Adam exploded as he scowled down the length of his aristocratic nose at her. 'I have several things in need of my attention on my estate in Cambridgeshire, and it is my wish for you and Amanda to accompany me there.'

'To Cambridgeshire?'

He nodded tersely. 'That is what I have just said, yes.'

'Oh…'

He flicked a black brow. 'There is some problem with that course of action?

It was a county in England that Elena had never visited

before, but of course she had no objection to accompanying Lord Hawthorne and his daughter there.

Not as such...

The truth of the matter was that Elena had made a conscious decision to move to London after her grandfather had died so suddenly, and following the terrible scene with her cousin, which had occurred after the funeral.

Her grandfather, once a soldier, had told her that the best way to hide from the enemy was in plain sight, which was the reason Elena had chosen to change her appearance as far as she was able and adopt an assumed name, before accepting the post as governess to Amanda Hawthorne, a post that largely involved staying inside the house with her charge. Even if Neville Matthews, her cousin and abuser, and the new Duke of Sheffield, did decide to come to town, then he was unlikely to accept any but private invitations following the recent death of their grandfather.

She did not believe that she had any acquaintances living in Cambridgeshire, but she nevertheless felt safer in the anonymity of London...

'Perhaps,' Adam continued relentlessly as he saw the uncertainty in her expression, 'it is that you have...acquaintances, here in London, you would be reluctant to be parted from, even for a week or so...?' Just because the woman had been widowed for almost two years, and she still wore her black clothes as a sign of her continued mourning, did not mean that she had not taken a lover during that time. Several, in fact.

Indeed, Adam had heard it said that physical closeness was one of the things most lamented when one's husband or wife died. Not true in his case, of course; he and Fanny had not shared so much as a brief kiss from the moment he had learnt of her first infidelity just a month after their wedding.

But Elena Leighton was a young and beautiful woman, and she had already explained that she still wore her widow's attire for financial reasons rather than emotional ones. It was naïve on Adam's part to assume that she had not taken a lover. Quite when she met with that lover—perhaps on her one afternoon off a week?—he had no wish to know!

'We would only be gone for a week?' Her expression had brightened considerably.

Irritating Adam immensely. Which was in itself ridiculous; the woman's obvious eagerness not to be parted from her lover for any length of time was of absolutely no consequence or interest to him. 'Approximately,' he qualified. 'At the moment, the exact length of time I will need to stay in Cambridgeshire is undecided.' Mainly because Adam felt a certain inner discomfort about this departure for Cambridgeshire at all.

It was true that there were several matters there in need of his attention, but he had no doubts they were matters he could have settled by the sending of a letter to his man who managed the estate in his absence. His decision to visit the estate in person had more to do with his conversation with Royston last night, than any real urgency to deal with those matters himself.

Not because Adam was in any real fear of his grandmother being successful in her endeavours to procure him a suitable wife—that, he had vowed long ago, would never happen!—but because, much as his grandmother might irritate him on occasion, he did have a genuine affection for her, and as such he had no wish to hurt her. Like Royston, removing himself from London, far away from his relative's machinations, seemed the best way for him to avoid doing that.

However, he could not avoid having dinner at Lady Cecily's home this evening, when no doubt a suitable number of eligible young ladies would be produced for his approval—or otherwise, as he absolutely knew would be the case!—but as it would also give Adam the opportunity of telling his grandmother in person of his imminent departure for Cambridgeshire, he was willing to suffer through that particular inconvenience.

He frowned as he saw the look of consternation on the governess's face. 'I repeat, is there some objection to your travelling into Cambridgeshire with myself and Amanda?'

Elena drew herself up stiffly. 'No, of course there is not. And to answer your earlier question, I can have my own and Amanda's things packed and ready for departure in a matter of hours.'

Adam gave a tight smile. 'It is not necessary that you be quite so hasty,' he drawled. 'I have a dinner engagement this evening. First thing tomorrow morning will be quite soon enough. I trust that will give you sufficient time in which to…inform any relatives and friends that you are to be absent from Town for the next week?'

'Approximately.'

'Indeed,' he conceded drily.

The only relative Elena had left in the world was Neville and the moment *he* learnt of her whereabouts he would no doubt call for her immediate arrest!

And Elena had decided at the onset that the less she involved her friends in her current unhappy situation—and

she did have several who still believed in her innocence—
the better it would be for them.

She necessarily had to accept a small amount of financial
help from her closest friend, Lizzie Carlton, after fleeing
the duke's estate in Yorkshire in late February, and she had
also informed Lizzie by letter that she had safely reached
London and secured suitable lodgings. But Elena could not,
in all conscience, allow her friend to become embroiled in
this situation any further than that.

Indeed, she had resolved to completely become the widowed Mrs Elena Leighton, a schooled young lady who had
fallen on hard times since her husband's untimely death. As
she must, if she were to be successful in her endeavour of
hiding in full view of the populace of England's capital; it
was sad, but true, that the *ton* rarely noticed the existence of
the people whom they employed, let alone those employed
by the other members of England's aristocracy.

'There is no one whom I would wish to inform, my lord,'
she answered her employer coolly. 'If I might be allowed to
return to the schoolroom now?'

'Of course.'

'Thank you, my lord.'

Adam tapped his cheek thoughtfully as he watched her
quietly exit the study before closing the door behind her,
irritated at the realisation that she had once again avoided
revealing anything about herself or her connections. As she
was perfectly entitled to do, he allowed; her family connections, or even her romantic ones, had been of no significance
to him at the commencement of her employment with him,
and they should not be of any import now.

Except he could not prevent himself from wondering—

despite her denial of the need for her to inform anyone of her imminent departure for Cambridgeshire—as to which gentleman might currently be the lucky recipient of the ministrations of those full and sensuous lips...

Chapter Four

'She is merely ill from travelling in the carriage.' Elena looked up at Adam apologetically as he opened the door of the carriage just in time for Amanda to lean out and be violently sick on his black, brown-topped Hessians already covered in dust from where he had ridden on horseback all day beside the carriage. 'Oh, dear.' Elena moved forwards on her seat to help her distressed charge down the steps on to the cobbled courtyard of the inn they were to stay in for the night, cuddling Amanda against her before turning her attention to those now ruined boots. 'Perhaps—'

'Perhaps if you had informed me of Amanda's discomfort earlier it would not have come to this.' Adam glowered down at her.

Elena gasped her incredulity at an accusation she believed completely unfair. 'Amanda was perfectly all right until a short time ago and has only found this last few bumpy miles something of a trial. Also, my lord, as you had ridden on ahead I could not inform you of anything…'

'Yes. Yes,' Adam snapped, waving his hand impatiently.

'I suggest you take Amanda upstairs to our rooms while I speak to the innkeeper about organising some water to be brought up for her bath.'

Elena kept her arm about the now quietly sobbing Amanda. 'And some food, my lord. Some dry bread and fresh water will perhaps settle Amanda's stomach before bedtime.'

'Of course.' Adam turned his attention away from his ruined boots to instead look down at his distressed daughter. Amanda's face was a pasty white, her eyes dark and cloudy smudges of blue in that pallor, her usually lustrous gold hair damp about her face. Nor had her own clothing escaped being spattered, her little shoes and hose in as sorry a state as his boots. 'There, there, Amanda, it is not the end of the world— You are soiling your clothing now, Mrs Leighton,' he warned sharply as Elena ignored the results of Amanda's nausea, moving down on her haunches beside the little girl and gently wiping the tears from her face with her own lace-edged handkerchief.

'My clothes are of no importance at this moment, sir.' Her eyes flashed up at him in stormy warning, before she returned her attention to the cleansing of Amanda's face, murmuring soft assurances to the little girl.

Adam clamped down on his feelings of inadequacy. 'I was merely pointing out—'

'If you will excuse us?' She straightened, obvious indignation rolling off her in waves. 'I should like to see to Amanda's needs before considering my own.'

A praiseworthy sentiment, Adam admitted as he stood in the courtyard and watched her walk away, her back ramrod straight as she entered the inn, her arms about Amanda.

Except for the fact that he knew that parting comment had

been made as a deliberate set down for what she perceived as his lack of concern for his young daughter…

A totally erroneous assumption for her to have made; Adam knew his behaviour to be yet another example of his own lack of understanding in how to relate to a six-year-old girl, rather than the lack of concern Elena Leighton had assumed it to be. No excuse, of course, but Adam had no idea how to even go about healing the distance which seemed to yawn wider with each passing day between himself and Amanda.

Nor had the governess's anger towards him abated in the slightest, Adam realised an hour or so later when she joined him for dinner in the private parlour of the inn, as he had requested when the maid went to deliver food and drink to Amanda. Her eyes sparkled a deep and fiery green-blue as she swept into the room, with a deep flush to her cheeks and her whole demeanour, in yet another of those dratted black gowns, one of bristly disapproval and resentment—the former no doubt still on Amanda's behalf, the resentment possibly due to the peremptory instruction to join him for dinner.

'Would you care for a glass of Madeira, Mrs Leighton…?' Adam attempted civility. Bathed and dressed in clean clothes and a fresh pair of boots, he felt far more human; he tried not to think about the fact that his man Reynolds was probably upstairs even now, crying as he attempted to salvage the first pair!

'No, thank you.'

'Then perhaps you would prefer sherry or wine?'

She looked at him coolly. 'I do not care for strong liquor at all.'

Adam frowned. 'I do not believe any of the refreshments I offered can be referred to as "strong liquor".'

'Nevertheless…'

'Then perhaps we should just sit down and eat?' He could barely restrain his frustration with her frostiness as he moved forwards to politely pull back a chair for her.

'I had expected to dine in my bedchamber with Amanda,' she stated.

'And I would prefer that you dine here with me,' he countered, looking pointedly towards the chair.

She frowned as she stepped forwards. 'Thank you.' She sat rigidly in the chair, her body stiff and unyielding, ensuring that her spine did not come into contact with the back of the chair.

Adam gave a rueful grimace as he moved around the table and took his own seat opposite her, waiting until the innkeeper himself had served their food—a thick steaming stew accompanied by fresh crusty bread—before speaking again. 'Should I expect to be subjected to this wall of ice throughout the whole of dinner, or would you perhaps prefer to castigate me now and get it over with?' He quirked one dark brow enquiringly.

'Castigate you, my lord?' She kept her head bowed as she studiously arranged her napkin across her knees.

Adam gave a weary sigh. 'Mrs Leighton, I am a widower in my late twenties, with no previous experience of children, let alone six-year-old females. As such, I admit I know naught of how to deal with the day-to-day upsets of my young daughter.'

Elena slowly looked up to consider him across the table, ignoring his obvious handsomeness for the moment—difficult as that might be when he looked so very smart in a deep-blue superfine over a beige waistcoat—and instead trying to see the man he described. There was no disputing the fact that he was a widower in his late twenties. But Lord Adam Hawthorne was also a man whom senior politicians were reputed to hold in great regard, a man who ran his estates and a London household without so much as blinking an eye; it was impossible to think that such a man could find himself defeated by the needs of a six-year-old girl.

Or was it…?

He was a man who preferred to hold himself aloof from society. From all emotions. Why was it so impossible to believe he found it difficult to relate to his young daughter?

Some of the stiffness left Elena's spine. 'I think you will find that six-year-old young ladies have the same need to be loved as the older ones, my lord.'

He frowned. '"Older ones", Mrs Leighton…?'

She became slightly flustered under that icy gaze. 'I believe most ladies are desirous of that, yes, my lord.'

'I see.' His frown deepened. 'And are you questioning my ability to feel that emotion, Mrs Leighton?'

'Of course not.' Elena gasped softly.

'Then perhaps it is only my affection for my daughter you question…?'

Her cheeks felt warm. 'It is only the manner in which you choose to show that affection which—well, which—'

'Yes?'

'Could you not have hugged Amanda earlier rather

than—' She broke off, suddenly not sure how far to continue with this.

'"Rather than…?"' he prompted softly.

She took hold of her courage and looked him straight in the eye. 'Amanda was upset and in need of comforting—preferably a physical demonstration of affection from her father.'

He looked obviously disconcerted with her candour.

Perhaps she had gone too far? After all, it was really none of her concern how Lord Hawthorne behaved towards his young daughter; she had briefly forgotten that she was no longer Miss Magdelena Matthews, the privileged and beloved granddaughter of a duke who was allowed to speak her mind, but was now an employee. And employees did not castigate their employers!

Elena lowered her gaze demurely. 'I apologise, my lord. I spoke out of turn.'

Now it was Adam's turn to feel discomforted. Elena Leighton's disapproval apart, he was fully aware that he had difficulty in demonstrating the deep affection he felt for Amanda; she had been only two years old when her mother died and had been attended to completely in the nursery until quite recently. Not that Fanny had ever been a particularly attentive mother when she was alive, but she had occasionally taken an interest and showered Amanda with gifts completely inappropriate to her age, whereas, perhaps partly because of his experiences with Fanny, Adam now found it difficult to show that deep affection he felt for his six-year-old daughter. Which he knew was not a fault of Amanda's, but due to his own emotional reserve as much as his lack of experience as a father.

He looked enquiringly at her. 'I thought it normal for men in society to spend only an hour or so a day in the company of their female offspring?'

'You do not strike me as the sort of gentleman who would be concerned as to how others might behave.'

'Possibly not,' he allowed slowly. 'But I am often at a loss as to know how I should behave. Perhaps you might endeavour to help guide me, as to how a father should behave towards his six-year-old daughter?'

Elena blinked. 'My lord...?'

Adam tried not to feel vexed at her surprise. 'I am suggesting, as Amanda's governess, that you might perhaps aid me in how best to take more of an interest in the happenings in my daughter's life.'

Her lips thinned so that they did not look in the least plump and inviting. 'Are you laughing at me, my lord?'

His top lip curled back derisively in response to that. 'I believe you will find, Mrs Leighton, that I rarely find reason to laugh at anything, so I very much doubt I will have made you the exception.' He eyed her closely, no longer sure he had any appetite for the rich and meaty-smelling stew that had been provided for them.

He had actually been anticipating the evening ahead when he dressed for dinner earlier, could not remember the last time he had dined alone with a beautiful woman—apart from Fanny, whom he had despised utterly, when those rare evenings they had dined at home together had been more a lesson in endurance than something to be enjoyed.

Just as his grandmother's dinner the evening before had been something to be endured rather than enjoyed!

Lady Cecily had totally outdone herself in that she had

provided not one, not two, but four eligible young ladies for his approval. All of them young and beautiful—and all of them as empty-headed as Fanny!

He already knew that Elena Leighton was not of that ilk, that she was educated, learned and that he found her conversation stimulating. As he found her physically stimulating… Except on those occasions when she was determined to rebuke him for what she perceived as his lack of feeling for Amanda!

'Perhaps we should just eat our dinner before it cools any further.' He didn't wait for her response, but turned his attention to eating the food in front of him.

Elena ate her own stew more slowly, aware that she had displeased him. Was he justified to feel that? She was, after all, employed to attend to his daughter, not to comment on his behaviour and attitudes.

Disconcerted at being summoned to join him for dinner, and the two of them sitting down to eat their meal together alone in this private parlour, she had again forgotten the façade of being the widowed Mrs Elena Leighton and instead talked to him as an equal, forgetting that she no longer had the right to do so.

If Adam Hawthorne were ever to discover her true identity, then no doubt he would not hesitate to turn her over to the authorities himself!

She placed her spoon down carefully beside the bowl, her food untouched. 'I must apologise once again for speaking out of turn, my lord. It is not my place—'

'And exactly what do you consider to be "your place", Mrs Leighton?' he rasped irritably as he looked across at her with stormy-grey eyes.

Elena chewed on her bottom lip before answering, once again disconcerted, this time by the intensity of that deep-grey gaze. 'Well, it is certainly not to tell you how you should behave towards your own daughter.'

'And yet you have not hesitated to do so.'

She gave a wince. 'And for that I—'

'Do not apologise to me a second time in as many minutes, Mrs Leighton!' Adam pushed his chair back noisily as he stood up.

Elena looked up at him warily as he stood glowering down at her. 'I did not mean to displease you...'

'No...?' His expression softened. 'Then what did you mean to do to me, Mrs Leighton?'

Elena's pulse leapt at the sound of that huskiness, the lacing of sensuality she heard underlying his tone, his piercing grey gaze now appearing to be transfixed upon her mouth. Disturbing her with sensations she was unfamiliar with.

Elena ran the moistness of her tongue nervously across her lips before speaking. 'I do not believe I had any intent other than to apologise for speaking to you so frankly about what is a private matter.'

'No...?' He was far too overpowering in the smallness of the room. Too large. Too intense. Too overwhelmingly male!

She found herself unable to look away from him, her heart seeming to sputter and falter, before commencing to beat a wild tattoo in her chest. A fact he was well aware of, if the shifting of his gaze to the pulse in her throat was any indication. A gaze that slowly moved steadily downwards before then lingering on the ivory swell of her breasts as she continued to breathe shallowly.

As Miss Magdelena Matthews, she had of course attended assemblies and dinner parties in Yorkshire, as she had many other local social occasions. But her mother had unfortunately died shortly before her coming-out Season two years ago, and her grandfather had not been a man who particularly cared for town or London society, and his visits there had been few and far between, usually only on business or with the intention of attending the House of Lords.

As a consequence, even following her year of mourning for her mother, her grandfather's preference for the country meant that Magdelena had spent no time at all in London, and so had not learnt how to recognise or to deal with a gentleman's attentions. Indeed, Elena's only experience with a gentleman of the *ton* was of such a traumatic nature that she had feared ever becoming the focus of a male ever again.

Except Adam Hawthorne did not incite that same fear within her...

Rather the opposite.

The warmth she detected in the grey softness of his gaze, as he continued to watch the rise and fall of her bosom, filled her with unaccustomed heat. Her heart once again fluttered wildly and caused her pulse to do likewise, and her breasts—those same breasts he continued to regard so intently—seemed to swell and grow, the rose-coloured tips tingling with the same unaccustomed heat, making the fitted bodice of her gown feel uncomfortably tight.

It was an unexpected, and yet exhilarating, sensation, every inch of her skin hot and almost painfully sensitive, and she felt almost light-headed as she continued to shyly meet his gaze through the sweep of her dark lashes.

Adam had no idea what he was about!

The fact that he had anticipated enjoying Elena Leighton's stimulating presence for a few hours, her obvious intelligence and sensitivity, did not mean he had to take their relationship any further than that. Indeed, he would be foolish to ever think of doing so.

Not only was she a splendid addition to his household, in that she appeared to have already developed a very caring relationship with his young daughter, but she *was* in his employ. And whilst some of the male members of the *ton* might feel few qualms in regard to taking advantage of their pretty and young female household staff, Adam had certainly never done so. Not even at the worst moments of his marriage to Fanny had he stooped to seeking comfort or solace from one of the young women working in any of his own households. Nor was it his intention to start now with this one.

He straightened abruptly. 'I suggest that we eat the rest of our meal before making an early night of it.' Adam gave a pained wince as her face became a flushed and fiery red. 'By that, I meant, of course, that we should then retire to our respective bedchambers.'

'I did not for a moment suppose you meant anything other, my lord,' she answered sharply.

Adam pulled his chair out noisily and resumed his seat. 'Good,' he growled, more than a little unsettled himself, both by their conversation, and the things which had not been said…

Thankfully Amanda seemed to have recovered fully the following day as they resumed the last part of their journey, the weather warm enough that Elena had been able to lower the windows and so allow some air into the carriage, and also making it possible for Amanda to poke her head out of the window when she saw something that interested her.

Lord Hawthorne had been noticeably absent when Elena and Amanda ate their breakfast earlier in the private parlour of the inn and he had again ridden on ahead once they resumed their journey, no doubt anxious to arrive at his estate so that he might begin to deal with whatever business had brought him to Cambridgeshire in the first place.

Elena sincerely hoped that it had nothing to do with his wishing to avoid her own outspoken company.

She had woken early this morning to the sounds of certain other inhabitants of the inn already being awake: the grooms chatting outside in the cobbled yard as they fed the horses prior to travel and the sounds of food being prepared for the guests in the kitchen below.

A quick glance at the neighbouring bed had shown that Amanda was still asleep, thus allowing Elena the luxury of remaining cosily beneath her own bedcovers for a few minutes longer, as she thought of the time she had spent alone with Adam Hawthorne yesterday evening.

It had taken only those few minutes' contemplation for Elena to convince herself she had imagined the intimate intensity of his gaze, both on her lips and breasts; her employer was not a man known for displaying desire for women of the *ton*, let alone the woman who was engaged to care for his daughter.

'Is it your intention to spend the evening, as well as all of the day, seated inside the carriage, Mrs Leighton?'

Elena's cheeks were flushed as she came back to an awareness of her present surroundings, looking out of the open carriage door to see Lord Hawthorne standing outside on the gravel looking in at her mockingly. While she'd been lost in contemplation, the carriage had come to a halt in the courtyard in front of two curved-stone staircases leading up from either side to the entrance of Hawthorne Hall. Amanda had already stepped down from the carriage and was even now skipping her way up the staircase on the left to where the huge oak door already stood open in readiness to welcome the master of the house and his entourage.

Elena stepped slowly down from the carriage to look up at the four-storeyed house; it was a grand greystone building, with a tall, pillared portico at the top of the two staircases, with two curved wings abutting the main house, dozens of windows gleaming in the late evening sunshine.

It was, Elena noted with some dismay, a house very like the one at her grandfather's estate in Yorkshire, where she and her mother had moved to live following the death of Elena's father, and where the late Duke of Sheffield had met his end so unexpectedly two months ago.

'Mrs Leighton…?'

She smiled politely as she turned to look at Hawthorne. 'You have a beautiful home, my lord.'

For some inexplicable reason Adam did not believe her praise of Hawthorne Hall to be wholly sincere. Indeed, the strained look to her mouth and those expressive blue-green eyes convinced him of such.

He turned to look at the house with critical eyes, looking for flaws and finding none. All was completely in order. As it should be, considering the wages he paid his estate manager.

He turned back to Elena Leighton. 'Then do you suppose we might both be allowed to go inside it now?' he prompted drily.

'Of course.' She nodded distractedly, her smile still strained as she preceded him up the stairs, her dark curls hidden beneath another of those unbecoming black bonnets, her black gown reflective of that drabness.

A drabness that suddenly irritated Adam intensely. 'If I might be allowed to speak frankly, Mrs Leighton?' He fell into step beside her as they neared the top of the stairs.

She glanced up at him. 'My lord?'

'I intend to ask Mrs Standish to arrange for a local seamstress to call upon you at her earliest convenience.'

A frown appeared between the fineness of her eyes as she came to a halt at the top of the staircase. 'Mrs Standish, my lord?'

Adam had spent all of his adult life answering to that title—but it had never before irked him in the way it did when this woman addressed him so coolly!

Which was utterly ridiculous—what else should she call him? She was not his social equal, but a paid servant, and as such her form of address to him was perfectly correct. Should he expect her to call him Adam, as if the two of them were friends, or possibly more? Of course he should not!

He scowled his irrational annoyance. 'She is the housekeeper here and as such in charge of all the female staff, and consequently the clothing they are required to wear within the household.'

Elena's expression became wary. 'Yes, my lord…?'

Adam sighed. 'And I am tired of looking at you in these— these widow's weeds.' He indicated her appearance with a dismissive wave of his hand. 'I shall instruct Mrs Standish to see to it that you are supplied with more fitting apparel.'

She raised surprised dark brows. 'More fitting for what, my lord?'

Oh, to the devil with it! Another of those questions this particular woman seemed to ask and which took Adam into the realms of the unacceptable.

As it did now, as he instantly imagined Elena Leighton as his mistress, all of that glorious ebony hair loose about her shoulders, her naked body covered only by one of those delicate silk negligees Fanny had been so fond of parading about in. Not black as with Fanny, but rather white or the palest cream, in order to set off the almost luminous quality to this woman's ivory skin and allowing the tips of her breasts to poke invitingly and revealingly against that silky material. What colour would her nipples be? he wondered. A fresh peach, perhaps? Or, more likely, considering the colour of her lips, a deep and blushing rose—

His mouth tightened with self-disgust as he realised that he had once again allowed himself thoughts of this woman that were wholly inappropriate to the relationship that existed between the two of them. 'For spending so many hours a day with a six-year-girl who has already suffered the loss of her mother, without your own clothing reminding her of death on a daily basis,' he rasped harshly.

'Oh!' She gasped. 'I had not thought of that! And I should have done so. I am so sorry, my—'

'I believe I have already made clear my feelings regarding this constant and irritating need you feel to apologise to me for one reason or another.' Adam looked down the long length of his nose at her.

'But I should have thought—'

'Mrs Leighton…' He barely controlled his impatience at her continued self-condemnation. Damn it, he had thought only to get her out of those horrible clothes— Well, not exactly *out* of them— Oh, damn it to hell! 'Mrs Leighton, I am tired and I am irritable, furthermore I am in need of a decent glass of brandy, before sitting down to enjoy an even more decent dinner cooked by my excellent chef here, before then spending a night in my own bed!'

She blinked at his vehemence. 'I—please do not let me delay you any further.'

'If you will excuse me, then? Jeffries will see to it that you are shown the nursery and schoolroom as well as your own bedchamber.'

'As you wish, my lord.' Her lashes lowered with a demureness Adam viewed with suspicion.

'It is indeed as I wish.' He scowled, adding, as she made no further comment, 'Goodnight, Mrs Leighton.'

'My lord.' She nodded without so much as glancing up.

Adam gave her one last irritated glance before entering the house, pausing only long enough to hand his hat and cloak to the patiently waiting Jeffries, before striding down the hallway to his study without so much as a second glance.

Where, Adam sincerely hoped, he would not be haunted by any further lascivious thoughts about the widowed Mrs Elena Leighton.

Chapter Five

‘I believe there has been some sort of mistake…’ Elena viewed with consternation the brightly coloured materials the seamstress had laid out on the *chaise* in the bedchamber for her approval. They were predominantly green and blue, but there was also a cream silk and a lemon, all with matching lace.

Mrs Hepworth was aged perhaps thirty and prettily plump, that plumpness shown to advantage in a gown of sky blue in a high-waisted style that perfectly displayed her excellence as a seamstress. ‘Mrs Standish was quite specific in her instructions concerning which materials I should bring with me for your approval, Mrs Leighton.’

‘Are you sure?’

‘Oh, yes, I am very sure of Mrs Standish’s instructions, Mrs Leighton,’ the seamstress confirmed cheerfully.

And Mrs Standish, as Elena knew, had received *her* instructions from the infuriating Lord Hawthorne…

‘Come,’ Adam instructed distractedly as he concentrated on the figures laid out in the ledger before him. The study door opened, then was softly closed again, followed by a lengthy silence. So lengthy that Adam was finally forced to look up beneath frowning brows, that frown easing slightly as he saw a flushed and obviously discomforted Elena Leighton standing in front of his wide mahogany desk. 'Yes…?'

She moistened her lips. 'I am not disturbing you, my lord?'

'I believe you have used the wrong tense, Mrs Leighton— you have obviously already interrupted me,' he drawled pointedly as he leant back in his chair to look across at her.

He had seen Amanda only briefly these past two days, and her governess not at all, having been kept busy dealing with the myriad of paperwork involved in running the estate. He frowned now as he saw the governess was still wearing one of those unbecoming black gowns that so infuriated him. 'Has Mrs Standish not yet engaged the services of a seamstress—?'

'That is the very reason I am here, my lord,' she rushed into speech. 'I fear there has been some sort of mistake. The seamstress brought with her materials that are more suited to—to being worn by a lady than a—a child's governess.'

Adam arched one dark brow. 'And is that child's governess not also a lady?'

'I—well, I would hope to be considered as such, yes.' Elena looked more than a little flustered. 'But the materials are of the finest silks and of such an array of colours, when I had been expecting—I had expected—'

'Yes?'

She bit her lip. 'I had thought to be wearing serviceable browns, with possibly a beige gown in which to attend church on Sundays.'

Adam gave a wince at the thought of this woman's ivory skin against such unbecoming shades. 'That would not do at all, Mrs Leighton.' His top lip curled with displeasure. 'Brighter colours, a deep rose, blues and greens, are more suited to your colouring, with perhaps a cream for Sundays.'

Exactly the colours, Elena realised, that the plump Mrs Hepworth had just laid out for her approval.

'And I am not a churchgoer,' Adam continued drily, 'but you may attend if you feel so inclined.'

'But is it not your duty to attend as—?' Elena broke off abruptly, aware she had once again almost been inappropriately outspoken in this man's presence. Inappropriate for the widowed Mrs Elena Leighton, that was. Which, considering she had not set sight on, nor heard sound of Adam Hawthorne these past two days, she probably should not have done.

'You were saying, madam?'

'Nothing, my lord.' It really was not her place to rebuke him for not attending church, even if she knew her grandfather had made it his habit to always attend the Sunday service. Not because he was particularly religious, but because he maintained that conversation afterwards was the best way to mingle with and learn about the people who lived and worked on his estate.

'This reticence is not what I have come to expect from you, Mrs Leighton,' he drawled mockingly.

'No. Well…' She pursed her lips as she thought of the past two days, the time that had elapsed since she had last irritated him with her outspokenness. 'Perhaps I am finally learning to practise long-overdue caution in my conversations with you, my lord.'

Adam stared at her in astonishment for several seconds before he suddenly burst out laughing. A low and rusty sound, he acknowledged self-derisively, but it was, none the less, laughter. 'Did you tend to be this outspoken when you were employed by the Bamburys?' He continued to smile ruefully.

'I do not understand.'

Adam knew Lord Geoffrey Bambury slightly, from their occasional clashes in the House in the past, and knew him as a man who believed totally in the superiority of the hierarchy that made up much of society; as such Adam did not see him as a man who would suffer being rebuked by a servant, which the other man would most certainly have considered Elena Leighton's role to be in his own household.

He shrugged. 'I merely wondered if I was the exception to the rule as the recipient of this...honesty of yours, or if it is your usual habit to say exactly what is on your mind?'

'Oh, I do not believe I would go as far as to say I have done that, my lord—oh.' She grimaced. 'I meant, of course—'

'I believe I may guess what you meant, Mrs Leighton,' Adam said. 'And as such, I should probably applaud your efforts at exercising some discretion, at least.'

'Yes. Well.' Those blue-green eyes avoided meeting his amused gaze.

'You were about to tell me my religious duty, I believe?' he prompted softly.

Too softly, in Elena's opinion; she really did seem to have adopted the habit of speaking above her present station in life to this particular gentleman! Perhaps, on this occasion because she was still slightly disconcerted by the sound and sight of his laughter a few minutes ago...

He had informed her only three evenings ago that he found very little amusement in anything, and yet just now he had laughed outright. Even more startling was how much more handsome, almost boyish, he appeared when he gave in to that laughter.

She swallowed before speaking. 'Of course I was not, my lord. I just—I merely wondered if attending the local church would not be of real benefit to you, in terms of meeting and talking with the people living on your estate and the local village?'

'Indeed?' The suddenly steely edge to his tone was unmistakable.

Elena felt the colour warming her cheeks. 'Yes. I—I only remark upon it because I know it was Lord Bambury's habit to do so.' Her grandfather and Lord Bambury had discussed that very subject over dinner one evening at Sheffield Park…

Adam raised dark brows over cold grey eyes. 'And you are suggesting I might follow his example?'

Her cheeks burned at his icy derision. 'Perhaps we should return to the subject of the materials for my uniform, my lord?'

'What uniform?' He looked at her blankly.

Elena's eyes widened. 'Did you not say two days ago that it was your wish for me to wear a uniform whilst I am attending Amanda?'

He gave a slow shake of his head. 'I do not recall ever using the word "uniform" when I made the request for you to wear less sombre clothing in future.'

'But—' Elena frowned, thinking back to that conversation when they had arrived at Hawthorne Hall. 'I assumed…'

He gave a tight smile. 'It is never wise to make assumptions, Mrs Leighton.'

When it concerned this gentleman, obviously not. 'So it was your intention all along to supply me with new, prettier gowns, rather than simply a uniform?'

'Yes.' There was no mistaking the challenge in his monosyllabic reply.

Elena drew in a sharp breath. 'And is this—would this be your way of—of circumventing my earlier objections about this matter?'

'It would, yes.'

Elena clenched her fists tightly to rein in her frustration as Adam Hawthorne continued to look up at her calmly, one eyebrow raised in mocking—and infuriating!—query. 'In that case…perhaps I might ask something of you in return?'

That dark brow rose even higher. 'In return for what, madam?'

'In return for my making no further objections to the procuring of new gowns for me to wear.' In truth, Elena's heart had leapt in excitement earlier just at sight of those wonderful colours and delicious fabrics. True, she should out of respect for the recent death of her grandfather insist upon retaining her mourning clothes, but having already worn black for her mother for half a year, and then greys and dull purple for the rest of the year, with only a matter of months to enjoy wearing brighter colours, her youth and vivacity now chafed at thoughts of having to wear the sombre clothing any longer. Especially when she thought of those beautiful coloured silks and exquisite lace draped on the *chaise* in her bedchamber…

'In return for?' Adam felt incredulous. 'You make it

sound as if you are the one doing me a service rather than the other way about?'

She arched a dark brow. 'And am I not?'

Adam's lids narrowed. Could this young woman possibly know how much he wished to see her in something other than those unbecoming black gowns she habitually wore? Or preferably in nothing at all!

He drew in a sharp breath. 'You are being presumptuous again, madam.'

'If that is so, then I apologise.' She looked flustered again. 'I am merely—I only wished to—' She broke off to gather herself and tried again, more calmly. 'Several days ago you asked for my help, for suggestions in how you might deal better with your daughter. It is Amanda's dearest wish to own her own pony and to learn to ride it, my lord.'

Adam stared at her, not sure that he had heard her correctly. Not sure he had ever met anyone quite like Elena Leighton before. 'Let me see if I understood your terms correctly?' he spoke slowly. 'You are willing to accept the new gowns, without fuss, if I agree to buying Amanda a pony and allowing her to learn to ride?'

'No.'

'No?' Adam looked perplexed as he sat forwards. 'But did you not just say exactly that?'

Elena's chin rose determinedly. 'I did say that it is Amanda's dearest wish to own her own pony and learn to ride, yes. It is also my suggestion that you should be the one to teach her.' The idea had come to her after those days of travelling into Cambridgeshire, when she had noticed that Amanda seemed the most attentive to the scenery outside when there were horses to be seen grazing in the fields.

Several minutes' casual conversation with her charge had revealed Amanda's deep love of equines and her secret yearning to own a horse or pony of her own so that she might learn to ride.

The second part of Elena's suggestion—an inspired one, she had thought!—arose from her conversation with her employer in which he had asked for her help in finding ways of taking more of an interest in his young daughter's life. The stunned look on his face now would seem to suggest he had not meant that request to be taken quite so literally as this! 'Would it not be a perfect way for you to spend more time with Amanda, whilst also doing something she would enjoy?'

Adam was starting to wonder if he had not seriously underestimated this young woman, if he had not been fooled, both by her widow's weeds and her demur demeanour during those first few days in his employ, into thinking that she was both complacent and obliging.

Their last few conversations together had revealed her as being neither of those things!

He stood up to move around the desk until he was able to lean back against it, knowing a certain inner satisfaction as he noted her discomfort at his proximity. At the same time as he recognised, and appreciated, the way in which she remained standing exactly where she was, despite that discomfort, as testament to her spirited nature. 'Do you ride yourself, Mrs Leighton?'

She gave him a quick glance before as quickly glancing away again, a blush to her cheeks. 'Why do you ask?'

The reason Adam asked was because the more time he spent in this woman's company, the more convinced he became that there was something about her, an inborn lady-like elegance and a certain self-confidence, which did not sit well with her role as paid governess to a young girl.

She had also had no difficulty whatsoever in recognising that the seamstress had brought with her the finest silks for her approval, as Adam had instructed, rather than the inferior ones which might normally have been requested in such circumstances. Adam seriously doubted that most employers would ever buy expensive silks for a woman who was a member of their household staff. Unless that woman was also his mistress...

Of course he knew nothing of Elena Leighton's life before her employment with the Bamburys, so she could have been the daughter of an aristocrat, who had eloped with her soldier husband, for all Adam knew of that situation; he could certainly more easily believe that to be this elegantly lovely woman's history than he could see her as having been the daughter of an impoverished vicar or a shopkeeper!

He looked down the length of his nose at her. 'Do I need to give a reason in order to ask a question of one of my household staff?'

'No. Of course you do not.' The colour deepened in her cheeks—as if she had once again briefly forgotten that was now her place in life? he wondered. 'But to answer your question—yes, I have ridden since I was a child, my lord. I only thought this might be the perfect opportunity in which you might give pleasure to Amanda, whilst at the same time allowing you to spend more time with her.'

Adam's mouth twisted derisively. There was definitely something about this young woman—her background before she married Private Leighton?—which Adam found himself becoming more and more interested in knowing.

That, in itself, was unexpected…

His brief marriage to Fanny had succeeded in revealing all too clearly the many vagaries of human nature to him—the lies, the greed, the utter selfishness—until his own character, out of self-protection perhaps, had become that of the true cynic, to the extent that Adam rarely saw good in people any more—most especially the female of the species.

For whatever reason, Elena Leighton remained a mystery to him, yet at the same time there was a burning honesty about her, a determination, a desire to right injustice—such as she perceived his own lack of interest in Amanda to be. It was so at odds with the selfishness Adam had come to believe to be the motivation behind every human action— even his own, to a great extent, an example being that he had dragged his daughter and her companion off to the wilds of Cambridgeshire, in the middle of the Season, with the intention of dealing with matters on the estate, but also for the purpose of escaping the matchmaking machinations of his own grandmother!

Yes, he had become both selfish and cynical these past six years. And yet… And yet this little governess had brought something to life in him that was neither of those things, a desire not to act in his own interest, but instead for the pleasure of others. A desire to please her that had nothing to do with the physical attraction he felt towards her…

Adam straightened abruptly before moving back round his desk and sitting down behind it, his tone cool and controlled when at last he spoke. 'The seamstress will think you have forgotten about her.'

In truth, Elena *had* forgotten that lady's presence upstairs in her bedchamber during this past few minutes' conversation. Indeed, she had forgotten everything but the disturbing gentleman who now looked across the desk at her so disdainfully. A gentleman who suddenly looked so very different to the handsomely boyish one who had burst into spontaneous laughter only minutes earlier...

'And Amanda's pony and riding lessons?'

His mouth thinned. 'I will see what can be arranged.'

Elena's heart sank in disappointment as she turned to leave, inwardly knowing that any 'arrangements' Adam Hawthorne chose to make about Amanda's riding lessons were unlikely to include him.

'And, Mrs Leighton...?'

She turned back slowly, her expression wary. 'Yes?'

He sighed his exasperation. 'You have a look on your face like that of a beast in fear of being whipped!'

Elena stiffened in outrage. 'I trust that is not the case?'

'It was not a personal threat, madam, but a figure of speech!' Adam scowled, knowing he had once again been wrong-footed by this exasperating woman.

'Then it was an exceedingly unpleasant one,' she protested.

Adam gritted his back teeth together so tightly he feared they might snap out of his jaw, knowing he should not have delayed her departure from his study, but let her return upstairs to the attentions of the seamstress. And he would have done so, if not for the look of disappointment on her face after he had dismissed both her and her request that he be the one to teach Amanda to ride.

He took a steadying breath. 'I believe you take delight in misunderstanding me!'

She raised dark brows. 'I assure you, I take no delight at all in imagining you—or, indeed, anyone else—whipping an innocent beast of any kind.'

'I merely said—' Adam rose to his feet once again to round the desk with a sudden burst of frustrated energy before grasping her by the slenderness of her shoulders and shaking her slightly to emphasise his next words. 'I have never been a party to whipping a woman, man, nor beast, damn it!'

'I am glad to hear it.' Her voice had softened huskily.

Bringing Adam to an awareness of the fact that he still had hold of her by the shoulders, that he could feel the delicacy of her bones through the thin material of her black gown, the soft pads of his thumbs actually touching the silky softness of the flesh just above the ivory swell of her breasts...

And it was very silky skin, so soft and smooth as Adam lowered his gaze to watch as he gave in to the temptation to run the pads of his thumbs caressingly over that delectable flesh, his hands appearing dark and very big against that delicate and unblemished ivory.

Standing this close to Elena, he could once again smell lemons, and something lightly floral, the top of her dark head barely reaching his shoulders, her figure slender in any case, but appearing more so when measured against his own height and breadth. Even the firm swell of her breasts, above the scooped neckline of her gown, was delicately tempting rather than voluptuous.

Damn it, he should have stayed seated behind his desk, safely removed from that temptation! Should never have— His gaze became riveted on the full pout of Elena's mouth as she ran the moist tip of her tongue nervously across her lips whilst looking up at him from between silky dark lashes.

'My lord…?'

Adam drew in a deep, controlling breath even as he closed his eyes in an effort not to look at those now moist lips. Moist and utterly kissable lips. 'Do not—Elena…!' he groaned huskily in defeat as he opened his eyes and saw she had now caught her bottom lip between tiny, pearly-white teeth.

Her eyes widened slightly, those long, dark lashes framing those blue-green orbs, her throat moving when she swallowed as Adam slowly began to draw her closer towards him. 'My lord…?' she whispered again.

'Adam,' he encouraged gruffly.

Elena would have protested his request for such informality—if he had not chosen that moment to draw her closer still before lowering his head and she felt the gentle, intimate touch of his lips against the curve of her throat.

Surprisingly warm and sensuous lips, considering how cold and abrupt this man so often was. Instead of the fear and recoil that she might have been expected to feel, after Neville's harsh treatment of her, Elena relaxed into the safety of Adam Hawthorne's arms, safe in the knowledge that he was not a man to ever use force on any woman.

It was at once a surprise and yet the most thrilling experience of her lifetime, to be held by and touching Adam so intimately, and to feel the warmth of his breath heating her flesh, even as his lips tasted and caressed the slender column of her throat, the gentle bite of his teeth on her earlobe causing her to tremble as her breath hitched in her throat.

Her breasts became full, the tips full and sensitive, as those warm lips trailed along the line of her jaw before finally claiming her parted mouth in a deep and searching kiss that caused the heat to course through her, from the top of her head to the tips of her toes, settling at that secret, intimate place between her thighs. Elena's head was swirling, thought impossible, denial even more so as Adam's hands moved down from her shoulders to encircle her waist as he crushed her against him, his lips even more fiercely demanding against her own.

Then, just as suddenly, his mouth was wrenched away as he put her firmly apart from him before releasing her. Elena stumbled slightly as she attempted to regain her balance on legs that seemed to have all the substance of jelly, her lips feeling bruised and swollen, her cheeks flushed, breasts full and aching inside the bodice of her gown.

Elena blinked several times as she attempted to focus on Adam, only to step back in alarm as she found herself looking into the hard grey chips of ice that were his eyes.

'That was a mistake on more levels than I care to contemplate,' he rasped harshly, his face all sharp and disapproving angles, the tousled darkness of his hair the only indication that moments ago this man had kissed her, as Elena had kissed him back, and her fingers had become passionately entangled in his thick raven locks.

'A mistake…?' She felt a sharp tightening in her chest almost akin to pain, knowing that she felt the opposite, that kissing Adam had been the most wonderful of pleasures, more delicious than she had ever dared to hope a kiss ever could be. A kiss so unlike the ones her cousin had forced upon her—

No!

There were some things Elena could not—would not think about.

'On so many, many levels,' Adam repeated grimly as he saw the way in which her face had paled.

No doubt in reaction to the realisation that her employer had just kissed her with an intimacy and passion totally unacceptable to her, or the disparity in their social positions. Not that the raging of his libido cared one way or the other about that, but Adam must!

'For which you have my heartfelt apology,' he added, mortified with himself. 'I do not know—it was not my intention—it will not happen again,' he vowed.

At least, Adam would do what he could to ensure that it did not happen again! In truth, he was not sure how it had happened a first time...

There had been perhaps a dozen or so women in his life since Fanny died, women he had spent a few hours of intimacy with and never seen again. Beautiful as Elena might be, for him to have stepped over that line, for him to not only have felt desire for one of his own servants, but to have acted upon it, was totally unacceptable to him. Quite how he was going to feel, to react to her, once she had ceased wearing these unbecoming gowns, he dare not think. With decency and restraint, it was to be hoped. But—

'You were about to say something earlier as I began to leave the room...?'

Adam scowled as he tried to remember what she was referring to, his mind and body both still dominated by only one thought: his desire for her.

Ah, yes… 'I believe I was about to suggest that a riding habit might also be a useful addition to your wardrobe.'

Her eyes widened dubiously. 'A riding habit, my lord?'

His jaw tightened. 'Yes. Perhaps in turquoise or blue?' he found himself adding—before instantly castigating himself for caring what the colour of her riding habit should be.

'Very well, my lord.' She looked at him for several seconds longer, before giving a brief curtsy. 'If you will excuse me, I must return to the schoolroom.'

'And the seamstress.'

'Indeed.' She did not look at him again before leaving.

Adam frowned darkly once Elena had departed his study, knowing that he had made life decidedly uncomfortable for himself just now.

The throbbing ache in his groin spoke of his obvious physical discomfort, but it was the inner dissatisfaction, with his own completely uncharacteristic behaviour of making love to a female servant in his own household, and Elena's reaction to it once she had found the time and privacy in which to reflect, which caused Adam to continue to soundly castigate himself.

Elena might choose to believe that he did not take enough of an interest in his daughter or her life, but Adam knew enough to know that Amanda had been happier in recent weeks, more contented, since the advent of her new governess into her life.

His unacceptable behaviour just now might have put that in jeopardy if, on reflection, Elena should decide that she could not continue working for a man who attempted to take liberties with her.

There was another aspect to consider, Adam realised with a heavy heart, and that was his loss of control in kissing her at all. A loss of control he certainly did not welcome. Most especially with a woman he was fast beginning to suspect was much more than she seemed.

Chapter Six

'I thought your lessons would be over for the morning?'

'We are just finishing now.' Elena deliberately kept her gaze away from Adam and on the textbook she had been using to teach Amanda some basic arithmetic, but that did not stop the colour from warming her cheeks as she re-called—how would she ever be able to forget!—being kissed by him so passionately.

In fact, Elena had lain awake in her bed these past two nights unable to think of anything else.

Neville's brutality two months ago had been…shocking. Horrendous. Something Elena knew she would also never ever forget and not in a good way like Adam's kiss. She had been sure the experience would prevent her from ever al-lowing another man to so much as hold her, let alone kiss her, in future. And yet, not only had she allowed her hand-some, charismatic employer to do so, but she knew she had kissed him back.

Because she felt safe with him? Could that be it? Yet how was it possible for her to feel safe with a man whom she also found so physically arousing? The feelings he'd created inside her still made her blush just to think of them.

'Papa?' Amanda looked at her father uncertainly as he stood in the doorway.

Elena's breath caught in her throat as she at last looked up and took in Adam's wide-shouldered appearance. He was pristinely attired in a deep-grey superfine, black waistcoat and pale-grey pantaloons tucked into black Hessians, with his dark hair brushed neatly back from his harshly handsome face. A face that looked every bit as remote as on the first occasion Elena had met him, grey eyes chillingly cold as he met her gaze unblinkingly. As warning, perhaps, that he deeply regretted the last time the two of them had been together? As if Elena had not already guessed that from the distance he had kept from her ever since then.

'What do you have in the basket, Papa?'

Elena, having also noted the wicker basket beside him in the doorway, had been wondering the same. Especially as it gave every appearance of being a picnic basket.

'Our picnic luncheon,' Adam confirmed that suspicion.

'A picnic, Papa…?' Amanda looked even more bewildered.

He nodded. 'It is the perfect day for it, if you two ladies would care to join me?'

Two ladies? Adam seriously expected Elena to join father and daughter for their picnic?

'Really, Papa?' For once Amanda completely forgot her usual reserve when in her father's company, as she instead jumped up and down excitedly. 'Oh, may we, Mrs Leighton? May we?' She looked up at Elena appealingly with those beguiling sapphire-blue eyes.

Much as Elena loved the thought of sitting on a blanket beneath one of the splendid oak trees in the garden, or possibly beside the huge lake beyond the gardens at the back of the house, and enjoying a leisurely alfresco luncheon, she was unsure of the wisdom of spending even that amount of time in close proximity with Adam, following the inappropriate behaviour between them, and her confusion, and his frosty demeanour towards her, ever since.

'Mrs Leighton?' Adam prompted when she didn't answer.

Elena deliberately kept her attention centred on Amanda. 'I am sure you do not need my permission to join your father for luncheon, Amanda,' she said with a smile. 'I, however, have some things in the schoolroom in need of my attention—'

'Such as…?' Adam challenged her coolly; he had initially been unsure of the wisdom of inviting Elena to join them in the first place, but now found, contrarily, that he was more than a little irritated at her reluctance to accept that invitation now he had made it, dash it all!

A frown appeared between those blue-green eyes. 'I have tomorrow's lessons to prepare—'

'And, as such, they can as easily be prepared this evening,' he dismissed briskly. 'It is too fine a day to spend all of it shut indoors.'

'I would not wish to intrude.' Her smile was overbright, her gaze not quite meeting his.

Adam's mouth tightened. It was as he had thought might be the case; after his appalling behaviour, she could barely stand to look at him, let alone spend any more time in his company than she had to. Perhaps if he tried to ease her nerves? 'It would be the ideal occasion on which to show off what I am presuming is one of your new gowns,' he ca-joled, while allowing himself to inwardly admire the way in which her deep rose-coloured gown perfectly comple-mented her ivory complexion and the darkness of her hair.

She wore those dark tresses in a less-severe style today, too, several loose curls at her temples and nape giving her a much more youthful appearance, bringing about a sud-den recollection of how she had not been altogether honest with him in regard to her true age when she had first ap-plied for the job.

His mouth tightened as he privately wondered what other secrets the puzzling Elena Leighton might be keeping from him…

Her cheeks blushed the same becoming rose as her gown. 'Mrs Hepworth was able to finish and deliver this first gown early yesterday evening.'

'Her promptness is to be commended.' He turned away to look at his daughter. 'Now, I believe Amanda, for one, is eager for her luncheon.'

Amanda beamed up at him. 'We are really to have a pic-nic together, Papa?'

'I have said so, yes.'

Amanda did a happy little skip. 'I have never been on a picnic before.'

A frown appeared on Adam's brow as he looked at his young daughter's glowingly excited face. His marriage to Fanny had been a mistake, for which he had paid dearly, and he had always been grateful that Amanda had been far too young, when her mother died, to have ever witnessed the unhappiness that had existed between her mother and father.

But Adam had sincerely believed, until his conversations

with Elena this past week, that he had been a good father to Amanda, given the circumstances, and his own lack of experience and knowledge in that regard. Amanda's excitement now, at the thought of such a simple pleasure as the sharing of a picnic together, once again led him to question that belief.

He forced the tension from his shoulders. 'Then it is for Mrs Leighton and me to do everything we can to ensure that you enjoy this, your very first one.'

Amanda reached out and wrapped both her arms about one of his as she gave him a hug. 'Thank you, Papa. Oh, thank you!'

'Mrs Leighton?'

Elena had watched the exchange between father and daughter with increasingly softening feelings; far from chastising Amanda for wrinkling his perfectly tailored superfine, as many gentlemen of the *ton* might have done, Adam had actually placed his hand on top of his daughter's in a gesture of affection. A gesture not lost on Amanda as she gazed up at him adoringly.

It took so little for Amanda to forget, for a time at least, to be that restrained little girl who normally spent only a very short time each day with her father; Amanda's eyes gleamed like sapphires, her face alight with anticipation at the prospect of such a treat.

'Mrs Leighton?' Adam repeated with unaccustomed patience at her continued silence.

Elena could not speak momentarily for the lump of emotion that had formed in her throat, her eyes having gone quite misty. She swallowed now to clear the dryness from her throat. 'If you are sure I will not be intruding…?'

'I would not have invited you if I had considered that to be a possibility,' he came back crisply.

No, of course he would not. Elena still continued to forget, on occasion, that she was now a governess rather than the beloved granddaughter of a duke. That same accomplished young woman who had once acted as mistress of her grandfather's estates, and as such, the person used to issuing the invitations, rather than the other way about. 'In that case, I should love to join you both, thank you.' She gave an almost regal inclination of her head—for she did not always have to forget she possessed the graciousness of extremely well-born manners!

'How are you liking Cambridgeshire, Mrs Leighton?'

Elena—sitting primly on the same blanket where Adam, hat removed, lay in relaxed repose a short distance away, their picnic luncheon eaten—turned from watching Amanda scamper about the garden chasing elusive butterflies. 'I like it very much from the little I saw of it on the drive here.'

He raised dark brows. 'Is that a complaint regarding the lack of any outings since your arrival?'

Elena's cheeks felt once again as if they had flushed the same deep rose as her new gown. Why did he constantly put her on the back foot? 'It is not my place to complain, my lord,' she murmured.

He snorted in patent disbelief. 'I seem to recall you telling me it is "not your place" to advise me how to bring up my own daughter—and yet you have done so, on several occasions. I believe you also claimed it is "not your place" to tell me how and when I should deal with the tenants on my estate, whilst at the same time pointing out that it is my duty to attend church on a Sunday, in order that I might converse with them.' One dark teasing brow flicked up to gently mock her. 'Tell me, madam, why should I now believe you when you say it is "not your place" to complain about the lack of entertainment provided since your arrival here?'

Elena's cheeks had grown hotter and hotter with each word that he spoke. Each damning, *truthful* word. For she had done those things. Out of a sense of rightness. The first for Amanda's benefit, the second out of consideration for the workers and tenants of Adam's estate. But Elena felt sure that the real Mrs Leighton would never have forgotten 'her place' as to be so forward, or so outspoken, in her views.

She winced. 'I was merely commenting on the fact that I cannot make an educated judgement as to the attractions or otherwise of Cambridgeshire when I have seen so little of it—have I said something to amuse you, my lord?'

Adam exploded into full-throated laughter at the look of indignation on Elena's beautiful face. Indeed, he had laughed more in this woman's company than he had for— in fact, he could not remember how long it had been since he had last laughed with such spontaneity!

Admittedly, he was laughing at her this time rather than with her, but it nevertheless felt good to once again experience that lightness of humour and heart, to truly enjoy a woman's company. 'Do not look so indignant.' He was tempted to lift his hand to reach up and smooth the frown from Elena's brow with his fingertips, and at the same time enjoy touching her smooth and velvet-soft skin. His laughter slowly faded as he strongly resisted that temptation. 'Perhaps I should consider organising a dinner party so that you might meet some of my neighbours?'

Elena looked more than a little alarmed. 'Even if you were to do so, the governess of your young daughter could not possibly be one of the guests at your dinner table.'

Adam raised an arrogant brow. 'I believe it is for me to say who may or may not be seated at my dinner table.'

She gave a sharp shake of her head. 'And, as such, you know it would not be fitting for me to be present, my lord.'

Yes, Adam knew better than most the dictates of society—he should do, Fanny had broken them often enough! Which was why he always took care to do the opposite, mainly by absenting himself from society completely.

What was it Royston had called him several evenings ago? Besides a prickly bastard? Ah, yes, Royston had accused him of being a recluse. Not completely accurate, but close enough; removing himself from inclusion in society was by far the easiest way of ensuring that Adam broke none of society's rigid rules. As a widower, his invitation for the beautiful governess of his young daughter to join his other guests for dinner would certainly cause every bit of that gossip and speculation he had managed to avoid since Fanny's death.

Adam frowned. 'You are far too beautiful to want to hide away in the schoolroom forever.'

'I am content there,' she insisted softly.

'You have no ambition in life other than to be a governess to a six-year-old girl?'

She blinked long dark lashes. 'Amanda will not always be aged six.'

He gave a tight smile. 'I believe you are being deliberately obtuse.'

Elena had no idea what she was being, what she was

thinking. How could she, when Adam was looking up at her with eyes as soft and dark a grey as a pigeon's wing? 'What—what else should I be if not governess to Amanda, or someone like her?'

The black of Adam's pupils seemed to expand so that they almost encompassed that soft velvet grey even as he moved closer. 'Have you never considered—?'

'Papa, come and see the tiny kitten I have found!' Amanda, totally relaxed in her father's company following their picnic, called excitedly to him from across the garden.

Elena continued to be caught in the spell of those velvet grey-eyes for several long seconds more before she made a deliberate effort to break away, turning and looking across to where Amanda held a black kitten cradled gently in her arms. 'Careful it is not feral!' She gathered her skirts before rising quickly to her feet. 'My lord…!'

She looked at Adam imploringly as he rose to his booted feet beside her.

Adam cursed himself for being a fool even as he hurriedly crossed the garden to Amanda and quickly relieved her of the tiny black kitten, knowing he had been about to make a scandalous suggestion to Elena that would have resulted in her either accepting that offer or slapping his face for daring to voice it. Neither of which he wanted.

He did not want nor need a mistress.

Not even one he found as amusing and desirable as Elena Leighton. Most especially one he found as amusing and desirable as Elena Leighton!

And if she had slapped his face, for daring to make her such a reprehensible offer, then she would no doubt have given him notice only seconds later, too. For they could not continue in the way they had been if he were ever to make such an offer and she were to refuse it.

Leaving Amanda without a governess she liked and Adam without the unexpected source of pleasure, and amusement, the brief times he spent with Elena were becoming to him. It was an unpalatable thought and one he swiftly pushed out of his head.

'It is all right, is it not, Papa…?' His daughter looked up at him uncertainly.

Adam focused on the tiny kitten in his hand, knowing by the healthy glow to its grey-green eyes, as it looked up at him so trustingly, that it was not diseased. The soft rumbling purr that shook its little body was indicative of it not being feral, either. 'Perfectly all right.' Adam nodded as he gently replaced the kitten back into Amanda's waiting arms. 'But it is not wise to pick up stray animals, pet.'

'Where do you think it came from, Papa?' Amanda stroked the kitten even as she looked about the otherwise deserted garden.

His expression softened as he appreciated how pretty his daughter looked today in her yellow gown, a ribbon of the same colour tied about her golden curls. Tall for her age, and already giving indications of the beauty she would possess when she was older, Adam had no doubts that he would one day be beating his daughter's beaus away from his door. 'I suggest you try looking in the stables for its mother and siblings,' he murmured indulgently. 'There is usually a litter or two hiding in there.'

'You are not hurt, Amanda?' A slightly breathless Elena prompted huskily.

Adam's expression tightened as he looked down at the

woman he had moment ago considered asking to become his mistress, damn it!

Admittedly, Elena looked very beautiful today, in that rose-coloured gown and with her hair in that softer style. And, yes, she had once again succeeded in amusing him, in making him laugh, in a way no other woman ever had, but he could not and would not lower his guard by inviting any woman to become his permanent mistress. Most especially he could not ask it of the widowed Elena Leighton. If she accepted, he would no doubt be provided with amusement for a matter of days or possibly weeks, but ultimately it would deprive Amanda of her governess forever.

Much better if he were to remove himself from this situation, if only briefly, and find some other woman—a woman who offered far fewer complications—to scratch the sexual itch that presently demanded satisfaction!

He looked over at his daughter. 'Perhaps Mrs Leighton would care to accompany you to the stables?' He turned to address Elena. 'I have some business to attend to this afternoon before my departure later this evening.'

Elena looked at him sharply. 'You are going back to London?' There had not even been so much as the suggestion of it whilst they were eating their picnic luncheon, or of him going anywhere else today. Not, she acknowledged ruefully, that he owed her any explanation as to his movements.

A sentiment he completely echoed, if the expression of arrogant disdain on the haughty handsomeness of his face was any indication. 'As it happens, I am not returning to London, but have a business appointment elsewhere—'

'You are going away, Papa?' Amanda, momentarily distracted from where she now sat on the grass playing with the kitten, looked up at him in pouting disappointment. 'How long will you be gone?'

'Two, perhaps three days—'

'Do you have to go?' Amanda cut in pleadingly. 'I have so enjoyed our picnic today that I thought we might have another one tomorrow?'

Her father smiled slightly. 'Picnics can only be considered fun if they are a treat rather than an everyday occurrence.'

'But—'

'Amanda,' he reproved softly.

'But I so wanted another picnic tomorrow!' Amanda stated mutinously—a mutiny that Elena, at least, recognised as a precursor to one of the little girl's rare temper tantrums.

He shook his head. 'There is urgent business in need of my attention.'

'There is always urgent business in need of your attention!'

'Possibly because my estates do not run themselves—'

'Go away, then!' Amanda jumped to her feet, two bright spots of angry colour in her cheeks as she stamped one slippered foot on the grass in temper. 'You always do!' She gave a sob before turning and running across the lawns, then disappearing inside the house with a flourish of golden curls.

'Do you see where your interference has led?' Adam accused as he continued to look across at the house with narrowed and disapproving eyes.

Elena's own eyes widened indignantly. '*My* interference…?'

He shot her an impatient glance. 'I have never, before today, needed to explain my movements or actions to my six-year-old child!'

She gasped. 'And you believe *I* am to blame for that?'

'I believe your suggestion that I needed to "spend more time with my daughter" is to blame for that, madam,' he bit out. 'In the past Amanda has always been content with the time we spend together each day. Now I've spent more time with her, she's suddenly not satisfied.'

Elena frowned at the unfairness of these accusations. 'She has perhaps *seemed* content with only a half hour, perhaps—'

'She *was* content, damn it!'

'In *your* opinion.'

He turned to look down at her with chill grey eyes. 'Yes, in my opinion. Which, unless you have forgotten, is not only the opinion of Amanda's father, but also that of your employer.'

Elena's gaze lowered at this timely reminder of her position in this gentleman's household; she was becoming far too fond of forgetting that fact. 'I will go and talk to her.'

'Does she often throw such tantrums?' Adam asked grimly. He realised he was probably overreacting, but Amanda's display of temper just now had been far too much like that of her late mother for him to be able to address the matter in his usual calm manner.

Fanny had been wont to throw such tempers, in public as well as privately, whenever she could not get her own way, but Adam had never before witnessed such a display from his young daughter. Perhaps because he had spent so little time in her company in the past? If that should be the case, then it was perhaps as well that he had discovered Amanda's temper before it was too late to be rectified, for there was no way, absolutely no way that he would tolerate the same selfish wilfulness in her as he had experienced so often in his late wife.

'No, she does not,' Elena assured him firmly. 'And I am sure it has only happened on this occasion because Amanda is a little upset at your imminent departure, after having enjoyed such a lovely afternoon in your company.'

Adam's gaze narrowed ominously. 'Do you think to humour me, madam?'

Warmth entered her cheeks. 'I was only—'

'I am well aware of what you were doing, Mrs Leighton.' He grimaced. 'Nor was there anything "little" about Amanda's display of bad manners.' Adam's frown didn't bode well for the child. 'It was a spoilt and wilful display which cannot be overlooked.'

Elena looked dismayed. 'Oh, but—'

'No, Mrs Leighton, it is my belief that it is my having listened to you which has brought about this unpleasantness in the first place,' he insisted.

She looked up at him pleadingly. 'If you will only allow me to talk with Amanda—'

'I advise that, whilst you are doing so, you are sure to convey my deep displeasure in her behaviour just now,' Adam said as he crossed to the blanket to pick up his hat before placing it upon his head. 'I will speak to her on the matter upon my return.'

'And when might we expect that to be?' Elena dared to venture, only to rear back slightly as she now found herself the focus of his displeasure. 'I should not have asked,' she acknowledged quickly.

A nerve pulsed in his rigidly clenched jaw. 'I trust that your inclusion in our picnic today has not caused you to once again misunderstand your "place" in my household, madam!' He gave her one last dismissive glance before striding forcefully across the lawn towards the house.

Elena had felt the colour drain from her cheeks as she was very firmly—and with a touch of deliberate cruelty, perhaps?—reminded that her 'place' in Adam Hawthorne's household was only that of a servant.

Chapter Seven

'Why didn't you let us know you were to be here this evening, my lord?'

Adam kept his gaze guarded as he looked up at the blousily beautiful woman currently pouring the red wine the same ruby colour as her painted lips, which he had ordered to be served with his late evening meal at the coaching inn he was to stay at for the night, situated thirty miles or so from his estate in Cambridgeshire.

Josie was the widow of the late innkeeper and a woman whose favours Adam had accepted a time or two when he had travelled through to Cambridgeshire in the past. A woman with auburn hair and come-hither brown eyes, her low-necked red gown doing very little to hide the voluptuous swell—and nor was it intended to do so!—of her considerable charms.

Charms that, unfortunately, were of absolutely no interest to Adam this evening. Nor were those of any other woman but the one he could not, should not, even think of wanting... 'Do not fret, Josie,' he drawled drily, 'I am well aware that some other lucky gentleman has already beaten me into sharing your bed tonight.' Josie was as generous with her invitations as she was warm in her bed.

She gave him a saucy grin. 'None that I wouldn't see off in a minute if'n you was to say the word…?'

'I fear I am too exhausted tonight to do you justice, Josie.' Adam smiled to take the sting out of his refusal, knowing the fault lay with his desire for another woman rather than any diminishing of the charms of this woman's warm invitation for him to enjoy her plump and alluring curves.

She returned his smile to show she had taken no offence at that refusal. 'In that case, I hope it's because ye've found yourself a decent woman to satisfy ya needs.'

Adam's smile grew rueful. 'Is that not a contradiction in terms?' He frowned as he realised how pompous he had just sounded. Incomprehensible, perhaps, to a woman who felt no qualms whatsoever in admitting she could neither read nor write, but could count any amount of money accurately and quickly. He shook his head. 'What I meant to say—'

'I knows as what ye meant, my lord,' Josie dismissed unconcernedly. 'Even so, I would've expected a good-looking gent, and an expert and satisfying lover such as yerself, to 'ave found a suitable lady and remarried afore now.'

'I thank you for the compliment, Josie.' Adam smiled.

'Ain't no compliment when it's the truth,' she insisted.

Gratified as he was for Josie's praise, it was nevertheless a little difficult for him to completely accept the second part of Josie's compliment, when his own wife had admitted to being adulterous with another man only a month after their wedding!

Not that he had ever heard any complaints from any of the

women he had taken to his bed before he married Fanny, as those liaisons had always resulted in the enjoyment of mutual pleasure. Since Fanny had died, however, he had preferred to pay for that pleasure, so he supposed it was not in the best interest of any of those women to show dissatisfaction in his performance, was it?

Josie gave him a shrewd narrow-eyed glance. 'I hope you'll excuse me for being so bold, my lord, but that wife o' your'n didn't know 'ow to appreciate a good thing when she were married to it!'

Adam let out a bark of laughter as he leant back in his chair. 'You are very good for a man's ego, Josie.' He raised his glass to her in a toast before taking a sip of the ruby-red wine.

'But the answer's still no, I'm guessing...?' She quirked an auburn brow knowingly.

'I am afraid so, yes.' Adam frowned his inner irritation as he slowly placed his glass back down onto the table, knowing that he had lied just now when he claimed to be too tired to do this lady justice in her bed; the reason for his uninterest lay much closer to home. *His* home.

Out of sheer contrariness—or perhaps desperation!—he had been away from Hawthorne Park for a total of four days now, tomorrow, the day he expected to return there, being the fifth day. And not one of those days had passed without his having thought more of the beautiful Elena Leighton than he ought to have done. Dear Lord, a single moment's thought, given to a young woman in his employ, beautiful or otherwise, was one moment too many!

And yet...

Her beauty had continued to haunt and beguile him. Her

air of inborn elegance intrigued and bedevilled him, as well as her ability to puzzle and tempt him, to amuse him, to the extent that he actually laughed in her company—all despite his previous decision not to give in to the weakness of this unexpected and unwanted attraction!

They had parted badly four days ago. Very badly. He had been both cold and condescending towards her. Attitudes which should not have been directed at Elena at all, but towards his young daughter. Amanda's temper tantrum that day, even the words she had used as to his 'always being busy with estate affairs', had been far too reminiscent of the accusations her mother would fling at him in her fits of pique or temper.

As a result, Adam had responded to Amanda's wilfulness instinctively, but unfortunately his own anger had rained down on Elena's innocent head rather than his absent daughter's. Something that had continued to bother him in the four days that had passed since, along with his ever-weakening determination to withstand the deep attraction Elena held for him.

While his libido had been totally uninterested in any other woman the last few days, he only had to think of Elena to become aroused. He imagined her now, perhaps in her bedchamber getting ready for bed, with her long ebony hair loose about her sweetly swelling, rose-tinted breasts, the slenderness of her waist above the gentle swell of her hips—

'I hope she appreciates her good fortune,' Josie said, unwittingly breaking into his pleasant thoughts.

'Sorry?' Adam looked up to raise a questioning brow.

Josie gave another of her saucy grins. 'Whoever the lady

was you was just thinking about 'as brought a devilish gleam
to your eyes and a hardness to your thighs!'

It was true, damn it!

Obviously he could not speak for the 'devilish gleam' in
his eyes, but the other part, at least, was without a doubt
true, that hot and throbbing arousal evident in the obvious
bulge pressing against the front of his breeches. An arousal
he would probably have to deal with himself when he retired
to his bedchamber later this evening. As he'd had to do this
past four nights. Unless… 'Best bring me another flagon of
this wine, Josie,' he advised ruefully as he refilled his glass;
inebriation was another way of banishing these intruding
thoughts of the delightful governess from his mind. And
quelling the raging desire of his shaft!

Josie gave a throaty chuckle. 'Just say the word and I'll
shimmy 'neath the table and see 'e's settled quick as a wink.'
She gave a slow and pointed lick of painted ruby red lips as
she looked down at the bulge in his breeches.

'Tempting…but let me try the wine first, hmm,' Adam
murmured evasively.

'You knows where I am if'n ye should change ya mind.'
She shrugged her shoulders good-naturedly, jiggling her
ample breasts temptingly, before leaving the parlour to collect a second flagon of wine.

Adam sat back with a sigh, knowing he had to find a
suitable solution to this dilemma, of desiring a woman he
had no right to desire, that he could not go on living in this
physical and mental purgatory indefinitely; both he, and
his estates, would suffer if he did not soon find some way
of putting an end to what had become a hellish situation.

This past four days' absence from Hawthorne Hall, of

thinking constantly of Elena Leighton rather than the business he should be dealing with, had more than proved that point. And it provided him with only two solutions going forwards.

Elena must either leave his household forthwith, and so be removed from both his sight and temptation, or Adam must give in to his desire and offer her the role of his mistress and hope—or fear—that she would accept…

'Do you think Papa will be cross about Samson…?' Amanda looked at Elena anxiously as she stroked the soft black fur of the rapidly growing kitten currently purring in her lap.

In truth, Elena had absolutely no idea how Adam would react to his daughter having adopted the black kitten they had found after the picnic. He had left in his carriage for his business appointment later that very same day, without so much as saying goodbye to Amanda or leaving instructions for Elena.

Elena did know that Amanda had been sobbing inconsolably when she had sought out the little girl in her bedchamber that day, Amanda's disappointment at her father's imminent departure having been replaced with regret and remorse for having behaved so badly. A regret Amanda had unfortunately not had the opportunity to voice to her father before he'd left.

And ever since he'd been gone, Elena had tried but failed in her attempts to forgive the dratted man as she witnessed her young charge's misery.

Amanda was aged only six, Adam Hawthorne was eight or possibly nine and twenty, and that disparity in years between father and daughter should have carried a similar disparity in their maturity. Unfortunately, in this case, that did not appear to have been the case.

Consequently Elena was very angry with Adam. More angry than she could remember being for a long, long time—if ever. As a result, when it transpired that the black kitten was a stray, unaccepted by any of the mothering she-cats in the stables, Elena had taken it upon herself to give her permission when Amanda had asked if she might have the kitten for her own. And if Lord Adam Hawthorne did not like that decision, then Elena would tell him exactly why she had made it!

'Not at all,' she assured Amanda briskly. 'I have every reason to believe your father is a fair and reasonable gentleman—'

'I am glad to hear it,' that very same 'gentleman' drawled from the schoolroom doorway. 'Just as I would dearly love to hear what I have done to be deserving of such an accolade…?'

'Papa!' Amanda's previous anxiety disappeared like a summer mist as she ran across the schoolroom to launch herself into his arms.

'Careful, pet,' her father advised gently as the kitten looked in danger of being squashed between them. 'What do we have here?'

He gently took the kitten and held it up for his inspection.

'I have given Amanda permission to keep the kitten,' Elena, sensing another crisis looming on the horizon, rushed in to claim decisively.

'Indeed?' Adam spared her only a cursory glance before turning his attention back to his daughter. 'What do you call him?'

'Samson,' Amanda supplied almost shyly.

He smiled. 'You called this little fellow Samson...?'

'He will grow into his name, I am sure,' Elena defended briskly, feeling slightly indignant on behalf of both Amanda and the tiny kitten. Admittedly the kitten was probably the runt of whatever litter he had come from, which was perhaps why he had been cast out, but he had huge paws that must surely one day support an equally as large body.

Her employer gave her another enigmatic glance before smiling down at Amanda as he gave the kitten back into her care. 'He is a fine little fellow.'

'And I may keep him, Papa?' Amanda prompted.

'How can I possibly decide anything else when Mrs Leighton herself has declared me to be such a fair and reasonable gentleman?'

The underlying sarcasm of that comment was completely lost on the now-beaming Amanda. Not so on Elena, who was only too well aware that he had to be mocking her.

'It is so good to have you home again, Papa.' Amanda's pleasure shone in her sapphire-blue eyes.

'It is very good to be home again, pet,' he assured gruffly. 'I have missed you.'

Elena eyed him sceptically; if he truly had missed the company of his young daughter then he should have returned sooner, rather than leaving Amanda in an agony of anxiety for the past five days over their strained parting.

'As a special celebration of my return, perhaps you and Mrs Leighton would care to join me downstairs for dinner this evening?'

'Really, Papa?' Amanda's eyes were wide with disbelief at the offered treat.

Elena, on the other hand, was still too irritated and annoyed by his long absence to be able to contemplate spending the evening in his company, or to enjoy how dashingly handsome he looked now in a deep-green superfine and buff-coloured pantaloons and black Hessians. 'You will have to excuse me, I am afraid, Lord Hawthorne.'

'Indeed?'

Elena ignored the coolness of his tone. 'My evenings are my own to do with as I wish, I believe, and I have several other, personal and more important things in need of my attention this evening.'

Adam eyed her mockingly. 'Such as?'

She gave him a reproving frown. 'Such as my ironing and washing my hair, sir!'

So now he knew where he stood in Elena Leighton's list of considerations, Adam acknowledged ruefully—obviously placed after her ironing and hair-washing!

Her manner had been more than a little frosty since he first entered the schoolroom, Adam acknowledged ruefully, and also defensive in regard to Amanda and the kitten. The latter might be attributed to the protective role she held in Amanda's young life and the manner in which father and daughter had parted five days ago. Yet he sensed there was more to it than that, that whether she was aware of it or not, the indignation was also on her own behalf.

Because of the way in which he had spoken to her before his departure?

No doubt about it.

Amanda had obviously already forgiven him for going away so suddenly and remaining away longer than he had anticipated. Elena Leighton, apparently, was of a less forgiving nature altogether...

'Both of those chores might wait another day, I am sure,' Adam briskly dismissed her excuse. 'Perhaps it would help if you were to look on this evening as a lesson to Amanda in manners and etiquette,' he added persuasively as he saw Elena was about to refuse his dinner invitation a second— or was it a third?—time.

She arched dark brows. 'In that case, might I expect to be allowed another afternoon off this month in lieu?'

His mouth thinned at the stubborn defiance she made little or no attempt to disguise. 'And what would you do with that second free afternoon, when, by your own admission, you do not know the Cambridgeshire area well?'

She looked at him coolly. 'I could use that free afternoon in which to know it better.'

Adam bit back his instinctive reply, knowing that it would suffice nothing, change nothing, except to make her more determined not to dine with him rather than the opposite. 'Then perhaps I might offer to be your guide?' he came back with a good attempt at that reasonableness she had attributed to him earlier.

She looked more alarmed than pleased at the suggestion. 'You are such a busy man, my lord, I could not possibly ask or expect that you waste any of it on showing me Cambridgeshire.'

'Or you to Cambridgeshire?'

'I very much doubt, my lord, that the county has feelings one way or the other about meeting the governess of your young daughter!'

Yes, whether she acknowledged it or not, she was indeed frostily indignant on her own behalf, as much as Amanda's!

It was an indignation totally at odds with her role of governess, an indignation that had given a flush to her ivory cheeks that was slowly moving down over the plump slope of her breasts visible above the low neckline of the turquoise gown she wore. Another of Mrs Hepworth's creations, no doubt, Adam mused, approving of this gown even more than he had the rose-coloured one, admiring the way in which it deepened the colour of Elena's eyes as they met his gaze unblinkingly and gave a soft glow to the ivory texture of her skin.

Adam continued to hold that gaze with his as he spoke to his daughter. 'Amanda, should you not consider taking Samson outside for a short time?'

'Oh, yes.' She gave a little giggle. 'May I be excused, Mrs Leighton?'

Those blue-green eyes narrowed slightly on Adam. 'Yes, of course you may, Amanda. With your father's agreement, I believe our lessons are over for today.'

'Papa?'

He smiled down at her approvingly. 'I will see you at dinner, Amanda.' Adam waited until his daughter had left the room before speaking again. 'I believe, Elena, that I owe you an apology for my…brusqueness the last time we spoke together.'

She raised haughty brows. 'Is it now my turn to dismiss the repetitiveness of your own apologies, my lord?'

'Adam.'

She blinked. 'I beg your pardon…?'

'I believe I once asked that you call me Adam,' he reminded her.

Her cheeks warmed with colour as she obviously recalled the occasion on which he had made that request and the exact circumstances under which he had made it. 'And I believe that I declined that invitation.'

His mouth tightened. 'Do you decline it still?'

She gave a gracious inclination of her head. 'As I must.'

'Why must you?'

Elena was unsure of how he came to be standing only inches away from her. She had not seen or heard him move, yet here he was, so close to her that she could see that black circle about the deep-grey iris as she looked up into his eyes and smell the sandalwood cologne he wore. The darkness of his hair looked slightly damp, seeming to imply he had bathed and changed before coming to the schoolroom.

She lowered her lashes to hide the expression in her eyes. 'It is not fitting for me to address you so informally.'

'Elena—'

'Do not!' She stepped back in alarm as he would have reached out and taken hold of her arms.

He released a heavy sigh even as his hands fell back to his side. 'Will you at least allow me to explain—to try to explain—why I was so ill-humoured on the last occasion we spoke together?'

She clasped her hands tightly together. 'I am sure there is no reason for you to either apologise or explain your moods to me, my lord.'

'In this instance I should like to do so,' he insisted huskily.

Elena continued to avoid meeting that soft grey gaze, so unlike that chilling coldness of five days ago. 'I am fully aware that Amanda's loss of temper had angered you—'

'Would you not like to know the reason why it did so…?'

Would she? Did Elena want to know anything more about the dynamics of this small family than she already did? To have Adam's emotions explained to her?

Elena had believed, when she fled Sheffield Park as if the hounds of hell were at her heels, that her future was bleak, her only course of action to cease being the fugitive Miss Magdelena Matthews and instead become a woman whom no one noticed, a servant in the household of one of the very people who believed her guilty of murder and theft.

And for a short while she had succeeded in doing exactly that, quietly going about her business as Amanda Hawthorne's governess and seemingly invisible to Lord Adam Hawthorne. Quite when, or why, that had changed, she was not quite sure—she only knew that for some inexplicable reason he had indeed noticed her, that he had actually sought out her company on several occasions. To the point that he had kissed her the previous week! A kiss, which although surprising, she had been unable to forget. Or her unexpected response to it.

Making her position here untenable?

She was very much afraid that was exactly what was happening...

If it had not already done so!

The fact that she knew her cousin would never give up his search for her meant she could not allow Adam to see her as anything more than his daughter's governess, that to do so would place her in a position of danger and vulnerability.

To her loss of freedom.

As well as her heart...

Because she was becoming attached to this family in spite of herself. Amanda, although given to those occasional tempers, was on the whole adorable, and as for Lord Adam Hawthorne—Elena found herself thinking about that gentleman far more often than was wise. Admittedly it had been mainly in annoyance most recently, and a certain sense of injustice at becoming the focus of his displeasure following Amanda's outburst, but even so she had still found herself thinking of him often. Of how much she admired his handsome looks. Of how charming he could be when he relaxed his guard and appeared to forget to be coldly reserved. She also found herself thinking of that kiss far more often than she ought…

Everything came back to that kiss. The surprise of it, the unsuitability of it, and the unexpected *pleasure* of it, when Neville's brutality to her two months ago should have caused her to feel only nausea.

The same pleasure still caused Elena to tremble every time she thought of those chiselled and yet softly questing, lips pressed so intimately against her own…

She straightened her spine. 'As I have said, it is not necessary, my lord.'

'Damn whether or not you think it necessary—!' Adam broke off his angry retort, fully aware that it was caused by the tension of awaiting her reply rather than any real anger he felt towards her. A tense wait that had been rewarded by another of her cool set-downs. 'Look at me, Elena.' He raised his hand beneath her chin and lifted her face up towards his when she did not obey him. 'I reacted in the way that I did because—'

'Adam, I—am I interrupting something…?'

Adam stiffened with shock, his hand dropping back to

his side as he turned sharply at the sound of that familiar voice. A familiar voice, which by rights, should have been many miles away from here. 'Grandmama…?'

Chapter Eight

Lady Cicely stepped into the schoolroom, grey brows raised in query. 'You look surprised to see me, Adam.'

That surely had to be the understatement of the Season! Adam was not only surprised to see his grandmother here, but he was less than happy about it too, bearing in mind his recent suspicions concerning her matrimonial machinations in regard to himself.

Adam turned briefly to give Elena a censorious frown. 'Why did you not inform me immediately of my grandmother's arrival here?' If he had known his grandmother was in the house, he would most certainly have delayed his conversation with her. Delayed, but not dismissed it completely…

How could he dismiss it, when just to look at her again, to briefly touch her, had caused a bulge in his pantaloons he was forced to cover with the fall of his jacket!

Her eyes widened. 'It was my assumption that Jeffries would have informed you on your arrival of Lady Cicely's presence, your lordship.'

A perfectly logical assumption to have made—except

that Adam, having made up his mind as to his future re-
lations with this woman, had been more intent on bathing
and going to the schoolroom rather than listening to anything Jeffries might wish to impart to him. 'Obviously not,'
Adam muttered.

'I fail to see what all the fuss is about concerning who
did or did not tell you of my arrival?' his grandmother said
querulously. 'I am here, as you can clearly see.'

And Adam's instant reaction to that was 'and for how
long do you intend staying?' Which was not only rude of
him, but also less than familial, considering he and Amanda
were Lady Cicely's closest relatives.

His mouth quirked and he forced the tension to ease from
his shoulders. 'I am merely surprised at seeing you so far
from London, and your dear friends there, in the middle of
the Season, Grandmama.'

'I missed you and Amanda so.'

His brows rose. 'We have only been gone a few days...'

'If you will excuse me, my lord, Lady Cicely, I believe I
must go and check on Amanda and the kitten.' Elena gave a
brief curtsy, her head remaining bowed as she crossed and
then departed from the room.

Adam's mood was one of pure frustration as he watched
her leave. Not only had he been unable to talk privately to
Elena, but he also apparently now had to deal with having
his grandmother visit for goodness knew how long.

'There is...something about that young lady, which does
not quite...sit right, with the role of a governess, my dear...'

Adam scowled darkly as he turned to look at his grandmother, a scowl completely lost on her as she continued to
look in the direction of the doorway through which Elena

had just passed. But he couldn't ignore the fact that his grandmother echoed some of his own doubts about Elena Leighton's suitability as a governess; she was very ladylike and elegant in her manner, and she often, but not always, appeared to forget to treat him with the deference of his other servants. Of course, a governess was an occupation slightly above that of the maids or footmen, but surely no more so than Jeffries or the housekeeper, neither of which ever forgot either that Adam was Lord Hawthorne, or that he was their employer.

Nevertheless, they were doubts which Adam had no intention of sharing with his grandmother. 'I believe it is time we both had tea and then you can explain to me exactly why it is you have chosen to leave London in order to visit me here.' He offered her his arm.

Lady Cicely gave him a sideways glance as she placed her gloved hand on that arm. 'Is that your polite way of saying that the subject of Mrs Leighton is at an end?'

Adam could not prevent a burst of laughter escaping him. 'I do believe you have been spending far too much time in the company of the forceful and forthright Dowager Duchess of Royston, my dear!'

She gave him a coquettish smile as she preceded him through the doorway, waiting outside for him to join her before they strolled down the hallway together towards the wide staircase. 'In that case, you will not be at all surprised if I also comment on your reluctance to discuss your newest, rather beautiful employee?'

Adam's mouth tightened. 'Because there is nothing to discuss. Mrs Leighton was employed as governess to Amanda, and I can find no fault with her in that regard.'

'But what do you know of her background? Her family? Her connections?'

He controlled his impatience. 'Not a thing above her widowhood—nor is it necessary for me to know anything else about her, Grandmama,' he added firmly as he saw how the curiosity had deepened in his grandmother's expression.

Lady Cicely frowned slightly. 'She has a look about her, seems to remind me of someone that I know, or have known, in the past…'

Adam glanced at her sharply. 'Do you have any idea who that someone might be?'

'It escapes me for the moment.' His grandmother gave a vague shake of her head. 'Perhaps she is some gentleman of the *ton*'s illegitimate daughter—'

'Grandmother!'

She raised a grey brow. 'I am not too old to be unaware of these things, Adam.'

'I was not for a moment suggesting that you were, but still—'

'It is the elegant tilt of her head, and possibly that abundance of silky dark hair, which seem so familiar.' Lady Cicely continued to muse softly. 'And, of course, her eyes are quite magnificent.'

Considering that Adam inwardly echoed that sentiment he wisely kept silent, knowing that to comment at all on the fineness of Elena's eyes would only result in deepening his grandmother's curiosity, if that were even possible. Much better if he were to appear uninterested in the whole subject.

'I am certain I have seen eyes of that unusual colour before.' Lady Cicely gave a pained moue as she searched for the memory that continued to elude her. 'Never mind.' She shook her head as she straightened. 'I am sure it will come back to me at some later date...'

Adam was unsure as to whether or not he wished his grandmother to recall that knowledge, his curiosity to know more of Elena Leighton warring with the possibility of his learning that she was not who she claimed at all, but some other man's runaway wife.

Elena, having gone briefly to her bedchamber, in order to collect her bonnet and gloves before going outside in search of her small charge, had emerged out into the hallway behind her employer and his grandmother, just in time to hear their conversation.

And now trembled at the significance of it.

For she knew who it was that Lady Cicely had previously met with these same unusual blue-green eyes: Elena's father, the late Lord David Matthews, youngest son of the previous Duke of Sheffield. He had caused many a female heart to swoon over the years with eyes of such an unusual blue-green. He would have been at least twenty or so years younger than Lady Cicely, of course, but her parents had been much a part of society before her father's death, an occurrence that would have ensured Lady Cicely saw them both even if she did not know them intimately. And Elena's mother, Lady Maria Matthews, had been the lady with an 'abundance of silky dark hair' so similar to Elena's own.

'It really is too bad of my grandson to have dragged you away from London in the middle of the Season.' Lady Cicely smiled at Elena sympathetically as the two of them sat in the green salon together, where they had retired to drink tea following a sumptuous dinner, after leaving Adam alone in the dining room to enjoy his brandy and cigars.

Adam had kept to his invitation for Amanda and Elena to join him for dinner, an invitation which also included his grandmother. And if Lady Cicely found it strange to find herself sitting down to dine with her great-granddaughter and her governess, then she did not show it by word or deed, her conversation pleasant and kept to subjects that both Amanda and Elena could contribute to, if they wished.

On several occasions Elena had felt she had no choice but to do so, when Adam, magnificent in his black evening clothes and snowy white linen, remained broodingly silent at the head of the table for the most part, eating little but enjoying several glasses of ruby-red wine.

Elena had left the room for a short time following dessert, when it was decided that Amanda had stayed up quite long enough for one evening, and Elena had gratefully risen to her feet in order to take the little girl to her bedchamber. Only to feel her heart sink again when Lady Cicely had expressed a wish for Elena to return downstairs and join her for tea once she had seen that Amanda was safely abed.

'As I am not part of society it is of little significance to me whether I am here or in London, Lady Cicely,' she answered smoothly now.

'But it is always so much more…lively, in London, during the Season. And I see you are no longer in mourning…' The older woman smiled approval of Elena's cream gown, delivered yesterday by Mrs Hepworth, in plenty of time for attending church tomorrow, and the only gown Elena had which was suitable for wearing to a formal dinner such as this evening's had been.

Elena sat stiffly in the armchair facing Lady Cicely as she sat on the green-velvet sofa. 'Lord Hawthorne did not think my black gowns suitable attire for when I am in Amanda's company.'

'No?'

'He feared it was too much of a reminder to Amanda of her deceased mother.'

The older woman's smile faded as she nodded slowly. 'And I am sure none of us needs to be reminded of the absence of Amanda's mother from this household.'

It was, Elena decided, a strange way to refer to the death of Adam's wife. 'No,' she answered slowly; she knew from Adam that he had been a widower for some years, but she had no idea of the happiness or otherwise of that marriage before Fanny Hawthorne's death.

Strangely, there had been no talk below stairs in regard to Adam's brief marriage, at Hawthorne House in London or since their arrival in Cambridgeshire. Which was unusual in itself; most household servants took delight in discussing the private lives of the family for whom they worked. But perhaps in this case the marriage had been of such short duration that no lasting impression had been made in regard to her ladyship?

Whatever the reason for that silence, Elena found that she was becoming increasingly more curious about Fanny Hawthorne. To wonder what manner of woman she had been that she had managed to ensnare the heart of a man as cold and arrogant as Adam could be. Or perhaps he had not been quite so cold and arrogant all those years ago? He could only have been in his early twenties when he married, hardly old enough for his true nature to have emerged and become quite so set in stone. Literally. For there was no doubt that, apart from his obvious affection for his daughter and grandmother, Adam Hawthorne now possessed a heart as cold as ice.

'Do you have any children of your own, Mrs Leighton…?'

Elena's attention sharpened as she realised she had allowed her thoughts to wander into conjecture regarding her employer's marriage. A serious lapse in attention, when, despite all outward appearances to the contrary, Lady Cicely was far more sharply astute than she gave the impression of being. 'Sadly, no.' Elena smiled briefly.

'I should have loved to have been blessed with a daughter, but unfortunately it was not to be. Nor a granddaughter, either.' The older woman sighed wistfully.

'But you have a great-granddaughter now,' she consoled the elderly lady.

'So I do.' Lady Cicely brightened briefly before that smile faded once again. 'Which is all well and good, of course, but it is a male heir that is needed if we are to keep the title within the family—'

'The last I heard, Cousin Wilfred was still a member of this family?' came a cool voice Elena knew only too well.

She gave a guilty start as she turned in the armchair to face Adam, knowing that guilt was reflected in the flush that also warmed her cheeks as those cold grey eyes raked over both women. Rightly so, perhaps, when it was obvious they had been gossiping about his succession.

'Being your third cousin, he is not a Hawthorne by name and is currently employed as a lawyer.' Lady Cicely showed no outward sign of apology at being caught discussing her grandson in his absence, or to hide her distaste for her distant relative's occupation. 'Furthermore, he has a shrew for a wife and at least half-a-dozen unruly children.' She wrinkled her nose delicately. 'I cannot even bear to think of him and his family being invited here on a visit, let alone imagine them all residing here!'

Adam had delayed joining the ladies for as long as he had felt able, not wishing to appear too eager, but at the same time only too well aware of how artfully his innocuous-looking grandmother could draw information from people when she chose to do so. And despite having claimed earlier that she had decided to come to Cambridgeshire on a whim, that she had missed the company of both himself and Amanda, she had also made her interest in learning more about Elena Leighton only too obvious during their earlier conversation.

He entered the salon and quietly closed the door behind him before answering his grandmother. 'If it is any consolation, I very much doubt that you will still be alive when the time comes for Cousin Wilfred and his family to reside here!'

Lady Cicely gave a grimace. 'No, Adam, I do not believe that to be of any consolation to me whatsoever!'

Adam lowered hooded lids as he saw that Elena was doing her best to hold back a smile at their conversation. 'I thought only to cheer you.'

'Then you failed utterly.' His grandmother gave him a knowing look before turning to Elena once more. 'As you may have gathered, my grandson finds the discussion of his heir to be a disagreeable subject,' she confided ruefully.

Adam's mouth tightened. 'Your grandson finds it a ridiculous subject, because I have stated, on more than one occasion, that it is not my intention to ever remarry, so leaving Cousin Wilfred in possession of the title when I die, whether that is what the rest of the family wants or not.' He looked arrogantly down the length of his nose.

Lady Cicely rose gracefully to her feet, very slight and delicate in a gown of pale grey. 'And on that cheerful note I believe it is time I retired for the night...'

Elena matched her action, equally as elegantly. 'I believe I might also retire, my lord.'

Adam studied her beneath lowered lids, the cream gown she wore seeming to give a moon-glow to the ivory of her skin. With an ebony sheen to the dark arrangement of her hair and her cheeks a pale rose, she was a vision of loveliness that had taunted and tempted Adam all the evening, her every move increasing the throb of his desire, to a degree that he had grown more and more silent and surly as the time passed.

'I, too, am fatigued from my long journey today,' he made his own excuses, only to then find himself irritated by the expression of relief Elena was not quick enough to mask as she quickly turned away. 'Unless Mrs Leighton finds the hour too early for sleeping?' Adam gave an internal grin of satisfaction as she stiffened. 'In which case, I will, of course, offer to act as her escort if she wishes to take a stroll outside before bedtime?'

'Is it not a little cold and late for strolling outside, Adam?' His grandmother glanced out into the darkened garden.

Adam kept his gaze firmly fixed on the tense and still Elena. 'I will happily wait here while Mrs Leighton goes upstairs to collect her bonnet and cloak.'

Elena was totally at a loss to know how to deal with a

conversation that seemed to have progressed to the acceptance of her strolling outside in the moonlight with Adam Hawthorne, without the inclusion of so much as a single word of encouragement or agreement from her!

A totally inappropriate and improper stroll... 'I really would prefer to go straight to my bedchamber,' she refused primly. 'But I thank you for the offer, my lord,' she added awkwardly.

'I will do my best to bear the disappointment, Mrs Leighton,' he drawled, a derisive smile tilting his lips as those dark-grey eyes met hers mockingly.

Telling Elena more clearly than anything else could have done that he had not been serious in his offer, but simply playing with her all along. A part of her longed to wipe that mocking smile from his lips by telling him that she had changed her mind, and would, after all, like to go for a stroll outside. But another part of her, the more sensible part, warned that she would be playing with fire by daring to challenge this gentleman when he was in this dangerously unpredictable mood.

'Shall we go upstairs together then, Mrs Leighton?' Lady Cicely linked her arm with Elena's. 'Adam?' She offered her cheek to her grandson.

As a consequence Elena was standing far too close when he bent down to pay his respects to his grandmother. So close that she could not mistake the challenge in those dark-grey eyes when he continued to look down at her as he lingered over kissing Lady Cicely's powdered cheek.

'Darling boy.' His grandmother patted his own cheek affectionately when he finally straightened. 'I am so glad I decided to visit you.'

'As are we, Grandmama,' Adam replied noncommittally.

'Am I not the most blessed of grandmothers, Mrs Leighton?' Lady Cicely turned to beam at Elena as the two of them crossed the room together to where the door was even now being opened by the attentive Jeffries.

Adam could almost have laughed out loud as he witnessed the way in which Elena's natural frankness warred with the politeness expected of her as a member of his household staff; those blue-green eyes glittered at him briefly with that scathing honesty as she stepped aside to allow his grandmother to walk out into the hallway first. 'You are indeed blessed in many ways, Lady Cicely,' Adam heard her murmur ambiguously as the door was closed softly behind them both.

An answer that had no doubt pleased his grandmother, but did not fool Adam for a moment; Elena obviously did not number *him* amongst Lady Cicely's many blessings.

Adam sighed deeply as he turned to stare sightlessly out at the moonlight gardens beyond the windows, becoming lost in thought as the silence of the night covered him like a shroud.

He would have to talk to Elena in private, and at the earliest opportunity. Not necessarily with a view to asking her to become his mistress—not only because, as things stood between the two of them, she would no doubt deliver a sharp and painful blow to his cheek for even daring to voice such a suggestion—but because Adam now felt that he should ask Elena to tell him more about herself before thinking in such terms, as well as attempt to clear the air between them.

For Amanda's sake, nothing more, Adam assured himself briskly as he moved to the window to stare out at the dark starlit sky. It would not do for Amanda's father and her governess to be constantly at odds with each other—

Adam turned sharply as he heard the door softly open behind him, his eyes widening as he saw that Elena had returned.

Alone…

Chapter Nine

'Oh!' Elena felt consternation as she stepped back into the green salon and found herself face to face with Adam. 'I did not mean to interrupt, my lord—I thought you would have retired to your rooms by now,' she hurried to excuse.

'As you can clearly see, I have not,' he drawled softly in reply, arms behind his back.

'Yes.' Elena avoided looking at the man whose very presence disturbed and yet somehow excited her. 'I believe I may have dropped my handkerchief earlier.' She began to look about the furniture and floor for the missing scrap of silk and lace, given to her as a gift by her late grandfather, with her initials, *MM*, damningly sewn into one of the corners—a realisation which had thrown her into something of a panic once she reached her bedchamber and noticed it was missing from the pocket concealed in her gown.

She should never have kept the scrap of silk and lace, of course, should have left that behind with all the other personal effects which identified her as Lady Magdelena Matthews. But she had wanted to keep something with her which had been given to her by her grandfather, and it was such a tiny piece of silk and lace…

'Ah.' Adam rocked back on his heels. 'Perhaps I might be of assistance—'

'No! No, I have found it now.' She straightened swiftly, the handkerchief crushed in her hand before being pushed into the pocket of her gown.

'Perhaps—' he broke off to look enquiringly towards the door.

Jeffries entered the room. 'May I get you anything further this evening, my lord?'

'No, that will be all for tonight, thank you, Jeffries.' Adam Hawthorne nodded dismissal of the other man.

Elena felt the jolt of alarm in her chest as she looked across at him sharply even as Jeffries bowed out of the room, leaving her alone with him, the very air between them seeming to crackle and dance in a manner that made her tremble. She cleared her throat before speaking. 'I am sorry for disturbing you—'

'Are you?'

'Of course.' Elena eyed him warily, not sure they were talking on the same subject. 'If you will excuse me, my lord, it has been a very long day.'

'Then a few minutes more should make little difference.' He eyed her calmly. 'I wish to speak with you, Elena,' he added huskily as she stared at him uncomprehendingly.

Elena's gaze dropped under the intensity of that unblinking grey one. 'Yes, my lord.'

Adam took a calming breath. 'You may safely dispense with your air of deference, Elena, when my grandmother is no longer present to witness it.'

She regarded him warily. 'My lord…?'

Adam had spent the past two hours or more, sitting at the head of his dining table, as he broodingly contemplated this woman from between narrowed lids. Had watched as she ate very little of the food placed before her. Listened as she added only the odd comment to the conversation between his grandmother and Amanda. Noted the way in which she rarely glanced in his direction.

And he had drawn but one conclusion from those observations. 'I have no idea how it may have occurred, but I am nevertheless of the opinion that you somehow overheard at least part of my grandmother's remarks to me earlier this evening concerning yourself?'

Her chin rose slightly. 'I don't know what you mean, my lord.'

Adam gave an impatient snort. 'Do not insult my intelligence by attempting to pretend otherwise!'

Those blue-green eyes snapped with her own impatience before she lowered dark lashes to veil those enticing orbs. 'I would not be so presumptuous, my lord.'

'Hah, every demure word you speak only confirms my suspicions!' he pronounced triumphantly.

A frown appeared on her brow. 'Just because I am being mindful of my manners—'

'Just because you are behaving in a most un-Elenalike manner,' he corrected derisively. 'The Elena Leighton I have come to know was not the woman who sat calmly silent during dinner this evening, her gaze lowered as much as it was a few minutes ago, adding very little to the conversation, and offering not a single opinion, despite the fact that I know she has many.'

Elena frowned her irritation with this summing up of her

character. 'You make me sound like an unpleasant cross between a harridan and a blue-stocking!'

Better, Adam noted with satisfaction, deciding that he liked this indignantly flushed Elena much better than the beautiful but mainly silent statue which had sat at his dinner table this evening. 'Whatever you may have decided to the contrary, I assure you that my grandmother was merely expressing her curiosity and did not mean to be in the least derogatory towards you in our conversation earlier.'

Elena raised dark brows. 'And I can assure both of you that far from being illegitimate my mother and my father had been married—to each other!—for almost two years on the day that I was born.'

'And in which part of England might that have been, Elena?' he prompted curiously.

'Subtlety is not your forte, is it, my lord?' she commented ruefully, the tension leaving her shoulders.

'Apparently not,' Adam muttered before he chuckled throatily. 'I have no idea how it is you always manage to do that…' He gave a slightly dazed shake of his head as he looked at her admiringly.

'Do what, my lord?'

He spread his hands. 'I can be in the blackest mood possible, feel beleaguered on all sides, by my family and other circumstances, and yet you nevertheless manage to say or do something which succeeds in making me smile or openly laugh. It is…a gift I had not expected.'

She moistened her lips with the tip of her tongue before answering him, not in artful invitation, Adam realised, but more in the way of a nervous gesture. 'It is a gift I had not known I possessed either until now, but if it has succeeded in lightening your lot in life then—then I am glad of it.'

Adam stared across at her for long, timeless seconds, aware that the very air seemed to have stilled between them. 'Will you stay and join me in a glass of brandy before retiring, Elena?' he finally requested. 'It would be pleasant to… linger together here awhile longer.'

Elena looked at him searchingly, knowing she should say no and straight away go upstairs to her bedchamber. Far away from the temptation of this gentleman's compelling handsomeness. And yet… 'Perhaps a very small glass, my lord.'

He smiled, not in triumph but in pleasure as he strolled across to the where the decanter and glasses sat upon a silver tray. 'My grandmother really did not mean any insult to you by her remarks earlier,' he assured as he poured the brandy into the glasses before carrying them across the room and offering one to Elena. 'She was merely voicing the fact that she finds you a woman of unexplainable contrasts. A puzzle, in fact. As do I,' he added softly.

Elena tensed warily, careful not to let her gloved fingers come into contact with his as she took the glass he offered. 'I am no puzzle, my lord, just a widow fallen on hard times who is in need of work in order to support myself.'

'You are a lady who has fallen upon hard times,' he corrected huskily.

She eyed him. 'I am not sure I care for that description, my lord. It sounds…somehow indecent.'

It was the perfect opportunity for Adam to put forward his offer, the ideal opening for him to ask this woman if she would consider becoming his mistress.

And yet he found he could not do so. Oh, he assured himself that it was because he now wished—needed—to find out all there was to know about her, before he considered entering into a relationship of intimacy with her. He told himself that. But the truth of the matter was, he did not wish to spoil the delicate ease that currently existed between the two of them…at the same time as he hungered to taste once again the perfect bow of her lips!

So much for his earlier concerns regarding the effect this woman had upon his self-control, the caution he had earlier decided he should practise with regard to her. If this was a lack of control, a weakness, then for the moment he knew he had no guard against it!

The top of Elena's silky black curls barely reached his shoulder, a delicate blush adding rose to her cheeks as she looked up at him with those luminous blue-green eyes through sooty dark lashes, her pulse pounding rapidly at the base of her long and slender throat, her breasts—oh lord, her breasts!

All of Adam's good intentions, all of those inner warnings for caution seemed to evaporate into mist as he gazed upon the wonderful swell of her breasts.

Besides which, there was a distinct possibility that Elena would turn down such an offer from him and that she might then leave his home altogether. Something which Adam currently found he did not even wish to contemplate.

'I toast you, Elena.' He touched his brandy glass gently against hers. 'You have worked wonders with Amanda,' he explained as she looked a little confused.

Elena made no effort to sip the brandy. 'She was very upset after you had departed last week.'

'And I, as a consequence, was just as upset when I departed,' he returned.

'You were?' She looked surprised.

Adam sighed. 'Contrary to what you so obviously believe, I do not enjoy being at odds with my daughter. But, conversely—' his mouth firmed '—I will not allow myself to be manipulated by emotional blackmail of the kind Amanda demonstrated that day. That sort of behaviour is too much like her mother's to be tolerated.'

Elena's curiosity quickened at Adam's mention of his wife. A lapse he already regretted if the bleakness of his expression was an indication. 'Amanda never mentions her mother—is it possible that she has memories of her?' she asked gently.

'Lord, I hope not!' A scowl darkened Adam's wide brow. 'No, I am sure not. She was not quite two when her mother died, could not possibly remember how Fanny screamed and ranted when she could not get her own way by persuasion or trickery.'

'My lord...?' Elena quietly gasped her shock.

Adam focused on her with effort—almost as if he had forgotten for a moment that she was there—before his jaw tightened. 'I do not believe it has ever been a secret in society that my marriage was far from a happy one.'

It had been to Elena because she had never had the chance to be a part of London society. Indeed, she had found herself wondering these past few weeks if Adam might have remained a bachelor after his wife died because he was still in love with her.

Elena admitted to feeling curious at the lack of conversation in the household, above or below stairs, in regard to the late Lady Fanny, as well as Lady Cicely's enigmatic comment earlier this evening, but there was no escaping the fact that Adam was a compellingly handsome gentleman of wealth and title, a gentleman in need of a male heir, who might take his pick of any of the young and beautiful single ladies of society as his second wife.

His remark just now would seem to imply his reason for not marrying again was not because he was still in love with his first wife, but because that marriage had been such an unhappy one he had no desire to repeat the experience.

'That is regrettable, my lord,' she murmured, only to open her eyes wide as Adam, after remaining silent for several seconds, now gave a loud shout of laughter.

Despite her confusion, she could not stop herself from once again appreciating how much younger, how much more compellingly attractive this man looked when he laughed or smiled.

Adam's shoulders shook as he took her brandy glass from her gloved fingers and placed it on the table with his own. He turned back to her, clasping both her hands in his own as he continued to grin widely. 'Do not look so offended, Elena,' he said as he saw her expression. 'It is only that "regrettable" does not even begin to describe my disastrous marriage to Fanny.' He could never remember finding that marriage a subject of mirth until Elena's understatement had made him see it as such. His fingers tightened about hers. 'For you see, Fanny, I am ashamed to say, was already two months along with my child when we married.'

'Are you sure you should be confiding any of this to me, my lord?' Elena looked alarmed as she tried to pull her fingers free of his.

Adam refused to release her. 'It is not a matter of should I tell you, but whether or not you wish to hear it?'

Did she wish to hear it? Miss Magdelena Matthews, granddaughter of a duke, and therefore Lord Hawthorne's equal, very much wished to know more of what had made him into the reserved gentleman he now was. But Elena Leighton, young and widowed governess of his young daughter, surely should not be made privy to such personal information as to the reason for her employer's hasty marriage and Amanda's subsequent birth seven months later.

Those two personalities warred inside Elena for several long seconds. But after all, she had been Miss Magdelena Matthews for far longer than she had been Mrs Elena Leighton... 'If you wish to tell me, then I will, of course, listen.'

He quirked a teasing brow. 'And not comment?'

A smile curved her lips. 'Oh I could not promise that, I am afraid.'

'I did not think so!' Adam eyed her ruefully. 'Nor do I think you a woman who is afraid of anything.'

In that he would be wrong, Elena acknowledged sadly. For she had been frightened in the past, and still was. Very frightened. Her cousin's forced attentions upon her had sickened her. His coercion, and then threats, when she had refused him, had terrified her. And hardly a moment had passed since that time when she was not afraid of Neville, still. Of someone discovering who she really was, then finding herself returned to Neville to pay for the crimes of which she was innocent, but which he had accused her of publicly as a cover to his own crimes against her.

She gave a shiver of revulsion. 'Everyone is afraid of something, my lord.'

He eyed her searchingly. 'Elena, what is it…?'

Elena gave herself a mental shake; Adam was a man of deep sensitivity as well as sharp intelligence—it would not do to alert his suspicions. She attempted a reassuring smile. 'I, for example, do not care for spiders.'

'Spiders…?' Adam echoed doubtfully.

She met his gaze unblinkingly. 'Yes, my lord, spiders.'

He gave her a wicked look. 'Does that mean that you might call upon my services one night so that I might rescue you from such a creature?'

Elena felt hot inside at the very thought of Adam entering her bedchamber, for whatever reason. 'I am not *that* afraid of them, my lord,' she assured huskily.

'Pity,' he drawled.

She swallowed before speaking. 'If we could resume our earlier conversation…?'

'Of course.' He straightened. 'You will try not to judge me too harshly?' He looked down at her searchingly.

Elena met that gaze openly. 'I do not believe I could ever think too badly of you, my lord,' she finally murmured. Truthfully. The man Adam kept hidden behind that mask of coldness and reserve was a gentleman Elena knew she was coming to like, and most of all to trust—to be attracted to!—far too much for comfort.

Adam's fingers tightened about hers momentarily before he released her to step away, his expression having turned grim once more. 'I was only young myself when I was first introduced to Fanny Worthington, who was the débutante of the Season that year. She was—' He drew in a deep breath. 'Her golden-haired, blue-eyed beauty was such that

I thought her an angel fallen to earth to dazzle and bewitch unsuspecting humans.'

Amanda's colouring and prettiness were already showing the promise of such dazzling beauty herself when she was older, and so easily allowing Elena to imagine the exquisite beauty of her mother.

She also felt a slight jolt of something—jealousy, perhaps?—at hearing how besotted Adam had been with the beauty of his wife. A beauty so unlike her own dark hair, and eyes that were neither blue nor green…

His mouth had become a firm, flat line. 'I was both dazzled and bewitched to such a degree that I did not notice the mercenary intent towards my fortune in the depths of those blue eyes, or realise that the marked preference Fanny showed towards my company was for that reason alone rather than a return of the love I believed I felt for her.'

'I think you underestimate your own…attractions, my lord,' Elena protested.

'Not where Fanny was concerned,' he insisted harshly. 'Although it is kind of you to say so,' he added.

Elena dare not look at Adam now, for fear that he might see the expression in her own eyes was far from innocent. 'I was not meaning to be kind, only truthful.'

'As you invariably are.' Adam smiled.

Elena felt a clenching in her chest, very aware that she had not been truthful with him at all about what was most important about her, namely her true identity and the circumstances that led her to come here. An oversight that she doubted Adam, with his obvious loathing for deceit of any kind, would willingly forgive.

'You are grown very quiet, Elena…?'

She kept her lashes lowered. 'I am merely waiting for you to continue.'

He sighed heavily. 'It is such an unpleasant tale.'

'Then do not tell it, if it makes you so uncomfortable.'

'I am more concerned that I may be making *you* feel uncomfortable?'

Elena's own emotions were in such confusion she did not know how she felt about these ridiculous feelings of jealousy, while at the same time she had a desire—a yearning—to know about Adam's marriage to the beautiful Fanny. 'I am not discomforted, only sorry that your marriage was such an unhappy one.'

'I was young. And very foolish. To a degree I allowed myself to be seduced into Fanny's bed—I think perhaps this is not a fit conversation for one such as you, after all!' he muttered as he heard her gasp.

'"One such as me"…?'

Adam saw the way her little chin had risen defensively, as if Elena imagined he somehow meant to insult her. 'I now realise that it is both a sordid and unpleasant tale, and not for the ears of a lady.' And he knew, innately, that Elena was far more of a lady than Fanny had ever been, for all that she had been the daughter of a baron.

Also, strangely, despite the fact that she was a widow, Adam found he was uncomfortable talking to Elena of the physical intimacies he and Fanny had obviously shared before their marriage—and for a very short time after it!

There was an innocence to Elena which he found he had no wish to besmirch with the sordid details of the reason for his marriage to Fanny, or the hell that marriage had become just a short month after their wedding day.

He smiled tightly. 'I am sure I have already told you enough that you realise my marriage to Fanny was not a love match.' He grimaced. 'By the time she died I believe we heartily despised one another.'

'Surely not...?' Elena looked dismayed. 'You shared Amanda, if nothing else.'

Adam shrugged. 'Fanny saw my love for my baby daughter as nothing more than a weakness which she could, and did, exploit in her constant attempts to emotionally blackmail me into doing exactly as she wished.'

'Is that the reason—?' She broke off with a self-conscious moue.

'"Is that the reason"...?' He quirked dark brows.

'I wondered if that was the reason you were now...occasionally aloof towards Amanda?' A heated blush warmed her cheeks. 'Because in the past your love for her was exploited and used against you?'

He gave her a shocked look. 'I had not thought of it as being so, but perhaps you are partly right... But only partly, I am afraid.' He frowned. 'The rest of my fatherly bungling really is due to a complete lack of experience in dealing with six-year-old children.'

'But which you are now attempting to rectify.'

'But which I am now attempting to rectify,' Adam agreed.

'What happened on the occasions when your wife's attempts to emotionally blackmail you failed?' Elena prompted curiously.

He smiled thinly. 'Ah, then she would have fits of temper which occasionally resulted in my sporting physical evidence of her displeasure!'

'She was violent towards you?' Elena gasped.

He grimaced. 'Her attacks were usually of a verbal variety, but I do recall suffering three scratches down my cheek from her fingernails on one occasion, and a bite on my bottom lip on another,' he recounted grimly. 'I very quickly grew to dislike such excessive displays of emotional temperament, and even all these years later, I still shy away from them.'

'Ah.' Elena breathed. 'Which is no doubt the reason you were so displeased when Amanda appeared to have a temper tantrum of a similar nature last week.'

'Yes...'

Elena realised now exactly why this man gave the appearance of being so cold and haughty, when she now had good reason to believe he was neither of those things. Well... perhaps Adam was naturally haughty, she allowed ruefully. But, after the things he had chosen to reveal to her, she now believed that coldness to be a barrier, one that he had deliberately erected in order to keep from suffering the same hurt as he had time and time again during his ill-fated marriage to the volatile Fanny; no doubt it also served to warn others to keep their distance.

Except Elena, standing but inches away from him, was not at a safe distance.

She moistened her lips with the tip of her tongue. 'I am... honoured that you have chosen to share this information with me, but—but perhaps it is time I now retired for the night.' It was a question as much as a statement.

One that caused Adam's eyes to darken with an emotion she could not fathom. 'Is that what you want?'

'It is very late.'

He smiled slightly. 'That is not what I asked, Elena.'

The tension between them was palpable. 'I— Surely that would be for the best?'

'Again, that is not what I asked. Is it what you *really* want to do?' He pressed as he reached out to grasp both her gloved hands in his.

Elena's fingers trembled within the firmness of that grasp.

Because it was not what she wanted at all. What she *wanted* was to remain here with Adam awhile longer, drinking the brandy in her glass as the two of them sat quietly together and talked some more, of pleasanter things than his unhappy marriage to Fanny, and then—then she would like it very much if Adam were to take her in his arms and kiss her again!

The memory of the last kiss they had shared, a kiss of warmth and pleasure, had helped to wipe away some of the nightmare of the memory of Neville's brutality. To a degree that Elena had thought of that kiss often this past few days: while she was teaching Amanda, eating her meals, strolling about the garden, or alone in her bed at night, but most of all when she was alone in her bed at night. Instead of the revulsion and nausea she might have expected, Elena had instead felt warm and satisfied just at the delicious memory of Adam's gentleness and passion.

She had only to think of that kiss to once again feel Adam's lips against her own, to remember how wonderful, how utterly safe, it had felt to be held in his arms, to feel the hardness of his body pressed against hers, that sensuous mouth moving softly, assuredly, over her own, wiping out those other horrific memories and instead igniting a passion, a desire, within Elena that she had never realised existed.

A passion and desire she had longed to feel again.

Adam's breath caught in his throat, as he now saw the emotions he'd been waiting for burning in Elena's beautiful blue-green eyes as she gazed at him silently.

Emotions—and a woman—Adam knew he did not have the strength to resist as all doubts and caution fled his brain, along with those fears for the tight control he had held over his life for so long, the blood swiftly travelling from his brain and going southwards. 'Elena…!' He released her hands only long enough to take her into his arms, the intentness of his gaze locked with hers, his lips parting as he slowly lowered his head to claim the delicious softness of hers.

Chapter Ten

She tasted of honey and brandy, her lips warm and compliant as they moved shyly beneath his, and her skin smelt of the strawberries and cream which had been their dessert at dinner earlier. A heady combination that Adam could not, did not, want to resist and one that all too quickly took him to a height of desire he had not felt in a very long time.

Too long, Adam realised with a groan as he very quickly became completely engorged inside his breeches, thickening and lengthening to an almost painful degree as he continued to kiss and taste, to tenderly nibble on the fullness of Elena's bottom lip. His tongue ventured into the moist and heated cavern of her mouth, seeking out each sensitive and secret place as he heard her breath catch in her throat and felt her gloved fingers reach up to cling to the broad width of his shoulders.

His arms tightened about her and his lips continued to devour and claim hers as he pressed his burgeoning thighs against Elena's much softer ones, as he sought, craved, to find some relief for the fierce ache of his pulsing erection.

A relief he could not, should not, press upon the woman who had borne so much of his temper these past few weeks, only to then be ignored, before becoming a willing listener this evening to his torments, both past and present!

A woman Adam employed as governess to his daughter.

And a woman who could not afford, quite literally, to deny the liberties he was taking, for fear that he might dismiss her.

He knew that his disastrous marriage to Fanny had made him cold and occasionally cruel, but was he now guilty of also becoming a man one who took advantage of unprotected females? That thought did what nothing else could and threw a bucket of ice-cold water on his libido.

Elena stumbled as Adam suddenly wrenched his mouth from hers before holding her at arm's length, those grey eyes blazing darkly in the fierceness of his face. She blinked in an effort to clear her muddled brain, having been totally swept away by the rage of passion created by the taste and feel of Adam's mouth possessing hers. 'I do not understand. Did I do something wrong?'

His expression was harsh as he released her to step back. 'It is I who am the one in the wrong,' he rasped harshly. 'I should not have—I apologise for—' He gave a self-disgusted shake of his head. 'You have my permission to slap my face, without fear of reprisals.'

Elena noted the tension in his shoulders and spine, the nerve pulsing in his tightly clenched jaw and the fierce glitter of those dark-grey eyes, his hands once against clasped tightly behind his back. She also recognised that he had just invited her to inflict physical retribution upon him in the same way that his wife had once taken such pleasure in doing.

'I could not possibly do that. But perhaps you regret what just happened?' she queried gently.

He gave a humourless smile. 'How could I possibly do that when I obviously enjoyed it so much?'

Some of the tension eased from Elena's own shoulders. 'As did I,' she admitted, knowing it was true. She trusted Adam not to hurt her. Physically, at least…

He drew in a deep, controlling breath. 'It is not right for me to take unfair advantage of you or force my attentions upon you.'

She gave a frown of confusion. 'Did I give the impression that I felt forced or taken advantage of?'

'No… But you must feel as if you have been—'

'Adam.'

'—and as such I—' He broke off his explanation to stare at her. 'That is the first time that you have voluntarily called me by my given name.'

'Yes.'

'Why now?'

The softness of her gaze met his levelly. 'Possibly because I enjoyed being kissed by you, as much as you enjoyed kissing me, and that I now think of you as Adam.'

The strong column of his throat moved as he swallowed before speaking. 'Did you enjoy it enough to repeat the experience?'

Elena knew that she should refuse him. That if she didn't, it would irrevocably change their relationship. Except…after the things Adam had just told her about his marriage, and after being held in his arms and kissed by him again, she accepted that it was already irrevocably changed.

She might only have that one nightmare experience with

Neville with which to compare Adam, but even so she recognised that his kisses were nothing like her cousin's, that
Adam had kissed her as a starving man newly arrived at a
feast, or a man dying of thirst in a desert, a man who longed
to eat and drink until that hunger was sated.

Elena knew she should be frightened of such an intensity of passion, that she should resist—should not want or
crave the compelling and irresistible attractions of her employer. Yet she found she did, that she needed to erase those
memories of Neville's attack upon her once and for all with
Adam's gentleness.

It had also been months since she had felt anyone wanted
so much as her company, let alone desired her with the intensity of passion Adam had just displayed so readily; Neville did not, could not, count. Indeed, Elena wanted another
memory, a much pleasanter one, to put in its place!

'I believe I might, yes,' she whispered, then stepped forwards until she was once again pressed up against the lean
and muscled length of his body, her gaze clear and steady
as she raised her face invitingly to his.

It was an invitation that Adam did not, could not, refuse.
He swept Elena up in his arms and once again claimed those
full and pouting lips with his own, the kiss questioning and
yet fiercely demanding at the same time as he moulded her
slender curves to his much harder ones.

But, as Adam had already knew only too well, it was not
enough, not with this particular woman. He wanted more,
so much more of Elena than the taste of her lips or the feel
of the soft skin of her throat as his own lips sought out each
and every sensitive dip and hollow with teeth and tongue,
as the insistent pulse of his desire told him only too clearly!

As it must also be telling her!

Elena was not an innocent young miss, but a widow, a woman, not a girl, who would recognise the depths of Adam's desire for her when his arousal pressed so insistently against her.

Adam's teeth closed on the lobe of her ear as he murmured. 'I have been dreaming, imagining, wondering...'

'Yes?' she breathed softly, her neck arched as she leant into him.

'While I was away I thought endlessly of your breasts...'

Her breath caught sharply. 'You did?'

He nodded. 'And I have wondered...are they tipped with rose or peach?'

The breasts Adam spoke of so candidly suddenly felt hot and swollen inside the bodice of Elena's gown, the tips now swelling, tingling, becoming painfully sensitive against the material of her chemise.

It was at once shocking and yet strangely exciting to imagine Adam thinking so intently about her breasts and the colour of her nipples. Should she be so bold as to respond to that? 'They are rose,' Elena answered him huskily. 'A deep rose.'

'Ah,' he moaned, his lips a trail of fire across the full swell of her breasts. 'May I touch you, Elena?' Adam raised his head to look at her, his eyes an intense glittering grey, a dark flush across the sculptured planes of his cheekbones. 'May I look at you there, touch you and then kiss you?'

Elena could no longer breathe, felt as if she were drowning in the unfathomable depths of his eyes, finally dragging her own gaze away to instead look at his lips. Sensuously soft lips. Lips that he'd asked if he might kiss her with. Not on her own lips, but on her breasts. As he would perhaps wish to kiss that other, even more intimate place between her thighs, too?

Elena felt a sudden warm rush of moistness just at the thought of Adam touching her there. With his hands. With his lips. With his tongue, perhaps?

Did men and woman do that to each other? Would Adam expect her to touch and kiss him with the same shocking level of intimacy?

Elena thought that he might.

Because Adam believed her to be a widow. A woman who had been married, and was therefore perfectly familiar with the physical intimacies that took place between a man and a woman. He thought she would not be shocked by the things he was saying to her, the things he was describing he wished to do to and with her.

She trembled with longing, but had to be prudent. 'We cannot—I could not permit—' She gave an embarrassed shake of her head even as she straightened her shoulders, determined to get her point across. 'I could not permit full intimacy.' There, she had said it! And surely, now that she was aware of the reason for Adam's hasty marriage to Fanny Worthington, he would not want to take the risk of impregnating her, either?

'I would not ask for it,' Adam reassured her immediately.

'Then…yes, you may.' Elena's stomach gave a sickening lurch of anticipation even as her heart skipped several beats. 'But—is it not overly bright in here?' She glanced self-consciously about the candlelit room.

Adam gave her an understanding look. 'Would you feel more relaxed if I were to blow out some of the candles?'

'Or all of them,' she suggested ruefully.

He made a throaty sound of protest. 'Then I would not be able to see you at all!'

Of course he would not. And Elena knew she should not allow him to see her. Except her breasts now ached so as they pressed and throbbed against the confines of her gown, bursting to be free, as if they at least knew, and ached, for the pleasures of Adam's hands and mouth.

If Adam had been in the least rough with her, or demanding, or seemed in the least arrogantly triumphant about her obvious responses to him, then Elena knew she would not have hesitated to refuse him. It was Adam's very gentleness—his gentlemanliness, his regard for her own comfort and pleasure—which now piqued Elena's curiosity to know, to experience the desire of a man not intent upon hurting her.

'A few less candles alight would be…preferable,' she conceded.

'Then fewer candles you shall have.' He reached up to cup her chin, the soft pad of his thumb a caress against her bottom lip as he looked down at her searchingly. 'I will not do anything you do not wish for, Elena.'

Her eyes widened. 'I never thought that you would.'

'No?' Adam was sure he was not mistaken about the trepidation he had seen in the depths of her eyes. As if she feared he might somehow hurt her. As someone else—her husband, perhaps?—had once hurt her? Adam had never been able to understand why a man, any man, would ever wish to hurt a woman rather than give her pleasure.

Even in the depths of the despair over his awful marriage with Fanny, despite several times suffering the painful provocation of her scratching and biting, Adam had never once felt a desire to instigate physical retribution of his own.

Partly, perhaps, because Fanny seemed to want, even crave him to lose control and strike her, before taking her in a sexually violent manner, which Adam had refused to do. He'd found it totally abhorrent and against his very nature to dominate a woman in that way.

He already knew Elena well enough to know she was Fanny's complete opposite, in looks as well as temperament. A woman of dignity and elegance, gentleness, and yet at the same time deeply hidden passions. A quietly self-contained woman, who did not need to be constantly reckless in her efforts to prove her feminine power over men. Over him.

As if sensing some of the unpleasantness of his thoughts, Elena reached up to gently smooth the frown from between his eyes. 'I fear we have both been hurt in the past.'

'Yes…'

She nodded. 'I will make myself comfortable on the *chaise* and unbutton my gown whilst you blow out some of the candles.'

Adam looked down at her intently for several more seconds before nodding his satisfaction with the trust he could see in her eyes. 'I should like that very much.' He released her before turning away, primarily to give her the privacy to unfasten the back of her gown, but also so that he might move about the room extinguishing half a dozen of the eight lit candles.

The room was thrown into golden shadow by the time Adam crossed the room to join Elena on the *chaise*, his eyes glittering even more brightly in the soft glow of the dimmed candlelight as he looked down at her. 'It hardly seems fair if I remain fully dressed.'

She blinked those long dark lashes. 'And if Jeffries should decide to return, after all?'

'He will not.'

Elena paused for a second to think before speaking. 'I— is Jeffries accustomed to your bringing women here and making love to them—?' She fell silent as Adam placed his fingertips against her lips.

'No, he is not, he merely knows when he is dismissed for the evening,' Adam answered firmly, evenly, knowing it was a fair question for Elena to ask, but resenting it all the same. 'I never bring the women I...take to my bed, to my estates, Elena. Nor would I ever think of doing so now, when my grandmother and daughter are both abed upstairs.'

Her smile was strained once he had removed his fingertips. 'Perhaps, then, it is nothing more than a convenience that I am already here?'

Adam closed his eyes briefly. 'My desire for you is not in the least "convenient",' he assured ruefully. 'Indeed, it is most *in*convenient. It is just—I can no longer resist wanting to kiss and touch you, Elena,' he admitted gruffly.

Her cheeks coloured warmly. 'I apologise. I—' She moistened her lips, unknowingly drawing the heat of Adam's gaze to that provocative movement. 'I am only—I have never— this is not something I have ever done—allowed—before.'

He knew that, had been aware of her shyness when she asked for most of the candles in the room to be extinguished before she allowed him to look upon her breasts.

Elena might be a widow, but Adam knew beyond any shadow of a doubt that she had not become promiscuous after her husband died, and her very youth, and the brief duration of her marriage, implied that she could not been so beforehand, either. Nor did that marriage itself appear to have given her the physical satisfaction she deserved and that Adam wished to share with her, if her continued shyness was any indication.

His gaze continued to hold hers as he stepped back slightly. 'I believe it only fair that I join you in partially disrobing.' His hands moved up to remove his superfine and untie his neckcloth, before putting them both aside, his waistcoat joining them seconds later. He unfastened the three buttons of his shirt and then pulled it free from the waistband of his breeches to leave it hanging free about his thighs.

Elena sat unmoving as she watched Adam between thick dark lashes, her heart beating a wild tattoo in her chest as she looked at the gold smoothness of his skin revealed at this throat, the fine dusting of hair on his chest also just visible. She was barely breathing as she waited to see if he would remove the shirt completely.

She had taken off her gloves so that she could unfasten the buttons at the back of her gown, the release having somewhat lessened the pressure against the fullness of her breasts, but that very freedom of movement serving to heighten the full and tingling sensation at their tips.

Quite what happened next, Elena had no idea, but she was happy—indeed, she quivered with eagerness!—at the thought of putting herself into Adam's gentle and more experienced hands. And lips. And tongue. And teeth…

Adam did not remove his shirt, but sat down beside her on the *chaise*, the warmth of his thigh resting against the length of hers. He reached out and slowly slid the loosened material of her gown from her shoulders and down the length of her bare arms before slipping the bodice down completely, her breasts only covered by the thin material of her chemise now. 'You have beautiful hands…' he murmured even as he raised one of those hands to his lips to kiss each individual finger before once again looking up into her eyes. 'I should very much like to feel them against the bareness of my chest, so if you will help me to remove my shirt…?'

Elena was moved beyond words by Adam's continued tenderness, knew that most men—how that past memory was still burned within!—would have simply made an eager grab at her breasts rather than take the time to kiss her fingers, totally uncaring as to whether or not she enjoyed the experience. Which, with Neville, she most certainly had not.

'Do not think of the past, love.' Adam reached out to gently touch Elena's cheek as he saw the shadows that had once more entered her eyes. 'This is you and me. Adam and Elena. And there is no room for anyone else here, not between the two of us.'

Tears glittered in those blue-green depths. 'Why are you being so kind to me?'

How could he not be kind to her? How could any man not wish to show kindness to this beautiful and entrancing woman? 'Help me off with my shirt, love?'

Instead of continuing to sit beside him as she reached up to help him, as Adam had expected she would, Elena now stood up, causing her unfastened gown to fall to the carpet at her slippered feet, and leaving her clothed only in that revealing white chemise over her drawers, and delicate white stockings held in place at her thighs by white garters adorned with rosebuds.

Drawing Adam's gaze unerringly to those other rosebuds

now visible through the thin material of her chemise, full and delicious red berries that were clearly and temptingly outlined against that gauzy material.

Adam continued to gaze hungrily at those pouting red berries as Elena slowly raised his shirt up his chest and then over his head before discarding it completely, only looking up into her face as he heard her gasp softly. 'What is it, love?'

'You will think me silly.' Her cheeks had flushed a fiery red, her eyes overbright.

'I am currently sitting half-naked in the salon where I usually receive guests, and I will think *you* are the silly one?' he teased huskily.

'I am standing here half-naked in that very same salon,' she came back ruefully. 'And the reason for my shock was that you are very beautiful, Adam,' she said shyly.

His own breath caught in his throat at her unaffected candidness, then he ceased to breathe altogether as those long and slender hands moved tentatively to the nakedness of his chest, fingers tracing a delicate and seductive path across the muscled width of his shoulders before moving down to touch the silky dark hair covering his chest. Adam let out a hoarse exclamation of pleasure as her fingernails rasped lightly across the flat nubbins hidden there. His arousal surged and leapt inside his breeches to the same rhythm as those caressing fingers, causing him to shift uncomfortably.

Elena flattened her fingers against those hardened nubbins. 'Am I hurting you?'

'Only with pleasure,' Adam acknowledged throatily.

Her eyes widened. 'You enjoy being touched?'

'By you, yes, very much so.' Adam reached up to slide the

thin shoulder straps of her chemise down to her elbows, finally baring those breasts to the avidness of his heated gaze.

Surprisingly full breasts, considering the slenderness of her body. They were round and pert, and tipped with delectable rosy-red nipples that seemed to swell and deepen in colour the longer he continued to look at them hungrily.

'May I?' Adam moistened his lips in anticipation of the taste of those ripe berries as he slipped the straps down completely, allowing her chemise to fall down to her waist.

'Please…!' Elena stepped forwards to stand between his parted thighs, her bared breasts swinging temptingly close to his mouth.

Adam placed his hands on her hips to steady her as he leant forwards and gently kissed each rosy-red nipple, one after the other, before lingering to lave one engorged berry with his tongue, around and around, urged on by her softly keening cries. She reached out to cling to the bareness of his shoulders as he slowly, skilfully drew that sensitive nubbin fully into the heat of his mouth.

Elena's knees threatened to fold completely and she knew she would have fallen, if Adam had not tightened his grip on her hips to hold her in place. Her throat arched, head thrown back. She became totally consumed with the pleasure he gave with his lips and tongue—ah, yes, his teeth!—as he laved and suckled and nibbled upon that engorged berry.

This was nothing like that terrible memory of her cousin's touch, Adam's causing her drawers to become wet with moisture, her folds there swollen and aching, and a throbbing between her thighs that she could not explain.

She whimpered as Adam ceased his ministrations to her breasts and turned his attention to its twin, no longer gentle as he drew deeply on that nubbin, his breathing laboured as he suckled hard and long until it grew bigger still, elongating as he rasped his tongue across the tip over and over again until Elena thought she might go mad with the pleasure. The ache inside her was now so great that it caused her to thrust her thighs forwards, her movements restless as she burned, ached, begged for a release from the torment, at the same time as she never wanted this pleasure to stop.

Her back arched as she leant into him, pleading, asking, needing—for what she did not know. She groaned in protest as Adam released her nipple with a loud popping sound, that berry red and moist as Elena looked down at him with dark and sultry blue-green eyes.

'Part your legs, love,' Adam encouraged throatily as he pushed her chemise up her thighs to her waist. 'I want to touch you here, too,' he breathed, looking at her long and deeply before once again slowly, deliberately, latching on to the engorged pout of her nipple. Her legs slowly parted, allowing his hand to seek out the slit in her drawers.

Elena felt his fingers part her silky curls to seek out her swollen folds, dipping those fingers into the moisture there before parting those folds and moving higher, circling, caressing, moistening her there but not quite touching the part of her that throbbed, ached for his touch. 'Please, Adam…!' She moved her thighs restlessly against those caressing fingers, seeking, wanting— 'Yesss!' Elena cried out at the first touch of those fingers against that ache, fingers that now alternately stroked and circled that swollen and moistened nubbin to the same rhythm that he suckled deeply on her nipple. His free hand moved from her hip to cup her other breast, finger and thumb tweaking, pulling on that second nipple.

The triple assault upon her senses was too much. Too many different sensations at once. Too much pleasure. Too much, too much, too much—

That pleasure released, climaxed so suddenly, that it took Elena's breath away as it rippled and surged, then exploded in a cascade of overwhelming sensations, the moisture rushing freely between her thighs, wetting Adam as he thrust one finger deep inside her even as he continued to stroke her into ecstasy.

On and on it went, as the tears coursed hotly, unknowingly, down Elena's cheeks.

Chapter Eleven

'We are not finished yet,' Adam said as Elena, flushed and obviously self-conscious after her loss of control, turned her face away and would have moved out of his reach. Instead he continued to hold her lightly with one arm about her waist as he reached up to release the pins from her hair, so that he might admire those long silky dark curls as they cascaded down the length of her spine and fell softly about her flushed face. 'You are a very beautiful woman, Elena…'

She moistened full and swollen lips, those blue-green eyes slightly unfocused from her recent climax. 'I—thank you.'

Adam chuckled softly at the obvious absence of her usual calm and composure—he was feeling less than calm or composed himself! Nor had he had his fill of her beautiful body. 'Come, lie here beside me, love,' he encouraged as he turned with her in his arms to place her down gently upon the *chaise*.

His gaze darkened appreciatively at the totally wanton picture she presented as he sat back to look at her, those dark curls falling wildly about her shoulders and breasts, breasts swollen from his ministrations, the nipples tight red buds, becoming even more so as Adam's gaze lingered there before moving down to the slenderness of her waist where her chemise was gathered.

'These need to come off.' He suited his actions to his words as he rolled both her chemise and her drawers down over her thighs and legs before discarding them completely, Elena now wearing only those white stockings held up by rosebud-adorned garters. 'Please do not.' Adam reached out to clasp Elena's hand in his as she would have self-consciously covered the curls between her legs, dark and silky curls that he could see were slightly damp from her recent release. 'Will you allow me to kiss you here?' He allowed his fingers to tangle lightly with those silky dark curls as he raised his soft grey gaze to hers.

Elena's eyes widened. Adam wished to—he wanted to place his mouth against her *there*?

She had not known what to expect from Adam's love-making, her past experience with Neville—both painful and terrifying, and one she had tried in vain to erase from her memory—having in no way prepared her for the pleasure she had just known. He had been so gentle with her, so careful not to hurt her, as he showed her that lovemaking could be a pleasurable and caring experience. With him, at least.

Even so, could she—dare she—allow him to kiss her *there*, to feel those sensual lips against her most intimate place?

'Your husband did not deserve you, love!' Adam rasped as he obviously saw, and understood, the uncertainty in her expression, though he did not know the correct person to

blame for it. 'Lovemaking is for the enjoyment of both parties, Elena,' he continued gently. 'And it would give me as
much pleasure to kiss you here as I believe it would for you
to be kissed. But I appreciate that some ladies do not even
like the thought of such intimacy. Do you trust me, Elena?'

She looked up at him. 'I trust you, Adam.'

His eyes darkened. 'Thank you.'

She nodded. 'You have been very kind and gentle and I
have enjoyed our time together up to this point.'

'I promise I will stop if you decide you do not like what
I do to you now.' His caressing fingers gently parted her
legs so that he might separate the dark curls and stroke
against that already swelling nubbin between her thighs as
he draped the leg nearest to him across the muscled hardness of his own thighs before his head began its slow de-
scent. 'I so badly wish to taste you!'

Elena swallowed the saliva that had gathered in her
mouth, that swallow turning to a breathless sigh, her lids
closing, at the first touch of Adam's lips against her swollen folds, pleasure coursing through her anew as she felt the
rasp of his tongue against her most sensitive place.

'You taste divine, Elena.' The warmth of his breath
moved lightly, arousingly, against her moist heat. 'So sweet
and creamy,' he murmured.

Elena's hands seemed to move of their own volition as
her fingers became entangled in the darkness of Adam's
hair. Her back arched as her hips began to undulate in the
same rhythm as the almost unbearable rasp of his tongue,
his fingers moving to stroke the little nubbin, causing Elena
to shift restlessly.

He raised his head only slightly. 'Do you wish me to stop?'

'Heavens, no!' Elena's husky laugh caught on a sob— she wished him to do the opposite!—as she glanced down into those dark-grey eyes rimmed by black, allowing her to see lips damp from her. 'Unless… Do you wish to stop?'

His gaze continued to hold hers as he once again lowered his head and resumed that skilful flicking of his tongue, at the same time as both his hands moved up to cup her breasts, capturing the nipples between thumb and index finger and pinching gently. This combined assault upon her senses was altogether too much for Elena as she felt the burn of that pleasure coursing through her once again, hotly, frantically, until she exploded a second time, even more fiercely than the first, her back arched up as wave after wave of pleasure consumed her.

'Does that answer your question, love?' Adam asked as he lay his head against her bare thighs. 'I would kiss and caress you here all night long if you allowed it,' he assured her. 'You are as beautiful here as you are everywhere else.' His gaze lowered as the gentleness of his fingers stroked against her sensitive flesh. 'So, so beautiful, Elena.'

She chewed lightly on her bottom lips before answering him shyly, 'And you…you really enjoy performing such… such intimacies?'

'Any man would, love.' A smile curved those sensual lips as he looked up at her. 'To give you pleasure is to give myself pleasure also.'

'Would you not enjoy it more if I—if I were to touch you now?' She looked at him anxiously, unsure if she had gone too far as she saw his eyes widen. Except…she ached to touch Adam, to explore the hardness of his arms and chest, the flatness of his abdomen, and perhaps lower still?

'You do not have to do so,' Adam said gruffly, that reassurance belied by the heated glitter that had entered his eyes and the deepening flush in his cheeks, the bulge in his breeches seeming to grow larger still.

Elena had only seen a man's rampant rod once before in her life, seconds before it was pushed painfully inside her, ripping through her innocence and causing her immeasurable pain. What had followed had been even more excruciating and unpleasant.

But this, here and now with Adam, was so unlike that last time, both the man and the experience. Adam was intent only on giving her pleasure, to a degree that he had asked nothing of her in return. She *wanted* to give something back to him, to perhaps be able to give him the same release he had given her—twice.

Well, perhaps she should not expect it to happen twice for Adam, for Elena had overheard two of the maids gossiping once at Sheffield Park, in regard to one of the footmen, a gentleman with whom it seemed that both young ladies occasionally engaged in love-play, and there had been much giggling between them over that gentleman's need to rest for several hours before he could 'perform' a second time.

She looked up at Adam shyly once again. 'And if I should wish to?'

His throat moved as he swallowed before answering. 'Then I would like that very much indeed. You are sure, love?'

She nodded as she tucked her legs beneath her before moving up on her knees and placing her hands upon his bare shoulders as she knelt in front of him. 'If you will help to instruct me as to what I may do, how to touch you, so as best to please you?'

Adam's breath caught in his throat as he gazed at her un-ashamed nudity: those firm, uptilting breasts, reddened now from his ministrations as they peeped through the ebony waves of the long hair cascading over her shoulders and down her spine, the curve of her waist, her legs slender and shapely, slightly parted so as to reveal the dampness of the curls between her thighs.

'You would perhaps find such intimacies...unpleasant.'

She gave him a calm, trusting look. 'I do not believe that I should. Not with you.'

Something welled up in Adam's chest. Something too fleeting to be recognised. Something he had no time or inclination to analyse, as Elena reached down and began to unfasten the buttons at the sides of his breeches.

His shaft, already a painful throb, surged to even greater heights as those slender fingers brushed lightly against his heat, a small amount of liquid moistening his smalls as it eagerly escaped.

'I believe you will have to be the one who now lies down.'

Adam dragged his gaze away from Elena's flushed face to glance down and see that she had his breeches completely unbuttoned and pulled down to his thighs, along with his smalls, his manhood bobbing free and far longer and thicker than Adam could ever remember seeing it before. 'I believe he is pleased to see you,' he murmured ruefully as he lay down on the *chaise* in order to completely divest himself of his clothing.

'"He"?' She gave an uncharacteristic giggle as she moved to kneel between his parted thighs.

'All men call that part of their anatomy "he", love,' he teased.

'As if "he" is an entity apart from yourself?'

'Sometimes I believe he is,' Adam drawled ruefully. 'Certainly, men have allowed themselves to be led about by it. Myself included—' He broke off as once again Elena smoothed the frown from between his brows caused by memories of the past.

'We will not talk of anything but the here and now,' she spoke firmly, as if she too had memories she would rather not dwell on. As no doubt she had. 'My instinct is to curl my fingers about him, is that correct?'

'Your instinct is perfectly correct.' Adam nodded, watching between narrowed lids as Elena moved her hand to allow her fingers to curl about his girth. Well, almost to curl about his girth, for it was now so thick and throbbing that her fingers were too tiny to span him completely. 'Perhaps you should use both hands?' he teased, only to catch his breath in a gasp as she did exactly that, those fingers tightening and relaxing at the same time as she began to pump lightly and rhythmically.

Elena was obviously completely enthralled by what she was doing and Adam was more aroused by her wonder in his response than he had ever been aroused by anything, or anyone, in his life before. It was almost as if she were seeing a man's responses to her for the first time—and perhaps she was? Her surprise earlier, when she had reached her first climax, would seem to imply that whatever manner of man her husband had been, he had not seen to Elena's physical needs before his own. That he had not seen to her needs at all, or shown her how to please him!

Not so unusual, in any marriage. Indeed, the marriages of the *ton* especially tended to be arranged or loveless affairs, forged only to produce an heir and a spare, before the gentlemen returned to their mistresses and the woman very often took a lover of her own. Why should he have assumed it would be any different between men and women of the lower classes? Elena's lack of experience in what pleased her or the man in her bed made a complete nonsense of any such assumption. He—

'Dear God…!' Adam groaned low in his throat as he felt Elena's tongue against him, trailing up the velvety side, seconds before she parted her lips wide and took the sensitive tip fully inside the hot cavern of her mouth. 'Elena!' His fingers became entangled in her hair as she took him deeper still, at the same time as her fingers tightened about him and her other hand moved to cup him beneath.

At which time Adam knew he was never going to hold!

Elena had never seen or felt anything as beautiful as the shapely length of Adam's rod: long and thick and hard, the skin surprisingly soft to the touch. It was no longer enough for her to merely hold him; she needed to taste him fully, in the same way he had tasted her.

Instinct had told her to part her lips and take him into her mouth. The same instinct that told her to pump her fingers lightly along the shaft as Adam began to thrust his rod into her mouth, slowly at first, and then faster, his breathing laboured.

'It is all over for me, Elena,' he cried out in a strangulated voice. 'I cannot hold any longer. I am going to—oh, dear God…!' The last was a low and husky cry as hot and creamy spurts of Adam's release poured out of him like molten lava.

'We should both dress and go upstairs to bed.'

'Yes.'

'The candles have both burnt out.'

'Yes.'

'The fire will soon have burnt down, too.'

'Yes.'

'Elena…?'

'Yes?'

He chuckled softly and glanced down at her as she lay in his arms upon the *chaise*, the darkness of her hair a silky curtain across his bare chest. 'I believe you would make that same reply to anything I were to say to you at this moment!'

'Possibly.'

'Ah, a different reply, after all.'

'I would not wish to become boring.' There was a smile in her voice.

'I doubt you could ever be that, Elena,' Adam murmured, and, to his surprise, meant it.

Women had become a necessary inconvenience to him before and since Fanny had died, something Adam had need of every now and then in order to assuage his physical needs, but none of those women had been for conversation, certainly not for lying in each other's arms once he had found his release, or sharing a conversation which did not appear to be conversation at all but what he believed to be lovers' nonsense.

Was that what Elena was to him now? His lover? Had he taken her as his mistress, after all, without so much as even asking her?

Without any of the finer details of that relationship having been discussed and agreed upon?

That very much appeared as if it might be the case.

An occurrence he should have thought of sooner.

Adam scowled the following morning as he walked through the capacious entrance hall and through to the breakfast room. He paused only long enough to bestow a kiss upon his grandmother's powdered cheek, as she sat at the table drinking the herbal tea she favoured in the mornings, before turning his attention to where the array of breakfast foods were laid out in covered silver dishes and plates for his selection. Jeffries had already disappeared to the kitchen to collect the pot of strong tea he knew Adam preferred with his breakfast. His stomach gave a sickening lurch as his nostrils were assailed with the smell of the breakfast foods.

'No appetite this morning, Adam?' his grandmother prompted as he sat down opposite her at the table.

'None whatsoever,' he muttered gruffly.

His grandmother nodded. 'You did not sleep well?'

Adam was uncertain as to whether or not he had slept at all after being assailed with the worst feelings of guilt once alone in his bedchamber. Guilt. And uncertainty as to what the future held, if anything, in regard to his relationship with Elena. The latter emotion was due, he knew, to his feeling out of control whenever he was with her. An iron control he had maintained over all of his emotions since shortly after his wedding to Fanny. For his own protection. A protection that he could not, dared not, allow to be pierced. Even by a woman as sweetly responsive as Elena. *Especially* by a woman as sweetly responsive as Elena!

'Obviously not,' his grandmother said drily. 'Perhaps that is because you did not sleep alone?'

Adam stiffened. 'Grandmama!'

'Adam,' she bit back with uncharacteristic firmness. 'I am not so old that I am unaware of a man's desire for a woman. And my insomnia is such that I heard you and Mrs Leighton talking softly together as you passed my bedchamber late last night. Very late last night. Had the two of you arranged an assignation after I had retired?' She arched questioning brows.

Adam and Elena had parted outside Elena's bedchamber, a long and lingering goodnight, neither of them in any hurry to bring the night to an end. Except Adam's euphoria, his physical satisfaction, had ended the moment he entered his own bedchamber and realised the enormity of what he had done.

He had not realised she had heard them and would not have wished for his grandmother to have done so if he could have helped it. 'I do not—'

'Ah, thank you, Jeffries.' Lady Cicely turned to bestow a smile on the butler as he entered with Adam's pot of tea.

'That will be all, thank you, Jeffries,' Adam dismissed distractedly.

'Shall I pour?' his grandmother offered once the two of them were once again alone.

Adam scowled darkly. 'I am quite capable of pouring my own tea, thank you, Grandmama.'

'As you wish.' She gave him a nod before continuing to sip her own cooling brew.

Adam poured his own steaming tea from the fresh pot, his thoughts in turmoil as he contemplated his grandmother guessing what had taken place between himself and Elena the night before. It was not only embarrassing, for any man of eight and twenty to be 'caught out' by his own grandmother, it was also damned inconvenient.

'Oh, do stop looking so po-faced, Adam,' Lady Cicely said briskly. 'I only mentioned the subject at all because I wished, if you intend to continue the relationship with Mrs Leighton, to offer a few words of warning.'

Adam's spine stiffened even further. 'This really is not a fit conversation for the breakfast table.'

Grey eyes twinkled at him merrily over her teacup. 'Would you prefer I wait until luncheon?'

'I would prefer that we not discuss the subject at all!' He glared at her down the length of his nose.

'I feel I must, my dear.' She placed a hand upon his. 'I have no wish to see you hurt or disappointed again—'

'I shall not be.'

'How can you be so sure?' she asked gently. 'Mrs Leighton is a beautiful young woman. And one whom you obviously desire. But there can be no future in such a relationship. None that would not see both of you hurt—'

'There is not a relationship to continue!'

'I sincerely hope not, my dear.' His grandmother patted his hand. 'Because not only do I seriously doubt that really is her name, but I have other reservations, too.'

'Do you know something about Elena that I do not?' He eyed his grandmother suspiciously.

'Nothing definite, no.' She sighed. 'Only the doubts I expressed to you yesterday. But whether or not that really is her name, or she really is a governess, I am sure I do not have to remind you, of all people, to have a care. For I have no doubt that somewhere in the world, as was the case with Fanny, Elena Leighton will have a father, or a brother, or perhaps even a husband still alive, who will be just as desirous that their daughter or sister, or wife, was not debauched and disgraced by Lord Adam Hawthorne!'

'I do not believe a mutual passion can be called debauching, Grandmother!' Adam's expression had turned icy again.

'If that is the case, then Mrs Leighton must now have some idea of her value.'

Adam stilled. 'Value…?'

Lady Cicely nodded. 'You may be lucky, of course; she does not seem like a particularly grasping sort of gel to me.' His grandmother smoothed the already-smooth skirt of her gown. 'A pretty piece of jewellery and a suitable reference will perhaps suffice.'

'Reference?' he echoed again, sharply.

'Really, Adam—' she sounded exasperated '—whether you choose to continue the relationship or otherwise, you cannot be so naïve as to think that the gel can continue to be employed by you and live in the same household as your own daughter?' Lady Cicely arched disapproving brows.

No, he was not that naïve. Just as his grandmother's comment had also reminded him, all too forcibly, of his own earlier doubts and suspicions about Elena's background and identity.

Doubts and suspicions which he had chosen to ignore, or

simply forget the night before, in his desire, his eagerness, to make love to her.

But which he could ignore no longer.

Chapter Twelve

Elena found herself smiling inwardly and often as she spent the following morning in the schoolroom with Amanda. She hugged memories to her of being with Adam the night before, her thoughts drifting time and time again to the wonders of his lovemaking even as she distractedly attempted to teach Amanda her lessons.

Adam had been so gentle with her, so solicitous of Elena's needs, that there had been no thoughts of denial inside her. Nor had there been any reminder of horror and pain to mar the experience. Rather, she had responded eagerly to each new pleasure Adam gave and shared with her. Shy and inexperienced though her own caresses had been, she also believed that she had given him that same pleasure back tenfold.

Even now, Elena felt a moist and burning heat between her thighs every time she so much as thought of having Adam's mouth upon her there. And the warmth of colour entered her cheeks at the memory of how wonderful it had been to kiss and touch him just as intimately, to taste and hold him as he lost his normally icy control to pleasure.

Those long precious minutes of being in his arms afterwards had been almost as rewarding, a time of shared contentment, when their conversation had been of little import in comparison to their physical closeness. And they had laughed with the lightness of children when they had thought themselves discovered going up the stairs together. She could still feel his long and lingering goodnight kisses upon her lips.

Elena had not seen him as yet this morning, having breakfasted in the nursery with Amanda, as was her habit, before the two of them had then gone through to the schoolroom. But Elena very much hoped that they might see each other again at luncheon now that Lady Cicely had joined the family.

And if they did, how would they greet each other? Elena wondered dreamily. With Amanda and Lady Cicely present, Elena knew she and Adam would not be able to reveal, by word or deed, the intimacies they had shared the night before, or the closeness that had followed. But surely he would be able to give some indication, some small gesture that only she would know and understand, to acknowledge the change in their relationship?

The hours until luncheon, until she saw him again, could not pass quickly enough for Elena…

Adam was aware of the exact moment that Elena entered the salon where the family gathered before luncheon, could feel her presence behind him as much as he could hear Amanda's excited chatter at being allowed to join the adults.

It had not been Adam's suggestion for them to do so, but his grandmother's, with the added comment that he 'would have to face Mrs Leighton at some time today, so he may as well get it over with at luncheon'.

'Getting it over with' was not paramount in Adam's mind at this moment—finding the right way in which he might do that was his greatest concern!

He had been too aroused, and then too satiated after making love to Elena, to give much thought as to how they would proceed from there. It had only been later, alone in his bedchamber, that the full import of his actions had struck him.

Indeed, it would seem his impetuous behaviour the previous night had placed Elena in a position of power, one that now required Adam to either offer her monetary or similar recompense for last night, or, if Elena were agreeable to continuing the relationship, then he would be expected to set her up in a household of her own until such time as that relationship ended, before again offering her monetary or similar recompense.

Either way, it seemed that Elena could not remain as a member of his household.

Either way it would seem that last night Adam had behaved just as foolishly as he had with Fanny all those years ago, in that he had allowed his physical attraction to a woman to influence his actions rather than the cold logic that had stood him in such good stead in the years since Fanny died. And that lapse, enjoyable as it might have been at the time, had once again placed a woman in the position of dictating the tenure of their future relationship.

An unpleasantly familiar feeling, which he found totally unacceptable...

* * *

Whatever Elena had secretly hoped would be Adam's response to her today, she was doomed to be disappointed as the luncheon progressed without his so much as glancing at her, let alone addressing a word to her directly!

Not only was his behaviour bewildering, but it was hurtful in the extreme.

Elena could come to only one conclusion: the time which had passed since they were together had given Adam the opportunity to reflect, and regret, the closeness they had shared yesterday evening.

'—a little distracted today, Mrs Leighton...?'

Elena gave a start as she realised that, while she had been lost in her misery, Lady Cicely had addressed a remark down the table to her. Had her misery been noted? As well as the surreptitious glances Elena had occasionally given Adam beneath the sweep of her dark lashes? Elena hoped not; it would not do for Adam's grandmother to become suspicious of the tension that now existed between her grandson and the governess of his young and motherless daughter.

She forced a smile to her lips. 'I was merely enjoying this delicious dessert.'

'Really?' Lady Cicely gave the barely touched mousse in front of Elena a pointed glance.

Embarrassed colour warmed her cheeks as she acknowledged she had, in fact, eaten very little of the luncheon. But how could she possibly eat, when she felt so nauseous?

'I was remarking upon the pleasantness of the weather for the beginning of May.' Lady Cicely appeared to take pity on her confused state.

Goodness, yes, today was the first day of the new month.

And the sun, as Lady Cicely had observed, was shining brightly. Elena only wished that her own feelings of inner turmoil allowed her to appreciate that warmth. 'It is very pleasant, yes,' she instead answered noncommittally.

Lady Cicely turned to her grandson as he sat stony-faced and silent at the head of the table, his own dessert as untouched as Elena's. 'Perhaps we might all take a stroll outside in the sunshine after luncheon?'

His eyes were flinty between narrowed lids. 'You must do as you please, Grandmama, as must Mrs Leighton and Amanda; I am far too occupied with estate business for such frivolity.'

'All work and no play makes for a very dull fellow,' Lady Cicely came back drily.

'Then I must remain dull,' her grandson ground out, 'for I have neither the time, nor the inclination, for walks in the sunshine.'

His grandmother gave him a long and measured look before turning to Amanda. 'If you have finished your meal, dear, shall we go upstairs together and collect our bonnets? No, do not trouble yourself, Mrs Leighton.' She smiled gently at Elena as she would have risen too. 'You obviously have not finished eating as yet and I am sure that Amanda is perfectly capable of collecting a bonnet for you, too.'

And Lady Cicely and Amanda's departure would leave Elena alone at the table with Adam...

It was an occurrence which obviously pleased him as little as it did Elena, if the chilling gaze Adam swept over her, as he stood politely to his feet when the ladies of his family rose to leave, was an indication of his feelings on the matter. 'If you will excuse me, there is work in my study urgently in need of my attention.'

A frown creased Lady Cicely's brow as she paused in her own departure. 'Perhaps you might accompany Amanda upstairs after all, Mrs Leighton?'

'Of course.' Elena was only too relieved to have this opportunity to absent herself from Adam's icily unapproachable company.

That he deeply regretted their closeness of the evening before had become painfully obvious. So painfully obvious that Elena had to force herself not to run from the dining room.

'I advise you not to interfere in this matter, Grandmama,' Adam warned as he guessed that was exactly what she was about to do now that they were alone in the dining room.

'When the icy demeanour you have shown that poor woman all through luncheon is already working so well, you mean?' She eyed him with gentle reproof.

'I would hardly refer to her in those terms,' he said.

'Perhaps that is because you appear to be completely impervious to the obvious distress you are causing her?' his grandmother accused.

Of course Adam was not so unfeeling as to be completely unmoved by her response to his recent attitude. But what else was he to do? Any warmth or kindness on his part would surely be seen as an encouragement, after the events of yesterday evening, and Adam could not, would not, allow any woman to lead him about by his libido ever again!

His mouth thinned. 'This is a turnaround, isn't it? After

all, you were the one to point out to me earlier on the un-suitability of such a...relationship.'

'I believe I advised caution, not cruelty, my dear.'

'I do not consider it a cruelty to make clear my regret for my previous actions.'

A frown marred his grandmother's creamy brow. 'Am I to understand, then, that your present behaviour is some-what in the form of being cruel to be kind?'

'Exactly,' he confirmed tersely.

Lady Cicely looked exasperated. 'It is one way of doing things, I suppose...'

'It is the only way I know how to deal with this delicate matter.' Adam turned away to stare sightlessly out of one of the dining-room windows. 'I freely admit I made a mis-take last night. A mistake that can only be rectified by Mrs Leighton's immediate removal from my household. In the circumstances, I believe it would be better, for all concerned, if she were to be the one to make that decision.'

'I am not disputing that decision, but I am sure there must be a kinder way of going about it.'

Adam's top lip curled back with self-derision as he con-tinued to stare out of the window before him. 'Kindness has never been my forte—'

'If you are ready to go outside, Lady Cicely? Amanda is even now awaiting us in the entrance hall.'

Adam swung round at the first sound of Elena's brisk tone, a single glance at her unwavering blue-green gaze in the pallor of her face beneath the straw bonnet she now wore enough to tell him that she had once again overheard the last part of his conversation with his grandmother, at least.

Despite those remarks to his grandmother, cruelty was

not a natural part of Adam's nature, but something he'd had necessarily to learn during his marriage to Fanny, out of a sense of self-preservation. Nor, whatever decisions he might have made regarding Elena, was this the manner in which he would have chosen to make her aware of them.

He turned to his grandmother. 'If you would care to take Amanda outside whilst I talk briefly to Mrs Leighton, my dear?'

'Of course—'

'I assure you, it is unnecessary for us to talk on this matter any further,' Elena burst out, colour warming her cheeks as she recognised her own rudeness in doing so.

But she was not herself. How could she be, when she had just overheard Adam, the gentleman to whom she had felt closer than any other, not only discussing the events of last night with his grandmother, but also how best to now rid himself of her embarrassing presence from his household!

And Elena had believed herself to be half in love with him. Had thought that Adam felt some measure of affection for her in return. His remarks to Lady Cicely just now had served to show her just how foolish she had been in that regard. Lord Adam Hawthorne had taken what he wanted from her last night and now he just wanted to be rid of her embarrassing presence. And the sooner the better, as far as he was concerned.

Her chin rose proudly. 'I shall pack my things and make my arrangements to leave here first thing tomorrow morning.'

'You will leave when I give you permission to leave,' Adam bit out harshly.

Elena gave him a stony stare. 'I was under the impression that you had already done that, my lord.'

'It was my intention to return to London tomorrow,' Lady Cicely put in softly. 'There is a ball I must attend on Saturday evening,' she turned to inform her stony-faced grandson. 'You are more than welcome to accompany me in my carriage to London, if that is where you wish to go, Mrs Leighton?' she added gently.

It was a gentleness that brought tears to Elena's eyes; no matter what Lady Cicely's private thoughts might be, as to the relationship that now existed between her grandson and his young daughter's governess, the elderly lady was not so disgusted with her that she did not show compassion for her present dilemma. And Elena now wished to be as far away from Adam Hawthorne as he wished for her to be from him!

'Thank you,' she accepted politely, her gratitude for the older woman's compassion shining in her eyes. Alongside the tears…

But Elena would not cry. Refused to allow herself to cry in front of Adam. The tears could come later, once she was alone in her bedchamber. For now she would maintain a calm demeanour—along with her dignity.

Adam did not at all appreciate the arrangements for Elena's departure tomorrow being made without any input from him. 'And what do you intend saying to Amanda in regard to your hasty departure?'

Lowered long dark lashes hid the expression in Elena's eyes as she answered him drily, 'Obviously not the truth.'

Adam felt the warmth of colour enter his cheeks at the obvious rebuke. 'If you would leave us now, Grandmama…?'

'Of course.' She moved forwards to briefly to place her hand gently on Elena's arm in obvious sympathy before leaving the room and closing the door softly behind her.

Damn it, his bungling of this affair had his own grandmother believing him to be not only cruel, but heartless, too! A belief so far from the truth as to be ludicrous...

Those hours Adam had spent with Elena last night had been some of the happiest he had ever known. Free of artifice and pretence, he had believed. Just two people enjoying each other's bodies and company.

Before he'd had the time to realise the consequences of their actions, that is.

But the thought of her leaving as early as tomorrow morning, of never seeing her again, was just as unacceptable to him. 'There is no need for leaving in such haste—'

'There is every need, my lord.' She did not look at him, but kept her beautiful blue-green gaze fixed on the unlit fireplace.

Allowing Adam to admire the alabaster perfection of her face in profile, similar to the beauty of a cameo brooch once owned and worn by his mother... He drew in a sharp breath. 'I regret that you obviously overheard at least some of my conversation with my grandmother—'

'Do you?' Elena turned slowly to look at him with cool blue-green eyes.

Adam gave a small frown at that unwelcome coolness. 'Of course I regret it. It was not the way in which I wished for you to hear of my concerns about the change that recently occurred in our relationship.'

Elena choked back a bitter laugh at this major understatement. As she saw it, Adam's only 'concern' amounted to nothing more than a desire to have her removed from his sight, and his home, as quickly as was humanly possible! So that was what she was going to do.

Her mouth firmed. 'Perhaps, after all, it was for the best that I overheard. It has achieved what you wished it to achieve, in that I am now leaving your household tomorrow morning, without any further embarrassment, or for the need for you to tell me to go.'

He stepped forwards quickly. 'Have you considered that we might perhaps come to some other sort of arrangement agreeable to both of us? A discreet house in London, perhaps, paid for by me, of course,' he added hastily. 'Where we might meet when I am in town—'

'No!' Elena gasped her shock.

And her outrage.

She had believed this man cared for her—had truly thought last night to be beautiful and sincere.

How foolish of her. How utterly, utterly foolish of her to have ever thought their lovemaking last night meant anything to him at all; he might just as well have called her a whore just now, with his insulting suggestion of setting her up in a house in London. His own personal whore, whose bed he proposed visiting whenever he was in London.

How strange it was, that the man who had raped her had wished to make her his wife, and the man who had made love to her only wished to make her his mistress…

'No, my lord,' she repeated flatly.

'Why the hell not?' He glared his irritation at her intransigence to what he could see was an ideal solution to their dilemma.

Elena gave him a pitying glance. 'I am sure I must have

made many mistakes in my life, my lord, but I would hope that they are mistakes I will have learnt from. And never repeated,' she added stingingly.

A nerve pulsed in his tightly clenched jaw. 'You consider last night to be one of those mistakes?'

She nodded distantly. 'I am sure that we both do.'

'You will not even try to understand the awkwardness of this situation from my point of view—'

'If I might be permitted to interrupt, my lord…?'

Adam turned fiercely to face his butler as Jeffries stood in the doorway. 'What is it, man? Whatever it is, can it not wait until I have finished speaking with Mrs Leighton?'

Jeffries looked unruffled by Adam's aggression. 'There is a person outside, wishing to speak with you, my lord. He says you are expecting him.'

Adam scowled. 'Who is he?' The condescending tone of his butler's voice clearly implied that Jeffries did not consider the visitor to be of any note at all.

'A groom, my lord. He says he is—'

'I know who he is,' Adam cut in wearily; he knew exactly who the other man was, and why he was here, but the events of these past few hours had put the matter completely from his mind. 'Ask him to go round to the stables and inform him I will join him there shortly.'

'Yes, my lord.' Jeffries remained stoic as he quietly left the room.

Elena waited only long enough for the door to close behind the butler before turning to look coolly at Adam. 'I really should go and begin my packing—'

'You will remain exactly where you are!' he instructed succinctly, halting Elena's escape as she came to an abrupt halt, her back stiffly unyielding as she continued to face away from him.

'Elena…' his voice gentled '…we need to discuss this situation without allowing emotion, either yours or my own, to cloud the situation—'

'Emotions?' Her eyes glittered as she whirled to face him, angry colour in her otherwise pale cheeks. 'I confess, I no longer believe you to be capable of such frivolity as experiencing genuine emotions!'

'Just a minute—'

'I do not intend to waste so much as another second of my time on a man such as you, my lord, let alone a minute.' Elena gave a scathing snort.

'What do you mean, a man such as me?' he exclaimed indignantly.

Elena spread her hands. 'What sort of man is it that would discuss one woman's virtue so openly with another? Moreover, a kind and gentle woman whose respect and liking I valued?' Her voice broke emotionally. 'You have humiliated me in the worst way possible, have allowed Lady Cicely to believe you have ruined me. I shall never forgive you for that. Never!' She turned on her heel and almost ran to the door.

'Elena!'

'Leave me alone, Adam.' She wrenched the door open before glancing at him over her shoulder. 'I shall accept your grandmother's offer to share her carriage when she leaves tomorrow for London. After which you will never have to see or hear from me again.'

'Damn it, I want—'

'I have heard what it is you want from me, my lord.' Elena

fought to contain the tears, refusing to allow the final humiliation of actually crying in front of him. 'And I have informed *you* that such an arrangement is completely unacceptable to me. Now, if you will excuse me—I advise that you remove your hand from my arm this instant, sir!' she instructed levelly as, having crossed the room in pursuit, Adam had his fingers now curled about her upper arm. She was not at all sure how much longer she could hold back those tears, or be forced to employ some other method of expressing her anger and disappointment.

She had believed Adam to be a better man that this. Had thought him so much *more*. And instead he was no better than Neville Matthews. Worse, in fact, because Neville had at least offered her marriage. Or the asylum...

Those had been the choices Neville had offered to Elena two months ago. A loveless marriage to him, her cruel and sadistic cousin, or for Neville, as her closest male relative and guardian, to have her placed in an asylum for the rest of her life.

Elena had searched for and found a third option, which was to assume another identity and run away, as far and as fast as she could, from Yorkshire. From Neville.

Only to now find herself the victim of her own heart. A heart that had cried out for love, for protection, only to learn that she had instead found a desire equally as selfish as Neville's had been.

Her chin rose proudly. 'I do not believe we have anything more to say to each other, on this subject, or any other, my lord.'

Adam continued to grasp her arm as he stared down at her in frustration. He freely admitted he had handled this situation badly, from start to finish. For it was the finish, he could see that clearly in Elena's contemptuous gaze as she looked up at him unblinkingly, and leaving him in no doubt that she now utterly despised him.

He had been expecting cajoling or threats, a demand in one form or another, that Adam must now provide for her. Instead Elena had turned down his suggestion—a suggestion Adam could still not believe he had made, considering his earlier decision to remove her from his household as soon as possible—that he set her up in a discreet house in London.

He frowned in bewilderment. 'What is it you want from me?'

She blinked long lashes at last. 'I have told you, I wish for you to release me—'

'I do not mean this exact moment!' He scowled.

'If it is not too much trouble, I would appreciate it if you would give me a reference so that I might find another situation.'

'I meant, what is it you want from me as recompense?' he grated impatiently. 'For last night?'

Elena did not wait any longer for Adam to release her, but instead wrenched her arm out of his grasp, no doubt bruising herself in the process, although she did not seem concerned by this, her face now as pale as snow, her eyes dark unreadable pools as she shook her head violently. 'You are without doubt the most *despicable*—'

'Papa? Papa!' Amanda burst into the room unannounced, her face alight with excitement as she ran to him. 'Papa there is a man come into the stables leading the most beautiful pony you ever saw!' She bounced up and down on her heels in her excitement. 'Come and see, Papa! Oh, Mrs Leighton...' she turned to grasp Elena by the hand '...do come and see!'

Elena's expression softened at the complete lack of the reserve Amanda had so often shown in her father's presence in the past. 'I am sure your father would love to come and see the pony, but I have something else I need to do—'

'You must come, Mrs Leighton...' Some of Amanda's excitement faded as she now looked up appealingly at Elena.

'Yes, do come and see the pony, Mrs Leighton,' Adam drawled, feeling stung, both by Elena's dismissal of his ability to feel emotion, as well as the tirade of names she had obviously been about to inflict upon him before Amanda interrupted them.

He freely admitted—to himself, at least—that he appeared to have seriously misjudged Elena; despite what he had assumed, she appeared to want nothing from him. Except never to see him again once she had departed from here tomorrow...

Which made absolutely no sense to him. He shouldn't have made love to a woman employed in his household and it was a mistake Adam had fully expected to be made to pay for, in one way or another. As he had learnt the hard way, no woman gave of herself without expectation of payment, of some kind. Admittedly Elena was not a member of the highest society, but she was a respectable widow and the wife of a dead soldier. Yet she maintained she wanted nothing from him except a reference before she left so that she might seek other employment.

She perplexed Adam totally.

He straightened. 'Yes, Mrs Leighton, as you had a

hand in its appearance, you must certainly come and see Amanda's pony.'

'*My* pony, Papa?' Amanda was the one to answer him in awed breathlessness. 'Is it really mine?'

Adam's expression softened as he looked down at his daughter. 'It is really yours, pet,' he confirmed tenderly.

Elena took the opportunity of Amanda's launching herself into her father's arms, amidst squeals of excitement, in which to edge closer towards the doorway.

Only to have that progress halted as Adam reached out to once again grasp the top of her arm to prevent her from going any further. 'You will accompany us to the stables, Mrs Leighton,' he commanded in a voice that brooked no further argument.

No argument that Elena could put forwards in front of Amanda, at least. And so, with Adam's fingers still curled firmly about her arm, as he carried Amanda in his other arm, Elena was left with no other choice but to accompany father and daughter out of the house and round to the stables where Lady Cicely stood in conversation with the head groom, and another man who was holding the leading rein of the pony.

Elena was pleased for Amanda that her father had obviously acquired a pony for the little girl during the days he had been away from the estate. It truly was a beautiful little mare, with a gleaming coat of golden honey and a mane and tail of pale cream, its eyes the softest brown as it gazed down adoringly at Amanda as, having squirmed to be put down by her father, she hurried forwards to pet its silky soft nose.

'Ah, there you are, Adam.' Lady Cicely turned towards them, allowing a better view of the two men she had been conversing with—and at the same time allowing the two men to have a better view of Elena...

Adam's visitor, the man holding the leading rein of the pony, stared at her in disbelief and recognition.

Elena gasped with horror. Darkness eclipsed the sun and the world went completely black.

Chapter Thirteen

'I appreciate you catching Mrs Leighton as she fell and carrying her up to her bedchamber, Adam, but you really cannot continue to remain in the room now!'

'I can and damn well will! I apologise for swearing, Grandmama.' There was the sound of a heavy sigh. 'But I am sure you will admit, it has been something of a trying day.'

'I realise that. And I am sure we are all anxious to know why Mrs Leighton fainted, but I really do feel it is best if I am the one to continue to sit with her rather than you. As you instructed, Bristol is giving Amanda her first riding lesson and Jeffries has taken the visiting groom to the servants' hall for some tea, but I am sure the young man will wish to be on his way soon.'

'Not until after I have questioned him.'

Elena had been awake for the past several minutes, but had continued to keep her lids firmly closed, so as not to alert grandmother and grandson to the fact that she was no longer lying unconscious upon the bed. In truth, also in an effort to delay having to face the questions which were sure to be asked of her.

She had fainted because she had recognised the 'visiting groom' and, despite the changes in her appearance and circumstances, she knew that Jeremiah had recognised her, too, as Magdelena Matthews.

What was she going to do? What *could* she do to avert further disaster? And disaster it most certainly would be, once Adam Hawthorne and Lady Cicely learnt she was the runaway granddaughter of the Duke of Sheffield. The same young woman accused by her own cousin of murder and theft. A claim Elena could not disprove, and which had given Neville the leverage to threaten her with the choice of marrying him or being sent to an asylum. Needless to say, she had chosen to escape than suffer either of those horrors.

Jeremiah's appearance at Hawthorne Park would seem to have put an end to that escape…

There was another sigh, from Lady Cicely this time. 'I did try to talk to the groom myself before coming upstairs, but the poor man refused to answer any of my questions. I do believe he may be suffering from some sort of shock.'

'I shall shake the answers out of him if I have to!'

Elena had heard enough. 'There will be no need for any physical violence towards Jeremiah,' she murmured huskily, opening her eyes at the same time as she moved up the bed to sit back against the pillows; thankfully someone had removed her bonnet. 'I fear that poor young man will have thought he was seeing a ghost, Lady Cicely,' she added as she looked up at the older woman, not feeling strong enough as yet to face the cold accusation she knew would be in Adam's haughtily aristocratic face.

'A ghost...?' the older lady repeated uncertainly.

Elena nodded. 'Until he saw me here, no doubt Jeremiah believed me either dead or, as so many others were also led to believe, that I had gone abroad somewhere I would never be found.'

Lady Cicely frowned her confusion. 'You and the young groom are acquainted, then?'

Elena would hardly call Jeremiah young, at aged thirty or so, but no doubt he seemed so to the much older Lady Cicely. 'Yes,' she confirmed.

Adam gave a disgusted snort. 'What eclectic taste you appear to have in your choice of male friends, Elena! First a groom and now a lord—will a duke be the next to share your bed, I wonder?'

'Adam!' His grandmother widened scandalised eyes even as Elena felt her face go even paler.

These past few minutes since Elena had fainted had been decidedly unpleasant ones for Adam as his imagination had run amok and he speculated wildly as to the nature of the acquaintance between her and the young man she had just referred to so familiarly as Jeremiah.

A familiarity Adam found less than pleasing following the intimacies they had shared the previous evening. 'Then perhaps Mrs Leighton would care to explain how it is that she and Lord Stapleton's groom come to be so well acquainted that she refers to him by his first name?'

Elena blinked. 'I beg your pardon?'

Adam gave her a confused look. 'It was from his estate in Warwick that I purchased the pony for Amanda, which his own daughter had outgrown.'

She stared at him with puzzled blue-green eyes. 'Jeremiah now works for Lord Stapleton?'

'Have I not just said so?' Adam snapped his impatience with what to him seemed merely a delaying tactic in answering his previous question.

She frowned. 'When I knew him before he worked for—' She broke off abruptly, her lips clamping firmly together.

'Who? Who did he work for?' Adam prompted, still unaccountably jealous that she'd known the good-looking groom at all.

'Someone else.' That blue-green gaze no longer met his as she stared down at the coverlet her fingers were nervously plucking. 'I—I should like the opportunity to talk with him before he leaves, if that is permitted?'

'What the—!' Adam broke off his angry tirade to glare down at her in disbelieving exasperation. 'If you are expecting me to allow that young man to come up to your bedchamber then you are sorely mistaken.' He looked down the length of his nose at her. 'You may talk with whom you wish, where you wish, once you have left my household, but until that time you will behave in a manner befitting that of my daughter's governess.'

She gave him an exasperated glare. 'I do not believe that I either requested or implied that I wished to speak to Jeremiah here in my bedchamber.'

'No, I do not believe that she did either, Adam,' his grandmother joined in the conversation. 'Now, might I suggest that we all calm down,' she added soothingly, 'so that Mrs Leighton may explain to us why seeing the groom Jeremiah—what a charmingly old-fashioned name that is!—should have such an effect upon her that she fainted dead away?'

Elena almost laughed at the disgusted expression on Adam's face at his grandmother's aside concerning the charm of the groom's name. Almost. Because there really was nothing in the least amusing about her present situation...

She would have liked nothing better than to be able to just continue to lie here with her eyes closed until all of this just went away. All of it. The love-making of last night. The scene with Adam earlier. Her dismissal and departure tomorrow. Jeremiah's unexpected arrival. The disclosure as to who she really was that must surely follow...

Most of all Elena wished that she did not have to witness the disgust in Adam and Lady Cicely's expression and demeanours once they learnt the truth about her.

But she knew it was unavoidable. Just as Adam's actions, following that disclosure, would be just as unavoidable...in that he would have no choice but to call the local authority and have her arrested. After which, she would surely find herself transported to the gaol closest to her grandfather's estate, where she would then be accused and tried by the local magistrate. Who just so happened to be Neville Matthews, the evil eleventh Duke of Sheffield.

Elena feared being at Neville's mercy as much as she dreaded seeing the disgust and dislike in Adam's face once it was made known to him who she really was.

'Well?'

Elena blinked as she glanced up at Adam, her breath catching in her throat as she saw the bleak expression in his unyielding grey eyes, assuring her that she should expect no mercy there! She moistened the dryness of her lips before speaking. 'Once Jeremiah has had chance to drink his tea and recover from his shock, then he will no doubt tell you that—that my name is not, and never has been, Mrs Elena Leighton.' She inwardly trembled even as she forced herself not to flinch under the sudden fierceness of his gaze.

'Not Mrs Elena Leighton…?' Adam's tone was dangerously soft.

She swallowed hard. 'No.'

'You are not the widow of Corporal Leighton, late of his Majesty's Royal Dragoons?'

'No.'

Adam breathed deeply in an effort to hold on to his rapidly rising temper. A temper he had not truly lost in all the years since Fanny died. 'Then perhaps you would care to tell us what your real name is and exactly who you are?'

The slenderness of her throat moved as she swallowed, her face now as pale as alabaster. 'Once I have told you my name, I doubt there will be any need for me to tell you who I am.'

'Adam—'

'Leave this to me, Grandmama,' he instructed tautly, his gaze remaining fixed on Elena.

'But—'

'Grandmother!' He turned sharply to glare her into silence. 'Please allow Mrs—this person to tell us who she is and exactly what she is doing in my household masquerading as someone else!' Adam's voice rose on those last two words, as he could no longer hold his anger in check. He turned to scowl that displeasure down at the woman on the bed. 'Are you even a governess?'

'No.'

'I do not see what difference it makes as to whether or not she is a governess,' his grandmother put in mildly.

'It makes a difference to me!'

'I do not see why, Adam,' Lady Cicely soothed. 'When Mrs—this young lady has obviously done such a wonders for Amanda's education and social demeanour.' She beamed at Elena approvingly.

An approval, Elena recognised heavily, which must surely turn to the same anger and suspicion with which Adam now viewed her once Lady Cicely knew the truth.

'It will make a great deal of difference if this young woman is someone less than suited to being companion to my daughter,' Adam insisted stiffly.

Elena noted that he'd said 'woman' rather than 'lady' as Lady Cicely had.

'Perhaps you should leave me to talk with Mrs—er—the young lady?' Lady Cicely suggested lightly. 'I have always considered myself a good judge of character, and I believe that Elena—is that your real name, dear?' She looked down kindly at Elena.

'Yes…well, sort of.'

The older woman nodded before turning back to her grandson. 'I am sure that this is all just a misunderstanding, Adam.'

'The only misunderstanding made was by this person, when she came into my household falsely masquerading as the governess she is not.' He looked down his aristocratic nose at Elena. 'Now, madam, you will tell me exactly who you are and what your association is with this Jeremiah.'

Elena gave a start. 'I do not have an "association", as such, with Jeremiah—'

'So you would have me believe that you fainted at the sight of him because he is merely a past and casual acquaintance, then?' he scorned.

Elena frowned; if anything, Adam seemed more angry about Jeremiah than he was about her working for him under a false identity. 'I only know Jeremiah because he worked for—he worked for my—'

'I do believe that Mrs—Elena is in danger of fainting again, Adam; perhaps you should go and get some of your best brandy to revive her?' Lady Cicely gently pushed her grandson aside so that she might sit on the side of the bed before taking one of Elena's hands into both of hers.

Elena gave the older woman a searching glance, sure she detected something more than casual concern in Lady Cicely's gently lined face—sympathy for her plight in those faded grey eyes, perhaps?

A suspicion that seemed to be borne out as the other woman gave Elena's fingers a reassuring squeeze before she looked up at her grandson. 'Adam?'

He crossed his arms across his muscled chest. 'I am not going anywhere until El—this young woman has answered my questions to my satisfaction.'

'I admit to feeling a little in need of a restorative myself, after all this upset,' his grandmother murmured weakly.

'And I repeat, I am going nowhere, Grandmama, until this puzzle has been solved,' Adam repeated firmly, his gaze remaining stubbornly fixed on Elena.

In truth, his imagination was once again running amok at Elena's obvious reluctance to reveal her identity. Who, or what, was she that she had lied in order to obtain a position in his household?

If she was merely a woman left alone in the world and desperate to find a way of supporting herself, then it should not have been necessary for her to lie about her name. Unless she was, after all, that runaway wife Adam had once suspected her of being?

The mere thought that she was another man's wife was enough to drive him completely insane.

Adam needed to know—*now*—exactly who she was and what she was doing here! 'Well?' he demanded.

Her lashes lowered. 'If I might be allowed to sit up, Lady Cicely...?'

'Of course.' The older woman stood up so that Elena might sit up on the side of the bed.

Her face was a pale oval against her dark and dishevelled hair as she looked up at Adam. 'My name is Magdelena Matthews.'

Adam's face remained a blank following Elena's announcement, but she heard a slight gasp of recognition from Lady Cicely's direction. Needing every ounce of courage she possessed, in order to continue, Elena did not so much as glance in the direction of that lady, but continued to look up at the stony-faced man standing in front of her. 'My grandfather was—' Her voice broke emotionally as she talked of her grandfather in the past tense. 'He was George Matthews, the late Duke of Sheffield.'

Adam recoiled away from her as realisation of her identity finally dawned on him. 'You are the same granddaughter suspected of murdering that gentleman and robbing his home?'

Elena's vision blurred as the tears came readily to her eyes. 'Yes.'

'Good God…!' Adam exclaimed in horror; this was worse, so much worse than he had even imagined. He had been harbouring a murderess in his household! A young woman who had cold-bloodedly done away with her own grandfather before then stripping his home bare of every jewel she could carry.

Good God, she might have murdered them all in their beds this past month before robbing them too!

'*That* is why— You have your father's eyes, my dear,' Lady Cicely murmured.

'Yes.'

Adam turned to his grandmother incredulously. 'How can you stand there and talk of the colour of her eyes when she is nothing more than a murderess—?'

'I believe you just stated she was a suspected murderess,' his grandmother reproached him. 'Personally, I have always had my suspicions as to the validity of that claim—'

'The only reason she is not presently in a prison cell awaiting sentence is because she ran away before the authorities could charge her with such!' Adam growled, pinning her to the bed with his piercing gaze. 'You were about to tell us who the man Jeremiah is?'

She drew in a deep breath. 'He is one of the grooms who worked on my grandfather's estate—'

'You were romantically involved with one of your grandfather's grooms?' he barked incredulously.

'No, of course I was not.' Irritation flickered in those blue-green eyes. 'Jeremiah merely recognised me as being the Duke of Sheffield's granddaughter.'

Another thought occurred to Adam at the full import of this statement. Rather than making love to his daughter's governess yesterday evening, as he had thought, he'd dallied with the granddaughter of a duke. An occurrence that would, in normal circumstances, have resulted in his being forced by the dictates of society into offering marriage to that same person.

His mouth thinned. 'You realise that this disclosure means I shall have to call in the authorities and have you taken into custody?'

Her face paled to the colour and stiffness of white parchment. 'Yes, of course—'

'Let us not be too hasty in our actions, Adam,' his grandmother put in firmly.

'Hasty?' he echoed incredulously. 'It appears to me, as the Duke of Sheffield met his end two months ago, that her arrest is long overdue!'

Lady Cicely tutted. 'Adam, I have come to know and like Amanda's governess this past few days, and believe that you are now allowing your…personal involvement to rob you of your natural sense of fairness and logic.'

'Indeed?' He eyed her frostily.

'Most certainly,' she said, unrepentant. 'Think, Adam,' she continued impatiently as he remained impervious to her look of reproach. 'Why would a young lady accused of those crimes now be working in your household as a governess?'

He gave a scornful snort. 'As a safe place to hide from capture, of course.'

'And why would she not have used the money and jewels she is reputed to have stolen to have taken herself as far away from England as possible? To the Continent, at very least? Indeed, that is where the gossip in society these past few months has said she is rumoured to be.'

Adam gave a sudden frown as the logic of his grand-mother's comments permeated what she had referred to as his 'personal involvement'. 'It is my belief that we should leave it to the relevant authorities to decide as to her guilt or innocence.'

'Did you wish to say something, my dear?' Lady Cicely prompted as Elena gave a strangled sound of protest at Adam's suggestion.

Elena swallowed before answering. 'Only that the authority to which Lord Hawthorne refers consists of my cousin Neville, the new Duke of Sheffield, and that he—that he—' She swallowed anxiously. 'He is the same gentleman who, for reasons of his own, levelled the accusations of murder and theft against me at the outset!'

'Can that possibly be so, Adam?' Lady Cicely looked wide-eyed at her grandson. 'Surely, for the sake of impartiality, that cannot be allowed?'

He shrugged. 'I know nothing as to the authority in York-shire.'

This past few minutes had been more excruciatingly pain-ful for Elena than she could ever have imagined. As well as having to live through some of the events of two months ago she also had to listen to and see, in Adam's cold and re-morseless eyes, his condemnation of her as being the guilty party, without so much as a second thought or doubt. It was beyond bearing, when only hours ago Elena had believed herself to be falling in love with him.

A shy and hesitant love, which now withered and died in her breast as if it had never been. 'If you did, then you would know that my cousin Neville has inherited my grandfather's magisterial role in that area, as well as his title and estates,' she spoke flatly, unemotionally—indeed, what point was there in her pleading when Adam so obviously believed her to be guilty without benefit of a trial? 'And that, once safely in his custody, no matter what the evidence, I have every reason to believe he will not hesitate to ensure that I am immediately hanged by the neck until I am completely dead.'

Adam's gaze moved instinctively to that long and delicate throat, wincing slightly as he easily imagined the crudeness of a thick rope about it, squeezing and bruising that soft and ivory flesh until all life had been extinguished from the young and beautiful woman to whom it belonged.

He shuddered at the very thought of it...

Chapter Fourteen

'I believe that a certain amount of hysteria has been allowed to enter into this conversation—'

'Hysteria?' Elena stared at Adam incredulously as she began to pace the bedchamber, her skirts swishing about her ankles at the briskness of the movement. 'Perhaps you, too, would feel less than calm, sir, at thoughts of your own demise in such a horrible fashion?' Her eyes glittered brightly, partly with anger, and partly with those unshed tears Elena refused to allow to fall.

'Hold your tongue, Adam.' His grandmother rounded on him with unaccustomed sharpness, as he would have replied. 'And let me remind you that you certainly liked Miss Matthews well enough—perhaps too well!—before being told of her identity.' Her expression gentled as she turned back to a now blushing Elena. 'I knew and liked your mother and father very much, child.'

Elena felt an emotional lump rise in her throat. 'It is very kind of you to say so.'

'Not at all.' Lady Cicely reached out to clasp both of her

hands in her own, at the same time halting Elena's pacing. 'Your grandmother—Jane—was also a friend of mine in her younger days. And your grandfather—'

'How long is this trip down memory lane going to last, Grandmama?' Adam asked with a sigh.

Lady Cicely's eyes, so like his own, flashed as she cast him a brief and censorious glance. 'Perhaps if you had not become so rigid in your thinking, Adam, you would not only see, but also hear that I am endeavouring to point out that Miss Matthews has a fine pedigree—'

'I believe that every family, even those in possession of a "fine pedigree", has been known to have its black sheep, Grandmama.'

'Your sarcastic sense of humour is not welcome in this conversation, Adam!'

Elena stared at Lady Cicely. The older woman did not truly believe that her grandson was jesting? For, if she did—

'Admittedly it is usually a gentleman who is referred to as such,' Adam continued regardless, 'but I see no reason why it should not occasionally be—'

'Adam!'

'Very well, Grandmama.' He sketched her a mocking bow, that levity swiftly fading as he turned to Elena. 'May I ask what has happened to the real Mrs Leighton?'

'She is in Scotland, living with the parents of her dead husband.'

'And you know this because…?'

'Because I was acquainted with the Bambury family and so was aware of Mrs Leighton's decision not to accompany them to the Continent.'

'I am relieved to hear it.' Adam frowned. 'My grandmother is obviously of the opinion that the respectability of your antecedents renders you incapable of murdering anyone.'

Elena looked at him guardedly, no longer sure herself as to whether he was jesting or serious, and the cool derision in his expression did not give an indication either way. She drew in a deep breath before speaking. 'Even without my antecedents I am incapable of harming so much as a fly—' She broke off as she recalled the blows and scratches she had rained upon Neville as she'd attempted to fight off his attack. 'Unless I am sorely provoked,' she corrected huskily.

Adam raised dark brows. 'And were you given such provocation by your grandfather?'

She hesitated. 'No.'

His eyes narrowed shrewdly. 'By another person?'

Her lids lowered. 'Yes.'

'Would you care to tell us who that person is?'

Could she tell the Hawthornes the awful truth of what had really happened two months ago?

Elena looked first at Lady Cicely, seeing only gentleness and understanding in that lady's countenance, before turning to Adam; his mood was now much harder to gauge, hooded lids lowered in order to shield the emotion in his eyes, his general demeanour unreadable.

But what other choice did Elena have other than to confide in these people? She either told them the truth and threw herself upon the mercy of their compassion, or she found herself removed from Cambridgeshire forthwith and placed in Neville's vindictive clutches, where she knew she would receive no mercy whatsoever.

Elena drew in a deep and controlling breath, determined

to relate past events with a calmness and precision Adam would appreciate, if not condone. Where to start, that was the problem.

Adam kept his gaze narrowed as he watched the conflicting emotions flickering across Elena's face, as he waited for her to answer. Or not. He hoped she did as he had no idea how to proceed if she did not.

Contrary to what his grandmother might think, he was not in the least unemotional about this situation. If anything, he felt too much. The surprise of learning Elena's true identity as well as the shock of realising she had been accused of a terrible crime.

Admittedly, Adam's immediate reaction had been to go into protective-father mode; but what parent would not feel concerned at learning their child had, for the past few weeks, been in the care of a woman who was accused of murdering her own relative?

But, despite his grandmother's rebuke, his own good sense had prevailed almost immediately. Elena Leighton, as he had known her to be until a few minutes ago, had shown nothing but kindness and concern in regard to Amanda's happiness; indeed, she had made every effort to bring father and daughter closer together, and he had bought the very pony upon which Amanda was now riding because Elena had told him it was his daughter's fondest desire to have a pony of her own.

And as for the woman he had made love to last night—

Adam drew in a deep, controlling breath as he thought of that woman. A shy and yet responsive young woman, who had given as much pleasure as she had received. A woman who had asked nothing of him in return. Not last night. Nor when they had spoken again this morning. She had even decided to leave his employment rather than be the cause of any further embarrassment to him or his family.

In truth, Adam could not seriously believe that woman to be capable of theft, let alone the murder of her own grandfather.

'Proceed, if you please,' he instructed curtly, only to see Elena flinch as if he had struck her, the paleness of her face taking on such a look of fragility, it took every ounce of his will not to stride across the bedchamber and take her into his arms and offer her comfort.

A comfort that would solve nothing, if it should emerge that Elena really was responsible for her grandfather's death, by whatever means. There was also the accusation of theft to consider. But, as his grandmother had already so astutely noted, that accusation did not at all tally with the young woman who had entered his household three weeks ago as a governess. Or the fact that she had not possessed the money with which to replace those black mourning dresses she wore. Mourning dresses which it now appeared she had worn out of respect for her grandfather's death rather than that of a husband…

The confusion of emotions Adam now felt at knowing there was not, nor had there ever been, a husband in Elena's life, was enough to make him scowl anew.

Elena turned away from Adam's harshly condemning face, knowing she would not be able to talk about what had happened to her if she continued to look at him. Instead she walked over to the window of the bedchamber to gaze out over the beautiful rolling grounds at the back of the house. Such an idyllic picture of the Cambridgeshire countryside, when here inside the house, her life was falling apart for the second time in as many months.

This past two months had been an illusion, of course, a delaying of the inevitable—but she knew she could delay it no longer. 'My grandparents had two children, two sons, the younger being my own father, David,' she began, her voice husky but steady enough. 'His older brother, Howard, was killed in a hunting accident many years ago, after which his wife and son moved to live in the Dower House on the Sheffield Park estate. My own father died fighting against Napoleon, and as my mother and I were visiting with my grandfather when we received the news, we remained living with them.'

'Your cousin being the heir?'

Elena could not help but smile tightly at his astuteness in going directly to the heart of the problem. 'My cousin Neville.' She nodded. 'He is not the most likeable of men.' She repressed a shiver at how unlikeable she personally found him.

Oh, Neville was handsome enough, with his golden blond hair and his deep-blue eyes, his regular features and trim form not displeasing to look upon. It was his nature, cruel and vindictive, apparent at an early age, which had always caused Elena to avoid his company even when they were children together. As adults it had quickly become clear to her that Neville intended to rob her of her virginity at the earliest opportunity. A deed he had finally succeeded in doing after their grandfather's funeral in February...

'And I suppose he became your guardian on the death of

your grandfather?' Once again Adam showed himself to be a man of both astuteness and intelligence.

'Yes, Neville is now my guardian.' Elena suppressed another shudder at all that now meant to her. 'My grandfather, in his wisdom, left me well provided for and Neville—he made it known to me, shortly after my grandfather's death, that he wished for the two of us to marry.'

'Indeed?'

Elena looked down at her clasped hands, the knuckles showing white even through her gloves. 'It was not a match I either wished for or encouraged.'

'Of course it was not,' Lady Cicely spoke for the first time since Elena had begun her halting explanation. 'I am slightly acquainted with that young gentleman,' she spoke to her grandson, 'and he is not at all the sort of man I would wish any granddaughter of mine, if I had one, to ever contemplate marrying and spending the rest of her life with.'

'I do not recall ever meeting him?' Adam frowned darkly.

'That is because you have chosen not to be in society for so many years, Adam.' There was censure in his grandmother's tone. 'For if you had been, you would know that Neville Matthews is not only a known reprobate, but is also responsible for the ruination of several young ladies in society! Edith St Just will not so much as have his presence in her ballroom, let alone seated at her dinner table,' she added as if that settled the matter regarding Neville Matthews's nature and reputation.

Which, Adam acknowledged ruefully, it probably did; Edith St Just, the Dowager Duchess of Royston, was not only a close friend of his own grandmother, but also a much-respected matriarch of society, and if the Dowager Duchess had decided Neville Matthews was unacceptable, then so must the majority of society.

And this was the man who was now Elena's guardian? Not only her guardian, but also the man who had wished for her to become his wife? A man known as a reprobate and despoiler of innocents?

Had he—would he have dared to try to despoil her, too? The blood chilled in his veins at the thought.

'Elena?' Adam prompted sharply.

'Lady Cicely has divined his character perfectly,' she confirmed, the slenderness of her back and shoulders now stiff and unapproachable. 'I turned down his offer of marriage, of course. A refusal he did not—did not take kindly to, shall we say. And which, as my legal guardian, he chose to ignore.'

'He is in love with you?'

'Love?' Elena scorned as she finally turned to face him, her face paper-white, and her eyes a dark and unfathomable blue-green. 'I do not believe love to be an emotion Neville is capable of feeling. Self-indulgence. Lust. Greed. Those are the only emotions he understands.'

'Greed?' Adam chose to ignore the first two emotions, for fear of where those thoughts might take him, his gaze intent on the pallor of her face.

She drew in a shaky breath. 'As I said, my grandfather did not wish for me to be left destitute as well as alone after his death and so made financial provision for me in his will. In that, I would come into my own considerable personal fortune on the advent of my coming of age or my marriage, whichever came first.'

'Your grandfather did not expect his demise to occur before your majority.' Adam made it a statement rather than a question.

'No, he did not.'

His eyes narrowed. 'How did he die, Elena?'

Her breath caught in her throat. 'A heart attack, brought on by shock.'

'What sort of shock?'

'Does it matter?' she came back defensively. 'The fact is he died, ten months before my twenty-first birthday. And Neville, as my legal guardian, made it clear to me, after my grandfather's funeral, that he did not intend for any of the Sheffield money to be settled outside of the family and that I was to become his wife as soon as the arrangements for the marriage could be made.'

'A marriage you were opposed to.'

'Oh, yes,' she assured vehemently.

'And so you ran away, taking the money and jewels with you so as to—' Adam broke off, shaking his head. 'You did not take any money or jewels with you, did you?' How could she have done? For, as he had realised earlier, if Elena had stolen those things, then there would have been absolutely no reason for her to seek employment as a governess.

'Neville Matthews made up the story about your having taken the money and jewels,' Lady Cicely stated firmly. 'As he also made up the story of your having been responsible for your grandfather's death.'

Elena turned away, the tears now falling softly down her cheeks as she could no longer bear to so much as look upon the sympathy she saw in that kindly lady's face. 'I—not exactly,' she answered huskily.

'How not exactly?' Adam demanded harshly.

'It is true I did not take anything from the house when I left, apart from a few personal belongings.' Elena gave a shake of her head. 'But if I had not fought off Neville's attentions that evening—if I had not called out for help—if I had not screamed, then my grandfather would not have taxed himself by running to my bedchamber to discover—to see—'

'I believe we have distressed Miss Matthews quite enough for the moment,' Lady Cicely cut in firmly. 'You will go down the stairs for the brandy now, Adam,' she instructed as she crossed the room to Elena's side and placed an arm gently about her shoulders.

Lady Cicely's kindness was too much for Elena to withstand after talking of, remembering, the night of her grandfather's death and the terrible days that had followed, when she had lived in constant fear of what Neville would do next, and she turned in that lady's embrace as she began to sob in earnest. For the death of her grandfather, for all that she had lost, and lastly, because of the disgust she knew would be on Adam's face if she had dared to look at him again.

Which she did not, hearing instead his departure to do as his grandmother bade him and fetch the brandy.

'Now, my dear,' Lady Cicely spoke again with firmness. 'You will tell me exactly what further outrage that excuse for a man inflicted upon you to cause you to run away as you did, without even the means of supporting yourself. A confidence I promise you I shall not share with my grandson, if that is what you wish,' she added at Elena's obvious hesitation.

Elena looked at the older woman searchingly, easily seeing the compassion in that kindly face, but also some of

Adam Hawthorne's strength of character in the directness of Lady Cicely's unwavering and encouraging gaze. A compassion and strength, which now gave her the courage to tell Lady Cicely the whole truth of the day of her grandfather's funeral, when she had been left with no choice but to run away from Sheffield Park, penniless and alone.

'I understand from my own conversation with the gentleman that you spoke with Jeremiah prior to my own conversation with him?'

Elena could discern none of Adam's feelings on the matter as she looked across at him from the doorway of his study, where she had been summoned by Jeffries to attend him after earlier refusing to join the family for dinner.

She had known she would have to see and speak with Adam again some time during this evening, of course, and had chosen not to burden the dinner table with her presence, but rather accept Lady Cicely's suggestion that she have a tray sent up to her bedchamber. Not that Elena had been in the least hungry, but she had not wished to disappoint Lady Cicely when she had been so kind to her.

Unfortunately, with only a single candle alight on the front of Adam's desk, his face remained in shadow, so making it impossible for Elena to read his expression to gauge what he might be feeling. 'I thought it best that I try to reassure him, yes,' she confirmed.

He nodded. 'Come in and close the door behind you. There is absolutely no reason why the whole of my household should be privy to our conversation,' he added gently once Elena had done as he requested. 'And having now spoken to Jeremiah yourself, you will also know that Matthews dismissed the majority of your grandfather's household staff seven weeks ago, and replaced them with his own?'

She gave a sigh. 'Yes.'

'What do you make of such behaviour?'

Elena frowned slightly, having expected Adam's next question to be something entirely different. And her own feelings, upon learning of the summary dismissal of the household staff that had been so loyal to her grandfather for so many years, had been ones of distress. Mrs Hodges, for example, had been housekeeper at Sheffield Park for many years, and only two years away from her retirement, when she might have expected to receive a small pension to keep her. Instead, after being dismissed, she had been left with no pension and no choice but to go and live with her eldest son in Skegness. Younger members of staff, like Jeremiah, had simply been tossed out into the world, to seek other employment where they could.

She gave a shrug. 'I would say that it is a typical example of Neville's complete disregard for the welfare of others.'

'And that is all you make of it?'

Elena frowned slightly. 'What else should I make of it?'

'The possibility that Matthews perhaps dismissed the staff at Sheffield Park so that they could not be called to give evidence in your favour at your trial?'

Elena's stomach cramped nauseously at the mention of a trial. 'I believe it is not uncommon for the new incumbent to replace the original servants with his own?'

'Not uncommon, no,' Adam allowed grimly. 'But in this particular instance, it is certainly convenient.'

'Not to those household servants.'

'No,' he acknowledged. 'Jeremiah also seemed to be of

the opinion that you were incapable of harming a single silver hair upon your grandfather's head.'

Elena's chin rose defensively. 'Then Jeremiah is an excellent judge of character.'

Adam gave a tight smile at the implied criticism of him. 'My grandmother has also informed me that she still intends for you to travel back to London with her when she leaves here tomorrow morning.'

'I have not encouraged her in that decision—'

'Did I say that you had?'

'No, but—' Elena grimaced. 'I accept that you cannot be best pleased at the idea.'

'And would my displeasure bother you?'

'Of course it would bother—' She broke off abruptly to draw in several calming breaths. 'I am sure that you would much rather I just removed myself from here without involving any of your family further in my—in my personal problems.'

As Lady Cicely had encouraged her to do, Elena had confided the whole of the truth as to the reason for her hasty flight from Sheffield Park two months ago, secure in the knowledge that Lady Cicely would not break her promise to her. Nor did she believe for a moment that that dear lady had broken that promise. No, Elena had no doubt that Adam's request for her to attend him immediately in his study once dinner had ended was as a direct result of his conversation with Jeremiah. A conversation he had not indicated yet whether or not he believed.

'You appear to be attributing me with thoughts and wishes which I do not believe I have expressed, either by word or deed.'

Elena wished that she could at least see Adam's face clearly rather than just those hollows and shadows created by the flickering candlelight. 'Perhaps you have not stated them,' she allowed. 'But that does not mean you have not thought them.'

'Indeed,' Adam allowed drily after a brief pause, no longer sure what he 'thought' about this situation. His conversation with the groom had been…enlightening, to say the least, that gentleman having immediately leapt to Elena's defence, after expressing his delight in knowing that no harm had come to her since her disappearance from Yorkshire.

That Lady Cicely knew more of that situation than he, Adam had no doubts. He was also certain that Elena did not intend to share those same confidences with him. So Adam had little choice but to draw his own conclusions regarding the reasons for Elena's flight from the unwanted attentions of her cousin.

And, in view of his grandmother's summing up of that young man's character, a damning statement of fact completely vindicated by the Dowager Duchess of Royston's social aversion to Sheffield, those conclusions were extremely unpleasant ones.

All the more so when Adam considered the physical liberties he himself had taken with Elena so recently.

It was a wonder she had not run screaming into the night, if what he suspected had happened to her should prove to be correct.

Just the possibility of it was enough to warn Adam to exert caution with her now. 'I have no objection to your accompanying my grandmother to London tomorrow,' he stated evenly. 'Although I have reservations as to what she hopes to accomplish by it. No matter what the circumstances leading up to your leaving Sheffield Park…' he scowled as she saw Elena flinch '…the fact remains, innocent or guilty, that you still have the accusation of murder and theft to answer before you may even begin to think of rejoining society.'

She gave him a sad smile. 'I have never been a part of society, my lord,' she explained as he raised a questioning brow. 'My father's death, followed by my mother's, and then my grandfather's, has meant that I have never been out of mourning long enough to ever venture into society.'

'You have not missed much,' Adam drawled dismissively. 'But the fact remains, you must eventually return to Yorkshire in order to answer the charges made against you.'

She repressed a shudder. 'Where my cousin Neville is now magistrate.'

'That is…unfortunate.' Adam nodded grimly at this reminder. 'But that does not prevent you from being represented by a reputable lawyer, a man who is able to point out the unfairness of such a trial taking place in that vicinity, given the circumstances.'

She released a shaky breath. 'With Neville in charge of my fortune until I reach the age of one and twenty, I do not have the means to employ such a lawyer—'

'But I do.' Adam stood up decisively.

Elena blinked as he suddenly loomed very large and intimidating in the small confines of his private study. 'You—you would be willing to help me in that regard?'

'I feel someone must,' he stated grimly. 'And if I do not do so, then I believe my grandmother will choose to embroil herself in this affair even more than she has already done,' he added.

It was too much to hope, Elena acknowledged heavily, that Adam had made his offer of help because he believed her to be innocent of the accusations; instead he made it clear he was intervening solely to prevent his grandmother from involving herself any further in the tangle of Elena's affairs.

Adam knew, by the fact Elena now avoided meeting his gaze, that she believed his interest in this matter to be for his grandmother's benefit only. An understandable assumption for her to have made, given the circumstances. It was also an erroneous one.

The truth of the matter was, Adam dared not show any sign of personal preference for Elena in this situation, for fear that Matthews, once he knew of the Hawthorne family's intervention in his affairs, should then claim that Adam's interest in Elena was far from impartial.

Which it undoubtedly was.

Despite his initial reaction earlier, to learning Elena's identity, Adam's natural sense of logic had very quickly reasserted itself, allowing him to see her as incapable of killing anyone, let alone the grandfather she had so obviously loved.

Nor, despite their intimacies the previous night, had she asked anything of him, as so many women would have done, other than that he at least listen to what she had to say in her defence, before he condemned her.

That Elena had been treated so cruelly, and by one who should have been her protector, filled Adam with a burning rage completely at odds with the veneer of cool practicality he now presented to her. But he had no choice but to present that side to her, and everyone else, if he were to be of any help to her in this matter.

'It is very kind of you, my lord—'

'Kindness, be damned!' he growled, wishing he dared take her in his arms and comfort her, but knowing that he could not, dare not, for fear he would want so much more from her if he once touched her again. For this to work at all he must remain aloof, from both her and her present situation. 'I am not a kind man—'

'I beg to differ.'

'The truth is, I have never cared for men of Matthews's ilk.'

'You have only heard what manner of man I believe him to be.'

'An opinion that my grandmother and the Dowager Duchess of Royston share.'

'Even so—'

'Do not forget I have also spoken to Jeremiah,' Adam bit out firmly. 'He is to return to Warwick tomorrow morning, but he has promised to be available if his testament as to your character should be needed at your trial—Elena!' He barely had the chance to move forwards in time to catch her, as her face paled and she swayed on her feet, as if in danger of fainting a second time today.

A move Adam knew to be a mistake the moment he held her in his arms again. He smelt and felt the softness of her dark hair beneath his chin, a mixture of lemons and flowers and ebony silk, as he lifted her lightness up into his arms and carried her across to the chair beside the unlit fireplace, before sitting down with her fragility cradled against his chest as she began to cry.

'You really must cease your tears now,' he murmured gruffly several minutes later as he offered her his silk handkerchief.

Elena felt as if her heart were breaking, the tight control she had kept about her emotions this past two months having disintegrated completely under first Lady Cicely's, and now Adam's kindness. Admittedly, Adam claimed he was offering his assistance in an effort to spare his grandmother from any further involvement in her scandalous affairs, but his reasons for that kindness were unimportant at this moment; Elena felt as if she had been alone, and lonely, for so long now, her emotions frozen, that any show of kindness, for whatever reason, was sure to be her undoing.

As it had been, the tears she should have shed two months ago, for the loss of her grandfather, and her innocence, were now falling hotly, and unchecked, wetting Adam's waistcoat and shirt, she realised as she felt that dampness beneath her cheek.

She sat up to take Adam's handkerchief and begin mopping up those tears. 'I am so sorry—'

'There is no need for apology,' he rasped, stilling the movements of her hand against his chest.

'But—' The words froze on Elena's lips as she looked up to find Adam staring down at her intently in the candlelight even as she felt the wild tattoo of his heartbeat beneath the palm of her hand. An intensity of gaze levelled on the fullness of those parted lips even as she felt the stirring, swelling, of Adam's arousal beneath the roundness of her bottom. 'Adam…?' she breathed her uncertainty at his physical response.

His jaw clenched. 'I believe it is time—past time!—you retired for the night.'

'But—'

'Do not argue, Elena—just go!'

The tightness of his jaw and lips might be telling her to go, but the arms he still kept about her, and the increased swell of his arousal beneath her bottom, said the opposite. 'Could I not just sit here, with you, for a little while longer?'

He bared his teeth in a humourless smile. 'I believe we both know that would not be a good idea.' As if in confirmation of that claim, the stiffness of his erection moved hard and demanding against her tender flesh.

Elena looked up at him shyly in the candlelight, at this physical display, despite all that he had learnt and heard of her today, that Adam still desired her. Against his will, perhaps, if his coolness towards her earlier today at luncheon, and the grimness of his expression now, was an indication, but that physical evidence of his desire was undeniable. Of course, physical desire was still not the love she had last night hungered for and craved from this man, but it was so much more than Elena had believed she would ever know from him again.

Besides which, Neville's actions two months ago had ensured that in future she could never ask, or expect, anything more than desire from any man! 'I believe it is.' She settled more comfortably against him.

Adam breathed in deeply through his nose, his normal iron control far more tenuous than he would have wished it to be as Elena snuggled against the warmth of his chest, knowing he should insist that she go, that she leave him, but for the moment unable to find the words, or the willpower, to insist she do so.

'Why were you so aloof during luncheon today?'

Adam flinched. His intention earlier today, of distancing himself from Elena, in an effort to put their relationship back on an acceptable footing, had been rendered completely redundant in light of her revelations this afternoon.

He no longer had any choice in the matter; he had to remain aloof from her, for Elena's own benefit as much as his own.

He dug deep inside himself to add the necessary steel to that resolve as he grasped hold of Elena's arms and raised her to her feet before standing up himself and moving away from her. 'I should have thought that was obvious.'

'Not to me.' She looked utterly bewildered.

Adam's mouth firmed. He had to be cruel to be kind and force her away from him before he kissed her again and they were both lost. 'Because I had decided you are not a woman I wish to become involved with, either as Mrs Elena Leighton or Miss Magdelena Matthews.'

Elena drew into herself as if struck, as Adam's complete rejection of her hit with the force of a blow, bringing a return of those stinging tears to her eyes. Tears she could not allow Adam to see fall for a second time. 'I am sorry if I—I shall do as you suggest and return upstairs to my bedchamber.'

He nodded. 'Amanda and I will accompany the two of you to London tomorrow. I really cannot allow my grandmother to go haring about the English countryside alone in the company of a young woman who has been accused of murder!'

Elena gave a pained gasp even as her face paled once again.

Causing Adam to clench his hands at his sides in an effort to prevent himself from going to her and taking her in his arms once more; he dared not allow himself to so much as touch Elena again until this situation had been sorted out once and for all. Her safety came first. She was in such terrible danger from that villainous cousin of hers.

He had every intention of ensuring that she would be safe, and as soon as possible.

Chapter Fifteen

'This has just arrived for you.' Lady Cicely smiled warmly as she bustled into the bedchamber Elena had occupied this past four days and nights at the lady's London house in Grosvenor Square, her arms occupied with carrying a large oblong box.

Since she'd been here Elena had not so much as set eyes upon that lady's grandson. Nor had he spoken a single word to her during their two-day journey back to town, Adam having ridden on horseback whilst the three ladies travelled in the carriage, and his parting had been brusque in the extreme once they reached Lady Cicely's home. Elena had been left in a constant state of nerves as to what he intended doing with the information he now had as to her real identity.

'For me...?' Elena now eyed the older woman doubtfully as Lady Cicely placed the large box down upon the bedcovers.

She nodded. 'Open it up and let us take a look inside.'

'But who can it be from?' Elena eyed the box as if were a snake about to strike.

'Who else should it be from but Adam, of course,' Lady Cicely said impatiently. 'I do so hope that for once he paid heed to my instructions...' she added worriedly.

Elena felt her heart sink to the black boots she wore with one of the black gowns she had once again donned before travelling back to London, the pretty new gowns and bonnets Adam had purchased for her seeming entirely inappropriate to her present situation. 'Adam? I mean, Lord Hawthorne has sent me a gift?'

She was even less inclined to open the box now that she knew who it came from.

Lady Cicely made herself comfortable on the side of the bed. 'Are you not curious to see what is inside?' she encouraged.

It would be very rude of her, in view of this lady's kindness to her, to reply as she wished to, with 'not in the least'! For Elena could not think of anything that Adam might wish to send to her which in the least warranted Lady Cicely's present air of expectation.

'I do not understand...' Several minutes later she stared down nonplussed at the beautiful gown of white silk and lace that had been revealed nestled within the tissue paper inside the box, a turquoise ribbon sewn beneath the bodice, several matching ribbons accompanying it obviously intended to adorn her hair.

'He did listen!' Lady Cicely nodded approvingly. 'And the ribbon is a nice touch.' She held up one of the hair ribbons. 'An exact match in colour with your eyes. Perhaps there is hope for my grandson, after all,' she added speculatively.

Elena looked dazed. 'Why would Lord Hawthorne order an evening gown made and be delivered to me here…?'

'So that you may wear it when Adam escorts us to dinner this evening, of course.' Lady Cicely stood up briskly. 'I shall send my own maid to attend you, for you must look your very best—does the gown not meet with your approval, my dear?' She frowned as Elena simply continued to stare down at the gown.

'It is a beautiful gown.' She nodded distractedly.

'But?'

'But you must know, as must Lord Hawthorne, that I cannot be seen out and about with you in London, this evening or any other. Not only have I not been presented at Court, but for obvious reasons I am like to be arrested if I so much as show my face in society.' She had not even stepped outside of this house since arriving back in London. Indeed, Elena had spent those same four days constantly waiting for the sound of the knock upon the door, which would herald the arrival of the authorities, come to arrest her and lock her away in a prison cell.

'You will not be seen out and about in town, and you are allowed to attend a private dinner party without being presented,' Lady Cicely assured her.

Elena made no attempt to hide her bewilderment at this plan. 'As what? I would not be invited to a private dinner party as Mrs Elena Leighton and I certainly cannot attend as Miss Magdelena Matthews.'

Lady Cicely grasped both Elena's hands in her own, her expression intense. 'Do you trust me not to do anything which would bring you further unhappiness?'

'Of course.'

The older woman nodded her satisfaction with the swiftness of her answer. 'And do you trust Adam to do the same?'

Elena hesitated, unsure of her feelings towards Adam Hawthorne since the evening he had stated his own lack of interest in continuing any sort of relationship, even friendship, with her. 'I trust him not to do anything which would bring *you* unhappiness,' she finally answered guardedly.

Lady Cicely smiled ruefully. 'Your manners do you great credit, my dear,' she said. 'And I will admit that Adam has been irritating in his absence recently, but—'

'I expected nothing less,' Elena assured hastily. 'He has already been more than kind in allowing me to remain here with you for this amount of time.'

'Nevertheless, he could have been a little less…elusive.' Lady Cicely pursed her lips disapprovingly. 'But, he did make the arrangements for the dinner party this evening, so I expect I shall forgive him for—'

'We are dining at Lord Hawthorne's home tonight?' Elena gasped.

'Oh, no, my dear Elena.' Lady Cicely beamed. 'Tonight we are to dine at the home of my dear friend, Edith St Just, the Dowager Duchess of Royston!'

'Is it Lord Hawthorne's intention to publicly humiliate me by having me arrested in front of witnesses?' Elena backed away, from both Lady Cicely and the box containing that beautiful silk evening gown, tears now glistening in the deep and pained blue-green of her eyes.

Lady Cicely looked shocked. 'How could you think I would ever allow such a thing to happen? Or that Adam would ever do something so callously unfeeling?'

Elena had no idea what Adam was capable of anymore,

as she no longer felt as if she knew him at all; certainly the man who had dismissed her so coldly that last evening at Hawthorne Hall had not been the same caring and sensitive man who had made love to her the evening before.

She shook her head. 'Then I do not understand the purpose of my inclusion in this private dinner party this evening.'

Lady Cicely wrinkled her nose. 'And, for the moment, I am not at liberty to tell you, I am afraid.'

Elena looked vexed. 'In that case I believe I would rather not accept the dowager duchess's invitation.'

'That will not do at all, my dear Elena,' Lady Cicely tutted. 'Indeed, there would be no purpose in the dinner taking place at all if you were not present.'

'But—'

'I believe, by insisting you be allowed to stay here with her, that my grandmother has given you her trust, unconditionally,' Adam Hawthorne said from across the room. 'Is it too much for her to ask that you now do the same for her?'

Elena had spun round at the first sound of his voice, a guilty blush colouring her cheeks before she paled, as she wondered how much of their conversation he had overheard.

Her breath stilled in her throat, as she now took in his appearance in black evening clothes and snowy-white linen, the darkness of his hair fashionably dishevelled about his ears and across his brow, the eyes beneath of a chilling grey as he returned her gaze with his usual haughty arrogance.

She moistened her lips with the tip of her tongue before speaking. 'I did not in the least mean to cast doubts upon Lady Cicely's good intentions.'

'Only my own?' Adam guessed drily as he easily took

in the scene before him: the evening gown revealed inside the open box placed atop the bed, the pallor of Elena's face against the black gown she presently wore, his grandmother's expression of exasperation as she looked across the bedchamber at him. 'Would you leave us alone for a moment, Grandmama?'

She frowned her disapproval. 'Is that wise, Adam?'

'I am sure it is not,' he allowed ruefully. 'But Miss Matthews's present demeanour makes it necessary.'

'Very well.' His grandmother gave Elena's hand a reassuring squeeze before she crossed the room with a swish of her taffeta skirts. 'Five minutes and I shall be sending my maid to attend Elena,' she warned softly.

His gaze remained steadily fixed on Elena as he gave his grandmother an acknowledging inclination of his head, waiting only until they were alone before speaking again. 'Do you not like the gown?'

'The gown is…lovely, as I am sure you are aware,' she dismissed agitatedly. 'It is the reason it's here that I find so…unacceptable.'

His mouth tightened. 'The dowager duchess does you a great honour by inviting you into her home.'

Elena may have spent most of her life hidden away in the country, but even there she had heard of how coveted invitations were to the Dowager Duchess of Royston's rare private dinner parties—making her own invitation this evening all the more extraordinary. 'Is she aware of *whom* she is inviting?'

'Yes.'

She spread her hands. 'I am not even acquainted with the lady.'

'But I am. As is my grandmother. And you are currently a guest in my grandmother's home…'

'And I understand from your grandmother that you are the one who instigated the dowager duchess's invitation—'

'*That* is something she should not have told you!' He scowled darkly.

'Why are you doing this?' Elena groaned. 'Is it as punishment for the deception I practised upon you when I took up employment in your household?'

His mouth tightened. 'If there was time I would put you over my knee for the insult you have just given me,' he growled. 'As it is, you have precisely one hour to bathe, change into the gown in that box and arrange the ribbons in your hair, all in readiness for dining out this evening.'

'You cannot make me go.' Her chin rose in challenge as she met his gaze defiantly.

'No?'

Elena felt a cold shiver down her spine at the soft menace she detected in his tone. 'Can you not understand that I do not wish to embarrass the dowager duchess, let alone myself, by appearing as a guest in her home?'

It had taken Adam the whole of the past four days to make arrangements for this evening's dinner party and he did not intend to allow Elena's stubbornness to jeopardise all that he had put in place. Nor could he tell her of those arrangements, for if he did, he knew she would certainly refuse to attend.

'How is Amanda?' Elena enquired. 'I have sorely missed her company recently.'

'As she has missed yours,' he said. 'And do not change the subject, Elena.' He crossed the room in long, predatory strides, until he stood only inches away from her, not quite touching, but close enough that he could feel the heat of her body. As Elena could no doubt feel his. 'Do you trust me?'

Her eyes widened. 'Your grandmother has just asked me that very same question.'

He reached out to smooth the frown from her brow, fingers lingering on the warmth of that silky-smooth skin. 'And what answer did you give?'

Her gaze lowered. 'That I believed you could be trusted not to cause Lady Cicely any unhappiness or embarrassment.'

His mouth twisted wryly. 'That is something, I suppose.' His hand fell back to his side as a knock sounded on the bedchamber door. 'That will be my grandmother's maid come to attend you. You have one hour to make yourself ready, Elena,' he repeated. 'And I should warn you that I will not appreciate it if you put me to the trouble of having to come back up here and button you into that gown myself!'

'You would not dare!' She gasped indignantly.

'I think you know that I would.'

Elena glared at him, knowing by the implacability of that unblinking silver gaze that Adam meant exactly what he said.

She drew in a ragged breath. 'Very well, I shall be ready to leave in one hour. But—'

'Pity,' he drawled. 'I believe I should, after all, have enjoyed helping you into your gown. Not as much as I would enjoy helping you out of it, of course, but that is perhaps something for another time…' Adam sketched her a mocking bow as she gasped again, his gaze lingering on those parted lips for several long seconds before he turned to cross the room and open the door to admit the maid.

* * *

Elena studied her appearance critically in the mirror once Lady Cicely's maid had left to attend her mistress. The ivory of her skin appeared almost translucent against the white-silk gown, the turquoise ribbons, beneath the low bodice of the gown and threaded through the darkness of her simply styled curls, enlarging and emphasising the colour of her eyes framed by stunningly long lashes.

She looked…innocently virginal, Elena realised with a choked sob. A young lady poised on the brink of woman-hood. Something she was not now, nor ever could be again.

'You look very beautiful.'

Elena turned slowly to face Adam as he stood in the open doorway, no longer surprised at the manner in which he walked in and out of her bedchamber as though he had the right to do so. 'Thank you, my lord.' She gave an elegant curtsy, silky dark lashes lowered so that he should not see the tears still glittering in her eyes.

To say that Adam had been rendered breathless by the beauty of Elena's appearance would be an understatement. This evening, in the white silk gown, she looked every inch the duke's granddaughter that she undoubtedly was: cool, delicately elegant, innocently ravishing.

'I have something for you. There is no need for you to look so alarmed, Elena,' he soothed as he quickly crossed the room to her side.

She kept her lashes lowered. 'You have been kind enough already in giving me this gown.'

Not nearly kind enough, Adam groaned inwardly, wish-ing he might shower her with all the kindnesses that had been absent from her life recently, as she was forced to run, and then hide, from the man who had made her life so unbearable after the death of her grandfather.

His gaze hardened, mouth thinning, as he thought of the things he would like to do to that man for daring to harm so much as one dark curl upon Elena's head. 'I wish you to wear this single strand of pearls—they were my mother's,' he explained as she raised startled lashes to look at the pearl necklace he had withdrawn from the pocket of his evening jacket. 'She wore them on the evening of her début into society.'

Elena shook her head in denial. 'Then I could not possibly wear them.'

'Of course you can.'

'No!' She moved away from him. 'I have allowed you to bully me into wearing this gown and attending the dinner party, but I will not—' Her voice broke emotionally. 'I cannot—I simply cannot wear your mother's pearls!'

Adam knew by the stubborn fragility of her expression, and the determination in her gaze, that she meant every word she said. Nor did he mean to 'bully' her—it was the last thing he wished to do; for this one evening he simply needed her to do as he asked without further argument or objection. 'Very well,' he acquiesced as he slipped the pearl necklace back inside his pocket. 'Shall we go downstairs now and wait for my grandmother to join us…?' He held out his arm to her.

Elena stared at the strength of that arm, knowing that once she placed her hand upon it she would have committed herself to spending the evening at the home of Edith St Just, the Dowager Duchess of Royston. She had no idea who the other guests were to be this evening, but she had no doubt that the arrival of Miss Magdelena Matthews in their midst would be a sensation which would keep the tongues wagging for weeks, if not months, to come.

Her gaze moved higher, to the unyielding hardness of Adam's arrogantly handsome face, the steadiness of that grey gaze asking—no, demanding!—that she do as he requested without further protest.

'I give you my word I will not allow any harm to come to you this evening,' he murmured encouragingly.

A frown creased her brow. 'And how do you intend to prevent that from happening?'

'Can you not trust me enough to see that it does not?'

Once again Adam asked that she trust him. When they had spoken together six days ago he had dismissed the passion they had shared, out of hand. When they'd parted four days ago he had been barely civil to her. And now, after days of silence, he asked that she trust him.

Could she, dare she now put her trust in him?

What other choice did she have?

Absolutely none, came the unequivocal answer as she moved her hand up slowly, hesitantly, and placed it upon Adam's forearm, allowing him to escort her from the safety of her bedchamber.

'Your grandfather was one of the gentlemen whose offer I considered accepting when I was a gel!' the Dowager Duchess of Royston informed her briskly upon introduction, a briskness which appeared to be her usual manner. 'I admit to being quite put out when Jane Witherspoon whisked him out from beneath my nose and married him.'

And an impressive nose it was too, Elena thought admiringly, Edith St Just's a forceful beauty rather than one of pale delicacy, as her own grandmother's had been. 'They were very happy together,' she assured shyly, slightly disconcerted by the forthright manner of the dowager duchess's greeting, after spending most of the carriage ride, to that lady's magnificent house, worrying as to what sort of reception she might expect from her hostess.

'Well, of course they were, George and I would never have suited. Both too fond of our own way.' The older woman smiled before turning to kiss Lady Cicely affectionately upon one powdered cheek, then stepping back to give Adam a considering glance. 'We have succeeded in bringing you back into society again at last, I see, Hawthorne.'

He smiled ruefully. 'It is for this one evening only, your Grace.'

'Then we must make the most of your company "for this one evening only",' the dowager duchess came back drily. 'Come, Cicely, let us take Miss Matthews and introduce her to my other guests.' She moved ahead of them, cutting a swathe through the other ten or so guests gathered in the salon.

Much like a battleship sailing through the midst of smaller, less prepossessing vessels, Elena thought dazedly as she found herself moving further and further away from Adam's side.

'I believe I understand more what this evening is all about now that I have seen the young lady in question...'

Adam turned slightly to look at Justin St Just, as the duke moved to stand beside him. 'Indeed?'

The other man grinned at him. 'Do not take that arrogant tone with me, Thorne, when any man with eyes in his head can see and appreciate that Miss Magdelena Matthews is a rare beauty.'

'A rare beauty who has been much wronged,' Adam reminded him grimly.

The other man sobered instantly, his expression becoming almost as severe as Adam's own. 'Which is why we are all here, is it not? The duke, the earl, the judge, the lawyer, the doctor? As well as several of my grandmother's closest friends, to act as witness to the proceedings? Indeed, I cut short my own escape to the country in order that I might be of assistance.'

Adam forced some of the tension from his shoulders as he reminded himself that Royston, despite his words of admiration for Elena, was not his enemy, that the other man had indeed brought himself back to town, at the risk of facing more of the dowager duchess's marriage machinations, solely at Adam's request. 'I apologise for my churlishness. It is only—' He gave a shake of his head. 'The reproachful looks Elena cast in my direction, during the carriage ride here, lead me to the conclusion that she believes I have only forced her into coming here this evening because I somehow intend to cause her further humiliation.'

The duke gave him a reassuring slap on the shoulder. 'She will understand exactly why we are all here before this evening is over.'

Adam glanced across to where Elena and Lady Cicely were presently engaged in conversation with Judge Lord Terence Soames and Lady Soames, as well as the Dowager Countess of Chambourne, and her grandson Lord Chris-

tian Ambrose, the Earl of Chambourne, and Lady Sylviana Moorland, the lady to whom he had recently become
betrothed. Elena's expression appeared to be one of shy
pleasure as she found herself welcomed by the prestigious
company in which she now found herself, instead of re-
buffed, as she must fully have expected to be. 'I can only
hope that you are right,' he murmured bleakly.

Adam's plans for this evening had been made carefully
and cautiously, with only a handful of people knowing the
true reason they were all gathered together here at the dowager duchess's home. Elena had not been one of them. For
her own sake, admittedly, but Adam was not sure that she
would agree with that decision once she became fully aware
of why they were all here. The secrecy was a risk, a calculated risk on Adam's part, and not one he was at all sure
would ultimately pay off.

'Too late for second thoughts now, Thorne,' Justin murmured beside him as he turned towards the door. 'I believe
I hear our guest of honour arriving.' The duke wasted no
more time on further conversation, but strode quickly across
the room to stand at Elena's side.

Just in time, as the salon door was opened by the butler
and the last of the dinner guests, a tall and confident young
gentleman, in possession of a blond-haired blue-eyed handsomeness, stepped into the room at the same time as his
presence was sonorously announced by the dowager duchess's butler.

'His Grace, the Duke of Sheffield.'

Chapter Sixteen

It seemed that, in the brief passing of a second, the evening that Elena was finding to be a surprisingly pleasant one had now turned into her worst nightmare. Her face paled to a deathly white as she looked across the room at the man who was her nemesis.

'Steady.'

She was barely aware of the gentleman who had moved to stand beside her, nor did she acknowledge the firm grip he took of her elbow as she swayed on her slippered feet. She had eyes and ears for only one man in the room. Her cousin. Neville Matthews. The eleventh Duke of Sheffield. The man who had stolen so much from her. Not only her inheritance and her identity, but, worst of all, her innocence…

His shrewd blue gaze moved restlessly about a room that had fallen silent at his arrival, nodding haughty acknowledgement as he recognised several of the other guests, that arrogant gaze then passing dismissively over Elena before just as quickly shifting back again.

Elena found it impossible to turn away as she saw the

malevolent gleam that instantly appeared in those narrowed blue eyes and felt much like the mouse that found itself mesmerised by the eyes of the cat stalking it. If not for the increased firmness of that grip upon her elbow, she knew her legs would surely have given way beneath her. As it was, she could neither move nor breathe, but only continue to stare at Neville with ever-increasing dread as she waited for him to speak, to denounce her to every other person in the room.

'What are *you* doing here?' Neville's words, no more than a vicious whisper, was nevertheless still heard by every person gathered in the dowager duchess's beautifully appointed but otherwise silent salon. When Elena made no reply—she could not have spoken if her very life had depended upon it, which it perhaps did—his contemptuous gaze shifted to his hostess for the evening. 'I am sure you can have no idea of the deception which has been practised upon you this evening, madam, but I am sorry to inform you that your grandson appears to have brought a wanted fugitive into your home!'

'Steady,' that reassuring voice once again murmured at Elena's side.

A voice, she realised, from Neville's accusation, that must surely belong to none other than Justin St Just, the dowager duchess's grandson.

She blinked her uncertainty, unsure of how that gentleman came to be standing next to her at all. Or why the Duke of Royston should have chosen to take such a proprietary hold upon her elbow, when the two of them had never met, let alone been formally introduced.

'Which fugitive would you be referring to, Sheffield?' Edith St Just was the one to coolly answer the accusation.

Neville shot Elena a scowling glance. 'My cousin, Miss Magdelena Matthews, is the woman now standing beside your grandson!'

The elderly lady gave Elena a cursory glance before turning back to Neville. 'And?'

'And she is both a murderess and a thief, madam!' A flush of displeasure had darkened Neville's cheeks. Obviously he had expected a completely different reaction to his triumphant announcement.

'I do not know much about the affair, but gossip would seem to imply that it is only an accusation rather than accepted fact.' Adam stepped forwards into the middle of the room, placing himself firmly between the cousins. 'And was it not you who levelled that particular accusation against Miss Matthews?'

Elena's heart began to beat rapidly in her chest as she looked across at Adam, the first glimmer of hope beginning to brighten the darkness which she had felt surrounding her since they had left Cambridgeshire.

Trust him, Adam had requested of her earlier this evening, when Elena had questioned his reasons for insisting she attend this dinner party. Could he—dare she hope that he had been referring to this present situation when he made that request? That he had known all along that Neville was to be here this evening? That he had perhaps planned for this very confrontation to happen?

'This is none of your concern, Hawthorne.' Neville looked surprised by the other man's intervention.

Adam raised dark brows, his expression bland. 'I should have thought it to be the concern of any decent member of society?'

Neville gave him a pitying glance. 'From which you are known to have voluntarily absented yourself these past years.'

Adam smiled humourlessly. 'And what bearing can that possibly have upon any of this?'

'I merely mentioned it in passing.' Neville looked more than a little irritated as he once again turned the focus of his attention on Elena and the man standing so solidly at her side. 'I am surprised at you, Royston, for knowingly bringing such a woman into your grandmother's home—'

'I would prefer—no, I positively insist, that you address me as your Grace.' Ice literally dripped from the Justin's coldly contemptuous voice.

The other man scowled. 'As your equal in rank—'

'I doubt there is another man alive equal to the depths to which you have fallen, Sheffield,' the duke informed him scathingly.

An angry flush now darkened Neville's cheeks. 'I did not come here to be insulted by one such as you—'

'Have a care, Sheffield,' Justin warned.

'This is ridiculous!' Neville shifted impatiently as he turned to the other guests in the room. 'The woman standing beside Royston has been sought this past two months, for both murder and theft. She is—'

'Innocent of both those charges!' Elena pulled out of the duke's grasp as she stepped forwards, her cheeks flushed as she faced up to the man she knew to be responsible for all that he now accused her of. Accusations, which she had listened to silently, her eyes downcast, as she was filled with tortured mortification at having such personal things discussed in such exalted company. But she could not just stand by and listen any longer, had to at least try to defend herself. 'It was your own behaviour, when you—when you attacked me, that so upset our grandfather he had a heart attack and died! And it was you who threatened to have me locked in the asylum if I did not agree to marry you!'

'I threatened the asylum because I believe you to be mentally ill, madam,' Neville announced scathingly. 'The fact that you ran away is in itself evidence of your guilt.'

'Not so.' Elena gave a fierce shake of her head. 'It was you who made it impossible for me to remain in Yorkshire!' She could not bring herself to say in what manner he had gone about that. 'And you made up those terrible things about me so that I could not make any accusations regarding your own monstrous behaviour towards me following our grandfather's funeral!' She was breathing hard in her agitation.

His jaw tightened. 'As already stated, you are deranged, madam.'

'And yet you wished to make her your wife? That does not make any sense at all.' Adam spoke softly, filled with pride for Elena, as she stood up to her accuser so bravely. A pride he dared not show. Not yet…

Sheffield scowled darkly. 'Perhaps we should take this conversation somewhere less public?'

Adam turned to their hostess. 'Your Grace?'

Edith St Just remained stoically imperious. 'I believe, having heard so much, that it would be in Miss Matthews's best interest if my guests and I remained to hear the rest of what is said.' She glanced at those guests, receiving several silent nods of confirmation, before turning back to Neville. 'It does seem…odd, in light of your other comments, that you then offered for Miss Matthews?'

'I was unaware of her dangerous mental state when I made the offer.'

'Correct me if I am wrong, but it sounded as if your offer of marriage was made to Miss Matthews immediately after your grandfather's death?' the dowager countess said with deceptive mildness.

'What does it matter when I offered for her, when that offer, for obvious reasons, has since been withdrawn?' Sheffield's top lip curled with distaste.

Edith St Just raised grey brows. 'I should have thought it was of great significance, if you made the offer of marriage whilst believing Miss Matthews to be deranged and responsible for the death of your grandfather.'

Sheffield scowled darkly. 'I do not have to justify my actions to you, madam—'

'I believe the dowager duchess is merely seeking to clarify the sequence of events,' Adam put in mildly, not wishing for Sheffield to become so annoyed that he turned and walked out. Having come so far, that would not do at all.

He did not remember meeting Neville Matthews before this evening, but just a few minutes in this man's company and he knew that he did not like him in the least. That he was not a man he would ever have liked, even without the knowledge of his treatment of Elena. Indeed, Adam had sought out, and spoken with, several members of society these past few days, some of them women, who could testify, and would if necessary, as to the vicious depravity of Sheffield's behaviour.

Having now met the man, Adam could see that he was beyond arrogant, and his past behaviour surely implied he believed himself to be above the law of the land, too. If anyone present this evening were to be called 'mentally ill' or 'deranged', then it was surely this man?

'I believe we were talking of your offer of marriage to Miss Matthews while fully believing that she was responsible for the demise of the grandfather you shared?' He gave the man another prod.

Neville's hands clenched at his sides even as he glared his anger at Adam. 'If we must finish this conversation, then should we not at least excuse the ladies from any indelicacies that might follow?'

'I believe I may speak for all of the ladies present,' the dowager duchess answered loftily, 'when I state that we are none of us so delicate as all that.'

Sheffield gave a sneering smile. 'On your own head be it, madam!'

'Indeed,' she said regally.

'Very well,' he snapped his displeasure. 'I offered for Elena because it was always intended that we should one day marry—'

'Intended by whom?' Adam prompted.

'By all of the family, of course.'

'I understood that there was only your grandfather, yourself and Miss Matthews left alive in that family? Miss Matthews does not appear to me to be a chit just out of the schoolroom and I do not recall your grandfather making arrangements for that match before his death?'

'Because he was too damned soft to force her when she declined the match!' Neville muttered disgustedly.

Adam raised his brows. 'You did not agree with his showing such an indulgence of emotions towards his only granddaughter?'

The other man snorted. 'Not when it resulted in the old fool accepting her refusal and then settling half the Sheffield money on her in his will!'

'Perhaps he made such a decision so that Miss Matthews might be independent after his death? Because Miss Matthews had voiced her aversion to marrying you? Her aversion to *you*?' Adam goaded again with as light a touch as possible in the circumstances. 'I seem to recall Miss Matthews stating earlier that it was witnessing that very aversion which resulted in the duke's heart attack and subsequent death?'

'I did not allow her to remain averse to me for long after the old man's death, I assure you, Hawthorne,' the other man sneered.

'No?' Adam kept a tight rein on his own temper; much as he longed to reach out and squeeze the life out of this excuse for a man, it would not serve his purpose. Not yet, at least.

Neville gave Elena a sweeping knowing glance. 'Perhaps you should try her for yourself once Royston has finished with her. I believe you will find that, like all women, she is only too willing after the initial fight.' He gave an arrogantly mocking smile as one of the female guests gave an audible gasp.

'You like your women to fight you, do you, Matthews?' Adam's voice had now taken on a dangerous edge.

'It adds a certain…spice, yes.' Neville gave a confident smile, still certain his position as a duke gave him an iron-clad protection.

'You do not see it as a sign that they are possibly unwilling?'

The other man gave Elena another scathing glance. 'Elena

fought a little more than most, admittedly, and earned herself a few bruises for her trouble. But that was only to be expected. I have found that virgins are always the most skittish.' He gave a feral smile. 'Married ladies are much more eager to try new things. Your own wife, for example, very much enjoyed a little rough play in the bedchamber—'

'I believe you are right, Sheffield, in that we have all heard quite enough!' the Duke of Royston rasped, turning slightly to nod at Adam, the two men then moving forwards to link an arm each under Neville's, before then walking him backwards towards the open doorway, his booted heels dragging on the carpet.

'What the—! Unhand me at once!' the other man demanded furiously as he fought to free himself from their steely grasp. 'At once, do you hear!'

'Oh, I assure you, we have all heard you, very loud and very clear,' Adam said icily as the three men stood in the doorway. 'We have heard your contempt for your grandfather. We have heard how it was your attack upon Miss Matthews which caused your grandfather's collapse and death. We have heard you admit to later threatening Elena with the asylum if she would not consent to marry you. We have heard of your brutality when she continued to refuse. We have also heard how you made the accusations against her as a way of covering up your own contemptible behaviour towards her.' He looked at the other man with cold, merciless eyes. 'Feel free to correct me if I have missed anything out?'

Elena felt numbed by this past few minutes, hardly daring to believe she might now be free of Neville and his lies.

'I am the Duke of Sheffield,' he now shouted angrily,

'and I will simply deny any and all accusations you might care to make against me—'

'You may deny it all you like, young man.' A grey-haired gentleman stepped forwards, his expression grim. 'I assure you, it will not do you a bit of good. Not when I, Judge Lord Terence Soames, will be one of the people giving evidence against you.'

'As will the Duke of Royston,' that gentleman assured coldly.

'And Sir Michael Bennett, lawyer.'

'And Dr Jonathan Graves.'

'And Lord Christian Ambrose, Earl of Chambourne.'

Elena was completely dazed as each gentleman stepped forwards to bow respectfully towards her before turning to look at Neville with complete contempt.

Surely the presence this evening of all these eminent gentlemen could not be coincidental?

'We shall remove him from the sight of all the decent people in this room, gentlemen,' the judge instructed as he crossed the room, pausing in front of Elena to take her hand gently in both of his much larger ones. 'You are a very brave young woman,' he complimented gently. 'And I trust you will accept my word that this excuse for a man...' his eyes turned steely as he glanced at Neville '...shall never again be allowed to threaten or bother you.'

She gave a tremulous smile. 'You are very kind.'

His expression softened. 'I believe kindness is the least that all in society should give you in future.'

'Which I shall personally ensure that they do,' Edith St Just spoke imperiously. 'Now remove that distasteful object from my home at your earliest convenience, if you please,

Hawthorne.' She looked down the length of her impressive nose at the still-struggling Neville Matthews.

'Your Grace.' Adam bowed briefly to the dowager duchess before glancing at Elena, relieved to see that she appeared to be recovering some of the colour back in her cheeks.

And hoping, sincerely hoping, as he and Royston carried away a protesting and vengeful Matthews, that she would one day forgive him for the ordeal he had put her through this evening…

'I feel as if I dreamt the first part of this evening.' Elena looked up at Adam uncertainly.

He had ridden back in the carriage with Elena and Lady Cicely at the end of the evening, the elderly lady having then announced that she was more than ready for her bed, after all the excitement, and would see them both in the morning, leaving Elena and Adam to retire to the privacy of the library.

Exciting was not quite how Elena would have described the events of the evening just passed. Terrifying. Shocking. Ultimately filled with a surprising warmth and kindness, as Edith St Just's guests made her feel welcome in their midst, both during the dinner the dowager duchess had insisted would be served, and afterwards, when the ladies had all retired to the salon for tea and conversation, leaving the men at the table to enjoy their brandy and cigars.

As if Neville had never so much as been in their midst this evening, let alone been revealed as the egotistical monster that he was.

'Do you think you will ever be able to forgive me?' Adam

looked down searchingly into her face, which seemed dominated by her huge blue-green eyes.

If he had needed further proof that Elena had been raised
as the granddaughter of a duke—which he had not—then it
had been all too apparent this evening, when he and Royston
had rejoined the dinner guests to find Elena guarded on
either side by Lady Cicely and Edith St Just, as they discussed fashions with several of the other ladies, prior to dinner being served. Adam believed that only a young woman
of refinement and innocence could possibly have behaved
in such a poised manner only minutes after being publicly
flayed by her nearest living relative.

And only someone who knew Elena well would have
noticed the way in which she kept her gloved hands tightly
clasped together in order to hide their trembling. Or the
way she smiled while at the same time tears shimmered
unshed in her eyes.

Tears which even now glistened in those beautiful blue-
green eyes as she answered him. 'Forgive you?' she repeated
incredulously.

He nodded. 'I wanted to tell you what I had planned for
this evening, but dared not, for fear that you might alert
Matthews, by some word or gesture, as to what was about
to happen. I wished him to believe that you were as stunned
as he by your meeting, and that it was Royston with whom
you were acquainted rather than myself, so that I was then
able to lull him into a false impression of a lack of knowledge of the situation on my part—not difficult to do when,
as he stated, I have long been absent from society.'

Neville's remark about Adam's wife had given Elena a
glimmer of the possible reason for that lengthy absence.

'I am heartily sorry that in the end Neville chose to make some personal remarks to you.'

'I have found that men of his nature cannot resist boasting of their conquests, willing and unwilling, given the opportunity to do so.' His lip turned back with distaste. 'In truth, it seems it would be difficult to find a gentleman in society with whom my wife had not been intimate!'

Elena gave a pained wince. 'It was nevertheless poor recompense for your efforts on my behalf.'

He sighed. 'I am long past being concerned over such remarks.'

Nevertheless, Elena knew it could not have been easy for Adam to have to listen to them again this evening and from such a vile man as her cousin.

'You do understand the reason for not revealing to you beforehand my intention of exposing Matthews this evening?'

'Oh, yes.' Elena nodded. 'Did Lady Cicely and the dowager duchess know of your plan?'

He nodded confirmation. 'Invitations from the dowager duchess are much coveted by the *ton*, and we had to find some way to draw Sheffield out from his imposed mourning for your grandfather. Soames, Royston and Chambourne were also aware of my intentions.'

'You have been very busy these past few days,' Elena acknowledged ruefully. She had believed Adam to be avoiding her. Instead, he had spent his time putting together a plan which would ultimately prove her innocent of any wrongdoing. 'I do not know how I shall ever be able to repay you for the way in which you have revealed Neville, to the dowager duchess's guests at least, as the cruel and heartless man that he is.'

'My actions this evening were not done with any thought of being deserving of your gratitude,' Adam said hotly.

Elena flinched as she once again felt the sting of Adam's rejection.

Giving her no choice but to accept that his actions this evening had not been meant personally, but were those of the noble gentlemen he was, and that, believing in her innocence, he had simply felt duty bound to correct the wrong inflicted against her.

She lifted her chin. 'Nevertheless, you have it, my lord, and always will have. As does the Duke of Royston. Judge Lord Soames. Sir Michael Bennett. Doctor Jonathan Graves. And the Earl of Chambourne.'

He nodded. 'Lord Soames believes it best if the worst of your cousin's offences against you were not made public.'

'I am sure he does.' She smiled sadly. 'But I doubt that will be possible after the things that have been said this evening.'

'The dowager duchess's guests were all, I assure you, chosen with their discretion in mind. I have their word that they will none of them ever discuss the events of this evening with anyone else.'

'For which I am very grateful.' She nodded. 'Unfortunately, that silence will also mean that I am not absolved of the crime in the eyes of the rest of society.'

Adam's mouth tightened. 'I believe we might find a way of achieving that too. With your agreement.'

Her gaze sharpened. 'My agreement?'

He frowned. 'The situation is a…delicate one. On the one hand we would obviously wish to see Matthews incarcerated for the rest of his life, for causing your grandfather's demise when caught forcing his attentions upon you, and the miseries he has admitted inflicting upon you afterwards. On the other hand there is your own reputation. We can prove to society that you are not a murderess or a thief, but it would be at the cost of—'

'Revealing my lack of—of physical innocence,' Elena supplied huskily, her face now rather wan.

Adam's eyes darkened to a stormy grey. 'Your innocence is not in question—'

'How can you, of all people, possibly say that?' she choked.

'Elena—'

'Just tell me Lord Soames's solution to the problem, if you please,' she asked curtly, no longer able to meet that stormy grey gaze as she turned away. 'It has been a stressful evening and I am very tired.'

Of course she was tired after such an emotional evening and Adam was a fool for not realising it before now. 'Soames has suggested that Sheffield make a heartfelt apology to you in the newspapers, explaining that his emotions were overset after the death of your paternal grandfather and causing him to wrongly accuse you, that your grandfather had been ill for some time and had succumbed to that illness. That he, Matthews, was also mistaken about any jewels and money having been taken when you chose to leave, both having now been safely found in a hidden safe in your grandfather's bedchamber. After which Matthews will remove himself to the Continent for the rest of his natural life.'

'How would we explain my disappearance this past two months?'

'That you have been living in the country, in private mourning for your grandfather, and did not know of the rumours and accusations circulating against you.'

Elena gave a pained wince. 'Do you think Neville would ever accept such a proposal?'

'At the risk of a public trial, which Matthews will most certainly lose, and which would result in his being incarcerated for some considerable time, or worse? Yes, I believe he might be…persuaded, into accepting Lord Soames's proposal,' Adam confirmed ruthlessly.

She arched dark brows. 'And do you think that society would believe any of it?'

'I think that the unknowing will believe what the Dowager Duchess of Royston tells them to believe,' he admitted drily.

'And the rest?'

'Already know Matthews for the out-and-out bounder that he is and will just be relieved to have him removed from decent society!' Adam scowled as he recalled now knowing of the scoundrel's past association with Fanny, along with some of the tales about him he had heard recently. Tales which had led Adam to believe, no matter how cruelly Elena had been treated by Matthews, that she had at least been spared some of the man's darker depravities. Although only the lord knew she had suffered badly enough at the bastard's hands!

'What do you think I should do?'

'It is not for me to say.'

'But it is.' Elena insisted firmly. 'You asked earlier that I trust you. I did then and I still do. As such, I would welcome your opinion on this, too.'

Adam turned away, knowing exactly what he wished for Elena to do, both now and in the future, but also knowing he could not impose upon her newly found freedom by verbally expressing those wishes to her now. That he could never do so.

The first part of Elena's life had been a protected and loving one, initially with both her parents, then with her mother and grandfather following her father's death. This past few years had robbed her of her mother, and more recently her grandfather, her innocence, and her very existence, when she was forced to flee the only home she was familiar with to take on the name and life of another woman so that she might hide from the man who should have been protecting her, but had instead wounded her deeply.

With the Dowager Duchess of Royston, Lady Cicely Hawthorne and Lady Jocelyn Ambrose as her sponsors, Elena's future in society was assured. She would likely fall in love with a handsome and uncomplicated young gentleman, one unencumbered by a scandalous first wife and a six-year-old daughter from that marriage. As such, Adam's advice to Elena must be given unselfishly, with only her future happiness in mind.

He turned decisively. 'I believe it to be in your very best interest to accept Soames's suggestion.'

Elena looked at him wordlessly for several seconds, before nodding equally as decisively, her gloved hands tightly clasped together. 'Then that is what I shall do. Thank you, Adam. For everything that you have done for me tonight.'

Which was, Adam accepted heavily, his cue to depart…

Chapter Seventeen

'I do not wish to intrude, Adam, but I really need you to explain to me exactly what it is you think you are doing.' Lady Cicely swept into the privacy of Adam's study at his London home during the first week of June, looking remarkably spry for a woman of almost seventy years, in her gown and bonnet of pale blue and her parasol of cream lace.

Adam sat back slowly in the chair behind his desk, having seen very little of his grandmother during the month of May, her time being spent much in the society Adam still chose not to be a part of. 'I am checking estate accounts—'

'I did not mean at this precise moment.' His grandmother eyed him impatiently. 'You were primarily responsible for returning Miss Magdelena Matthews to society some weeks ago—and you have completely ignored her existence ever since!'

He could never 'ignore' Elena's existence. How could he, when he had spent every waking moment of this past month, thinking about her! 'I think you are exaggerating, Grandmama,' he drawled. 'Nor do I think that Miss Matthews needs or requires any more gentlemen to tell her how beautiful she is.' His jaw tightened grimly.

'Ah.' Lady Cicely beamed her satisfaction.

Adam frowned warily. 'What does that mean?'

She continued to smile at him. 'It means that you appear to be as miserable as Elena is.'

He looked startled. 'I beg your pardon…?'

'You heard me,' Lady Cicely repeated remorselessly. 'Which is a little frustrating, as it happens.' She frowned. 'Edith, Jocelyn and I have worked tirelessly these past few weeks to see that Elena was launched into society, since it was decided that three months of mourning for her grandfather would suffice. We wished to have her formally presented as soon as was possible after that dreadful man rescinded all of his accusations and fled to the Continent. I am not sure if I said so at the time, but I am very proud of you, Adam, for the efficient way in which you cleared Elena of all wrongdoing.'

'No, you did not say, Grandmama,' he acknowledged drily. 'And I was only too pleased to remove Sheffield from Elena's life,' he added with satisfaction.

'I am sure you were.' Lady Cicely gave an appreciative chuckle, before sobering. 'Anyway, Elena has become quite the thing and I believe several young gentlemen may already be about to offer for her—did you just *growl*, Adam?' She raised mock-surprised grey brows.

He had, damn it! At the mere thought of Elena accepting the offer of one of those young cubs he had only a month ago decided would be the best thing for her.

Best for Elena, perhaps.

Not for Adam. He had missed her presence in his home

these past five weeks. Not just the passion they had shared. He had also missed their lively conversations—occasions when Elena invariably upbraided him over some mistake or other on his part, usually regarding Amanda. And he knew that Amanda had missed Elena, too. Although his grandmother had taken the little girl out on several occasions, allowing Elena and Amanda to spend time together in her home.

Occasions when his young daughter would return home to talk of nothing else but 'Miss Matthews' this and 'Miss Matthews' that—with the resilience of most young children, Amanda had accepted the change of her old governess's name and circumstance, without blinking a silken eyelash— all succeeding in emphasising the hollow in Adam's chest at his own lack of even the sight of 'Miss Matthews'.

In a word, Adam felt…lonely for Elena.

He gave his a grandmother a self-derisive smile. 'I believe it may have been, yes, Grandmama.'

She gave an exasperated shake of her head. 'I do not understand you at all, Adam! Why do you sit here moping, day after day, night after night, when you might have attended any number of social occasions and so spent time with Elena yourself? After which you could have—'

'Could have what, Grandmama?' he cut in harshly. 'I am a widower, with a young daughter and a scandalous marriage behind me; do you not think that Elena has had enough scandal in her life recently, without the notorious Lord Hawthorne showing her his marked attentions?' For Adam had no doubt it would be marked; he could not bear to be in the same room with Elena and watch other gentlemen, more eligible and younger gentlemen than he, fawn over and covet her. 'It will not do, Grandmama.'

'And if it is you whom Elena wants?'

Adam looked at her sharply, hopefully, before he as quickly dampened down that hope. 'If she ever felt even the smallest measure of affection for me, then I am sure it has been forgotten by now.'

Lady Cicely gave him a reproving look. 'Are all young men as ignorant in their knowledge of women as you appear to be?'

'Grandmama!' He eyed her incredulously.

'I am not about to apologise, Adam, so you may take that offended expression off your face!' She eyed him impatiently. 'Elena does not have a "small measure of affection" for you—'

'Good,' he grated through gritted teeth.

'—but instead, it's clear she feels emotions of the enduring and faithful kind,' his grandmother continued. 'No, you shall hear me out, Adam,' she added determinedly as he would have interrupted once more. 'Elena is not one of those flirtatious young débutantes who appear in society at the start of each new Season, but a poised young lady of almost one and twenty. Moreover, she is a young lady to whom life has dealt a harsh hand—'

'Which is why I have no intention of taking advantage of the gratitude she expressed to me when we last spoke together!' Elena's gratitude, whilst better than having her feeling nothing for him at all, was not enough for Adam. Not nearly enough!

Lady Cicely sighed deeply. 'It is my belief that gratitude is definitely not all she feels for you. Far from it! Oh, she has put a brave face on things these past few weeks, accepting all that Edith, Jocelyn and I have arranged for her, has been very gracious to all in society. But we are all three agreed, Elena cannot hide from us the fact that she searches for a particular face every time we attend a party or ball and that her disappointment is palpable when that face is never there.'

'And you believe that face to be my own…?' Adam was almost too afraid to believe what his grandmother was telling him, his own heart pounding furiously in his chest as she imparted this last piece of information to him.

'I know it is,' Lady Cicely stated positively.

'This is not another of your machinations to try to see me married again?' He eyed her suspiciously.

A delicate blush coloured her powdered cheeks. 'No, it is not,' she said huskily. 'My only wish has been to see you happy again, Adam.'

'I was not criticising, Grandmama, merely trying to ascertain whether or not this is all wishful thinking on your part.'

She met Adam's gaze unblinkingly. 'I assure you, it is not.'

Was it possible—could Elena really be missing him as much as he was missing her? Could she feel something more than gratitude for him, after all?

There was only one way for him to find out…

'Your hair is as dark and beautiful as a raven's wing.'

'You are too kind, Lord Randall,' Elena responded politely to the compliment as the two of them stood talking together at the musical soirée being given by his mother; it was Elena's usual response to the effusive praise and admiration which had been showered upon her over the last few weeks by so many of the eligible gentlemen of the *ton*.

It had been a very busy time for her, the mornings spent shopping for suitable gowns and other clothing considered necessary by Lady Cicely for her entrance into society, the evenings just as full and busy, Elena's popularity assured as she attended a different social occasion every evening, in the company of Lady Cicely, Lady Edith and Lady Jocelyn.

It should have been every young débutante's dream.

And yet…

There was something missing from Elena's life, an absence which had resulted in her feeling hollow inside, no matter how busy she was, or how effusive and genuine the gentlemen's compliments were.

Because those compliments were never given by the voice she ached to hear again. And the eyes, which gazed so admiringly into hers, were never of a soft dove grey. Nor were the hands, which lightly clasped hers in greeting or during a dance, ever the hands she longed to feel again.

Because they did not belong to Adam.

It was silly of her, Elena knew, to hunger for the sound, the sight, the touch, of a man who obviously had not given her a second thought since the evening of Neville's denouncement—yet she could not stop herself from doing so.

She longed to see Adam again, to speak with him—oh Lord, if she could just *see* him again! Just once—

'Lord Adam Hawthorne.'

'What the devil!'

Elena did not so much as spare another thought for Lord Randall, let alone have any interest in his sudden exclamation, as she instead turned sharply, as had all of the *ton*, to stare across to where Adam stood so tall and handsome in the doorway.

Her heart leapt with happiness at her first sight of him in weeks, that happiness glowing in her eyes as she drank in her fill of the man she knew she loved so deeply he seemed to have taken up residence in her heart, so that she could no longer see and think of anything but him.

Adam…

Adam paid not the slightest heed to the stunned silence which had fallen over the Countess of Livingstone's crowded salon after the butler had announced his presence. The *ton* were obviously extremely surprised to see him here, the first society function he had attended in the past four years, but Adam had eyes and ears for only one person in the room.

Elena.

Looking more wonderful, more beautiful than he had even imagined these past long weeks, in a gown of the softest turquoise, the darkness of her hair secured in a fashionable abundance of curls upon her crown, her eyes glowing that same deep, luminous turquoise as she gazed back at him in unadulterated pleasure.

Adam continued to meet that glowing gaze as, nodding tersely to his twittering hostess, he began to stride purposefully across the room to where Elena now stood alone, a blush in her cheeks and a welcoming smile parting those full and rosy-red lips by the time he reached her side.

They continued to drink their fill of each other with their eyes for several long, telling moments, totally unaware as the hushed conversation—speculative now—resumed around them.

'Elena—'

'Adam!'

They both began talking at the same time, only to both stop at the same time, too. Elena started chuckling, Adam joining in seconds later. 'Please tell me that I am not imagining your pleasure in seeing me again!' he urged gruffly.

She met his gaze unwaveringly. 'You are not.'

His breath left him in a relieved sigh. 'It is so very good to see you again, too, Elena.' His gaze roamed hungrily over her face. 'And looking every inch the much-praised and admired Miss Magdelena Matthews.'

Her smile faltered slightly. 'Thank you, but I—I—'

'Elena?' He looked at her concernedly as he reached out to grasp both her gloved hands in his own.

'I have missed you so, Adam!' The air seemed to be forced from her lungs. 'I—'

'I love you, Elena.' Adam could no longer bear to see that pained look in her eyes.

'You do?' Elena looked up at him wondrously.

'I should have told you before,' he confirmed huskily. 'But I did not want you to think—I could not bear to think that you might feel kindly towards me because you felt grateful for—for—' He shook his head, not wishing to talk of Neville Matthews's treatment of her now, or his own part in removing the bounder from her life once and for all time. 'And so I stayed away,' he continued determinedly. 'Wished for you to go out into the society to which you belonged, to find a more suitable gentleman to love you, to marry—' He ceased speaking as Elena released one of her hands to place gentle fingertips against his lips.

'I shall never marry, Adam.' Elena gave a sad shake of her head, her heart heavy.

'Why the hell not?' he demanded incredulously.

'We have never spoken of it openly but—you know the reason I can never marry, Adam!' Tears stung her eyes. 'I am no longer innocent!'

'That is not of your doing!'

She gave another despondent shake of her head. 'It does not matter whose fault it is.'

'Elena, I know what happened to you and it does not matter to me. You are everything that is good and beautiful, and—'

'And I shall never marry now,' she repeated firmly. 'Indeed, these past few weeks of missing you I have several times considered accepting the offer you once made for me to become your—'

'Do not say it!' Adam commanded. 'I must have been insane to have ever made you such an offer. I wish for you to be my wife, Elena, not my mistress.'

'You know I cannot.' Elena's heart felt as if it were breaking, as she listened to Adam tell her that he loved her, but knowing she could never be a proper wife to him. No matter how much she might long to be. 'Besides which, you do not intend ever marrying again, remember, and are quite happy for your third cousin Wilfred to inherit the title,' she reminded him in a broken attempt at teasing.

'To the devil with Wilfred!'

'People are staring, Adam,' she admonished softly, lashes lowering as she became aware of curious stares.

'Then let them stare!'

'Perhaps we should remove ourselves somewhere more private…?' Elena murmured.

Adam looked about them, conversation once again ceasing as he boldly met, and challenged, those curious stares, pausing briefly as he met that of his grandmother, before he turned back to a now white-faced Elena. 'I love you, Elena, dare I hope that you—could you ever love me in return?' he begged.

'I already love you. So very much, my darling Adam.' She looked up at him glowingly. 'More that words alone can ever express.'

Adam looked down at her hungrily for several long seconds, seeing that love for him blazing unconditionally in those beautiful turquoise eyes.

His fingers tightened about hers as he straightened to give her a respectful bow before dropping down on to one knee in front of her. She heard the gasps around them before the room once again fell deathly silent. Adam continued to look up at Elena as she stared down at him in shocked disbelief. 'I love you, Miss Magdelena Matthews, will you do me the honour of becoming my wife?' he spoke loudly enough for all in the room to hear.

The tears fell unchecked down Elena's cheeks as she continued to gaze down into the dear beloved face of the wonderful gentleman whom she loved with all of her heart. The same gentleman who had stated several times how much he hated any public display, that he never intended to marry again, but who was now on bended knee in front of her before many of the *ton*, as he asked her to become his wife.

And he asked in the full knowledge of what had been done to her. Indeed, he stated that her lack of innocence did not matter to him, that he loved her and wished to marry her.

Was it possible that she might accept? That she might

become Adam's wife, his to love, and for her to love him, for the rest of their lives?

She raised her eyes to look quickly across the room to where Ladies Cicely, Jocelyn and Edith stood together, three dear and beloved friends who knew all there was to know of her past, and whom Elena had come to deeply respect and love.

One by one they gave brief, approving nods, Lady Cicely's accompanied by a glowing smile.

'Elena, please…!' Adam encouraged hoarsely.

She turned back to him, her fingers tightening about his. 'I love you, Adam, and, yes, I will marry you—' She got no further as Adam rose swiftly to his feet before sweeping her up into his arms and kissing her with all the hunger and longing she could ever have wanted.

Chapter Eighteen

One day later—the London home of
Lady Cicely Hawthorne

'So, Edith, Adam is to marry Elena as soon as the banns have been read, which now leaves only Royston's future marriage to be settled.' Lady Cicely could not stop smiling, thinking about her own grandson's future nuptials.

'And only weeks of the Season left in which to do it,' Lady Jocelyn put in sympathetically.

'Plenty of time,' Lady Edith dismissed airily.

'And are you still of a mind that it will be to the lady whose name is written on the piece of paper you left in the care of Jocelyn's butler?' Lady Cicely looked doubtful.

'I am more certain of it than ever.' The dowager duchess gave an imperious nod of her regal head.

Eleanor—Ellie—Rosewood, stepniece and companion to the dowager duchess, and deeply in love herself with Justin St Just, felt her heart go cold at the determination she saw in that dear lady's face…

* * * * *

NOT JUST A WALLFLOWER

CAROLE MORTIMER

To Peter, the love of my life, for all of my life.

Chapter One

'You must be absolutely thrilled at the news of Hawthorne's forthcoming marriage to Miss Matthews!' Lady Jocelyn Ambrose, Dowager Countess of Chambourne, beamed across the tea table at her hostess.

Lady Cicely nodded. 'The match was not without its… complications, but I have no doubts that Adam and Magdelena will deal very well together.'

The dowager countess sobered. 'How is she now that all the unpleasantness has been settled?'

'Very well.' Lady Cicely smiled warmly. 'She is, I am happy to report, a young lady of great inner strength.'

'She had need of it when that rogue Sheffield was doing all that he could to ruin her, socially as well as financially.' Edith St Just, Dowager Duchess of Royston, and the third in the trio of friends, said, sniffing disdainfully.

Lady Jocelyn turned to her. 'How are your own plans regarding Royston's nuptials progressing, my dear?'

The three ladies, firm friends since their coming out together fifty years ago, had made a pact at the beginning of this Season, to see their three bachelor grandsons safely married, thereby ensuring that each of their family lines was secure. Lady Jocelyn was the first to achieve that success, when her grandson had announced his intention of marrying Lady Sylvianna Moreland some weeks ago, the wedding due to take place at the end of June. Lady Cicely had only recently succeeded in seeing her own grandson's future settled, his bride to be Miss Magdelena Matthews, granddaughter of George Matthews, the recently deceased Duke of Sheffield. It only remained for Edith St Just, the Dowager Duchess of Royston, to secure a future duchess for her own grandson, Justin St Just, the Duke of Royston.

Not an easy task, when that wickedly handsome and haughtily arrogant gentleman had avowed, more than once, that he had no intention of marrying until he was good and ready—and aged only eight and twenty, he had assured his grandmother that he did not consider himself either 'good' or 'ready' as yet!

'The Season will be over in just a few weeks…' Lady Cicely gave her friend a doubtful glance.

The dowager duchess nodded regally. 'And Royston will have made his choice before the night of the Hepworth ball.'

Lady Cicely gave a gasp. 'But that is only two weeks away!'

Edith gave a satisfied smile. 'By which time St Just will, I assure you, find himself well and truly leg-shackled!'

'You are still convinced it will be to the lady whom you have named in the note held by my own butler?' Lady Jocelyn also looked less than confident about the outcome of this enterprise.

At the same time as the three ladies had laid their plans

to ensure their grandsons found their brides that Season, the dowager duchess had also announced she had already made her choice of bride for her own grandson, and that Royston would find himself betrothed to that lady by the end of the Season. So confident had she been of her choice that she had accepted the other ladies' dare to write down the name of that young lady and leave it in the safe keeping of Edwards, Lady Jocelyn's butler, to be opened and verified on the day Royston announced his intention of marrying.

'I am utterly convinced,' Edith now stated confidently.

'But, to my knowledge, Royston has not expressed a preference for any of the young ladies of the current Season.' Lady Cicely, the most tender-hearted of the three, could not bear the thought of her dear friend being proved wrong.

'Nor will he,' the dowager duchess revealed mysteriously.

'But—'

'We must not press dear Edith any further.' Lady Jocelyn reached across to gently squeeze Lady Cicely's hand in reassurance. 'Have we ever known her to be wrong in the past?'

'No…'

'And I shall not be proved wrong on this occasion, either,' the dowager duchess announced haughtily, belied by the gleeful twinkle in faded blue eyes. 'Royston shall shortly find himself not only well and truly leg-shackled, but totally besotted with his future bride!'

An announcement, regarding this about the arrogantly cynical Duke of Royston which so stunned the other two ladies that neither of them felt able to speak further on the subject…

Chapter Two

Two days later—White's Club, St James's Street, London

'Is it not time you threw in your cards and called it a night, Litchfield?'

'You'd like it if I did so, wouldn't you, Royston!' The florid, sneering face of the man seated on the opposite side of the card table was slightly damp with perspiration in the dimmed candlelight of the smoky card room.

'I have no opinion one way or the other if you should decide to lose the very shirt upon your back,' Justin St Just, the Duke of Royston, drawled as he reclined back in his armchair, only the glittering intensity of his narrowed blue eyes revealing the utter contempt he felt for the other man. 'I merely wish to bring this interminable game of cards to an end!' He deeply regretted having accepted Litchfield's challenge now, and knew he would not have done so if he had not been utterly bored and seeking any diversion to relieve him from it.

Ennui. It was an emotion all too familiar to him since the fighting against Napoleon had come to an end and the little

Corsican had finally been incarcerated on St Helena once and for all, at which time Justin had considered it was safe to return to London, resign his commission, and take up his duties as Duke of Royston. A scant few weeks later he had realised his terrible mistake. Oh, he still had all of his friends here, the women willing to share his bed were as abundant, and his rooms in Mayfair were still as comfortable—he had long ago decided against taking up residence at Royston House, instead leaving his grandmother to continue living there alone after the death of Justin's father, and the removal of Justin's mother to the country—but all the time feeling as if there should be something…more to life.

Quite what that was, and how he was to find it, he had no idea. Which was the very reason he had spent the latter part of his evening engaged in a game of cards with a man he did not even like!

Lord Dryden Litchfield shot him a resentful glance. 'They say you have the devil's own luck, with both the cards and the ladies.'

'Do they?' Justin murmured mildly, well aware of the comments the *ton* made about him behind his back.

'And I am starting to wonder if it is not luck at all, but—'

'Have a care, Litchfield,' Justin warned softly, none of his inner tension in evidence at the as-yet-unspoken insult, as he reached out an elegant hand to pick up his glass and take a leisurely sip of his brandy. With his fashionably over-long golden hair, and arrogantly handsome features, he resembled a fallen angel far more than he did the devil. But regardless of how angelic he looked, most, if not all, of the gentlemen of the *ton* also knew him to be an expert with both the usual choices of weapon for the duel Litchfield was spoiling for. 'As I have said, the sooner we bring this card game to an end, the better.'

'You arrogant bastard!' Litchfield glared across at him fiercely; he was a man perhaps a dozen or so years older than Justin's own eight and twenty, but his excessive weight, thinning auburn hair liberally streaked with silver, brown-stained teeth from an over-indulgence in cheap cigars, as well as his blustering anger at his consistent bad luck with the cards, all resulted in him looking much older.

'I do not believe insulting me will succeed in improving your appalling skill at the cards,' Justin stated as he replaced his brandy glass on the table.

'You—'

'Excuse me, your Grace, but this was just delivered for your immediate attention.'

A silver tray appeared out of the surrounding smoke-hazed gloom, bearing a note with Justin's name scrawled across the front of it, written in a hand that a single glance had shown was not familiar to him. 'If you will excuse me, Litchfield?' He did not so much as glance in the other man's direction as he retrieved the note from the tray to break the seal and quickly read the contents before refolding it and placing it in the pocket of his waistcoat, throwing his cards face down on the table. 'The hand is yours, sir.' He nodded in abrupt dismissal, straightening his snowy white cuffs as he stood up to leave.

'Ha, knew you was bluffing!' the other man cried out triumphantly, puffing happily on his foul-smelling cigar as he scooped up Justin's discarded cards. 'What the—?' he muttered disbelievingly at a handful of aces as the mottled flush of anger deepened on his bloated face.

Dangerously so, in Justin's opinion; he had no doubt that

Litchfield's heart would give up its fight to continue beating long before the man reached his fiftieth birthday.

'The note was from a woman, then.' An even more pronounced sneer appeared on the other man's face as he looked up at Justin through the haze of his own cigar smoke. 'I never thought to see the day when the devilishly lucky Duke of Royston would throw in a winning hand of cards in order to jump to a woman's bidding.'

At this point in time 'the devilishly lucky Duke of Royston' was having extreme difficulty in resisting the urge he felt to reach across the card table, grab the other man by his rumpled shirtfront and shake him like the insufferable dog that he was! 'Perhaps it is her bedchamber into which I am jumping…?' He raised a mocking brow.

Litchfield gave an inelegant snort. 'No woman is worth conceding a winning hand of cards.'

'This woman is,' Justin assured him drily. 'I wish you joy of the rest of your evening, Litchfield.' With a last contemptuous glance, he wasted no more time as he turned to stride purposefully from the dimly lit room, nodding briefly to several acquaintances as he did so.

'Step aside, Royston!'

Justin's legendary reflexes allowed him to take that swift sideways step and turn all at the same time, eyes widening as he watched a fist making contact with the lunging and livid-faced Litchfield, succeeding in stopping the man so that he dropped with all the grace of a felled ox.

Justin's rescuer knelt down briefly beside the unconscious man before straightening, revealing himself to be Lord Bryan Anderson, Earl of Richmond, a fit and lithe gentleman of fifty years or so, the thickness of his hair prematurely white. 'Your right hook is as effective as ever, I see, Richmond,' Justin said admiringly.

'It would appear so.' The older man straightened the cuff of his shirt beneath his tailored black superfine as both men continued ignoring the inelegantly recumbent Litchfield. 'Dare I ask what you did that so annoyed the man?'

Justin shrugged. 'I allowed him to win at cards.'

'Indeed?' Richmond raised his brows. 'Considering the extent of his gambling debts, one would have thought he might have been more grateful.'

'One would have thought so, yes.' Justin watched unemotionally as the unconscious Litchfield was quietly removed from the club by two stoic-faced footmen. 'I thank you for your timely intervention, Richmond.'

'Think nothing of it, Royston.' The older man bowed. 'Truth be told, I perhaps enjoyed it more than I should have,' he added ruefully.

Justin knew, as did most of the *ton,* that the now-widowed Bryan Anderson had spent around twenty-five years tied to a woman who, following a fall from her horse during the first months of their marriage, in which she had received a severe blow to her head, had regressed to having the mind of a child and remained as such until her recent death.

Nor, despite having every reason to do so, had that gentleman ever betrayed his marriage vows. Publicly, at least. What Richmond did in private had been, and remained, his own affair, and would not have been frowned upon by the *ton* in any case; twenty-five years of marriage to a woman, who believed herself a child, must have been unendurable torture. No doubt the hours Justin knew the other man had spent sparring at Jackson's had been an attempt to alleviate some of his frustrations during that time.

As, in all likelihood, had striking Litchfield just now…

'I thank you anyway, Richmond.' Justin said, giving him a slight bow in acknowledgement. 'Now, if you will excuse me, I have another engagement.'

'Of course.' Richmond returned the gesture. 'Oh, and Royston…?' He gave him a significant look as Justin paused to raise questioning brows. 'If I were you, I would watch your back for the next few weeks where Litchfield is concerned; it would seem he is an even less gracious winner than he is a loser.'

Justin's top lip curled. 'So it would appear.'

Richmond nodded. 'I had the displeasure of serving in the army with him in India many years ago and know him to be a bully with a vicious temper. The men did not like him any more than his fellow officers did.'

'If that were the case, I am surprised one of them did not take steps to rid themselves of such a tyrant.' It was well known in army circles that the enlisted men—enlisted? Hah! They were usually men who had been forced into taking the king's shilling for one nefarious reason or another—occasionally chose to dispose of a particularly unpopular officer during the confusion of battle.

Richmond gave a rueful smile. 'That should have been the case, of course, and likely would have happened if he had lingered in the army overlong, but there was some indiscretion with another officer's wife, which caused his superior officer to see that he left India sooner rather than later.'

Justin studied the older man's bland expression for several seconds. 'And would that superior officer happen to have been yourself, sir?'

'It would,' Richmond said grimly.

'In that case I will bear your warning in mind,' Justin

said. 'I wish you a good night, Richmond.' He lost no more time in making his departure as he proceeded out into the hallway to collect and don his hat and cloak in readiness for stepping outside.

'Hanover Square, if you please, Bilsbury,' he instructed his driver tersely as he climbed inside the ducal coach and relaxed back against the plush upholstery, the door closing behind him seconds before the horses moved off smartly into the dark of the night.

If any woman was worth the loss of a fabulous hand at cards, then it was surely the one he now hurried to…

Miss Eleanor—Ellie—Rosewood paced restlessly in the vast entrance hall of the house in Hanover Square as she awaited for word of the response to the note she had instructed be delivered earlier this evening. Hopefully none of her inner anxiety showed on her face as she heard the clatter of horses' hooves on the cobbles outside, followed by a brief murmur of conversation. Stanhope moved forwards and opened the door just in time to allow the handsome Duke of Royston to sweep imperiously inside, bringing the cool evening air in with him.

As always happened, at first sight of this powerful and impressive gentleman, Ellie was struck momentarily speechless, as she could only stand and stare at him.

Excessively tall, at least a couple of inches over six feet, with fashionably ruffled hair of pure gold, Justin St Just's features were harshly patrician—deep blue eyes, high cheekbones aside a long and aristocratic nose, chiselled lips and a square, determined jaw—and his wide shoulders and tapered waist were shown to advantage in the black super-fine and snowy white linen, buff pantaloons and high black

Hessians fitting snugly to the long length of muscled calf and thigh; he was without doubt the most handsome gentleman Ellie had ever beheld—

'Well?' he demanded even as he swept off his cloak and hat and handed them to Stanhope before striding across the vast hallway to where Ellie stood at the bottom of the wide and curving staircase.

—as well as being the most arrogant—

She drew in a breath. 'I sent a note earlier this evening requesting that you call—'

'Which is the very reason I am here now,' he cut in.

—and impatient!

And considering that Ellie had sent the note over two hours ago, she found his delayed response to that request to be less than helpful! 'I had expected you sooner...'

He stilled. 'Do I detect a measure of rebuke in your tone?'

Her cheeks felt warm at the underlying steel beneath the mildness of his tone. 'I—no...'

He relaxed his shoulders. 'I am gratified to hear it.'

Her chin rose determinedly. 'It is your grandmother whom I believe may have expected a more immediate response from you, your Grace.' Indeed, that dear lady had been asking every quarter of the hour, since she had requested Ellie, as her companion, to send a note to her grandson, as to whether or not there had been any word from him. The duke's arrival here now, so many hours after the note had been sent, was tardy to say the least.

'This is my immediate response.'

She raised red-gold brows. 'Indeed?'

Justin looked at her as if seeing her for the first time— which he no doubt was; companions to elderly ladies were of no consequence to dukes!—his eyes glinting deeply blue between narrowed lids as that disdainful glance swept over her from the red of her hair, her slenderness in the plain brown gown, down to the slippers upon her feet, and then back up to her now flushed face. 'The two of us are related in some way, are we not?'

Not exactly. Ellie's mother had been a widow with a nine-year-old daughter—Ellie—when she had married this gentlemen's cousin some ten years ago. But as both her mother and stepfather had since been killed in a carriage accident, it rather rendered the relationship between herself and the duke so tenuous as to be practically non-existent. And if not for the kindness of his grandmother, the Dowager Duchess of Royston, in taking Ellie into her own household as her companion when she had been left alone in the world without a penny to call her own, Ellie very much doubted she would have seen any of the St Just family ever again following her mother's demise.

'We are stepcousins once removed, at best, your Grace,' she now allowed huskily.

He raised an eyebrow, the candlelight giving a gold lustre to his fashionably tousled hair, the expression in those deep-blue eyes now hidden behind those lowered lids. 'Cousin Eleanor,' he acknowledged mockingly. 'The fact of the matter is, I was not at my rooms when your note was delivered earlier this evening and it took one of my servants some time in which to…locate me.'

Justin had no idea why it was he was even bothering to explain himself to this particular young woman. She was only a distant relative by marriage. Indeed, he could not remember even having spoken to Miss Eleanor Rosewood before now. He had noticed her, of course—bored and cynical he might be, but he was also a man!

Her hair was an intriguing shade of red, despite attempts on her part to mute its fieriness and curl in the severity of its style. Her eyes were a stunning clear green and surrounded by thick dark lashes, freckles sprinkled the tops of her creamy cheeks and the pertness of her tiny nose, and her mouth—

Ah, her mouth… Full and pouting, and naturally the colour of ripe strawberries, it was far too easy for a man to imagine such a mouth being put to far better uses than talking or eating!

She was tiny in both stature and figure, and yet the fullness of her breasts, visible above the neckline of her plain and unbecoming brown gown, emphasised the slenderness of her waist and thighs, her hands also tiny and delicate, the fingers long and slender in wrist-length cream lace gloves.

Justin was well aware that his grandmother had lost no time in gathering this orphaned chick into her own household as her companion after Eleanor had been left alone in the world, following the death of her mother and stepfather, Justin's own profligate cousin Frederick; Edith St Just might like to give the outward appearance of haughtiness and disdain, but to any who knew her well, it was an outer shell which hid a soft and yielding heart.

'Your note implied the request was urgent in nature,' Justin now drawled pointedly.

'Yes.' Colour now warmed those creamy cheeks. 'I—the physician was called to attend the dowager duchess earlier this evening.'

'The physician?' he repeated sharply. 'Is my grandmother ill?'

'I do not believe she would have requested the physician be called if that were not the case, your Grace.'

Justin's eyes narrowed suspiciously as he privately questioned whether or not she was daring to mock him; the green of her gaze was clear and unwavering, with no hint of the emotion for which he searched. Which was not to say it was not there, but merely hidden behind that annoyingly cool façade. 'What is the nature of her illness?' he enquired coldly.

She shrugged. 'Your grandmother did not confide in me, sir.'

Justin barely restrained his impatience with her unhelpful reply. 'But surely you must have overheard some of her conversation with the physician?'

Her gaze lowered from his piercing one. 'I was not in the room for all of his visit—'

'Might I ask why the devil not?'

Eleanor blinked those long dark lashes as the only outward sign of her shock at the profanity. 'She asked that I collect her shawl from her private parlour. By the time I returned Dr Franklyn was preparing to leave.'

Justin's impatience deepened. 'At which time I presume my grandmother asked that I be sent for?'

She nodded. 'She also requested that you go up to her bedchamber the moment you arrived.'

A request this lady had obviously forgotten to relay to him until now. Because his arrival had diverted her from the task, perhaps…? It was a possibility he found as intriguing as he did amusing.

He nodded. 'I will go up to her now. Perhaps you would arrange for some brandy to be brought to the library for when I return downstairs?'

'Of course.' Ellie found she was relieved to have something practical to do, her usual calm competence seeming to have deserted her the moment she found herself in Justin's overpoweringly masculine presence. 'Do you wish me to accompany you?'

The duke came to a halt on the second step of the wide staircase in order to turn and give her a pointed look. 'I believe I am well aware of where my grandmother's bedchamber is located, but you may accompany me up the stairs, to ensure I do not attempt to make away with the family silver, if that is your wish.'

'Is that "family silver" not already yours?' she asked, trying hard to keep hold of her composure against his needling.

'It is.' He smiled briefly. 'Then perhaps you fear I may become lost in my own house, Cousin?'

Ellie was well aware that this was his house. As was everything connected with the Duchy of Royston. 'I believe my time might be better served in seeking out Stanhope and requesting the decanter of brandy be brought to the library.' Even the thought of accompanying the duke up the stairs was enough to cause Ellie's cheeks to burn—something she knew from past experience to be most unbecoming against the red of her hair.

'And two glasses.'

She raised surprised brows. 'You are expecting company?' The fact that the duke had been so difficult to locate this evening would seem to imply that he had been otherwise…occupied, and perhaps less than reputably. Even so, Ellie could not imagine him inviting one of his less-than-acceptable friends here, especially if he had been spending the evening in the company of a lady.

'It is you whom I am expecting to join me there,' he explained with a sigh.

Ellie's eyes widened. 'Me?'

Justin almost laughed at the stunned expression on her

face. A natural reaction, perhaps, when this was the longest conversation they had ever exchanged.

Surprisingly, he found her naivety amusing, and, Justin readily admitted, very little succeeded in amusing him.

His childhood had been spent in the country until the age of ten, when he had been sent away to boarding school, after which he had seen his parents rarely and had felt an exclusion from their deep love for each other when he did, to the extent that it had coloured his own feelings about marriage. He accepted that a duke must necessarily marry, in order to provide an heir to the duchy, but Justin's own isolated upbringing had dictated his own would be a marriage of convenience, rather than love. A marriage that would not exclude his children in the way that he had been excluded.

His three years as the Duke of Royston had ensured that he was denied nothing and certainly not any woman he expressed the least desire for—and, on several occasions, some he had not, such as other gentlemen's wives and the daughters of marriage-minded mamas!

Eleanor Rosewood, as companion to his grandmother, was not of that ilk, of course, just as their tenuous family connection ensured she could never be considered as Justin's social equal. At the same time, though, even that slight family connection meant he could not consider her as a future mistress, either. Frustrating, but true.

'Your Grace…?'

He frowned his irritation with her insistence on using his title. 'I believe we established only a few minutes ago that we are cousins of a sort and we should therefore address each other as Cousin Eleanor and Cousin Justin.'

Ellie's eyes widened in alarm at the mere thought of her using such familiarity with this rakishly handsome gentleman; Justin St Just, the twelfth Duke of Royston, was so top-lofty, so arrogantly haughty as he gave every appearance of looking down the length of his superior nose at the rest of the world, that Ellie would never be able to even think of him as a cousin, let alone address him as such.

'I believe that you may have implied something of the sort, yes, *your Grace,*' she said stubbornly.

He arched one blond brow over suddenly teasing blue eyes. 'But you did not concur?'

'I do not believe so, no, your Grace.'

He eyed her in sudden frustration. 'Perhaps it is a subject we should discuss further when I return downstairs?'

She frowned. 'I—perhaps.'

He scowled darkly at her intransigence. 'But again, you do not agree…?'

Ellie believed such a conversation to be a complete waste of his time, as well as her own. What was the point in arguing over what to call one another? They'd probably not speak to each other again for at least another year, if this past year—which consisted of this last few minutes' conversation for the entirety of it—was any indication! 'It is very late, your Grace, and I believe the dowager duchess, if she has been made aware of your arrival, will be becoming increasingly anxious to speak with you,' she prompted softly.

'Of course.' He now looked annoyed at having allowed himself to become distracted by talking to her. 'I will expect to find you in the library, along with the decanter of brandy and two glasses, when I return,' he added peremptorily before resuming his ascent of the staircase.

Almost, Ellie recognised indignantly, as if he considered her as being of no more consequence than a dog he might instruct to heel, or a horse he halted by the rein.

Chapter Three

'I must say, you took your time getting here, Royston.'

Justin, as was the case with most men, was uncomfortable visiting a sickroom, but especially when it was that of his aged grandmother, the dowager duchess being a woman for whom he had the highest regard and affection.

Tonight, the pallor of her face emphasised each line and wrinkle, so that she looked every one of her almost seventy years as she lay propped up by white lace pillows piled high against the head of the huge four-poster bed. A state of affairs that was not in the least reassuring, despite the fact that her iron-grey hair was as perfectly styled as usual and her expression as proudly imperious.

The St Justs, as Justin knew only too well, after learning of his grandfather's long and private struggle with a wasting disease, were a breed apart when it came to bearing up under adversity; his grandmother might only be a St Just by marriage, but her strength of will was equal to, if not more than, any true-born St Just.

He crossed the room swiftly to stand beside the four-poster bed. 'I apologise for my tardiness, Grandmama. I was not at home when Cousin Eleanor's note arrived—'

'If you lived here as you should that would not have been a problem,' she said querulously.

'We have had this conversation before, Grandmama. This is your home, not mine—'

'You are the Duke of Royston, are you not?'

Justin sighed. 'Yes, for my sins, I most certainly am.'

Edith eyed him disapprovingly. 'No doubt living here with me would put a dampener on your gambling or wenching—or both! Which diversion were you enjoying this evening to cause your delay?' She gave a disgusted sniff, but couldn't hide the twinkle in her eye.

Justin kept his expression neutral so as not to upset his grandmother; his reluctance to live at Royston House was due more to the fact that he associated this house with the frequent absences of his parents during his childhood, and his subsequent loneliness, than because he feared his grandmother would put a crimp in any supposed excesses of his in gambling and wenching, as she put it. As a consequence, he preferred to remain at the apartments he had occupied before the death of his father. 'I am sure this is not a suitable conversation for a grandson to be having with his aged grandmother—'

'Less talk of the aged, if you do not mind! And why should we not talk of such things?' She looked up at him challengingly. 'Do you think me so old that I do not know how young and single gentlemen of the *ton* choose to spend their evenings? Many of the married ones, too!'

'I believe I may only be called young in years, Grandmama,' he drawled ruefully; these past three years as the Duke of Royston, and the onerous responsibilities of that title, had required that Justin become more circumspect in his public lifestyle, and at the same time they had left him little or no time for a private life either.

Perhaps it was time he thought seriously of acquiring a permanent mistress, a mild and biddable woman who would be only too pleased to attend to his needs, no matter what the time of day or night, but would make no demands of him other than that he keep her and provide a house in which they might meet. It was an idea that merited some further consideration.

But not here and now. 'I did not come here to discuss my own activities, when it is your own health which is currently in question.' he changed the subject deftly. 'Cousin Eleanor has informed me that Dr Franklyn was called to attend you earlier this evening. What is the problem, Grandmama?'

'Might I enquire when you decided that Ellie is to be referred to as your cousin?' Edith raised those imperious grey brows.

'Ellie?'

'Miss Eleanor Rosewood, your Cousin Frederick's step-daughter, of course,' she supplied impatiently.

'I can hardly be so familiar as to address her as Ellie—a name I do not particularly care for, by the by—' Justin gave an irritated scowl '—when her mother, one supposes, bestowed upon her the perfectly elegant name of Eleanor. And Miss Rosewood is far too formal, in view of her connection to this family.'

'I agree.' His grandmother gave a haughty nod. 'And it is Ellie—Eleanor, whom I wish to discuss with you.'

Justin made no attempt to hide his astonishment. 'Are you telling me that you had me tracked down at my club, with all the fervour of a pack of hounds baying at the scent of fox—'

'Do not be melodramatic, Justin.' Edith eyed him with indulgent exasperation.

His brows rose. 'Do you deny having had a note delivered to my rooms late in the evening, one moreover that appeared to be of such vital urgency that my manservant instantly dispatched one of the other servants to track me down at one of my clubs?'

'I did instruct the note be written and delivered to you, yes. But it was not so late in the evening when I did so,' his grandmother added pointedly. 'Nor can I be held responsible for the actions of your manservant in dispatching a servant to seek you out so doggedly.'

Justin gave another scowl. 'But you do not deny that the reason for sending the note was so that you might bring me here simply in order to discuss your young companion?'

The dowager duchess sent him a reproachful glance. 'There is nothing simple about it, my dear. Ellie, and her future, have loomed large in my thoughts of late. Even more so this evening, when I am feeling so unwell—Justin, would you please refrain from pacing in that restless manner and instead sit down in that chair beside me? It is making my head ache having to follow your movements in this way.' She gave a pained wince.

Only one part of that statement was of any relevance to Justin at this particular moment. 'In what way are you feeling unwell?' He pounced on the statement, his expression distracted as he lowered his long length down into the chair beside the bed before reaching out to take one of his grandmother's delicately fragile hands into both of his.

Edith gave a weary sigh. 'I find I become very tired of late. An occurrence which has made me realise that—it has made me aware that I should have made much more of an effort to ensure that things were settled before now…' She gave another sigh, a little mournful this time.

Justin scowled darkly. 'Grandmama, if this is yet another way for you to introduce the unwelcome subject of my acquiring a duchess—'

'Why, you conceited young whippersnapper!' She gave him a quelling glance as she sat up straighter in the bed. 'Contrary to what you appear to believe, I do not spend the whole of my waking life thinking up ways to entice my stubborn and uninterested grandson into matrimony!' Then she seemed to collect herself and settled back once more on her pillows with another pained wince.

Justin gave a rueful shake of his head at hearing her berate him so soundly; not too many people would have dared speak to him like that and hope to get away with it! Oh, he was certain that many of the *ton* referred to him, behind his back, as being 'arrogantly haughty' or 'coldly disdainful', and even on occasion as being 'harsh and imperious' just like his grandmother was, but they would not have dared to do so to his face.

Not when they were sober, at least, Justin acknowledged derisively, as he thought of Litchfield's insulting behaviour earlier this evening. A rash and dangerous move on Litchfield's part, when Justin was acknowledged as being one of the finest swordsmen in England, as well as one of the most accurate of shots; no gentlemen would dare to talk to him in that way when they were sober, for fear they might incite—and subsequently lose—the duel that would undoubtedly ensue.

'I am glad to hear it,' he drawled in answer to his grandmother's comment. 'Pray, then, what are these "things", which need to be "settled", Grandmama?'

'Eleanor's future, of course.' She eyed him carefully, her gnarled fingers folding and then refolding the fine bedsheet beneath them. 'She is so very young, and has no other relatives apart from ourselves, and I cannot bear to think of what might become of her when I am gone.'

Justin tensed. 'When you are gone? Is there any likelihood of that happening in the near future?' he prompted sharply as he felt the slight trembling of the hand he still held in his own.

The fact that the love his parents shared had been exclusive and all-consuming, and not one which had allowed time or particular consideration for their only child, had, as a consequence, meant that it was Justin's paternal grandparents, Edith and George St Just, who were the constant influences in his life, and with whom he had chosen to spend the majority of his school holidays, as well as Christmas and birthdays.

'Doctor Franklyn is of the opinion that I am simply wearing out—'

'Utterly ridiculous!' Justin barked, sitting forwards tensely, blue gaze fierce as he searched the unusual delicate pallor of her face. 'He is mistaken. Why, you had tea with your two dear friends only a few days ago, attended Lady Huntsley's ball with them just yesterday evening—'

'As a consequence, today I am feeling so weak that I do not even have the energy to rise from my bed.'

'You have overtaxed yourself, that is all,' he insisted.

'Justin, you are no longer a child and, sadly, neither am I.' His grandmother gave another heavy sigh. 'And I cannot say I will not be pleased to be with your grandfather again—'

'I refuse to listen to this nonsense a moment longer!' Justin released her hand to stand up before glowering down at her. 'I will speak to Dr Franklyn myself.'

'Do so, by all means, if you feel you must, but bullying the doctor cannot make me any younger than I am,' Edith reasoned gently.

Justin drew in a sharp breath at the truth of that statement. 'Perhaps you might rally, find new purpose, if I were to reconsider my decision not to marry in the near future.'

'Generous of you, Royston.' She gave him an affectionate, understanding smile, which had the effect of shooting more fear into his heart than anything she might say considering she'd been so hell-bent on seeing him married off as soon as humanly possible. 'Unfortunately, the outcome would, I am sorry to say, remain the same.'

'I simply cannot accept that!'

'You must, Justin,' his grandmother chided gently. 'Gratified as I am to see how the thought upsets you, it is a fact of life that I cannot go on for ever. I should, of course, have liked to see you settled before my time comes, but I accept that is not to be…'

'I have already suggested I might give the matter of matrimony further consideration, if it would make you happy!' He scowled fiercely at the mere thought of it.

'You must, and no doubt will, do exactly as you wish. At the moment I am more concerned with my dear companion. I must know that Ellie—Eleanor's—future has been settled before I depart this world.'

'I would prefer that you not say that phrase again in my presence, Grandmama.' Justin had resumed his restless pacing, too agitated by his grandmother's news to be able to stand or to sit at her bedside any longer.

'Ignoring something will not make it go away, my dear,' Edith pointed out.

Justin was well aware of that, but even the thought of his grandmother no longer being here, gently chiding or sternly rebuking him for one misdemeanour or another, was anathema to him. She was only in her sixty-ninth year, and Justin had not so much as spared a thought for the possibility of her dying just yet; Edith St Just had been, and still was, the woman in his life on whom he had always depended, a woman of both iron will and indomitable spirit, always there, the steely matriarch of the St Just family.

'May we discuss Eleanor's future now, Justin?' Edith continued, uncharacteristically meek.

Eleanor Rosewood, and her future, were the last things that Justin wished to discuss at this moment, but a single glance at his grandmother's face was enough to silence his protests as he noticed once again how the paleness of her face, and the shadows beneath her eyes, gave her the appearance of being every one of those eight and sixty years.

He bit back the sharpness of his reply and instead resumed his seat beside the bed. 'Very well, Grandmama, if you insist, then let us talk of Cousin Eleanor's future.'

She nodded. 'It is my dearest wish to see her comfortably married before I dep—am no longer here,' she corrected at Justin's scowl.

He raised his brows. 'It seems to me that you appear to wish this dubious state upon all those close to you. I am heartily relieved it is not just me you have set your sights on.'

'Do not be facetious, Royston!' The dowager frowned. 'As I have already stated, you must do as you wish where your own future bride is concerned, but for a young woman in Ellie's position, marriage is the only solution.'

'And do you also have a gentleman in mind to become her husband? More to the point, does Cousin Eleanor have such a gentleman in mind?' He raised mocking brows.

His grandmother sighed. 'She has been so taken up with my own affairs this past year that I very much doubt she has given the matter so much as a single thought.'

'Then—'

'Which is not to say she should not have done so.' Edith frowned him into silence. 'Or that I should not have insisted she do so, before she is of an age that is considered as being unmarriageable.'

'Exactly how old is Cousin Eleanor?' Justin eyed his grandmother incredulously, thinking of the girl's fresh, dewy complexion and unlined brow.

'She has recently entered her twentieth year—'

'Almost ancient then!' he teased.

'I am being serious, Justin. A young woman of Ellie's meagre circumstances, if left alone in the world, will, as I am sure you are only too well aware, have very few opportunities open to her.' She arched a pointed brow.

Yes, Justin was well aware of the fate that often befell impoverished but genteel young ladies of Eleanor Rosewood's beauty and circumstance, being neither a part of society and yet not of the working classes either. 'And exactly what do you expect me to do about it? Settle some money on her as a dowry, perhaps, in order to entice a penniless young man of the clergy or some such into offering her marriage?' he suggested sarcastically.

'The dowry would certainly be a start.' His grandmother took his suggestion seriously as she nodded slowly. 'Heaven knows the Royston fortune is large enough you would not even notice its loss! But I do not see why Eleanor should have to settle for an impoverished clergyman. Surely, somewhere amongst your acquaintances, you must know of a titled gentleman or two who would willingly overlook her social shortcomings in order to take to wife a young woman of personal fortune, who also happens to be the stepcousin of the powerful Duke of Royston?'

Justin had meant to tease with his suggestion of a providing a dowry for Eleanor, but he could see by the seriousness of his grandmother's expression that she, at least, was in deadly earnest. 'Let me see if I understand you correctly, Grandmama. You wish for me to first settle a sizeable dowry upon your companion, before then seeking out and securing a suitable, preferably titled husband, for her amongst my acquaintances?' The suggestion was not only preposterous, but seemed slightly incestuous to Justin in view of his own less than cousinly thoughts about that young lady just minutes ago!

'I do not expect you to approach the subject quite so callously, Royston.' Edith eyed him impatiently. 'I am very fond of the gel and I should not like to see her married to a man she did not like, or whom did not like her.'

His brows rose. 'So you are, in fact, expecting me to secure a love match for her, despite her "social shortcomings" as you so tactfully put it.'

'A suitable marriage does not preclude the couple from falling in love with each other,' Edith snapped. 'Your grandfather and I loved each other dearly. As did your father and mother.'

Yes, and it was the example of that deep love his parents had for each other that had made Justin so leery of entering into matrimony himself; he could not bear even the thought of ever loving a woman so deeply, so intensely, that his own offspring suffered because of it.

He suppressed a shudder. 'I believe you may be expecting too much for Eleanor to secure such a love in her own marriage.'

'We will not know until you try,' his grandmother insisted.

'And how do you propose I go about doing that?' He gave a rueful shake of his head.

'As Ellie's closest male relative—yes, I know you're about to say that technically you're not really related to her at all—you might perhaps commence by accompanying her to—to a musical soirée or two, perhaps, in order that you might introduce her to these eligible if financially bereft young gentlemen of your acquaintance?'

'I—you expect me to attend *musical soirées?*' Justin stared at his grandmother incredulously as he once again rose to his feet out of sheer incapability to know what to do next; indeed, he was starting to feel like that toy he'd had as a child which had popped out of the box when the lid was lifted! 'I believe your current indisposition has addled your brain, Grandmama!' He shook his head. 'I do not attend music soirées or balls in the normal course of events, let alone with the intention of marrying off my young stepcousin to some unsuspecting gentleman!'

'But there is nothing to say that you could not make the exception in these special circumstances, is there?' she insisted defiantly.

'No, of course there is not. But—'

'It would make me very happy if you were to do so, Justin.'

He narrowed suddenly suspicious blue eyes on the supposedly frail figure of his grandmother as she once again lay back, so small and vulnerable-looking against those snowy white pillows. 'I thought it was Cousin Eleanor's happiness which was your first and only concern?'

'It is.' Edith's eyes snapped her irritation at his perspicacity. 'And I can think of no better way to secure that happiness than you publicly acknowledging Ellie as a favoured cousin.'

'A favoured cousin of such low social standing she has been in your own employ this past year,' he reminded her drily.

'I very much doubt that any of the *ton* would make the connection between that mousy young woman and Miss Eleanor Rosewood, the elegant and beautiful cousin of the Duke of Royston.'

He very much doubted the truth of that claim, in regard to the gentlemen in society, at least; he, for one, had certainly taken note of Eleanor's understated beauty!

'And even if they did,' Edith continued firmly, 'none would dare to socially cut or slight Ellie whilst she is seen to be under your protection.'

On that subject Justin did agree. But the cost to himself, of being forced into the tedium of attending what was left of the Season, was surely too much to expect of him? His grandmother did not seem to think so...

'I am to host the Royston Ball in four days' time and you are always gracious enough to make an appearance on that occasion,' his grandmother reminded him.

'The ball may have to be cancelled if you are still feeling so fatigued,' he said slyly.

'That will not happen during my lifetime!' the dowager duchess assured him imperiously. 'The Royston Ball has taken place for the past hundred years and this year shall be no different, not even if I have to spend the evening sitting in my Bath chair overseeing events,' she continued determinedly.

'And you seriously intend to introduce Eleanor into society that evening?'

She gave a haughty inclination of her head. 'As a guest in my home she will naturally attend.'

'And you expect me to act as her escort for the evening?'

'As her guardian, perhaps, which would be perfectly acceptable as you are her closest male relative.' She nodded briskly. 'It is also the perfect opportunity for Ellie to see and be seen by the *ton.*'

Justin had the uncomfortable feeling that somewhere in the course of this conversation he had not only been manipulated, but soundly outmanoeuvred. An unusual occurrence, admittedly, but somehow his grandmother seemed to have succeeded in doing so. He—

'There is one other subject upon which I shall require your assistance, my boy.'

He eyed the redoubtable old lady extremely warily now. 'Yes?'

'I believe it might be advisable, before any marriage were to take place, to attempt to ascertain the identity of Ellie's real father...'

Justin's eyes widened in shock. 'Her *real* father? Was that not Mr Rosewood, then?'

'As that gentleman had already been dead for a full year before Ellie was born, I do not believe so, no...' Edith grimaced.

This situation, one not even of Justin's own choosing,

suddenly became more and more surreal. 'And is Eleanor herself aware of that fact?'

His grandmother gave a snort. 'Of course she is not. I only discovered the truth of things myself when I had her mother investigated after that idiot Frederick ran off to Gretna Green so impetuously and married the woman.'

'So my stepcousin and ward is not only penniless, but is also a bastard—'

'Royston!'

Justin groaned out loud. 'And if I should discover that her real father is an unsavoury scoundrel fit only for the gutter?'

His grandmother raised imperious brows. 'Then you will do everything in your power to make sure that no one else is ever made privy to that information.'

'And how do you suggest I do that?'

'I have every confidence that you will find a way, Royston.' She smiled.

A confidence in his abilities which, in this particular instance, Justin did not share...

Ellie could not settle as she waited nervously for Justin to join her in the library. Even the warmth from the fire beside which she now sat, lit by Stanhope some minutes ago when he delivered the tray on which sat the two glasses and brandy decanter, did little to ease the chill of nervousness from her bones.

She had been in the dowager duchess's household for a year now and before this evening could have counted the number of words she had exchanged with the top-lofty Duke of Royston on the fingers of one hand. Nor had he ever deigned to address her by her given name until this evening.

Which was not to say Ellie had not been completely aware

of him, or that his full name was Justin George Robert St Just, the twelfth Duke of Royston—and a long list of other titles which escaped Ellie's memory for the moment. Aged nine years her senior, and so obviously experienced as well as worldly, the golden-haired, blue-eyed Justin St Just had also featured largely in every one of Ellie's romantic dreams, both day and night this past year, to a degree that she believed herself half in love with him already.

Which made awaiting his appearance in the library now even more excruciatingly nerve-racking. How embarrassing if she were to reveal, by look, word or deed, even an inkling of the sensual fantasies she had woven so romantically about the powerful and handsome duke! Fantasies that made Ellie's cheeks burn just to think of them as she imagined Justin returning her feelings for him, resulting in those chiselled lips claiming her own, those long and elegant hands caressing her back, before moving higher, to cup the fullness of her eagerly straining breasts—

'Your thoughts appear to please you, Cousin Eleanor...?'

Ellie gave a guilty start as she rose hastily from the chair beside the fireplace to turn and face the man whose lips and hands she had just been imagining touching her with such intimacy.

Justin did not at all care for the look of apprehension which appeared upon Eleanor Rosewood's delicately blushing face as she rose to gaze across the library at him. Apprehension, accompanied by a certain amount of guilt, if he was not mistaken. What she had to feel guilty about he had no idea, nor did he care for that look of apprehension either. 'Perhaps not,' he drawled as he stepped further into the room and closed the door behind him before crossing to where the decanter of brandy and glasses had been placed upon the desktop.

'I trust the dowager duchess is feeling better?'

As Justin's grandmother had elicited several promises from him before allowing him to leave her bedchamber, the condition of her health being one of them, he was not now at liberty to discuss the reason for Dr Franklyn's visit, with Eleanor or anyone else. That Justin would be having words with the good doctor himself was definite, but his grandmother had insisted that neither of her two close friends, or her companion, be made aware of the reason for her fatigue.

Justin schooled his features into an expression of amusement. 'She assures me she feels well enough to continue as usual with the Royston Ball to be held here in four days' time,' he answered evasively as he turned to carry the two brandy glasses over to where she stood so delicately pale beside the glowing fire.

She made no effort to take the glass he held out to her. 'I do not care for brandy, your Grace.'

'I have a feeling that tonight shall be the exception,' he said drily.

She blinked long silky lashes. 'It will…?'

'Oh, yes,' he said distractedly. The flickering flames brought out the red-gold fire in her hair, Justin noted admiringly as he placed the glass in her hand; she really did have the most beautiful hair, in a myriad of shades, from deep auburn to red and then gold. Her eyes were a bright green, the same colour as a perfect emerald, and surrounded by the longest silky black lashes Justin had ever seen. As for those freckles upon her creamy cheeks and nose…

Justin felt a sudden urge, a strong desire, to kiss each and every one of them! He determinedly brought those wayward thoughts to an abrupt end and his mouth compressed. 'My grandmother has requested that you…assist her in the matter of the ball.'

Her little pink tongue moved moistly across those full and pouting lips, making him shift uncomfortably. 'I am not sure what assistance I could possibly be in the planning of such a grand occasion, but I shall of course endeavour to offer the dowager duchess whatever help I am able.'

Justin gave her an amused look. 'You misunderstand, Cousin Eleanor—the assistance required of you is that you attend the Royston Ball.'

She nodded. 'And I have already said that I shall be only too pleased to help the dowager duchess in any way that I can—'

'You are to attend the ball as her guest—careful!' he warned as the brandy glass looked in danger of slipping from her fingers.

Ellie's fingers immediately tightened about the bulbous glass even as stared up at him in disbelief. Justin could not seriously be suggesting that she was to attend the ball as a member of the *ton,* was he?

The implacability of his expression as he looked at her down the long length of his aristocratic nose appeared to suggest that he was.

Chapter Four

'You may find a sip of brandy to be beneficial...'

Ellie was still so stunned that she obediently sipped her drink—and immediately began to choke as the fiery liquid hit and burned the back of her throat. A dilemma Justin immediately rectified by slapping her soundly upon her back.

Perhaps a little harder than was necessary?

Ellie shook her head as she straightened, her eyes watering, her face feeling hot and flushed as she spoke huskily, 'I have no idea what her Grace can be thinking! I could not possibly attend the Royston Ball as a guest.'

'My grandmother has decreed otherwise.'

As if that announcement settled the matter, Ellie realised dazedly. 'And what is your own opinion on the subject, your Grace?' she prompted, sure that he could not approve of such a plan as this.

He gave a shrug of those wide and muscled shoulders before drawling, 'I make it a point of principle never to disagree with my grandmother.'

Ellie knew that to be an erroneous statement from the

onset; if Justin listened without argument to everything his grandmother said to him, then he would have long since found himself married, with half-a-dozen heirs in the nursery! For Edith St Just made no secret of her desire to see her grandson acquire his duchess, and not long afterwards begin producing his heirs. A desire which Ellie knew he had successfully evaded fulfilling during this past year, at least.

Ellie looked up at him from beneath lowered lashes as she tried to gauge the duke's response to his grandmother's unexpected decision to invite her lowly companion to attend the prestigious Royston Ball. A fruitless task, as it happened, the blandness of Justin's expression revealing absolutely none of that arrogant gentleman's inner thoughts. Although Ellie thought she detected a slight glint of amusement in the depths of those deep blue eyes… No doubt at her expense, she thought irritably.

Ellie was not a fool and she might well consider herself half in love with Justin, and find him exciting in a forbidden way, but that did not preclude her from knowing he was also arrogant, cynical and mocking. Or that his mockery on this occasion was directed towards her.

She drew in a ragged breath in an attempt to steady herself. 'I shall, of course, explain to her Grace, first thing in the morning, exactly why it is I cannot accept her invitation.'

'And I wish you every success with that.' There was no mistaking the amusement this time in those deceptively sleepy blue eyes.

Deceptive, because Ellie was sure that nothing escaped this astutely intelligent man's notice! 'But surely you must see that it will not do?'

'I am not the one whom you will have to convince of that, Eleanor,' the duke pointed out almost gleefully, she thought crossly. 'My grandmother, once her mind is settled upon something, is rarely, if ever, persuaded otherwise.'

That might well be so—indeed, after this past year spent in that lady's household, Ellie knew for herself that it was!—but in this case it must be attempted. Only the cream of society was ever invited into the dowager duchess's home, to attend the Royston Ball or on any other social occasion, and Ellie knew that she was far from being that. Admittedly, her mother and father had been on the fringes of that society, her father because he was the youngest son of a baron. And although her mother had been merely a country squire's daughter, she had been elevated in society by her first marriage to the son of a baron, and again at the second marriage to the son of a lord, the dowager duchess's own nephew. Even so, Ellie's own place in society was precarious at best.

'Indeed, I see no reason why you should wish to do such a thing,' the duke continued. 'If my grandmother has decided that you are to be introduced to society, then you may be assured that none in society will dare to argue the point.'

'Even you?' she couldn't help asking, then flushed at her own temerity.

Justin frowned at this second attempt on Eleanor's part to ascertain his own views on the subject. Especially when he was now unsure of those views himself...

Admittedly, he had initially dismissed the very idea of her introduction into society, but second, and perhaps third thoughts, had revealed to him that it was not such an unacceptable idea as he had first considered. His grandmother's argument, in favour of doing so, in an effort to secure Eleanor a suitable husband, although a considerable inconvenience to himself, was perfectly valid. Most especially if Justin were to provide Eleanor with a suitable dowry, as his grandmother suggested he must do.

Eleanor was both ladylike in her appearance as well as her manner. The fact that she also happened to be impoverished should not prevent her from seeking the same happiness in the marriage mart as any other young lady of nineteen years.

There was that irritating question as to whom Eleanor's real father might be, of course, but Justin had his grandmother's assurances that Eleanor knew nothing of that, believing herself to be the daughter of Mr Henry Rosewood. And if Justin's investigations into that matter, at his grandmother's behest, should prove otherwise, then who needed to be any the wiser about it?

The father, perhaps, if he did not already know of his daughter's existence...

Only time, and investigation, would inform Justin as to whether or not the name of Eleanor's real father was of any relevance to this present situation.

His grandmother having elicited his next promise—that he would not speak to Eleanor on that particular subject either—Justin now turned to the reason for Edith's insistence on Eleanor's début into society. 'The dowager duchess has decided it is time for you to acquire a husband.'

Green eyes widened incredulously at his announcement, even as those creamy cheeks became flushed. With embarrassment? Or temper? Or perhaps excitement? He wished he knew.

Justin did not know her well enough to gauge her present mood, but he was certainly man enough to appreciate the added depth of colour to the green of her eyes, and the flushed warmth in those creamy cheeks, as well as the swift rise and fall of the full swell of her breasts. Indeed, if this young lady had been anyone other than his grandmother's protégée, then she would have been the perfect choice for the role of his mistress he had been considering earlier—

Justin called a sudden halt to his wandering thoughts. His grandmother's request had now placed him in the position of guardian to this particular young lady, and as Eleanor's guardian Justin would frown most severely upon any gentleman having such licentious thoughts, as his had just been, in regard to his own ward!

She drew in a deep breath, unwittingly further emphasising the fullness of those creamy breasts. 'I am sure I am very…gratified by her Grace's concern—'

'Are you?'

Ellie gave Justin a quick glance beneath lowered lashes as she heard the mocking amusement in his tone; grateful as she was to the dowager duchess for coming to her rescue a year ago, it had not been an easy task for Ellie to learn to hold her impetuous tongue, or keep her fiery temper in check, as was befitting in the companion of a much older lady and a dowager duchess at that, and they were faults her mother had been at pains to point out to Ellie on a regular basis when she was alive.

The duke's amusement, so obviously at her expense, which she once again saw in those intense blue eyes, was enough to make Ellie forget all of her previous caution, as she snapped waspishly, 'I am gratified to see that at least one of us finds this situation amusing and it is not me!'

'If nothing else, it has at least succeeded in diverting my grandmother's attention from my own lack of interest in the married state!' he lobbed back lazily.

Ellie eyed him in frustration. 'I am no more interested

in entering into marriage, simply because it's convenient, than you are!'

Her mother's marriage, to a youngest son, had resulted in Muriel Rosewood being left a virtually impoverished and expectant widow on Henry Rosewood's death, with only a small yearly stipend from the Rosewood family coffers, and no other interest in the widow and her daughter from that family, with which to support them.

Muriel's second marriage ten years later, to a rake of a man whom she did not love, but who offered her a comfortable home for herself and her young daughter, had not been a happy one. Far from it.

As a consequence, Ellie had decided that she would never marry for any other reason than that she loved the man who was to be her husband. Far better that she remain an old maid, she had decided, paid companion to the dowager duchess, or someone very like her, than that she should end up as unhappy as her mother before her, unpaid servant and bed partner of a man who did not love her any more than she loved him.

The duke chuckled huskily. 'My grandmother is not easily gainsaid.'

'You appear to have done so most successfully all these years,' Ellie pointed out smartly.

Justin gave an acknowledging inclination of his golden head at the hit. 'And with my grandmother's determined efforts now firmly concentrated upon your own marital prospects, my dear cousin, I fully admit I am hoping to continue that enviable state for several more years to come.'

She frowned. 'I do not have any "marital prospects"!'

'But you will have, once I have settled a sizeable dowry upon you.'

'A sizeable dowry!' Ellie repeated, staring up at him incredulously. 'And why, pray, would you wish to do that?'

He lifted a brow. 'Because it would make my grandmother happy if I did?'

Ellie continued to look up at him for several long seconds, a stare the duke met with unblinking and bored implacability. Bored?

So he found the idea of marrying her off, whether she wished it or not, whether she would be happy or not, to be not only amusing but boring as well?

And to think—to imagine that she had thought only minutes ago that she was in love with Justin St Just! So much so, that she had awaited with trepidation the announcement of his betrothal and forthcoming marriage to some beautiful and highly eligible young lady. Now she could not help but feel pity for whichever of those unlucky women should eventually be chosen as duchess to this arrogant man!

Indeed, as far as Ellie was concerned, Justin St Just had become nothing more than her tormentor, out to bedevil her with threats of arranging her marriage to a man she neither knew nor loved.

It could not be allowed to happen!

Except…Ellie had no idea how she was to go about avoiding such an unwanted outcome when the duke and the dowager duchess, both so imperious and determined, seemed so set upon the idea.

She placed her brandy glass down upon one of the side tables before commencing to pace the room, as she feverishly sought for ways in which she might avoid the state of an arranged, unhappy marriage, without upsetting the kind dowager duchess, or incurring the wrath of her devil of a grandson.

Justin replenished his brandy glass before strolling over to take a seat beside the warmth of the fire, observing Eleanor's agitated movements from between narrowed lids.

That she was displeased at the idea of an arranged marriage was completely obvious. A deep frown marred her brow as she continued to energetically pace the length of the library, which allowed Justin to appreciate the outline of her slender and yet curvaceous form in the plain brown gown and the creamy expanse of her throat above the swell of her breasts, as well as the fineness of those furiously snapping green eyes.

He couldn't help but wonder how much more beautiful she might look with that abundance of red curls loose about her shoulders and dressed in a clinging gown, or possibly a night rail, of deep green silk...

And to think he had been bored to the point of ennui earlier this evening!

Not so any longer. Now Justin felt invigorated, the future full of possibilities, as he considered the challenge ahead of him in procuring a suitable husband for the surprisingly feisty, and obviously unwilling, Miss Eleanor Rosewood.

He was not a little curious as to the reason for her obvious aversion to an arranged marriage, when, in Justin's experience, for the majority of the women of his acquaintance an advantageous marriage appeared to be their only goal in life.

Could it be—did Eleanor's tastes perhaps run in another direction entirely? No, surely not! It would be a cruelty on the part of Mother Nature if a woman of such understated beauty, and surprisingly fiery a temperament as Eleanor, was not destined to occupy the arms, the bed, of some lucky gentleman. In other circumstances, she would almost certainly have made the perfect mistress—

No, he really must not think of her in such terms. He must in future consider himself as purely a guardian where she was concerned.

Even if his extremely private inner thoughts strayed constantly in the opposite direction!

'Have you drawn any conclusions yet as to how you might thwart my grandmother's plans for your immediate future?' Justin teased after several long minutes of her pacing. 'If so, I wish you would share them with me, if only for my own future reference?'

Ellie came to an abrupt halt to glare across the library at the lazily reclining form of the relaxed duke, the glow from the flames of the fire turning his fashionably styled hair a rich and burnished gold, those patrician features thrown into stark and cruel relief, and causing Ellie's pulse to quicken in spite of herself.

The rapidity of her pulse, and sudden shortness of breath, told her that, although she now doubted herself in love with him any more, she was still not completely averse to his physical attributes, at least.

His arrogance and mockery, when directly aimed at her, as they now were, were something else entirely, the former frustrating her and the latter infuriating her.

She drew in a deep and steady breath before answering him. 'I do not see why I cannot, politely but firmly, inform her Grace of my feelings of aversion to an arranged marriage—you find something amusing in that approach?' she prompted sharply as he laughed out loud.

'Truth be told, I find it ridiculous in the extreme.' Justin flashed his even white teeth in an unsympathetic grin. 'My grandmother, as I am sure you are aware, has all the subtlety of a battering ram. That being so, I doubt your own feelings on the matter will even be considered. Nor will anything you have to say on the subject shake her unwavering certainty that she feels she knows what is best for you,' he added firmly as Ellie would have protested.

'Perhaps if you were to—no, I see that you are so entertained by the whole idea, you would not even consider coming to my aid!' Ellie eyed him in utter disgust as he continued to grin at her in that unsympathetic manner.

He eyed her mockingly. 'Perhaps if you were to tell me of the reasons for your reluctance in this matter, I'd feel more inclined to help you out?'

Ellie gave an impatient shake of her head. 'No doubt they are the same as your own. I could never marry anyone whom I did not love with the whole of my heart and who did not love me in the same way.'

All amusement fled as he stood up abruptly, his eyes now a cold and glittering sapphire blue. 'There you are wrong, Eleanor,' he rasped. 'My own feelings on that particular subject are in total opposition to your own,' he elaborated harshly as she raised questioning brows, 'in that I would never consider marrying anyone who declared a love for me, or vice versa.'

Ellie's eyes widened at his words and the coldness of the tone in which he said them. She had believed that the duke's aversion to marriage was because he had not yet met the woman whom he loved enough to make his duchess. His statement now showed it was the opposite.

Ellie could not help but wonder why...

She was aware, of course, that many marriages in the *ton* were made for financial or social gain, as her mother's had been to Frederick St Just. But often the couples in those marriages learnt a respect and affection for each other, and in some cases love itself. Again, that had not happened in her mother's case, her marriage to Frederick, an inveterate gambler and womaniser, tolerable at best, painful at worst, certainly colouring Ellie's own views on the subject.

But for any gentleman to deliberately state his intention of never feeling love for his wife, or to have her feel love for him, seemed harsh in the extreme.

And surely it was asking too much of any woman, if married to Justin St Just, not to fall in love with him?

Or perhaps the answer to his stated aversion to loving his future wife had something to do with why he could not initially be found earlier on this evening…?

Ellie knew that many gentlemen of the *ton* had mistresses, women society dictated they could never marry, but for whom they often held more affection than they did their wives. Perhaps he had such a woman in his life? A low-born woman, or possibly a married woman of the *ton,* whom he could never make his duchess, but for whom he had a deep and abiding love?

Yes, perhaps that was the explanation for his stated desire for a loveless marriage. 'Would such a situation not be unfair to your future wife?' she ventured softly.

He looked down the length of his nose at her. 'Not if she were made aware of the situation from the onset.'

She gasped. 'Surely no woman would accept a marriage proposal under such cold and unemotional conditions?'

He gave her a pitying smile. 'It has been my experience that most, if not all women, would maim or kill in order to marry a duke and love be damned.'

'But—'

'The hour grows late, Eleanor, and I believe we have talked on this subject long enough for one evening.' Justin abruptly placed his empty brandy glass down upon the mantelpiece before turning away, no longer in the least amused by this conversation. 'If I might ask that you send word to me tomorrow regarding my grandmother's health?'

'I—of course, your Grace.' Eleanor seemed momentarily disconcerted by the abrupt change of subject. 'Hopefully I might also be able to inform you of her change of mind in regard to my attending the Royston Ball.'

Justin grimaced. 'You are an optimist as well as a romantic, I see.'

A faint flush darkened her cheeks even as she raised her chin proudly. 'I would hope I am a realist, your Grace.'

He gave a slow shake of his head. 'A realist would know to accept when she is defeated.'

'A realist would accept, even with your generous offer of providing me with a dowry, that I am not meant to be a part of society. Indeed,' she continued firmly as he would have spoken, 'I have no ambitions to ever be so.'

Justin raised his brows. 'You consider us a frivolous lot, then, with nothing to recommend us?'

He found himself the focus of dark-green eyes as Eleanor studied him unblinkingly for several seconds before giving a brief, dismissive smile. 'There is no answer I could give to that question which would not result in my either insulting you or denigrating myself. As such, I choose to make no reply at all.'

It was, Justin realised admiringly, both a clever and witty answer, and delivered in so ambiguous a tone as to render it as being at least one of the things she claimed it was not meant to be!

Again he found himself entertained by this surprisingly outspoken young woman, to appreciate why his grandmother was so fond of her; Edith St Just did not suffer twittering fools any more gladly than he did himself.

He gave her a courtly bow. 'I greatly look forward to being your escort to the Royston Ball.' And it was true, Justin realised with no little surprise; it was diverting, to say the least, to anticipate what this young woman might choose to do or say next!

Her eyes widened in alarm. 'My escort?'

He shot her a disarming grin. 'Another request from my grandmother.'

'But why should I be in need of an escort, when I already reside here?'

Justin smiled. 'Because a single lady, appearing in society for the first time, must be accompanied by her nearest male relative and guardian, and it appears I have that honour.'

Panic replaced the alarm in those deep-green eyes. 'Everyone would stop and stare, and the ladies would gossip speculatively behind their fans if I were to enter the ballroom on the arm of the Duke of Royston!'

'I believe that to be the whole point of the exercise, Cousin.'

'No.' Eleanor gave a decisive shake of her head, several red curls fluttering loosely about her temples as she did so. 'If I am to be forced to attend, as you believe I will be, then I absolutely refuse to make such a spectacle of myself.'

He raised haughty brows. 'Even though *you* will have the honour of being the first young woman whom the Duke of Royston has ever escorted anywhere?'

She looked startled for a moment, but recovered quickly. 'That only makes me all the more determined it shall not happen.'

Justin's smile widened at her stubborn optimism. 'I do

not believe there is any way in which you might prevent it—other than your possibly falling down the stairs and breaking a leg before then!' He laughed in earnest as he saw by Eleanor's furrowed brow that she was actually giving the suggestion serious consideration. 'Would it really be such a bad thing to be seen entering the ballroom on my arm, Eleanor?' he chided softly as he crossed the room to stand in front of her. 'If so, then you are not in the least flattering to a man's ego.'

'I do not believe your own ego to be in need of flattery,' Ellie murmured huskily, totally disconcerted by Justin's sudden and close proximity. Indeed, she could feel the warmth of his breath ruffling those errant curls at her temple.

'No?' Long lean fingers reached up to smooth back those curls, the touch of his fingers light and cool against the heat of her brow.

Ellie swallowed before attempting an answer, at the same time inwardly willing her voice to sound as it normally did. 'How can it, when you are the elusive but much-coveted prize of the marriage mart?'

She sounded only a little breathless, she realised thankfully, at the same time as she knew her disobedient knees were in danger of turning to water and no longer supporting her.

'Am I?' A smile tilted those sculptured lips as those lean fingers now trailed lightly down the warmth of her cheek.

Her throat moved as she swallowed before answering. 'Elusive or much coveted?'

'Either.'

Ellie found she was having trouble breathing as his fingers now lingered teasingly close to, but did not quite touch, the fullness of her lips. Suddenly she possessed both dry lips and a throat she necessarily had to moisten before attempting to speak again. 'This is a ridiculous conversation, your Grace.'

'Ah, once again you seek to put me firmly in my place with the use of formality,' he murmured admiringly.

'I do no such thing!' Ellie attempted to rally her indignation—not an easy task when the soft pad of the duke's thumb was now passing lightly across her bottom lip, and sending rivulets of excitement to the tips of her breasts and an unaccustomed warmth to gather between her thighs. 'Your Grace—'

'Justin,' he correct softly. 'Or Cousin Justin, if you prefer.'

'I do not,' she stated firmly, knowing that if she did not stop his teasing soon she would end up as a boneless puddle at his highly polished, booted feet. 'It is late, and I— Perhaps there is some—someone anxiously awaiting your returning to her tonight?'

He stilled as those narrowed blue eyes moved searchingly over her flushed face. 'You implied something similar when I arrived earlier tonight…'

'Your Grace?'

'It becomes more and more obvious to me that you, like my grandmother, believe my delay in arriving here this evening to be because I was in the arms of my current mistress,' he said speculatively.

Ellie felt her cheeks flush even warmer, no doubt once again clashing horribly with the red of her hair, as well as emphasising the freckles across her cheeks and nose that had long been the bane of her life. 'I am not in the least interested as to the reason for the delay in your arrival—'

'Oh, but I think you are, Eleanor,' he contradicted softly. 'Very interested.'

She gave a pained frown as she looked up into those intent blue eyes and decided she had suffered quite enough of this gentleman's teasing for one evening. 'Is your conceit so great that you believe every woman you meet must instantly fall under the spell of your charm?'

'Not in the least.' Those blue eyes now twinkled down at her merrily. 'But it is gratifying to know that you at least find me charming, Eleanor—'

'What I *believe,* your Grace, is that you are a conceited ass—' She fell abruptly silent as Justin lowered his head and bit lightly, reprovingly, on her bottom lip.

Ellie stiffened as if frozen in place and her heart seemed to cease beating altogether as she acknowledged that the coldly arrogant Duke of Royston, the mockingly handsome Justin St Just, had just run the moistness of his sensuous tongue over her parted lips...

Chapter Five

Justin knew, almost the instant he began to gently nibble on the enticing fullness of Eleanor's bottom lip, tasting her heady sweetness against the sweep of his tongue, that he had made a mistake. A mistake of monumental proportions.

Admittedly he had been intrigued by that plump curve for some time now and had wondered at the depth of sensuality it implied, but to have acted upon that interest, given that his grandmother had so newly appointed him Eleanor's unofficial guardian, was unacceptable. To himself as well as it must be to Eleanor. Indeed, she appeared to be so horror-struck by his advances that she stood in front of him as still, and as cold, as the statue she now resembled.

Justin pulled back abruptly, his hands grasping the tops of her arms as he placed her firmly away from him, at the same time unable to stop himself from noticing that her lip was a little swollen from where his teeth had seconds ago nibbled upon it. 'Perhaps, in future, it would be as well if you desisted from challenging me by insulting me?' he added harshly in a desperate attempt to divert her attention away from his despicable behaviour.

'You—I—' Ellie gasped her indignation, eyes wide and accusing at the unfairness of being blamed for his shockingly familiar behaviour. She now wrenched completely out of his grasp to glare up at him. 'You are worse than conceited, sir! You are nothing more than—'

'Yes, yes,' he dismissed in a bored voice, knowing he had to carry on now as he had started. 'I have no doubt I am a rake and a cad, and many other unpleasant things, in your innocent eyes.' He eyed her mockingly as he straightened the lace cuffs of his shirt beneath his jacket. 'You will need to be a little more subtle, my dear, if you are to learn to rebuff the advances of the gentlemen of the *ton* without also insulting them.'

'And why should I care whether they feel insulted, if they have dared to take the same liberties you just did?' Ellie asked scornfully.

'Because it is part of the game, Eleanor,' he explained, hoping she would believe him.

She stilled, eyes narrowed. 'Game...?'

He gave a slight inclination of his head. 'How else is a man to know whether or not he likes a woman enough to marry her, let alone bed her, if he does not first flirt with her and take a liberty or two?'

She breathed shallowly. 'You are saying that you—that your reason for—for making love to me just now was your way of preparing me for the advances of other gentlemen?'

He raised a golden brow at her comment. 'A mere taste of your lips cannot exactly be called lovemaking, Eleanor.'

Her cheeks flushed. 'You will answer the question!'

He shrugged wide, indifferent shoulders. 'Are you now prepared?'

Was Ellie 'prepared' for the assault upon her senses that had resulted when he had nibbled upon, and tasted, her lips? Could anything have 'prepared' her for having her heart stop beating as it leapt into her throat? For the aching heat that had suffused her body? For the way her legs had turned to jelly, threatening to no longer support her? For the thrill of the excitement that had run so hotly through her veins!

And all the time she had been feeling those things he had merely been 'preparing' her for the advances of the other gentlemen of society...

She straightened, her shoulders back, chin held proudly high. 'I am "prepared" enough to know I shall administer my knee to a vulnerable part of any gentleman's anatomy should he ever attempt to take such liberties with me!'

The duke gave a pained wince. 'Then my time with you this evening has not been wasted.'

Had there ever existed a gentleman as arrogant, as insufferable, as this particular one had just proved to be? Somehow Ellie doubted it. Nor did she intend to suffer his company this evening for one minute longer!

She stepped back, her gaze cool. 'I believe it time that I went upstairs and checked upon the dowager.'

Blond brows rose in disbelief. 'Are you *dismissing* me, Eleanor?'

Her mouth set stubbornly as she refused to be cowed by his haughty arrogance. 'Did it sound as if I were?'

'Yes.'

She gave a small smile of her own. 'Then that is what I must have been doing.'

Justin gave a surprised bark of laughter at the same time

as he cursed the fact that he had realised only this evening that he found this particular young woman so damned entertaining. It was, to say the least, inconvenient, if not downright dangerous, to his peace of mind, if nothing else. As he had realised when he had kissed her just now. A mistake on his part, which Justin had felt it necessary to explain by dismissing it as a lesson for Eleanor's future reference—even if the lesson *he* had learnt had been not to kiss her again. 'I am a duke, Eleanor, you are an impoverished stepcousin; as such it is not permissible for you to dismiss me.'

She raised auburn brows. 'Another lesson in social etiquette, your Grace?'

Gods, this woman had enough pride and audacity to tempt any man— Justin brought those thoughts to an abrupt halt, a scowl darkening his brow as he looked down at her between narrowed lids. 'One of many ahead of me, I fear,' he taunted. 'Your social skills appear to have been sadly neglected, my dear.' And he, Justin acknowledged bleakly, would have to take great care in future not to 'enjoy' those lessons too much!

Colour blazed in Eleanor's cheeks at his deliberate insult. 'I assure you that I am perfectly well aware of how to behave in the company of both ladies and gentleman without your help, sir.'

'Your implication being that you do not consider me as being one of the latter?'

There was no missing the dangerous edge to his tone now, and Ellie—in keeping with her changed circumstances in life a year ago—wisely decided to heed that warning. This time. 'There was no implication intended, your Grace. Now, if you will excuse me…' She gave a brief curtsy before crossing to the library door.

'And if I do not excuse you?'

Ellie came to an abrupt halt, her heart pounding loudly in her chest, the hand she had raised to open the door trembling slightly as she turned to face Justin. 'Do you have something more you wished to say to me tonight, your Grace?'

What Justin 'wished' to do at this moment was place this determined but politely rebellious young lady across his knee and administer several hard slaps to her backside; indeed, he could not remember another woman infuriating him as much as this one did—or who tempted him to kiss her as much as this one did either, and all without too much effort on her part, it seemed. 'You will remember to send word to me concerning my grandmother's health,' he commanded instead.

'I have said I will, your Grace.' She gave another cool inclination of her head. 'Will that be all?'

Justin's hands clenched at his sides as he resisted the impulse he felt to reach out and clasp her by the shoulders before soundly shaking her. After which he would probably be tempted into pulling her into his arms and kissing her once again. And heaven—or more likely hell—only knew where that might lead! 'For now,' he bit out between clenched teeth.

She turned and made good her escape, closing the library door softly behind her.

Leaving Justin with the unpleasant knowledge that he might have given his grandmother's companion little thought until this evening—apart from noticing those kissable lips and the tempting swell of her breasts like any other red-blooded male would!—but he was now far too aware of the physical attributes, and the amusement to be derived from the sharp tongue, of one Miss Eleanor Rosewood.

* * *

'Would you care to explain to me exactly why it is I am out riding with you in the park this afternoon, your Grace, chaperoned by her Grace's own maid…' Ellie glanced back to where poor Mary was currently being bounced and jostled about in the dowager duchess's least best carriage '…when I am sure my time might be better occupied in helping her Grace with the last-minute preparations for the Royston Ball later this evening?' She shot the duke a questioning glance as she rode beside him perched atop the docile chestnut mare he had requested be saddled for her use.

His chiselled lips were curved into a humourless smile, blue eyes narrowed beneath his beaver hat, his muscled thighs, in buff-coloured pantaloons, easily keeping his own feisty mount in check, so that he might keep apace with her much slower progress as the horses walked the bridal-path side by side. 'I believe you are riding with me in the park because it is my grandmother's wish to incite the *ton*'s curiosity by allowing you to see and be seen with me before this evening.'

Ellie shot him a curious glance. 'And what of your own wishes? I am sure that you can have no real interest in escorting me for a ride in the park?'

Justin bit back his irritated reply, aware as he was that Eleanor was not the cause of his present bad temper. He had spent much of his time these past three days hunting down Dr Franklyn, determined as he was to learn the full nature of his grandmother's ill health and what might be done about it.

To his deep irritation, the physician, once found, had been adamant about maintaining his doctor/patient confidentiality. A determination that neither the threats of a duke, nor the appeal of an affectionate grandson, had succeeded in moving. Nor had he been in the least comforted by Dr Franklyn's answer, 'We all die a little each day, your Grace', when Justin had questioned him as to whether or not the dowager duchess was indeed knocking at death's door.

The physician's professionalism was commendable, of course—with the exception of when, as now, it was in direct opposition to Justin's own wishes. As a consequence, he had left the physician's rooms highly frustrated and none the wiser for having visited, and spoken with, the good Dr Franklyn.

His evenings had been no more enjoyable, spent at one gaming hell or another, usually with the result that he had arrived back at his rooms in the late hours or early morning, nursing a full purse, but also a raging headache from inhaling too much of other gentlemen's cigar smoke and drinking far too much of the club's brandy. Last night had been no exception, resulting in Justin having risen only hours ago from his bed. He had then had to rush through his toilet in order that he might be ready to go riding in the park with Eleanor at the fashionable time of five o'clock.

An occurrence which had made him regret ever having agreed to his grandmother's request today. 'My own wishes are unimportant at this time,' he dismissed flatly.

Eleanor eyed him with a slight frown. 'I had thought her Grace seems slightly improved these past few days?'

Justin gave her a rueful glance, having no intention of discussing his grandmother's health with this young woman, or anyone else. 'You believe my grandmother's possible ill health to be the only reason I would have consented to ride in the park with you?'

Eleanor shrugged slender shoulders, her appearance thoroughly enchanting today in a fashionable green-velvet riding habit and matching bonnet, the red of her curls peaking enticingly from beneath the brim of that bonnet. 'You obviously have a deep regard for your grandmother's happiness, your Grace.'

'But I have no regard for your own happiness, is that what you are saying?'

Ellie avoided that piercing blue gaze. 'I do not believe anyone actually enquired as to whether or not I wished to go riding in the park with you, no...'

'Then I shall enquire now,' the duke drawled as some of the tension seemed to ease from those impossibly wide shoulders shown to advantage in the cobalt-blue riding jacket. 'Would you care to go riding in the park with me this afternoon, Miss Rosewood?'

Ellie had tried in vain these past three days to persuade the dowager duchess into changing her mind about Ellie attending the Royston Ball, or accepting Justin St Just as her escort for that evening.

Having failed miserably in that endeavour, Ellie had then been forced to spend much of those same three days being pushed and prodded and pinned into not only the velvet riding habit she wore today, but also several new gowns, one of which she was to wear to attend the Royston Ball this evening. Tediously long hours when the poor seamstress had been requested to return again and again by the dowager duchess, in order that the fit of Ellie's new gowns should meet the older lady's exacting standards.

As a consequence, Ellie would much rather have spent the day of the ball composing herself for this evening, than putting herself through the equally unpleasant ordeal of first riding in the park with the arrogantly indifferent, and highly noticeable Duke of Royston. Especially when his taciturn mood and scowling countenance showed he was obviously as reluctant to be here as she was!

'No, I would not,' she now answered him firmly.

Once again Justin found it impossible not to laugh out loud at her honesty. 'Even though, as I have previously stated, it is well known amongst the *ton* that I never escort young ladies, in the park or anywhere else?'

'Even then,' she stated firmly. 'Indeed, I do not know how you manage to stand all the gawking and gossiping which has taken place since we arrived here together.'

Justin raised surprised brows as he turned to look about them. Having been lost in his own sleep-deprived drink-induced misery until now, he had taken little note of any interest being shown in them.

An interest that became far less overt when openly challenged by his icy-blue gaze. 'Ignore it, as I do,' he advised dismissively as he turned back to the young woman riding beside him.

Green eyes widened in the pallor of Eleanor's face. 'I find that somewhat impossible to do.'

'Perhaps a compliment or two might help divert you?' he mused. 'I should have told you earlier what a capable horse-woman you so obviously are.' Far too accomplished for the docile mount he had allocated to her. A horse, Justin now realised, whose chestnut coat was very similar in colouring to the red of her hair.

'Are you so surprised?' she taunted before giving him a rueful smile. 'My stepfather, your own cousin Frederick, may have been offhand in his attentions, but he possessed an exceptionally fine stable, which he regularly allowed me to use.'

Justin's gaze narrowed. '"Offhand in his attentions"…?' he repeated slowly. 'Was Frederick an unkind stepfather to you?'

'Not at all.' Eleanor gave a reassuring shake of her head. 'He was merely uninterested in either my mother's or my own happiness once his interest in bedding my mother had waned.'

'Eleanor!'

She shrugged. 'It is not unusual amongst the gentlemen in society to marry for lust, I believe.'

'No,' Justin acknowledged abruptly. 'And you are saying that Frederick married your mother for just that reason?'

Eleanor nodded. 'So she explained to me when I had attained an age to understand such things, yes. Frederick married my mother because he desired her, my mother married him in order to secure the future for both herself and her daughter. Once Frederick's desire for her faded, as it surely must have without the accompaniment of love—' she grimaced '—it was not a particularly happy marriage.'

Justin began to understand now Eleanor's own aversion to a marriage without love. How ironic, when his parents' exclusive love for each other had determined his own aversion to a marriage *with* love.

Ellie was unsure as to the fleeting emotions that had settled briefly on the duke's harshly etched features, before as quickly being dismissed in favour of him looking down the length of his nose at her with his usual haughty arrogance. 'Will your own mother be attending the ball this evening?' she prompted curiously, not having met Rachel St Just as yet.

Her son scowled darkly. 'My mother never leaves her country estate.'

'Never?'

'Never.'

He answered so coldly, so uncompromisingly, it was impossible for Ellie not to comprehend that his mother was a subject he preferred not to discuss. Not that she was going to let that stand in her way! 'Was your own parents' marriage an unhappy one?'

'Far from it,' he rasped. 'They loved each other to the exclusion of all else,' he added harshly.

To the exclusion of their only child? she pondered, slightly shocked. And, if so, did that also explain his own views on the married state? It was—

'Good Gad, Royston, what a shock to see your illustrious self out and about in the park!'

Ellie forgot her musings as she turned to look at the man who so obviously greeted the duke with false joviality. A gentleman who might once have been handsome, but whose florid face and heavy jowls now rendered him as being far from attractive, and his obesity was obviously a great trial to the brown horse upon which he sat.

'No more so than you, Litchfield,' Justin answered the other man languidly, causing Ellie to look at him searchingly before turning her attention back to the man he had addressed simply as Litchfield.

As if sensing Ellie's curiosity, the older man turned to return her gaze before his pale hazel eyes moved from her bonneted head to her booted feet, and then back again, with slow and familiar deliberation. 'Perhaps it is your charming companion we have to thank for your presence here today?' he suggested admiringly.

Justin's tightened. 'Perhaps.'

The other man raised pepper-and-salt brows. 'Not going to introduce us, Royston?'

'No.' The duke's steely gaze was uncompromising.

The other man's pale eyes, neither blue nor green nor brown, but a colour somehow indiscriminately between them all, returned to sweep over Ellie with critical assessment. 'You seem somewhat familiar, my dear. Have we met before?'

'I am sure I should have remembered if we had,' Ellie replied ambiguously.

Litchfield turned to grin at Justin. 'She's a beauty, I grant you that,' he drawled appreciatively.

Ellie might be slightly naïve herself when it came to the subtleties of society, but even so she was perfectly well aware that this Litchfield was, in fact, challenging the duke and he was using her as the means with which to do it. 'You are too kind, sir.' She gave Litchfield a bright and meaningless smile. 'If you will excuse us now? We were about to leave.'

'Indeed?' Litchfield gave her a leering smile, revealing uneven and brown-stained teeth in his unpleasantly mottled face, wisps of auburn hair, liberally streaked with grey, peeping out from beneath his hat and brushing the soiled collar of his shirt.

'Indeed,' Ellie confirmed coolly.

'If you would care to…ride, another afternoon, then I should be only too pleased to offer my services as…your escort. You have only to send word to my home in Russell Square. Lord Dryden Litchfield is the name.'

The man's familiar manner and address, considering the two of them had not so much as been formally introduced—deliberately so, on Justin's part?—were such that even Eleanor recognised it as being far from acceptable in fashionable circles. As she also recognised that Lord Litchfield was far from being a gentleman. Which begged the question as to how Justin came to be acquainted with such an unpleasant man.

'I will join you shortly, Eleanor,' Justin bit out harshly.

'Your Grace?' she said in surprise as, having turned her horse back in the direction they had just come, she now realised he had made no effort to accompany her, the two men currently seeming to be engaged in an ocular battle of wills.

A battle of wills she had no doubt the duke would ultimately win, but it was one which Ellie would prefer not take place at all; not only would it be unpleasant to herself, but she very much doubted the dowager duchess would be at all pleased to learn that Ellie had been present during an altercation in the park between her grandson and another gentleman.

Justin's hands tightly gripped the reins of his restive black horse as he continued to meet Dryden Litchfield's insolently challenging gaze. 'You will wait for me by the carriage, Eleanor,' he commanded firmly.

'But—'

'Now, please, Eleanor.' He did not raise his voice, but she must have realised by the coldness of his tone that it would be prudent not to argue with him any further on the matter, and he thankfully heard her softly encourage her horse to walk away from the two men. 'Do you have something you wish to say to me, Litchfield?' he prompted evenly.

The other man feigned an expression of innocence. 'Not that I recall, no.'

Justin's mouth thinned. 'I advise that you stay well clear of both me and mine, Litchfield.'

Those pale eyes glanced across to where Eleanor now sat on her horse, talking to the maid inside the waiting carriage. 'Is she yours, Royston?'

'Very much so,' Justin confirmed instantly.

'If you say so...' the other man taunted.

His jaw clenched. 'I do.'

'For now, perhaps.'

'For always as far as you are concerned, Litchfield.' Justin scowled darkly.

'And if the lady should have other ideas?'

Justin drew in a sharp breath at his insolent persistence. 'Do not say you have not been warned, Litchfield!'

'You seem mightily possessive, Royston.' The older man gave him a speculatively look. 'Can this be the same young lady whose missive caused you to end our card game so that you could run eagerly to her side?'

Eleanor's note was indeed responsible for that occurrence, but certainly not in the way in which Litchfield implied it had.

'Ah, I see that it is indeed the case.' Litchfield nodded in satisfaction at Justin's silence. 'As I said, she is certainly a rare beauty—'

'And as I have said, she is not for the likes of you,' Justin bit out tautly.

'Well, well.' The older man eyed him curiously. 'Can it be that the top-lofty Duke of Royston has finally met his match? Are we to expect an announcement soon?'

'You are to *expect* that I shall not be pleased if I hear you have made so much as a single personal remark or innuendo about the young lady who is my ward,' Justin snarled, wanting nothing more than to take this insolent cur by the throat and squeeze until the breath left his body. Either that, or take a whip to him. And Justin would cheerfully have done either of those things, if he had not known it would draw unwanted attention to Eleanor.

Litchfield's eyes widened. 'Your ward...?'

Justin gave a haughty nod. 'Indeed.'

The other man continued to look at him searchingly for several seconds before giving a shout of derisive laughter and then turning to look at Eleanor speculatively once again. 'How very interesting...' He raised a mocking gloved hand to his temple before turning his horse and deliberately riding in the direction of the Royston carriage, raising his hat to Eleanor as he passed and so forcing her to give an acknowledging nod in return.

Justin scowled as he recalled Anderson's previous warning for him to beware of Litchfield in future, with the added comment that the other man was at the very least a nasty bully, and at worst, a dangerous adversary. Indeed, if not for the fact that it would have been damaging to Eleanor's reputation, then Litchfield would have been made to pay for his insulting behaviour just now, possibly to the extent that the other man found himself standing down the sights of Justin's duelling pistol. As it was, Justin had dared not involve Eleanor in the scandal of a duel before she had even appeared in society!

Tomorrow, or possibly the next day, was another matter, however...

'What an unpleasant man.' Ellie could not resist a quiver of revulsion when Justin finally rejoined her and the two of them turned to walk their horses back to Royston House.

'Very,' he agreed.

'Will he be attending the ball this evening...?'

The duke gave a scathing snort. 'My grandmother would never allow one such as he to step over her threshold.'

She eyed him curiously. 'And yet he is obviously a man of your own acquaintance, is he not?'

'We have shared a card game or two, which he has invariably lost.' Justin shrugged dismissively. 'His reputation is such that much of society shuns him. And while we are on the subject,' he added harshly, 'I forbid you to so much as acknowledge him should you ever chance to meet him again.'

'You *forbid* it?' Ellie gasped incredulously.

The duke looked implacably at her. 'I do, yes. Unless, of course, I am mistaken and you would welcome Litchfield's attentions?'

She gave another shudder just recalling that unpleasant man. 'Of course I would not.'

'Then—'

'Whilst I accept that we are distantly related by marriage, *Cousin*—' Ellie's bland tone revealed none of her inner anger at his high-handedness '—and that you are the grandson of my employer—'

'—and your newly appointed guardian—'

'Perhaps that is so—'

'There is no perhaps about it!' the duke swiftly interjected.

'Even so, I cannot—I simply cannot allow you to forbid, or allow, any of my future actions,' Ellie informed him firmly, with far too many memories of how his cousin Frederick had held such sway over her poor mother for the last years of her life.

Justin reached out and grasped the reins of her horse as she would have urged her horse into a canter. 'In this instance I must insist you obey me, Eleanor.'

Tears of anger now blurred her vision. 'You may insist

all you please, your Grace, but I refuse to allow myself to be bullied by any man.'

Justin scowled his frustration as Eleanor wrenched her reins from his grasp, leaving him to sit and watch as she urged her horse forwards and away from him.

Damn Litchfield.

Damn his troublemaking hide!

Chapter Six

'I believe, Royston, that if you do not cease scowling, you are in danger of taking your duties as Ellie's guardian to such a degree that you will succeed in scaring away all but the most determined of eligible young gentlemen!'

Justin turned to raise one arrogant brow as he looked down to where his grandmother had moved to stand beside him at the edge of the crowded dance floor in her candlelit ballroom. Still slightly pale, and uncharacteristically fragile in her demeanour, the dowager duchess had, as she had said she would, rallied from her sickbed in order to take her place as hostess of the Royston Ball.

Justin's mood had not improved since he and Eleanor had parted so frostily upon returning to the stables behind Royston House. For the most part because Justin knew he had handled the situation badly, that issuing orders to a woman as stubborn as Eleanor was proving to be was sure to result in her doing the exact opposite of what was being asked of her—an accusation, which if repeated to Eleanor, would no doubt earn him the comment of 'the pot calling the kettle black'! Not that Justin thought for a moment that she would ever encourage Litchfield's advances, but he had no doubt she would find some other way in which to bedevil him for what she had considered his high-handedness this afternoon.

He had known, the moment Eleanor walked down the grand staircase at Royston House earlier, and he had seen the light of rebellion in those emerald-green eyes and the defiant tilt to her chin, that she intended for that punishment to begin this very evening…

At first glance Justin had wondered at his grandmother's choice of attire for her young protégée. But the longer he gazed upon Eleanor's appearance, the more he realised how astutely clever the old lady had been; brightly coloured silks were now the preferred fashion for the ladies of the *ton,* as were the garishly matching feathers and silks worn in their hair.

In contrast, Eleanor's gown was the palest shade of green silk Justin had ever seen, as were the delicate above-elbow-length lace gloves that covered her hands and arms. Her hair, those glorious red curls, had been swept back and up and secured at her crown, before being allowed to cascade gently down to brush lightly against the slenderness of her nape. Her bare nape. For, unlike the other women of society, of any age, who often chose to wear their wealth, quite literally, upon their sleeves and about their throats, Eleanor was not wearing a single piece of jewellery. Her wrists, her hair, the lobes of her ears, the creamy expanse of her throat and breasts, were all completely unadorned.

As a consequence, Justin realised that Eleanor Rosewood's understated elegance gave her the appearance of a dove amongst garishly adorned peacocks. A pure, unblemished, perfectly cut diamond set amongst roughly hewn and gaudy-coloured sapphires, emeralds and rubies.

As predicted, the crowded ballroom had fallen deathly silent the moment Stanhope had announced their entrance. But Justin was fully aware the speculative attention was not directed solely towards him this evening, but included the young lady standing so coolly self-contained at his side— admittedly, it was a façade of calm only, as hinted at by the slight trembling of her gloved hand as it rested lightly upon his arm, but to all outward appearances Eleanor was a picture of composure and elegance. She was also, as his grandmother had intended, instantly recognised as the same young woman who had been seen riding in the park with him this afternoon.

The ladies, as Eleanor had previously suggested might be the case, had gazed openly and critically at her from behind fluttering fans—with not a single sign of recognition, Justin noted ruefully, that the elegant Miss Eleanor Rosewood was also Ellie, the previously nondescript companion of the dowager duchess. The gentlemen, Justin had noted with more annoyance, had been much more open in their admiration.

An admiration confirmed by the fact that at least a dozen of those same gentlemen had crowded around begging to be introduced the moment Justin had finished presenting Eleanor to his grandmother and her two close friends, the Dowager Countess of Chambourne and Lady Cicely Hawthorne, all of them expressing a wish to claim a dance with her before the evening should come to an end.

As her guardian and protector, it had been Justin's duty to claim Eleanor for the first dance, of course, and he had politely done so—much to the increasing interest of his grandmother's other guests; the Duke of Royston never stood up to dance on these occasions. Indeed, Justin had always made a point of not doing so, making his attentions to Eleanor all the more noticeable. It would, as his grandmother had always intended it should, secure her place in society.

The two of them had not exchanged so much as a word as they danced that first set together, Eleanor's expression one of cool detachment as Justin studied her beneath hooded lids, finding himself pleasantly surprised by her grace and elegance on the dance floor; proving that she had indeed been shown how to 'behave in the company of ladies and gentlemen'.

Justin had not been quite so pleased by those same gentlemen who had rushed to fill Eleanor's dance card the moment he escorted her back to his grandmother's side. Or the fact that Eleanor appeared to blossom under their avid attentions.

His mouth thinned anew as he continued to gaze across to where Eleanor was now laughing merrily at something amusing her current dance partner had said to her. 'Lord Braxton can hardly be considered young or entirely eligible,' he remarked curtly to his grandmother.

'Nonsense!' Edith dismissed as she continued to smile benevolently at her young protégée. 'Jeremy Caulfield is a widower as well as being an earl.'

Justin grimaced. 'He is also twice Eleanor's age and in need of a stepmother for all of those children he keeps hidden away in the nursery at Caulfield Park!'

His grandmother raised iron-grey brows. 'There are but three children, Justin, the heir, the spare and a girl. And anyone with eyes in their head can see that Braxton is smitten with Ellie herself, rather than having any thoughts of providing his children with another mother.'

Justin was only too well aware that Jeremy Caulfield's admiration of Eleanor was personal; that was made more than obvious by the warm way the other man gazed upon her so intently, and the way in which Caulfield's hand had lingered upon hers as they'd danced together. That Eleanor returned his liking was obvious in the relaxed and natural way in which she returned the earl's smiles and conversation. Nor could Justin deny, inwardly at least, that it would be a very good match for Eleanor if Caulfield were to become seriously enamoured of her, enough so that he made her an offer of marriage.

It would, Justin also acknowledged, bring a quick end to his reluctant role as Eleanor's guardian.

An occurrence which, surprisingly, he found far less pleasing than he had thought he might.

'—am afraid that I have already promised to eat supper with the dowager duchess, Lady Hawthorne and the Countess of Ambridge, my lord,' Ellie shyly refused the invitation of the handsome and attentive Lord Jeremy Caulfield, Earl of Braxton, placing her hand upon his arm as they left the dance floor together.

After the disastrous end to her ride in the park with Justin earlier, Ellie had been in a turmoil of trepidation about attending the Royston Ball with him this evening, only to find, once the tension of dancing the first set with Justin had been dealt with, that she was actually enjoying herself. Mainly due, she admitted, to the genuinely warm regard of such gentlemen as the attentive earl.

Her smile faded somewhat as she looked up and saw the imposing Duke of Royston standing so disapprovingly beside his smiling grandmother; he had certainly made no effort to put Ellie at her ease this evening. How could he, when he had barely spoken two words to her since his arrival some hours ago, causing her to give a sigh of relief when their dancing together finally came to an end?

Surely it only confirmed how deeply Justin disapproved of his grandmother's determined interest in settling Ellie's future, and his own reluctant involvement in it? He had made it more than obvious he would never have contemplated agreeing to it if not for his deep regard for Edith and that lady's recent bout of ill health.

Thankfully, the dowager duchess really had seemed to improve a little over the last few days, and although she was still pale, she gave every appearance of enjoying the evening; Ellie knew that dear lady well enough by now to know that Edith St Just would never admit to it if she were not!

The Earl of Braxton looked genuinely disappointed by Ellie's refusal to sit with him at supper. 'Perhaps if I were to ask the dowager duchess's permission—'

'As Miss Rosewood is my own ward, it is my permission you would need to receive, Braxton,' the cold voice of Justin St Just cut in.

The older man turned, a pleasant smile curving his lips. 'Then perhaps you might consent to allowing me to escort Miss Rosewood into supper, Royston?'

'I am afraid that would not do at all, Braxton.' The duke looked down the length of his nose at the other man.

'Oh, but—'

'It will not do, Eleanor,' Justin repeated firmly as she started to protest. 'Forgive my ward, Braxton.' He turned back to the earl. 'I am afraid Eleanor is new to society. As such she is unaware of the attention she has already drawn to herself by her naivety and flirtatiousness.'

Ellie's eyes widened at the unfairness of the accusation. Admittedly she had not sat down for a single dance since that first one with Justin, but she believed that her popularity was only because she was considered something of a curiosity, an oddity, if you will. Certainly she had not sought out any of the attentions that had been shown to her, nor did she consider she had been in the least flirtatious!

'If you will excuse us, Braxton?' Justin did not wait for the earl's response as he took a firm grasp of Ellie's arm before turning away.

'Justin—'

'We will await you in the supper room, Grandmother,' he said to the old lady who had come up behind them, his expression grimly unapproachable as he strode rapidly towards the room in which supper was now being served, practically dragging Ellie along beside him.

'Now who is the one responsible for drawing attention? To us both?' Ellie's cheeks burned with humiliation as she stumbled to keep up with the duke's much longer strides, at the same time as she kept a smile fixed upon her lips for those watching them.

Justin's jaw clenched and he ground his back teeth together as he glared at the members of the *ton* who dared to so much as glance in their direction. Glances which were hastily averted under the fierceness of his chilling blue gaze.

'Your Grace—'

'Do not "your Grace" me in what can only be described as a feeble attempt to mimic my grandmother's disapproving tones!' Justin rounded on Eleanor sharply, only for his breath to catch in his throat as he saw how pale her cheeks had now become, those freckles more evident on her nose and cheeks, and that there were tears glistening in those deep-green eyes as she looked up at him reproachfully.

Damn it to hell!

He forced himself to slow his angry strides and loosen his tight grip upon her arm before speaking again. 'It may not appear so, Eleanor,' he explained, also attempting to soften the harshness of his tone, 'but I assure you I am only acting in your best interests. For you to have singled Braxton out so soon, by eating supper alone with him, would have been as good as a declaration on your part.'

A puzzled frown marred her creamy brow as she blinked back the tears. 'A declaration? Of what, exactly?'

'Of your willingness to accept a marriage proposal from him should one be forthcoming.'

'That is utterly ridiculous...' she recoiled with a horrified gasp '...when I have only just been introduced to him!' If anything her face had grown even paler.

Justin nodded grimly. 'And being new to society, you are as yet unaware of the subtle nuances of courtship.'

She shook her head, red curls bouncing against the slenderness of her creamy nape. 'But I am sure the earl meant no such familiarity by his supper invitation. He merely wished to continue our discussion, to learn my views, on the merits or otherwise, of engaging a companion or governess for his five-year-old daughter.'

Justin's breath caught in his throat. 'He discussed the future care of his young daughter with you?'

'Well, yes...' Ellie could see by the grim expression in his hard blue eyes that she had obviously done something else unacceptable. 'It was a harmless enough conversation, surely?'

He gave her a pitying glance. 'It is the sort of conversation that a gentleman has with the lady who might perhaps become the new mother of that child.'

Ellie eyes widened. 'Surely you cannot be serious? I hardly know the man!'

Justin gave a derisive snort. 'Can it be that you are really as naïve as you appear to be, Eleanor? Because if that is so, then I believe my grandmother should have waited a while longer before introducing you into society.'

'I do not—'

'This afternoon you were all but propositioned by one of the biggest blaggards in London,' Justin continued remorselessly. 'And this evening you have committed the *faux pas* of discussing a man's nursery with him!'

Ellie's cheeks now burned with humiliated colour, but she was determined not to give in without a fight. 'Must I remind you that I would not have so much as spoken to that "blaggard" this afternoon, if not for your own acquaintance with the man? And I truly believe the earl was merely making polite conversation just now—'

The duke cut her off with an incredulous look. 'By consulting with you on what is best for the future education of his young, motherless daughter?'

Ellie gave a pained frown. 'Well…yes.'

Had she been naïve in taking Lord Caulfield's conversation at face value? She had not thought so at the time, but Justin knew the ways of society far better than she, after all. Yet it had seemed such a harmless conversation, Jeremy Caulfield so terribly bewildered and at a loss as to how best to bring up a little girl on his own—

Oh, good lord…!

'I believe my evening has now been quite ruined!' Ellie almost felt as if she might quite happily sit down and cry rather than attempt to eat any of the delicious supper laid out so temptingly before her.

Justin gave her a humourless smile. 'Do not take on so, Eleanor, a single inappropriate conversation with a gentleman does not commit you to spending a lifetime with him. Indeed, I should not give my permission for such a marriage even if such an offer were forthcoming. And I have no doubt my grandmother is even now excusing your behaviour by reiterating to Braxton your inexperience in such matters.'

'And that makes me feel so much better!' Ellie snapped, her earlier feelings of well-being having completely dissipated during the course of this conversation.

She had believed herself to be doing so well, to be behaving with all the dignity and decorum as befitted the supposed ward of the Duke of Royston, and instead it now seemed she had been encouraging the Earl of Braxton into believing she was in favour of him furthering his attentions towards her.

She gave a forlorn sigh. 'How on earth have you managed to avoid the pitfalls of the marriage mart for so long and so expertly, your Grace?'

And just like that, Justin's scowling and dark mood of the past twelve hours became a thing of the past, and he began to chuckle even as he moved forwards to pull back a chair for her. 'I believe I may attribute my own success in that regard to both stealth and cunning!'

Eleanor pursed her lips as she sat down. 'Then perhaps you might consider tutoring me into how I might do the same, for I fear I am completely at a loss as to how to deal with it myself.'

Justin eyed her curiously as he lowered his long length into the chair beside her, waiting until one of the footmen

had placed plates of sweetmeats on the table for their enjoyment before answering her. 'You would not consider yourself fortunate in becoming Braxton's countess?'

She shook her head. 'He is a pleasant enough gentleman,
I am sure, but I—I have no ambition to become the wife
of any man who does not love me with all of his heart, as I
intend to love him.'

Justin studied her closely. 'Because of the unhappy circumstances of your mother's marriage to Frederick?'

Eleanor nodded. 'I can imagine nothing worse than suffering such a fate myself.'

Justin could not help but admire the strength of her conviction, even if his own feelings on the matter were in
total contradiction to her own. He thought it was far better
to marry a woman for her lineage and ability to produce
healthy children. On which subject… 'And what of children,
Eleanor?' he enquired. 'Do you have no desire to have a son
or daughter of your own one day?'

Green eyes twinkled mischievously as she looked about
them pointedly, the supper room now filling with other
members of the *ton* seeking refreshment. 'Is our present
conversation not as socially unacceptable as discussing the
education of Lord Caulfield's young daughter with him?' she
murmured softly before leaning forwards to pierce a piece
of juicy pineapple with a fork and lifting it up to her lips.

'Perhaps,' Justin allowed ruefully. Then he found himself
unable to look away from the fullness of her lips as they
closed about the juicy fruit.

Her expression was thoughtful as she chewed and swallowed the fruit before innocently licking the excess juice
from the plumpness of her lips. 'Then of course I would

dearly love to have children of my own one day, both a son and a daughter at least. But only—'

'If you were to have those children with "a man who loved you with all of his heart",' he finished drily.

Ellie smiled. 'Why are you so cynical about falling in love, your Grace…? Your Grace?' she prompted quizzically as he started laughing again.

He raised an eyebrow. 'You do not find it slightly ludicrous to ask me such a personal question at the same time as continuing to address me with such formality, Eleanor?'

'Perhaps,' she allowed huskily, colour warming her cheeks.

'Perhaps, Justin,' he insisted.

She blinked, aware that an underlying, inexplicable something seemed to have crept into their conversation, although she had no idea what it was or why it was there. 'Would calling you Royston as your grandmother does not be more appropriate?'

'Far too stuffy,' he dismissed gruffly.

Ellie lowered her lashes. 'I am not sure the dowager duchess would approve—'

'Not sure I would approve of what?' Edith prompted briskly as she joined them, Lady Cicely and Lady Jocelyn accompanying her.

Her grandson rose politely to his feet and saw to the seating of those three ladies in the chairs across the table from them, before resuming his own seat beside Ellie. 'I was endeavouring to persuade Eleanor into calling me Justin when we are alone together or in the company of family or close friends,' he explained with an acknowledging bow of his head towards Lady Cicely and Lady Jocelyn.

Lady Cicely looked flustered as she glanced nervously towards the dowager duchess. 'I am not sure…'

'Is that quite the thing, Edith…?' Lady Jocelyn frowned her own uncertainty as she too deferred to the dowager duchess for her opinion on the matter.

Edith gave her grandson a searching glance before answering the query. 'I do not see why not. They are cousins by marriage, after all.'

'Yes, but—'

'I am still unsure as to whether—'

'You were rather abrupt with Braxton just now, Royston,' the dowager duchess cut off her friends' continued concerns as she turned to look at her grandson.

'Was I?' the duke returned unconcernedly.

'You know very well that you were.' His grandmother frowned.

'I am sure he will recover all too soon,' he murmured distractedly as he reached out to pierce another piece of fruit before holding it temptingly in front of Ellie.

Something Ellie—even in her 'naivety and inexperience'—knew to be entirely inappropriate. Nor did she care for the piercing intensity of Justin's glittering gaze at it rested on her parted lips.

At the same time she realised that *this* was what had changed so suddenly between them just minutes ago; one moment Justin had been berating her for her 'flirtatiousness' in what he believed to be her encouragement of Lord Caulfield and the next he had been shamelessly flirting with her himself. Just what was he up to?

Was this perhaps another lesson, to see if she had learnt anything from their conversation just now?

Whatever the reason for his behaviour, it had resulted in

his drawing unwarranted attention to the two of them. As Ellie glanced nervously about them, she could see several of the older matrons in the near vicinity looking positively shocked at the intimacy of his gesture in offering to feed her the sliver of pineapple. Indeed, Lady Cicely and Lady Jocelyn both seemed to be holding their breath as they waited to see what Ellie would do next. Edith's expression was, unfortunately, as enigmatic and unreadable as her grandson's.

Ellie gave a cool smile as she sat back in her chair, not quite touching the chair back itself, as she had been taught to do by her mother long ago. 'I find I am no longer hungry for pineapple, your Grace,' she informed him repressively. 'Perhaps you should eat the fruit yourself? I can vouch for it being truly delicious.' She held her breath tensely as she waited to see what Justin would do or say next.

Chapter Seven

Madness.

Absolute bloody madness!

For there could be no other reason why Justin gave every appearance of behaving like a besotted fool, enticing his ladylove with succulent titbits of fruit.

Justin considered himself to be neither besotted nor a fool, Eleanor Rosewood was most certainly not his ladylove—nor would she ever be—and the only enticing that had ever interested him, where any woman was concerned, took place between silken sheets—and it was fruit of the forbidden kind!

He looked into those emerald-green eyes just inches from his own and knew from the uncertainty, the slight panic he detected in their depths, that Eleanor's casual dismissal just now was purely an act she had assumed for their audience. That the widening of her pupils, the bloom of colour in her cheeks, her slightly parted lips, and the barest movement of her breasts as she breathed shallowly, were indicative of what she was really feeling.

And Justin had no trouble at all recognising that.

Arousal.

For all that she might express her resentment of him in the role he now held in her life as her guardian and protector, and despite her rebelling against any and all restrictions he might choose to place upon her actions, she could not hide the fact she also found him physically attractive, despite her stated aversion to 'lust' being the reason for her mother's marriage to Frederick.

A knowledge that caused Justin's lips to curl into a satisfied smile as he straightened. 'Much better, Eleanor,' he drawled as he discarded both the fork and pineapple on to his plate before turning to the three older ladies seated across from them. 'I am endeavouring, at her request, to tutor Eleanor in how best to deter over-zealous gentlemen of the *ton,* without also offending them,' he explained wryly as Lady Cicely and Lady Jocelyn, at least, continued to look upon him in obvious shock.

His grandmother's expression was no less disapproving. 'And in that you appear to have been successful. Unfortunately,' she continued irritably, 'your chosen method of doing so has now also succeeded in rousing the speculation of the *ton* regarding the Duke of Royston's intentions towards his young ward!'

Justin gave a scornful laugh. 'An occurrence which will likely render Eleanor popular with the gentlemen and unpopular with the ladies!'

'It is not in the least amusing, Royston.'

'Of course it is, Grandmama.' He relaxed against the back of his chair. 'How can it be anything else when we all know I have no romantic intentions whatsoever where Eleanor is concerned.'

'I really must thank you for your most recent lesson, your Grace.' Ellie had heard quite enough of 'the Duke of Royston's' opinions for one evening. Arrogant, mocking, insufferable gentleman that he was!

Unfortunately, she also found him verbally challenging, dangerously handsome and physically exciting, to the extent that she suspected she might still be in love with him, despite previous private denials to the contrary.

Just to look at this man, to be in his company, to exchange verbal swords with him, still, in spite of her inner remonstrations with herself, caused her heart to beat faster, her breathing to falter and every nerve ending in her body to become thrillingly aware of everything about him. And Ellie knew she had almost succumbed to his dangerous allure as he had held that sliver of pineapple up in front of her so temptingly.

It had been so intimate an act, the noise and chatter about them seeming to disappear as the world narrowed down to just the two of them, and Ellie had found herself totally unable to look away from those piercing sapphire-blue eyes.

Much, she realised now, like a butterfly stuck on the end of a pin by its curious captor!

Certainly his next comment had shown that he had felt none of the physical awareness of her that she now had of him. Indeed, he had merely confirmed what she had suspected all along: that the arrogant Duke of Royston was merely being his usual insufferable self by teaching her another 'lesson'.

'If you will all excuse me, I believe I will go and tidy my appearance before the dancing recommences?' She placed her napkin down upon the table before standing up.

Justin also rose politely to his feet. 'I will accompany you.'

Ellie raised one mocking brow, in perfect imitation of the duke's own haughty arrogance. 'To the ladies' retiring room, your Grace?'

Those chiselled lips twisted. 'I will obviously wait outside in the hallway for you.'

Ellie frowned her irritation. 'I am sure that is unnecessary—'

'I beg to differ.' His mouth tightened. 'Unless you have a previous arrangement to meet with Braxton in one of the private rooms?'

She gasped. 'Of course I have not!'

He straightened his shoulders. 'Then I think it best that I accompany you to ensure he does not waylay you. Ladies.' He gave a polite bow to the three older women seated opposite them before pointedly raising his arm for Ellie to take, leaving her no choice but to place her gloved hand upon that arm and walk along stiffly at his side as he coolly nodded acknowledgement of acquaintances as they made slow progress across the crowded, noisy room.

But that did not mean Ellie did not bristle inside with indignation, at his highhandedness, for the whole of that time!

She removed her hand from his arm the moment they were outside in the less crowded Great Hall. 'How dare you! Who are you to embarrass me in front of other people, by questioning whether or not I might have behaved so scandalously as to have arranged to meet Lord Caulfield privately?'

Justin eyed her calmly, knowing himself to be once again in control—thankfully—of this situation. And himself. For he had not been as immune to Eleanor's physical awareness of him just now, when he'd attempted to feed her the pineapple, as he had given the impression of being...

No, indeed, he had risen to the occasion in spite of himself and had been forced to remain seated at the table for several minutes longer than necessary in order to wait until the bulge in his breeches became less obvious.

Much to his increasing annoyance.

Eleanor Rosewood's role as a protégée of his grandmother's, and his own ward, now rendered her as being completely unsuited to ever becoming his mistress. Nor did she meet the stringent requirements of a prospective duchess. As such there was no place for her in his well-ordered life, other than the annoyance of being forced by circumstance into acting as her guardian. All was not lost, of course; any number of women here this evening could, and in the past had, assuaged his physical needs.

'Who am I?' Justin repeated in a suddenly steely voice. 'I believe, for the moment at least, I am placed in the role of acting as your guardian and protector. Whether you feel you are in need of one or otherwise,' he added as she parted her lips with the obvious intention of protesting. 'As such, I have no intention of allowing you to embarrass me, or my grandmother, by behaving in an unsuitable manner through ignorance.'

Ellie eyed him hotly. 'You truly are the most insufferable man I have ever met!'

'So you have remarked before, I believe.'

'Then I must believe it to be true!'

The duke gave a deliberately weary smile. 'And I am fortunate in that I find your opinion of me to be of little interest.'

Just as Ellie knew she herself was of little interest to him either, other than as an appeasement to his grandmother's plans for her, the dowager the only woman whom he so obviously did care about; Ellie had heard a definite coldness in his tone when she had mentioned his mother to him.

Unfortunately, she now had no choice but to curl her fingers painfully into the palms of her gloved hands, in order to prevent herself from giving in to the temptation she felt to slap that supercilious and arrogant smile from his perfect lips!

She drew in a deep and controlling breath. 'Is it any wonder, then, that I have come to prefer the company of such polite gentlemen as the Earl of Braxton?'

Those blue eyes narrowed. 'I should warn you that it would be unwise to challenge me, Eleanor.'

Ellie's throat moved as she swallowed nervously, once again aware of the sudden tension that had sprung up between them, of how the very air that surrounded them now seemed charged with—with she knew not what.

The only thing she was sure of was the fluttering of excitement beneath her breasts, of the dampness to her palms inside her lace gloves, of the burn of colour blooming in her cheeks as his eyes continued to glitter down at her.

She swallowed again before speaking. 'I do not believe that is what I was doing.'

'No?'

'No,' she said defiantly.

A nerve pulsed in his tightly clenched jaw. 'I disagree.'

'That is your prerogative, of course—what are you doing?' she squeaked as the duke took a firm grasp of her arm before pulling her down the shadowed hallway, away from the crowded public salons, to where the private family rooms were situated. 'Justin?' she prompted sharply as he threw open the library door and pushed her unceremoniously inside the darkened room.

He followed her inside before closing the door firmly behind him. 'Of all the times I have asked you to do so, you must choose now to decide to call me Justin?' He towered over her in the darkness. 'I do believe you are challenging me, after all, Eleanor,' he murmured huskily.

It took Ellie several moments to adjust her eyes to the gloom of the library, at which time she realised it was not as dark as she had at first imagined, that the moonlight shone in brightly through the windows, giving his overlong-blond hair a silvery rather than golden sheen, his eyes glittering a much paler blue, the light and shadows giving his hard, chiselled face a darker, more dangerous sharpness, than it usually had.

Not that any of that was important, when placed alongside the scandal that would ensue if anyone were to discover them alone together in the darkness of the library! 'We should not be in here, your Grace.'

'Yes, you are most certainly challenging me, Eleanor,' he remarked in reproof. 'Did no one ever warn you that it is dangerous to wake the sleeping tiger?'

'You are likening yourself to a tiger?' she asked incredulously.

'Now I believe you are mocking me.'

He took a deliberate step forwards, causing Ellie to take a step backwards, only to find she could go no further as she came up against the closed door. Her eyes widened in alarm as she watched him place a hand flat against the door either side of her face, at once holding her captive between that door at her back and the hardness of his body just inches in front of her own.

Too few inches. Indeed, Justin stood so close to her now that she could feel the heat of his body through the thin silk of her gown, felt surrounded by the clean male smell of him as much as his impressive height and breadth. Her senses began to swim as she scented the sharp tang of his cologne, her breasts suddenly feeling fuller, firmer, the tips tingling with an almost painful ache, an inexplicable dampness between her thighs, the whole experience making her legs feel weak.

As clear evidence that she did indeed love this man...

The warmth of his breath brushed softly, sweetly, against her temple as he bent his head closer to her own before murmuring, 'Little girls who deliberately wake the tiger deserve to be...punished, just a little, do you not think?'

Ellie quivered in awareness, felt as if his close proximity had sucked all the air from the room, her head beginning to whirl as she tried to breathe, and failed. 'Please...!' she gasped at the same time as she lifted her hands to his chest with the intention of pushing him away, of allowing her to draw in a breath. Only to find she had no strength left to do so, that instead of pushing him away her hands lingered, as if with a will of their own, her fingers splaying almost caressingly against the heat of his broad chest.

'Please what, Eleanor?'

'I—' She moistened lips that had become suddenly dry. 'I should go...'

'You should, yes.' He nodded slowly as he moved even closer, so that the silk of her gown and his own clothing were all that now separated them. 'The question is, are you going to do so?'

She looked up at him searchingly, the shadows cast by the moonlight making it impossible for her to read the expression on the male face only inches above her own. Even so, she could see enough to know the duke's expression was one of hard determination and not the tender softness of a lover. 'I believe you are playing another game with me, your Grace,' she accused.

'Am I?'

'Yes!'

'Does this feel like a game to you, Eleanor?' He shifted slightly, allowing the length of his body to press against her much softer one, allowing her to feel the swollen hardness bulging in his breeches, which now pulsed insistently against the soft swell of her abdomen.

She raised startled lids; she might be young, and both naïve and as inexperienced as this man had called her earlier, but she was not so ignorant that she did not know what that throbbing hardness pressed against her meant.

As she had told him earlier today, her stepfather had kept a fine stable at the country house where Ellie had spent much of the ten years of Frederick's marriage to her mother, and she knew exactly what took place when the stallion was brought to the mare for breeding. And that impressive hardness, which had risen up between Justin's thighs, was the same as had been between the stallion's back legs when he had caught the scent of the mare in season.

Had he smelled her arousal and in turn had become aroused by her? she wondered.

If Justin had thought his behaviour earlier was madness, then this had to be insanity.

Complete insanity!

Not only should he not be here alone in a darkened room with Eleanor, but he should certainly have kept his distance from her, and definitely not given in to the temptation to feel her slender curves so soft and sensuous against his much harder ones.

He could not even put his rashness down to an overindulgence in brandy this evening, either, having been watching Eleanor so intently, as she danced with what seemed like a legion of other gentlemen, that there had not been the time to allow a single drop of the restorative liquid to pass his lips.

No, it was Eleanor herself who had intoxicated him this evening. Whose every word challenged him. Who had aroused him earlier, causing him to swell and throb inside his breeches, just by watching her lick the juice of the pineapple from the swell of her lips, until Justin had desired, hungered, for the sweet taste of those lips for himself. As he still hungered.

'Well, does it feel like a game?' he repeated as she didn't answer.

Her little pink tongue moved moistly across her lips before she finally responded in a breathy voice. 'Not any game I have ever played before, no.'

'Good.' Justin gave a hard, satisfied smile. 'And would you like to know what happens next in this particular... game?'

'Your Grace—'

'Justin, damn it!' He glared down at her, watching her face as he pressed his thighs against her, only to give a low and aching groan in his throat as pleasure immediately shot hotly down the length of his arousal.

Her eyes widened in alarm. 'Justin, are you all right?'

'Do not look so concerned.' He gave a strained smile. 'It may not appear so, but I assure you it is pleasure I am feeling, not pain.'

Ellie eyed him uncertainly now. 'Pleasure?'

Strange, because when she had secretly observed the stallion and the mare together in the stable yard, it had seemed to her as if the stallion were in pain, head tossing in agitation, eyes wide and wild, as he snorted and stomped on the cobbles beneath his hooves as he strained to get close to his quarry.

The terrified mare had seemed to fair no better, pinned restlessly in place as she was beneath those thrashing hooves, her silky neck bitten several times as the stallion mounted her, squealing and trying to move out from beneath him as that thick rod between his back legs disappeared inside her body, before being thrust in again, time and time without end it had seemed to Ellie, before she could stand to watch the wild coupling no longer and she had run crying from the stables in search of her mother.

Muriel had wiped away her tears, of course, soothing her fears as she explained that the mare had not been in pain as she had thought, that it was merely how baby horses were made, and that the mare would be happy enough when her foal was born in the spring.

It was in the course of that conversation that Ellie had added a codicil to her earlier conviction that she would never marry any man she did not love and who did not love her. Observing the stallion and mare together, Ellie had known that she could never be intimate in that way with a man she did not love and who did not love her, either. It was too personal, too carnal, too—too wild, for her to ever contemplate such personal intimacy taking place with a man whom she merely *liked*.

Justin's expression softened slightly as he obviously now

saw, or perhaps sensed, her uncertainty. 'You do not believe me?'

'I—I do not know what to think, or say...' A slow shake of her head accompanied the hesitancy of that denial.

He grinned. 'Well, that is certainly a novelty in itself!'

'You are laughing at me again.'

Justin sobered, glittering gaze fixed intensely on the pale oval of her face. 'What would you like me to do with you?'

She caught her bottom lip between small pearly white teeth, nibbling that tender flesh for several seconds before her chin rose in challenge. 'I believe I should like for you not to treat me as a child.'

He smiled. 'Oh, I assure you, Eleanor, at this moment you are far from appearing as a child to me.'

She nodded. 'Then you will please tell me what happens next in this game?'

Justin drew in a sharp breath. 'Usually the gentleman now nuzzles his lips against the lady's throat. Like this.' He suited his actions to his words, enjoying her perfumed and silky skin against his lips.

She gave a soft sigh even as she arched her throat to allow him easier access. 'And next?'

Justin continued to taste and kiss that tender column. 'Next he perhaps dares to venture a little lower...'

'Lower...?' Her breath caught and held, causing the fullness of her breasts to push against the low neckline of her gown.

'Here.' Justin trailed a path of kisses down to that magnificent swell, feeling himself grow even longer, thicker inside the confines of his breeches, as he tasted her breasts with his lips and tongue and breathed in her intoxicating, heady perfume.

* * *

Ellie heard another low and aching groan, only to realise that it was she this time who was making that sound, that the feel of Justin's lips and tongue against her swollen and heated flesh, the slow thrust of his throbbing hardness against the juncture between her thighs, did indeed give her pleasure. A hot and burning pleasure that coursed through the whole of her body, causing the rosy tips of her breasts to swell, and increasing the dampness between her thighs. 'I—oh…!' she gasped low in her throat, her back arching instinctively, as that slowly thrusting hardness against her thighs rubbed against a part of her there that also felt swollen and oh, so sensitive.

'Do you like that, pet?' he asked gruffly as he continued to kiss her breasts even as he slowly moved his thighs against hers a second time.

Ellie drew in a sharp breath. 'I—do—not—know.' The thrill of the sensations currently coursing through her body were so completely new to her, felt so strange, but not unpleasant, a mixture of both a shivery and hungry ache, and heated pleasure.

'Hmm, then perhaps we should continue until you do know.' Justin nibbled deliciously on the swollen flesh above her gown, his hips arched into hers as he continued that slow and leisurely thrusting.

And each time he did so Ellie felt that same pleasure, that swelling and moistness between her thighs becoming more intense as she now moved restlessly against him, seeking, wanting, oh God, aching for she knew not what…!

Her hands reached up to grasp tightly on to those impossibly wide shoulders, steadying her, anchoring her, even as she arched her thighs up to meet his thrusts, her breath now coming in short, strangled gasps. 'Please! Oh, Justin, please do not torture me any longer!'

Justin drew back slightly as he heard the anguish in her voice, knowing by the glazed look in her eyes, the flush to her cheeks, that she was close, so very close to orgasm. An orgasm, that in her innocence, she was completely unprepared for.

An innocence which he had been seriously in danger of shattering!

It took every effort of will he possessed to place his hands on her shoulders and pull away from her, feeling like the bastard he undoubtedly was as he saw the bewilderment in her expression. 'And it is for this reason, my dear Eleanor,' he drawled with deliberate lightness, 'why you would do well never to arrange private trysts with gentleman such as the Earl of Braxton!'

Chapter Eight

Ellie blinked dazedly, wrapping her arms about herself as she felt suddenly cold, bereft, now that the heat of Justin's body had been withdrawn from her, that chill entering her veins, and then her heart, as she saw the expression on his arrogantly disdainful face, and realised that the past few minutes had been all about teaching her yet another of those 'lessons' in how to *not* behave in society.

Physically roused he might have been, but it had been a controlled and deliberate arousal on his part, and obviously nothing like the unbelievable pleasure Ellie had experienced when he had kissed and caressed her. No doubt even the proof of his arousal had been deliberate on his part, as a way of showing her just how little she really knew about men, and the weakness of her own body in responding to them, while he seemed to have put the whole incident behind him as if totally unmoved by it.

Her arms dropped back to her sides as she drew herself up stiffly, determined that this arrogant duke should not see the humiliation she now suffered for having allowed herself to become so aroused by his deliberately intimate caresses. 'It seems I have reason to thank you once again, your Grace—' she gave him a cool smile '—in that I shall now know in future exactly how to deal with any gentleman who might attempt to take such liberties with me.'

His eyes narrowed. 'You will?'

'Oh, yes.' Ellie shot him another saccharine-sweet smile even as her hand rose in an swift arch before making sharp and painful contact with one of his arrogant cheeks. 'Tell me,' she continued calmly once he had straightened from the recoil of that hard slap, 'is that suitable punishment for such familiarity, do you think?'

Justin eyed her appreciatively as he slowly ran his fingers against his now-burning cheek. 'I am sure that it is,' he finally answered her drily.

'Good.' She stepped away from the door to straighten her gown. 'I believe it is now past time that I rejoined the dowager duchess in the ballroom.' She raised her brows as she gave a pointed glance towards the closed door.

Justin could not help but admire her coolness, in both her actions—painful as that forceful slap upon his cheek might have been!—and her demeanour. She looked, he decided, as he stepped forwards to open the door to allow her to sweep past him and out into the hallway, every bit as regally disdainful at this moment as his grandmother when she was least pleased with him.

Eleanor paused to turn in the hallway. 'I trust I may safely assume that you have no more "lessons" for me this evening, your Grace?'

'You may,' he confirmed, having already decided that he had attended his grandmother's ball for quite long enough. Far too long, in fact, when he considered how close he had been, just minutes ago, to making passionate love to Eleanor Rosewood in his grandmother's library!

Nor was that passion completely dampened even now, this distant, haughty Eleanor equally, if not even more challenging, than the defiant one of a few minutes ago. But it was a challenge Justin could not, dared not, allow himself to take up. Even if the uncomfortable throbbing of his unappeased shaft might demand otherwise.

As he already knew, there was an easy solution to that last problem. Instead of seeking one of the women here tonight, he would go to one of the houses of the *demi-monde,* settle on one of the pretty and willing woman to be found there and satisfy those demands in that way. Without expectation on either side. More importantly, without complication.

For it was quickly becoming obvious to Justin that his desire for Eleanor could become—indeed, if it was not already—a serious complication in his life.

'Royston?'

Justin, having already instructed Stanhope to bring his cloak and hat, with the intention of leaving Royston House following that less-than-satisfactory incident with Eleanor, now closed his eyes briefly before slowly turning to face the gentleman who had halted his departure. 'Richmond,' he recognised pleasantly. 'Forgive me, I had not realised you were here this evening.'

'Your grandmother was kind enough to invite me.' The older man nodded as he strode across the hallway to join Justin near the doorway. 'I rarely attend these things, but no one refuses an invitation from the Dowager Duchess of Royston,' he added ruefully.

'No.' Justin's reply was harder than was warranted as he

thought of the inconvenient, and deeply irritating, request his grandmother had made of him some days ago, regarding Eleanor Rosewood.

'You were just leaving,' Richmond stated the obvious.

Justin affected an expression of boredom as he smiled. 'There is only so much of the simpering misses and the over-eager young gentlemen that I can tolerate in one evening, even to please my grandmother.'

Bryan Anderson did not return his smile. 'I particularly noticed one of those young ladies as you danced with her earlier.'

'Indeed?' It was Justin's standard non-committal reply when he was unsure as to what it was the other person wanted from him. For, much as he liked Bryan Anderson, the only young lady Justin had danced with this evening had been Eleanor, and he was completely out of patience if Richmond was yet another middle-aged widower wishing to court her. 'I believe you are referring to my ward, Miss Eleanor Rosewood?'

'Just so.' Richmond ran an agitated hand through his prematurely white hair. 'I—would it be impertinent of me to enquire as to her exact age?'

'It would, yes.' Surely Eleanor was too young for him?

The earl's eyes widened as he realised what his question had sounded like to Justin. 'No, no, Royston, it is nothing like that. Miss Rosewood is far too young for my interest,' he assured hastily. 'I just—if not her age, would it be possible for you to tell me who her mother is?'

'Was,' Justin corrected guardedly, having absolutely no idea, now that Richmond had assured him so positively he had no marital intentions towards Eleanor, what this conversation was about. But he felt sure, from the intensity of the earl's mood, that it was something which would further add to the complication Eleanor had already become in his life. 'Eleanor's mother was married to my cousin Frederick and, if you recall, he and his wife were both killed in a carriage accident just over a year ago.'

The earl gave a thoughtful frown. 'Frederick's wife was previously Muriel Rosewood…?'

'I believe I have just said so.'

'I had no idea… Of course, I have not been much in society for many years, and but even so I had not realised—' He broke off with a shake of his prematurely white head.

'Look, Richmond—'

'Would you mind very much if I were to accompany you to wherever it is you are going?' The earl now looked at him appealingly. 'I would very much like to talk with you more on this subject, and here and now really is not the time or the place.' He looked pointedly at the attentive Stanhope, only to wince as several overly raucous young bucks also emerged from the supper room, glasses of champagne in their hands.

They all fell silent, however, the moment they were treated to a single infamously reproving lift of one of the Duke of Royston's eyebrows. 'Perhaps you are right, Richmond, and we should discuss this some other time?' Justin turned back to the earl. 'I am, however, presently on my way to a…private engagement, so perhaps we can make an appointment for some time tomorrow? In the afternoon would be best for me,' he added, thinking about spending a night of unbridled passion in some willing woman's bed, before making his leisurely way back to his own apartments in the late hours of the morning, and spending several hours sleeping off those excesses in his own bed.

The other man drew in a sharp breath. 'I suppose it could wait until tomorrow…'

'Best to do so, then.' Justin said. 'Perhaps we might have a late lunch together at White's?'

'As I said, I would rather we spoke on this matter in private,' Richmond insisted. 'Three o'clock suit? At your rooms?'

Justin looked taken aback. 'Now see here, Richmond, I do not—'

'Tell me, have you seen or heard any more of Litchfield?'

Justin's patience, never his strongest quality at the best of times—and this evening could certainly not be called that!—was almost non-existent as Richmond's conversation became even more obscure. 'As it happens we met him quite by accident whilst we were out riding in the park earlier today.'

'We? Miss Rosewood was with you?' the earl asked anxiously.

'What on earth does it matter whether Eleanor was with me or not?' Justin snapped.

'Everything! Or perhaps nothing,' the earl said vaguely. 'Did—is Litchfield now acquainted with Miss Rosewood?'

'I did not feel inclined to introduce the two of them, if that is what you are asking!'

Richmond sighed his relief. 'That is something, at least.'

'What does Eleanor riding with me earlier today have to do with the unpleasantness which exists between myself and Litchfield?'

'I shall not know the answer to that until we have spoken together tomorrow.'

Justin's previous interest in spending a passion-filled

night with a willing woman was now fading as quickly as his patience. 'You are being very mysterious, Richmond.'

'I do not mean to be.' The earl sighed heavily, his face unnaturally pale. 'It is just, having now seen Miss Rosewood, and realising that she is your ward, I feel I must—' He stopped and ran an agitated hand through his hair. 'Do not underestimate Litchfield, Royston.' His eyes glittered with intensity. 'I know him to be both a dangerous and vicious man and—we really must talk very soon!'

'Very well.' Justin acquiesced slowly. 'My rooms in Curzon Street at three o'clock tomorrow.'

'Thank you.' Richmond looked relieved.

Justin raised that infamous brow once again. 'And do I have your word that you will not attempt to approach my ward about this matter—whatever it might be—before the two of us have had chance to talk together tomorrow?'

'Good God, of course you have it!' The earl looked shocked at the suggestion. 'I would never discuss this with her—God, no.'

'I believed you the first time, Richmond,' Justin smiled wryly as he turned to finally allow Stanhope to place his evening cloak about his shoulders before donning his hat. 'Until tomorrow, then.'

'Tomorrow.'

Justin's mood was darker than ever as he walked rapidly down the steps to his carriage. What on earth could the other man want to discuss with him, about Eleanor of all people, that was so urgent and mysterious that Richmond had got himself into such a froth of emotion about it? And what did it have to do with Litchfield? Whatever it was Justin now felt almost as unsettled as Richmond so obviously was.

Perhaps he should not have delayed the conversation until

tomorrow, after all? It had been sheer bloody-mindedness on his part that he had done so in the first place; being guardian to Eleanor had already caused enough chaos in his life for one week—good God, had it really only been four days since his grandmother had made that ridiculous request of him?—and, as such, Justin had been unwilling to allow her to disrupt the rest of his plans for this evening.

'Where to, your Grace?' his groom prompted as he stepped forwards to open the door of the ducal carriage.

Justin ducked his head as he stepped up and inside. 'Curzon Street,' he said wearily as he sank back into the plush upholstered seat. 'You may take me home to Curzon Street, Bilsbury.'

Justin could see little point now in going on somewhere, or even in attempting to rouse his enthusiasm for any other woman, when his conversation with Richmond just now had succeeded in deflating any last vestiges of interest his libido might have had in partaking in such an exercise.

Damn his grandmother and her infernal interference.

Damn Richmond.

But, most of all, damn the irritating thorn Eleanor Rosewood had become in his side.

'It is such a beautiful day, ideal for a drive in the park!' Ellie smiled her pleasure at the outing as she sat in the open carriage beside Edith St Just during the fashionable hour of five and six. 'So kind, too, that so many of your guests from the ball yesterday evening have stopped to pay their respects and comment on their appreciation of the evening.'

'I would have been surprised if they had not.' The dowager nodded gracious acknowledgement of yet another group of ladies as they travelled past in their own carriage. 'Lord

Endicott seems to have especially enjoyed the evening, if his enthusiasm today is an indication,' she added with a knowing smile.

Ellie felt the warmth enter her cheeks, only to chuckle as she saw the mischievous twinkle in the dowager's eyes. 'He was very appreciative of your hospitality, yes.' Charles Endicott, having stopped to speak with them just a few minutes ago, had also been most complimentary to her.

'He is very appreciative of your own charms, child!' Edith insisted. 'As were many other gentlemen, if the florist's shop of flowers that has been delivered to you today is any indication.'

The blush deepened in Ellie's cheeks beneath her bonnet of pale lemon, a ribbon of deeper yellow secured beneath her chin, wearing a high-waisted gown of the same pale lemon, with another deeper yellow ribbon beneath her breasts. 'I have never seen so many flowers all together, have you, your Grace?'

Edith's eyes now warmed with humour. 'I do believe I may have seen almost as many at least once or twice in my own youth.'

Ellie smiled as she realised she was being teased. 'I am sure that you did. It is only—I have never received so much as a single bunch of freshly picked spring flowers from a gentleman before, let alone so many beautiful displays.' The dowager duchess's private parlour was awash with the vases of flowers that had been delivered throughout the day, following the Royston Ball the evening before. Half a dozen of them were for the dowager duchess herself, of course, sent by other society matrons, as acknowledgement of the success of the ball, but the other dozen or so were for Ellie alone.

Notably, she had not received so much as a single blossom from the Duke of Royston. Oh, no, that top-lofty gentleman would never deign to send a woman flowers, not even to his ward as a mark of the success of her introduction into society.

'I was only teasing, child.' Edith smiled across at her encouragingly. 'I could not be more pleased at your obvious success.'

Ellie forced the smile back to her lips. 'And you are not too tired from the ball and your late night?' Doctor Franklyn had been called to attend the dowager duchess this morning, but once again Ellie had been excluded from the bedchamber. Although she had not seemed to be too fatigued when she had joined Ellie for lunch in the small, family dining room earlier—it had been Edith's suggestion that the two of them go out for a carriage ride this afternoon.

Nevertheless, keeping true to her promise to Justin, Ellie had sent a short, formal note round to his rooms earlier today informing him of Dr Franklyn's visit this morning.

'Not too much, no,' Edith claimed.

'And will your grandson be calling upon you today, do you think?' Ellie posed the question as casually as she was able, in view of the unpleasant circumstances in which she and the duke had parted the evening before.

Not that she regretted slapping his arrogant face, for he had surely deserved it. The confusion of her own feelings for him aside, Justin St Just was, without doubt, the most infuriating gentleman she had ever known. Nothing at all like those charming young bucks who had clamoured to talk to her once it became known that her watchful guardian had departed the ball.

Ellie's own reaction to that abrupt departure was less

straightforward. To the point that she could not completely explain her feelings, even to herself...

A part of her had been so relieved not to have him scowling at her so darkly every time she so much as glanced across at him. But another part of her had known that the thrill of excitement had gone out of the evening for her and that she had merely played the role expected of her for the remainder of the evening, the charming and smiling Miss Eleanor Rosewood, ward of the Duke of Royston and protégée of the Dowager Duchess of Royston.

It...concerned Ellie, that she should feel this conflict of emotions. She had been so angry with Justin for the things he had said to her after he had kissed her. Furious at his mockery. And yet... To know that the duke was no longer even in the house, let alone the ballroom, had seemed to turn the evening flat, without purpose. Although what purpose a ball was supposed to have, other than dancing and flirtation, in which Ellie had engaged fully after Justin's departure, she had no idea!

She had fared no better, once the last guest had departed from Royston House and she was at last able to escape up the stairs to her bedchamber, her pillow seeming too lumpy for her to find any comfort, the covers either too hot or too cold. Unable to sleep, Ellie had not been able to prevent her thoughts from drifting to the time she had spent in the library with Justin.

Privately she could admit that it had been the most thrilling, the most physically sensuous, experience of her life. Of course, that might be because the only sensuous experiences of her life had been with Justin, rather than a confirmation of any softer emotions she might feel towards him.

There was some comfort to be found in that, she supposed. She had nothing, no other gentleman, with whom to compare her responses to Justin St Just. Perhaps any man turned a lady's legs to water when he kissed her and made her heart beat faster, caused her breasts to tingle and between her thighs to dampen? Ellie could only hope that might be the case.

'I doubt Royston will stir himself,' the dowager duchess answered Ellie's query dismissively. 'No doubt he will have gone on somewhere after he left us last night and will not have seen his bed until the early hours of this morning!'

Considering that Justin had not wished to attend the Royston Ball at all, he would most certainly have gone in search of more scintillating entertainment for his jaded senses after departing it. Indeed, Ellie had overheard the gossips fervently speculating as much the previous evening once he had left…

'Knowing my grandson—'

'Good afternoon, ladies.'

Ellie knew, just from looking at Edith's sudden and stiffly offended demeanour, that the gentleman who had now approached them on horseback was not someone the dowager considered as being an acceptable part of society, let alone of her social equal. One glance at that gentleman was enough for Ellie to know the reason for that.

Lord Dryden Litchfield appeared immune to both the dowager duchess's disapproval, and Ellie's unsmiling face, as he raised his hat to them both politely. 'Your Grace. And Miss Rosewood, too,' he added silkily. 'How gratified I am to have the pleasure of seeing you again so soon.'

Ellie had no idea what to do or to say in the face of such boldness as this. She had not liked this man when she met him yesterday and she knew from the duke that neither he or the dowager duchess approved of Lord Litchfield, either, but to cut the man direct, and a lord at that, was surely beyond Ellie's own low social standing?

'I was not aware that you were acquainted with my grandson's ward, Lord Litchfield?' Edith St Just was the one to answer coldly as she eyed him with chilling frost.

Dryden Litchfield bared those brown-stained teeth in a smile. 'Royston introduced us yesterday.'

Ellie gasped softly at the blatant lie; the duke had not even attempted to introduce the two of them—indeed, Ellie believed Justin had gone out of his way not to do so. For just such a reason as this, no doubt; without the benefit of a formal introduction, Lord Litchfield should not have approached or spoken to her at all.

'Indeed?' The dowager gave Ellie a long and considering glance before that gaze became icier still as she turned back to Dryden Litchfield. 'You must excuse us, Lord Litchfield, I am afraid Miss Rosewood and I have another engagement which we must attend.' She nodded to him dismissively.

'But of course,' he drawled with feigned graciousness. 'Perhaps I might be allowed to call upon Miss Rosewood at Royston House...?'

Ellie gave another soft gasp, this time clearly of dismay, and Edith's mouth thinned disapprovingly at the man's bad manners. 'I do not think—'

'Miss Rosewood's time is fully engaged for the next week, at least.' A steely cold voice, easily recognisable to them all as Justin's, cut firmly across his grandmother's reply.

Ellie looked at him, only to shrink back against the carriage seat as those icily contemptuous blue eyes glanced briefly in her direction before returning to Litchfield.

'Then perhaps the week following that?' the other man persisted challengingly.

'Not then, either,' the duke refused coldly. 'Now, if you will excuse us? I believe it is past time the two ladies and I returned to Royston House.'

'But of course. Ladies.' Lord Litchfield raised his hat once again in a mockery of politeness, before wheeling his horse about and urging it into an unhurried walk in the opposite direction.

'What a disgustingly dreadful man,' Edith muttered with distaste.

'Indeed,' her grandson agreed.

'Thank heavens you came along when you did, Royston.'

'I have no doubts you would have succeeded in routing him quite thoroughly yourself, Grandmama,' he said with a twinkle, 'once you had recovered from the shock of his incivility in daring to speak to you at all.'

'No doubt. I am nevertheless grateful for your intervention, Royston,' the dowager duchess said.

'Perhaps we should be thanking Stanhope. I called at Royston House earlier,' he explained, 'and it was he who told me that the two of you were out driving in the park.'

'I cannot imagine what Litchfield imagined he was doing by approaching my carriage in the first place.' Edith gave one of her disdainful sniffs.

'Perhaps that is because it was Miss Rosewood whom he wished to see again…?'

The dowager looked at her grandson sharply. 'What do you mean, Royston? Surely you are not meaning to imply that Ellie would ever encourage the interest of such an obnoxious gentleman as that?'

Ellie was wondering the same thing. Surely he did not

seriously imagine for one moment that she had encouraged Lord Litchfield in any way?

A single glance beneath lowered lashes at the duke's cold blue eyes, thinned lips and tightly clenched jaw, showed her that he was, to all intents and purposes, furious.

Was he furious with her? And if so, why?

The drive back to Royston House was completed in silence, but Ellie was only too aware of the duke's continued anger as he rode beside the carriage on his magnificent black hunter, the expression on his face daring any in society to approach or speak to them. Wisely, none did.

Why Ellie should continue to feel quite so much as if that anger was directed personally at her was beyond understanding; despite what the duke might think, she had done nothing to encourage Lord Litchfield.

And yet still she felt as if all of the seething emotions she sensed behind Justin's stony façade were directed at her: anger, irritation and, for some inexplicable reason, resentment.

Quite why he should resent her was a mystery. If anyone should be feeling *that* particular emotion, then it should be Ellie herself, for she was the one who had once again been made a fool of the evening before, with her undeniable responses to this impossible man. Yes, indeed, all of the resentment should be on her side, not his!

Justin handed his hat and gloves to Stanhope as he entered Royston House, knowing that if the two ladies had not been present in the park, he would have been unable to stop himself from committing a public scandal, by punching Dryden Litchfield on his drink-bloated nose!

But, of course, if they had not been present, Eleanor in

particular, then Justin doubted that such a confrontation would ever have taken place.

But it was only a matter of time before it did so, for Justin was certain that he and Litchfield would come to blows one day. And, after the things Richmond had related to him at their meeting earlier today, it was a day Justin anticipated with the greatest of pleasure.

But not yet. For the moment he intended to keep his own counsel and protect Eleanor without her knowledge. 'Perhaps we might partake of tea in your private parlour, Grandmama?'

'Tea, Royston?' His grandmother looked suitably surprised by this concession to civility by her wayward grandson. 'I had not thought you a great advocate of tea, my dear?'

'Brandy, then,' he conceded wryly.

'See to it, would you, Stanhope,' Edith instructed even as she walked up the grand staircase.

'At once, your Grace.' The butler departed for the back of the house, leaving Eleanor and Justin alone in the grand entrance hall.

He was very aware that it was the first time he had been alone with her since their strained parting of the evening before. And yet it seemed as if days had passed since that time instead of hours, so much had transpired.

Usually Justin had no trouble sleeping, but he had found it impossible to fall into slumber the night before, physically frustrated of course, which was never a good thing, but also angry with himself for having kissed Eleanor yet again, and more than a little troubled as to what Richmond wished to discuss with him.

But he would never have guessed, could never have envisaged the full horror of the things Richmond had related to him earlier this afternoon.

Justin could not help but frown now as he looked down at Eleanor's bent head, her innocent head, and wonder how, if Richmond's suspicions should turn out to be correct, he would ever be able to tell her the truth, without utterly destroying the spirit in her that he so admired, as much as the fragile hold she now had in society.

No doubt Eleanor, never having needed that society before, would dismiss the importance of it in her life now, but Justin found he could not bear the thought of her independence of spirit also being trampled underfoot, snuffing out that light of either challenge or mischief he so often detected in her unwavering green gaze during their lively exchanges.

No, he would not tell Eleanor anything of that conversation as yet, preferring to make his own private and discreet enquiries, at least going some way towards proving—or disproving—Richmond's fears, before so much as attempting to broach the subject to her. Fears, which, in view of his grandmother's own doubts on the subject, Justin had no choice but to take seriously.

For what decent young woman, especially a young and beautiful woman newly entered into society, would want to be burdened with the stigma of learning that her father, her real father, might be none other than Lord Dryden Litchfield, an inveterate rake and gambler, whom all of decent society shunned?

Chapter Nine

Ellie was painfully aware of Justin's sinfully handsome appearance as he stood beside her in a perfectly tailored superfine of sapphire blue, setting off buff-coloured pantaloons and brown-topped Hessians. There was an awkward silence between them, forcing her into making some sort of conversation.

She lifted her chin even as she tilted her head back in order to look up at him, feeling the physical discomfort at her nape in having to do so. 'Goodness, you are prodigiously tall!'

Blue eyes, the exact same shade as his superfine, widened briefly, before those chiselled lips twisted into a rueful smile. 'And you, brat, are incredibly rude, that you can never address a gentleman in the normal fashion of a well-bred young lady!'

'Perhaps I have been keeping company with you for too long?' she came back pertly.

'Perhaps you have,' he allowed. 'Shall we?' He held out his arm to her. 'Unless you wish to put my grandmother to the trouble of coming in search of us, which I am sure she will do if we do not soon join her in her parlour,' he prompted as Ellie hesitated.

No, she had no wish to involve the dowager duchess in this battle of wills that ensued between herself and that lady's grandson each and every time they met.

Her hesitation in taking his arm was for another reason entirely. Already aware of everything about him, she had no wish to place herself in the position of touching him, of once again feeling his warmth beneath her gloved finger-tips, the leashed strength of his tautly held muscles. To be so close to him that she could not help but be aware of that intensely seductive smell that was unique to him—clean healthy male and a fresh yet sensual cologne, which seemed to wind itself in and about her, until she longed for nothing more than to have him kiss her again, touch her again, make love to her again…

She straightened her spine in defence of that onslaught to her emotions as she deliberately placed her hand lightly upon the duke's arm. 'I should not at all wish to put the dowager duchess to such trouble as that.'

'And, in your opinion, how is she today?' her grandson enquired as they ascended the staircase together.

Ellie gave him a startled glance. 'You want my opinion…?'

He nodded. 'I received your note earlier, informing me of Dr Franklyn's visit this morning, and as that gentleman prefers to keep his opinion of my grandmother's health to himself,' he added with clear disapproval, 'it leaves me with no choice but to try to elicit the opinion on the subject from the one person who is with her the most.'

In truth, with all the excitement of the flowers arriving constantly throughout the day, the ride in the park, the encounter with the disagreeable Lord Litchfield, and then Justin's unexpected arrival a short time ago, Ellie had all but forgotten the note she had sent him following Dr Franklyn's visit.

Although Ellie could not help but admit to a certain grudging admiration for Dr Franklyn, in that he was insistent upon protecting his patient's confidentiality…much to the duke's obvious annoyance. She gave an inward smile.

'I believe her to be quite well, considering she was hostess to a ball yesterday evening, and the late hour at which we finally retired for the night,' Ellie said. 'Perhaps the doctor's visit was simply a precautionary one rather than a necessity?'

Justin pursed his lips. 'Perhaps.'

But, in Ellie's opinion, he did not sound at all certain. 'The dowager duchess did breakfast in her rooms, which is not her usual custom. But she did join me not long after that and we ate luncheon together. And it was her suggestion that we should ride in the park this afternoon.'

Justin's expression turned grim as he recalled who had been there with them when he had finally found Eleanor and his grandmother in the park earlier. 'I believe I warned you as to the unsuitability of Lord Litchfield's company?'

'You did, yes.'

'And?'

Two wings of angry colour brightened Eleanor's cheeks as she came to a halt in the hallway outside Edith's private parlour. 'And, as your grandmother has already informed you, Lord Litchfield chose to inflict his company upon us without the least encouragement. From either of us.'

Justin's nostrils flared. 'I cannot emphasise how strongly I wish for you to avoid that man's company!'

Not Just a Wallflower

'And I cannot emphasise how strongly I resent this second implication from you that I would ever wish to encourage the attentions of such an unpleasant man!' Green eyes sparkled with that same anger as Eleanor glared up at him.

Justin held back the sharpness of his own reply and instead drew in a deep breath in an effort to calm his own turbulent emotions, knowing the worst of them, his anger, was caused by fear—for her safety, for her emotional well-being.

Litchfield was proving to be something of a nemesis in their lives at the moment, somehow seeming to be there, whenever Justin turned around. And, after Richmond's revelations about the man, Justin did not wish for Dryden Litchfield to be anywhere near Eleanor. Or for Eleanor to be anywhere near him.

He forced the tension from his shoulders as he straightened. 'I believe you are determined to misunderstand me—'

'Is that you at last, Royston, Eleanor?' his grandmother, obviously having heard the sound of their voices outside in the hallway, now called out impatiently.

Justin bit back his own impatience at this interruption as he lowered his voice so that only Eleanor might hear him. 'We will talk of this again later.'

'No, your Grace, I do not believe we will,' she snapped back, and obviously tired of waiting for him to open the parlour door for her, opened it for herself and preceded him into the room.

'Do not believe you will what, my dear?' the dowager enquired.

Justin followed Eleanor into the room. 'Will not—Good God, it is like a florist's shop in here!' He almost recoiled from the overabundance of perfume given off by the multitude of flowers in the room, vases and vases of them, it seemed, on every available surface. 'How on earth can you possibly breathe in here, Grandmama?' He strode across the room to throw open a window before turning to glare across at Eleanor. 'I suppose we have your success last night to thank for this gratuitous display?'

'Royston!' his grandmother rebuked sharply.

Justin' continued to glare at Eleanor. 'I am only stating the obvious, Grandmama!'

'That is no excuse for upsetting Ellie.' The dowager duchess rose to her feet to cross to Eleanor's side and place an arm about her shoulders. 'I am sure Royston did not mean to be so sharp with you, my dear,' she soothed as the younger woman looked in danger of succumbing to tears.

He *had* meant to be sharp with her, Justin realised in self-disgust. In fact, that was exactly what he had meant to do!

Because he felt somehow…unsettled by this garish tribute to her obvious success the evening before, he acknowledged.

And also, he realised uncomfortably, because it had not so much as occurred to him to send Eleanor flowers himself.

Why should it have done? Even the women whose bodies he availed himself of for however long before he grew tired of them had never received flowers from him. A pretty and expensive piece of jewellery as a parting gift, perhaps, but never flowers. Justin considered flowers as being somehow more personal, a gift chosen for the woman herself, rather than with an eye to how much money they might cost.

And here Eleanor had received dozens of such tokens of admiration, probably from all those young bucks who had flocked about her at the ball!

Again Justin asked why that should bother him? If those young idiots wished to make fools of themselves over a

new and beautiful face, then who was he to care one way
or the other?

He stood stiffly across the room, arms behind his back.
'I was merely taken by surprise at—'

'—such a gratuitous display,' Eleanor completed challengingly as she straightened out of the dowager's embrace,
her chin held proudly high, sparks of anger in her eyes now
rather than tears as she glared across at him. 'If you will
both excuse me, I believe I will go to my room and tidy my
appearance before dinner.' She sketched a brief curtsy before leaving the parlour with a swish of her skirts.

'Royston, what on earth was that all about?'

Justin closed his eyes momentarily before opening them
again to look across at his grandmother, sighing deeply as he
saw the reproach in her steely blue gaze. 'You no doubt wish
for me to go to Eleanor and apologise for my churlishness?'

The dowager gave him a searching glance before replying. 'Only if that is what you wish to do yourself.'

Did he? Dare he follow Eleanor to her bedchamber?
Allow himself to be in a position, a place, where he might
be tempted into kissing her, making love to her once again?

'Obviously not,' his grandmother said acidly at his
lengthy silence. 'Ah, Stanhope.' She turned to greet the
butler warmly as he arrived with the brandy and tea. 'Wait
a moment, if you please, and take this cup of tea to Miss
Rosewood in her bedchamber.' She bent to pour the brew
into the two delicate china teacups.

Justin was still fighting an inner battle with himself,
aware that he had been overly sharp with Eleanor just now,
and that he did owe her an apology for his behaviour, if
not an explanation. For he had no intention of admitting to
anyone, not even himself—least of all himself!—the real

emotion that had washed over him when he had first looked upon all those flowers and realised they were tangible proof of the admiration Eleanor had received from so many other gentlemen the evening before.

Jealousy…

Insufferable, impossible, cruel, heartless man! Arrogant, hateful, *hateful* man!

And Ellie did hate at that moment. Hated his cynicism. His sarcasm. His mockery. His overbearing arrogance. His—

'I have brought you a cup of tea…'

Ellie turned sharply, from where she lay on the bed, to look across at Justin as he stood in the doorway to her bed-chamber, aware of her reddened cheeks and the soreness of her eyes from the tears that she had allowed to fall the moment she entered the room and which had been flowing unchecked ever since.

Tears of frustration and hurt, at the unfairness of his accusations.

Tears of pain and humiliation, at his unkindness about the flowers that had been sent to her today, and which she had so enjoyed receiving.

They were also tears which Eleanor had never intended for Justin to bear witness to!

She sat up and began dabbing at the evidence of those tears with the lace handkerchief she had retrieved from the pocket of her gown. 'Are you sure you should be in here?'

His answer to that was to step further into the room and close the door behind him. 'I have brought you a cup of tea,' he repeated. 'And I will bring it across to you if you promise not to throw it over me the moment I place it in your hand!' he teased gently.

Ellie replaced the handkerchief in her pocket. 'You are an exceedingly cruel man.'

'Yes.'

'An insufferable man.'

'Yes.'

She frowned. 'Hateful, even.'

'Yes.'

Ellie blinked at his unexpected acquiescence to her accusations. 'Why do you not defend yourself?'

He sighed deeply. 'Possibly because, on this occasion, I know you are correct. I am all of the things you have accused me of being.'

Ellie eyed him guardedly, looking for signs of that sarcasm or cynicism she had also accused him of to herself just minutes ago. He met her gaze unblinkingly, the expression in those blue eyes neither cynical nor sarcastic, but merely accepting. 'I do not understand...'

'I am merely agreeing with you, Eleanor.' He crossed the room until he stood before her, the delicacy of the saucer and teacup he held out to her looking slightly incongruous in his lean hand.

She reached up slowly and took the cup and saucer from him. 'That is what I do not understand.'

He looked down at her beneath hooded lids as he gave a shrug of those broad shoulders. 'I have no defence, when everything you accuse me of, I undoubtedly am.'

'And that is your apology for such insufferable behaviour?' Ellie asked.

A humourless smile curved his lips. 'No.'

'Because you offer no apology,' she realised. 'Only tea.'

'Is it not the panacea to all ills?' he drawled as Eleanor took several sips of the steaming brew.

'I believe I should have appreciated an apology more!'

'Would you?' he asked enigmatically.

Where had all her anger towards this man disappeared to? Ellie wondered crossly as she continued to sip her tea. Because, she realised, she was no longer angry. Or tearful. In fact, a part of her felt decidedly like smiling. Or perhaps even laughing at the incongruousness of seeing such a guilty-little-boy expression on the face of one as impossibly arrogant as he was. It was also totally illogical, in view of the way his sarcasm had hurt her just a few short minutes ago.

Except...

That ridiculous expression aside, she very much doubted that Justin had ever bothered himself to take tea to a woman in the whole of his privileged life before today. The fact that he had done so now, and to her, was in itself an apology of sorts. Not the grovelling appeasement that some would have made in the circumstances, but from this arrogant duke, Ellie recognised it was as good as another gentleman having got down upon his knees and begged her forgiveness.

She placed the empty teacup and its saucer on the bedside table. 'Thank you. I do feel slightly better now.'

'Good.' He moved to sit on the side of the bed beside her and took one of her hands in both of his much larger ones. 'And I do sincerely apologise for my bad temper to you just now, Eleanor.'

Ellie, already disconcerted at the touch of his hands on hers, now looked at him in surprise. 'You do?'

He nodded. 'I was boorish, to say the least. I was a little... unsettled after seeing Litchfield, of all people, beside my grandmother's carriage in the park. But I accept I should not have taken that bad temper out on you.'

Ellie's heart had begun to beat faster at his sudden proximity, her cheeks feeling warm, her breathing shallow, and he surely must be able to feel the way her hand trembled slightly inside his? 'I really do not think it quite proper for you to be in my bedchamber. The dowager duchess—'

'Made it plain to me just now that she, at least, considers me to be nothing more than an uncle to you and, as such, feels it is perfectly permissible for me to visit you here,' he revealed drily.

The utterly disgusted expression on his face that accompanied this revelation only made Ellie feel like laughing again. How strange, when just minutes ago she had felt as if she might never laugh again…

Justin was completely unprepared for the way in which Eleanor's lips now twitched with obvious humour, before it turned into an open smile, to be followed by husky laughter. 'I fail to see what it is you find so amusing?'

'That is probably because—' She broke off, still smiling as she shook her head. 'The thought of you being considered in an avuncular role by any young woman is utterly ridiculous!'

Justin scowled. 'I could not agree more.'

Those green eyes danced. 'Your reputation in society as a rake would be ruined for ever if that were to become the general consensus!'

He stilled. 'My reputation in society is that of a rake?'

'Oh, yes.' She nodded.

'And is that what you think of me, too?' He frowned darkly. 'That I choose to spend all of my days and nights bedding young women at every available opportunity?'

'Well…perhaps not all of your days,' Eleanor allowed mischievously. 'You do, after all, have to find the time in which to attend to your ducal responsibilities! And there was gossip, yesterday evening at the ball, that not all of those ladies have been quite so young or available…'

'I am accused of bedding married women, too?'

She raised auburn brows at his harshness. 'You sound surprised that your affairs are quite so widely known.'

'What I am surprised at is that you were subjected to overhearing such errant nonsense!' He released her hand and stood up to restlessly cross the room before standing stiffly in front of the window. 'Who made these scurrilous remarks?'

She looked puzzled. 'I am not sure that I remember who exactly…'

A nerve pulsed in his tightly clenched jaw. 'Try!'

She gave a slow shake of her head. 'The remarks were not made to me directly, I merely overheard several people speculating as to who your current mistress might be, and which husband was being made the cuckold last night.'

'I assure you—' Justin broke off, realising he was angry once again, but this time at remarks made in Eleanor's hearing as to what society thought of him—a reputation which had not bothered him in the slightest until he had heard it from her lips… 'I wish you to know that I have the deepest respect for the married state, and as such have never shown the slightest inclination to bed a married woman. Nor,' he continued grimly, 'do I have a "current mistress".'

Ellie could tell by his expression that by repeating such gossip she had somehow succeeded in seriously insulting him. 'I did not mean to give offence, your Grace.'

'I am not in the least offended,' he denied.

'I beg to differ…'

His expression softened slightly. 'I am not offended by

anything you have personally said to or about me, my displeasure is for those people who obviously have nothing better to do with their time than make up scandalous and inaccurate gossip!' His voice had hardened again over the last statement.

Ellie realised that his displeasure at hearing of society's opinion of him was completely genuine.

Gossip, which Ellie, in view of their own recent intimacies, had found extremely hurtful to overhear. So much so that just imagining Justin having a mistress, and that he had gone to be with her once he had left the ball, had only added to her inability to sleep the night before.

But Justin now appeared to be denying it most vehemently.

Too vehemently to be believed?

Somehow she did not think so. Justin was all of those things she had accused him of being earlier—he could be cruel on occasion, insufferable and hateful—but at the same time she knew him to be a truthful man; indeed, it was that very honesty, his bluntness, which was usually to blame for all of those other, infuriating traits!

As such, if he now said he did not have a current mistress, married or otherwise, then she believed him…

It was an acceptance which made her feel as if a weight had been lifted from her chest. A weight she had not even realised had been there until it was removed…and which once again caused her to question her feelings towards this unattainable duke. A question she knew, even as she asked it, that she shied away from answering!

She rose to her feet. 'I am sure the dowager duchess has been most forbearing, but perhaps it is time for you to rejoin her in her parlour?' She linked her gloved hands tightly together in front of her. 'I really do have to change before dinner.'

'You have not said yet whether or not you believe my denials.'

She shrugged. 'Does it matter whether or not I believe you?'

Justin narrowed his lids as he noted the challenging tilt of her chin and the directness of her unreadable gaze.

He also realised that his own mood just now had been a defensive one. A feeling which was surely totally misplaced; it should not matter to him what his young ward thought of him, or his reputation. 'Not in the least,' he finally drawled.

Her gaze dropped from his. 'As I thought.'

Justin gave her a terse bow before striding across to the doorway. 'I will see you at dinner.'

'What?'

He paused to turn, his hand already on the door handle. 'I said we will meet again at dinner.'

She blinked. 'I had not realised her Grace had invited you to dine here this evening.'

Justin smiled. 'Of course…you were not present just now during the last part of my conversation with my grand-mother.' He stood with his arms folded across his chest. 'If you had been, then you would know that it is my inten-tion to dine here every evening for the foreseeable future. Breakfast, too, on the mornings I rise early enough to par-take of it. I may be absent for the occasional luncheon—as you say, I do have other ducal responsibilities in need of my attention.'

Ellie gasped. 'I do not understand…'

His smile widened. 'It is quite simple, Eleanor. After years of my grandmother's interminable nagg—er, helpful suggestions, I have decided it is time that I moved back into the ducal home. As such I, and my belongings and personal staff, will be taking up permanent residence at Royston House as from tomorrow morning.'

Chapter Ten

'Why are you so surprised by my decision, Eleanor?' Justin asked as Ellie could only stare wide-eyed and openmouthed across the bedchamber at him in the wake of his announcement. 'After all, you are responsible for alerting me to the fact that Dr Franklyn made yet another visit to my grandmother this morning.'

That might be so, but she certainly had not thought it would result in his decision to move into Royston House!

No doubt the dowager duchess was beside herself with pleasure at this unexpected turn of events, but it was equally as unthinkable to Ellie that she would have to suffer this disturbing man's presence every hour of every day 'for the foreseeable future'!

She moistened suddenly dry lips. 'Well, yes, I did do that, of course. But I did not mean it to—I had not expected—'

'You did not envisage it would result in your now having to suffer my living here?' Royston guessed drily.

No, she most certainly had not! Nor did there seem any point in her denying that was her response, when she had moments ago gawked at the duke like a dumbstruck schoolgirl, no doubt with a look of horror upon her face. 'Will the dowager duchess not think it…strange that you have capitulated now, when you have always resisted her pleadings in the past?'

The duke's mouth quirked. 'My grandmother does not plead, Eleanor, she suggests or instructs. And, no, I do not see why she should find my decision in the least strange.'

Ellie nibbled her lower lip. 'Surely she will realise, eventually, that someone—notably myself—must have informed you of Dr Franklyn's visit earlier today?'

'Not unless you or I were to tell her of it.' He arched golden brows. 'Do you intend telling her?'

'No, of course I do not.' She frowned her agitation in the face of his infuriating calm. 'I just—your grandmother will be too pleased by your decision at the moment to question it, but once she does—what reason will you give her for this change of heart?'

He looked down the length of his arrogant nose. 'Why should I give her any reason? This is, after all, the official London home of the Duke of Royston. That I have not chosen to live in it for some years does not mean I was not at liberty to do so at any time I chose.'

Ellie was aware of that. But she was also aware that the dowager duchess was a woman of astuteness as well as intelligence, and once that dear lady had opportunity to think, to fully consider Royston's sudden unexpected change of heart, she would most assuredly question as to why it should have occurred now, of all times.

Ellie had dashed off that note to Royston this morning for the simple reason he had asked her to do so should such a thing occur, but she had not, as he so easily guessed and obviously found so amusing, expected to now have him thrust into her own life on a daily basis. Indeed, the very idea of it, given the circumstances of their own fraught relationship, was a total nightmare for her!

It was not too difficult for Justin to read the emotions flickering across her expressive face.

It was the last emotion—horror at the prospect of living with him—which irritated Justin the most. Especially when his real reason for moving into Royston House had everything to do with her, with the conversation that had taken place with Richmond this afternoon, and its possible repercussions upon Eleanor, rather than his grandmother's health, or any real desire on Justin's part to reside here.

It really was too insulting, given those circumstances, for him to have to suffer Eleanor's obvious dismay at the very thought of being under the same roof as him, of sharing even so large a residence as Royston House with him. But it was an insult he had no choice but to endure, unless he wished to tell her of the contents of his conversation with Richmond this afternoon, which, for the moment, he had no intention of doing.

Far better if Justin were to proceed with his previous decision to privately and quietly check into those details for himself, before facing the possibility of having to burden her with any of them.

She did not need to know, for instance, of the scandal that had ensued in India twenty years ago, in which Dryden Litchfield had been accused of attacking and raping the recently widowed wife of a fellow officer. A rape that Richmond, after seeing Eleanor the previous evening, and noting her likeness to Muriel Rosewood, and the richness of her auburn hair so like Litchfield's had once been, now believed might have resulted in Eleanor's very existence; Muriel Rosewood had not been with child when her husband had died, nor had there been any sign of it when she'd left India. The timing of the incident certainly suggested that Eleanor could well be Litchfield's daughter…

No, Justin wouldn't trouble Eleanor with any of that until he was sure, beyond any doubt, that Litchfield was, in fact, her biological father. And possibly not even then, either…

He straightened his shoulders. 'The decision has been made and tomorrow morning will be acted upon,' Justin said firmly. 'As such, I will see you at dinner this evening.'

'I—yes. Of course, your Grace—'

'I have repeatedly requested that you not call me that,' he growled.

Silky dark lashes lowered demurely over those expressive green eyes. 'Then perhaps I should consider calling you "Uncle" Justin?'

'Why, you little—!' He did not even bother to finish the sentence as he strode furiously across the room towards her.

Too late, Ellie realised her mistake in goading him, looking up just in time to see him powering towards her, fury blazing in those sapphire-blue eyes, causing her to step back even as she held her hands up defensively. 'Your Gr—er—Sir—Justin—'

'It's too late for that, Eleanor!' His arms moved about her waist as he pulled her in tightly against him, her hands trapped between the softness of her breasts and the muscled hardness of his chest. 'You are fully aware,' he grated, 'my feelings towards you are far from avuncular!'

How could she help but be aware of it when she could feel the evidence of his desire pressing into her abdomen!

Heat suffused her cheeks, her legs starting to tremble, as she looked at his face and saw evidence of that same desire blazing in the depths of the glittering blue eyes glaring down at her, high cheekbones thrown into sharp relief by the tight clenching of his jaw. 'You are crushing me, Your—Justin.' She turned her hands and began to push against the hardness of his chest in an unsuccessful attempt to free herself.

He bared his teeth in a humourless smile. 'And so now you learn, too late, my dear, the lesson that baiting the tiger is much worse than simply awakening him!'

She blinked. 'I was only—I merely—'

'I know exactly what you were doing, Eleanor—and *this* is my answer!' His head swooped downwards as he captured her lips with his own even as he took a step forwards, taking Ellie with him.

She gasped as her legs hit the mattress of the bed and she lost her balance, toppling backwards. Justin swiftly took full advantage of her parted lips in order to deepen the kiss, one of his hands moving to curve possessively about her chin as he followed her down, his heavier weight landing on top of her and crushing her into the mattress.

Ellie was so stunned to find herself lying on her back on the bed, Justin's body pressing intimately against hers, that she no longer fought the onslaught as his lips continued to devour hers. Instead, she felt compelled to return that fever of passion, her arms moving up and over his shoulders to allow her to entangle her fingers in the silky softness of the hair at his nape as she kissed him back.

Quite when his punishing onslaught changed—when Justin's lips became less demanding and instead sipped and tasted her own as he adjusted his position, the hardness of his arousal now pressing against her hip as one of his legs lay between hers, allowing the warmth of his hand to curve about the full softness of her breast—she had no idea.

Nor did she care, as the thrill of arousal coursed through her, causing her breast to swell into the heat of his palm as the soft pad of his thumb sought, and unerringly found, and began to caress, the swollen and sensitive berry pressing against the soft material of her gown.

Ellie felt hot, feverish, her throat arching as he continued to kiss and caress her, moving restlessly against him as she dampened between her thighs, groaning low in her throat, as his knee moved up to press gently against that sensitive nubbin she had recently discovered nestled there, even as his thumb and fingers plucked rhythmically at her now hardened and oh-so-sensitive nipple.

He dragged his lips from hers to trail kisses hotly across her cheek and down her throat, his breath warm, arousing, against the heat of her flesh, that tingling in her breasts rising to fever pitch as his lips and tongue now tasted the swell visible above her gown and causing another rush of dampness between her thighs.

'Justin!' she cried out achingly as his hand left her breast.

'Yes—Justin,' he growled intensely, his hand sliding up her back. 'Say it, Eleanor. Say it, damn it!'

'Justin,' she breathed obediently. 'Oh God, Justin, Justin, Justin…!' That last trailed off to a groan as she felt his tongue laving the throbbing, engorged tip of her bared breast, having no idea how that had come about, only knowing that it gave her pleasure beyond imagining as he now took that hardened tip fully into the moist heat of his mouth.

Her fingers became entangled in the silkiness of his hair even as she arched up into that demanding mouth, sensations such as she had never known existed coursing through her as she felt his hand now cup her other bared breast, thumb and finger capturing the ripe tip, and causing exquisite pleasure as he continued to caress and then squeeze that tingling, aching fullness.

Justin raised his head slightly, his movement releasing Eleanor's nipple from his mouth with a softly audible pop as he looked down in satisfaction at the swollen berry. The nipple and aureole were coloured a deep rose, the nipple engorged from the ministrations of his mouth and tongue, and continuing to flower as he blew on it gently, his gaze heating as his hand now lifted her breast until that nipple brushed against his lips.

He looked up into Eleanor's face as he slowly ran his tongue skilfully against that responsive berry, groaning low in his throat as he saw she was looking back at him with fevered eyes, several tendrils of her hair having escaped their confines and falling enticingly about the warmth of her cheeks. She looked gloriously, wantonly, beautiful!

And he should stop this now. Should put an end to this before it was too late—

'Justin…?' she moaned even as her fingers tightened in his hair and she arched her back, pushing her nipple between his parted lips and back into the moist heat of his mouth.

All thoughts of stopping fled, his lashes lowering as he obediently suckled deeply, drawing that nipple up to the roof of his mouth, tongue flicking, teeth gently biting, at the same time as his hand caressed a path down to her thighs to her knees, pushing the material of her gown aside so that he might touch the bare, silken flesh beneath.

The backs of her knees held the warmth of velvet, her

thighs as smooth as silk, satin drawers posing no difficulty as Justin sought, and found, the slit in that material between her thighs, allowing his fingers to slip inside to gently stroke her swollen, wet folds.

He dipped his fingers into that moisture even as he heard Eleanor's gasp, half in shocked protest, half in pleasure, stroking her again and again, bathing his fingers in that moisture between each stroke, drawing her nipple deeply into his mouth in the same rhythm, until she no longer protested but groaned her pleasure as she writhed beneath him.

Justin was aware of the moment her hands fell down on to the bed beside her in surrender, of her head moving restlessly from side to side on the pillows, and he at last parted the silky folds and bared her sensitive and swollen nubbin to his caressing fingers and began to stroke in earnest. Softly and then harder, each time increasing the pressure, measuring his strokes to the rhythmic lifting of her hips, as she met each and every one of them, until he knew she was poised on the brink of a shattering release.

'Oh, it is too much…!' she gasped in protest, yet at the same time unable to stop herself from arching up into those caresses, her fingers once again entangled tightly in his hair as she held his mouth against her breast. 'Justin, do something…!'

Justin knew he was damned if he did. Damned if he did not. Because, he knew, whether he gave her the release she so obviously craved, or stopped this before that should happen, no doubt leaving her aching and wanting for hours afterwards, that she was never going to forgive him for arousing her to such a pitch that she lost control so completely she begged him for satisfaction.

* * *

Ellie had never known such pleasure as this existed. Had never dreamt—never so much as guessed it was there for the taking.

It really was too much, overwhelming even, as Justin turned his attention to her other breast, at the same time as he stroked between her thighs, fingers dipping into her sheath, but never quite entering, those moist fingers then moving higher to stroke the hardened nubbin above.

Such a tiny nubbin of flesh, and one that she had barely been aware of until Justin touched her, and yet it was such pleasure to have him touch her there, stroking her, his fingertip now tapping lightly against it, driving her higher, and then higher still, taking her up to a plateau of exquisite pleasure, before just seconds later she felt herself falling over the edge and down into a sea of never-ending sensations.

Again and again mindless pleasure washed over her, becoming the centre of her existence, all of her senses concentrated on those sensations: the feeling of her sheath as it pulsed and contracted, the fullness of that nubbin as it swelled and throbbed, the pleasure-pain of Justin's lips and teeth capturing each of her nipples in turn, his breath so hot and arousing against her cooler flesh.

Ellie had no idea how long it lasted, how many minutes, hours, had passed as she lost herself to that release as Justin demanded and took every last measure of that pleasure.

But finally, immeasurable minutes later, he gentled those stroking fingers between her thighs, softened his tongue against her now throbbing and aching breasts, placing one last lingering kiss against each swollen tip before he rolled to one side and moved up on his elbow to look down at her. 'I did not hurt you, did I?'

The gruffness of his voice was a thrill in itself as it wound itself sinuously along Ellie's already sensitive nerve-endings. Yet at the same time it broke the sensuous spell she had been under, allowing her to become aware of exactly what she had allowed to happen.

The Duke of Royston had just made love to her, touched her, more pleasurably, more intimately than any man had ever dared to attempt before now. More intimately than Ellie should have allowed any man to touch her before her wedding night!

Something that would never happen for her with the cynically arrogant Justin St Just, who wasn't interested in loving his bride or having those feelings returned. And she had probably just added to that cynicism and arrogance, with her easy capitulation to his seduction!

She scrambled up into a sitting position, blushing as she drew her legs up beneath her defensively, to clutch her gaping gown against her to cover her now painfully aching breasts. It allowed her to see that he was still fully and impeccably dressed, necktie still in place, waistcoat still buttoned, his hair only slightly tousled, from where her fingers had entwined and clutched at that silkiness in the throes of her pleasure, whereas he had obviously remained unmoved throughout!

She drew in a shaky breath. 'I asked you to leave some time ago.'

'Eleanor—'

'Get out!' she instructed firmly as she averted her gaze from his, not wishing to see the disgust that must surely be in his eyes. Or perhaps it would be pity or triumph there and she knew she could not bear to suffer any of those emotions being directed towards her just now.

Dear lord, she was in love with this man. A love she could never, must never, allow him to find out about. It would destroy her utterly.

'Whatever you are thinking, Eleanor, I wish you to stop it this minute!'

Her eyes glittered with unshed tears as she turned back to him. 'Do not tell me what I should or should not think!' she flared, falling back upon anger to hide her real emotions.

His eyes narrowed. 'I could have stopped, should have stopped—indeed, I had thought of doing so—but you would not have thanked me for it if I had—'

'I am not thanking you now!'

'No,' he accepted heavily before standing up and looking down at her bleakly. 'Eleanor—'

'You "could have stopped"? You "thought of doing so"?' Ellie's voice rose indignantly as she realised what he had just said, knowing that she'd had no will to call a halt, no strength to resist his caresses. But he had. Oh, yes, the arrogant Duke of Royston had remained completely in control of his own senses, whilst her feelings for him meant that she had melted at his first touch. How humiliating. 'I told you to leave,' she repeated woodenly.

'Eleanor, listen to me, damn it!' He frowned down at her in frustration. 'If I had stopped you would now be berating me for leaving you in a state of dissatisfaction that would have clawed at you for hours, instead of which—'

'Instead of which I can now claim to have been the latest recipient of the irresistible Duke of Royston's expert lovemaking!' she threw back.

He drew in a sharp breath. 'I refuse to take offence at your insults. I realise that you are...upset.' He ran agitated hands through his hair, those golden waves instantly falling back into their artfully dishevelled style. As if he had made the gesture a hundred times before and knew its effect. After making love to a hundred different women, no doubt!

It infuriated Ellie all over again to know that she was nothing more to this man than another notch on his bedpost. 'Oh, by all means take offence,' she invited scathingly. 'For, I assure you, I am not so upset that I do not know exactly what I am saying when I warn you never to touch me ever again!'

'We will talk of this when you are calmer—'

'No, we will not,' she insisted firmly.

Too late, Justin realised the seriousness of the error he had made. Damn it, he was a man known for his icy control. A man who maintained his calm no matter what the provocation. A legendary control that had come about because of those lonely childhood years when he had felt the pain of his parents' exclusion and which he had eventually only been able to live with by learning and adopting that coolness of temperament for which he was now so well known. But Justin knew, had always known, that deep inside himself lay something else entirely, a heat, a quickness of emotions which he had no control over whatsoever. And it seemed Eleanor brought out that heat in him when no one else had managed it.

Tonight, with her, his control had been totally stripped away, his emotions so totally engaged in their lovemaking that his claim of thinking of stopping was an empty one. The unpalatable truth was, he could not have stopped kissing, caressing and making love to Eleanor if the devil himself had been at his back. That he had wanted, *ached,* to give her pleasure, as much as he had wanted to feel and see her in the throes of it, just because he had given it to her.

He sighed. 'It is a little naïve of you to expect us never to refer to this incident again—' He broke off as she gave a bitter laugh.

'Thanks to you I am no longer in the least naïve!'

'Oh, yes, Eleanor, in all the ways that matter you are still very much an innocent,' Justin argued, hands clenching into fists at his sides. 'Nor have we done anything this evening that in the least damages that innocence, or your reputation in society.'

She looked at him wordlessly for several long seconds before giving a slow shake of her head. 'I have little or no regard for my reputation in society, sir, but my innocence is certainly now questionable.'

'No—'

'Yes,' she hissed. 'You, of all people, must know that I had no idea—no knowledge of—' She stopped and gathered herself. 'My maidenhead may indeed still be intact, but my innocence is not.' Her cheeks were flushed. 'Now, would you please, please leave me.' Her voice finally wavered emotionally, the over-bright glitter in her eyes confirming that she was on the edge of tears.

Tears, which Justin knew with a certainty, she would not wish him to see fall. 'I trust you understand how impossible it is for me to even attempt to explain to my grandmother why I have changed my mind about moving into Royston House?'

Eleanor's shoulders straightened proudly. 'I understand. Just as I am sure that the two of us are adult enough, and both have enough affection for the dowager duchess, if not for each other, to do everything in our power to be polite to one another whenever we are in her company or that of others.'

Telling Justin, more surely than anything else could have done, that Eleanor had no intention of being in the least polite to him when they were alone…

He breathed out his frustration. 'Perhaps if you had listened to me when I advised you not to bait the tiger—'

'Are you saying,' Ellie interrupted with deceptive softness, 'that you consider this as being just "another lesson" you felt the need to demonstrate?'

He was taken aback. 'No, I am merely—Eleanor, put down that cup!' he instructed sharply as she turned to grab it up from its saucer. 'Eleanor!'

She did not so much as hesitate, drawing back her arm and launching the china cup across the bedchamber towards his arrogant head. Only to be thoroughly frustrated in that endeavour when he ducked at the last moment, allowing the cup to hit and smash against the door behind him.

He straightened, his face thunderous. 'My grandmother is very fond of those cups—'

Determined not to be thwarted, Ellie immediately took up the saucer and threw that at him too, succeeding in giving him a glancing blow on the side of his arrogant head, at the same time as it dishevelled the fashionably styled hair that had so annoyed her just minutes ago. 'How pleasant it is to know that my years of playing cricket with the local village children were not in vain!' She smiled her satisfaction with her accuracy.

'You are nothing but a damned hellion!' Justin winced as he raised a hand to gently probe the spot where the saucer had hit him. 'By all that's holy, you deserve to have your backside soundly smacked!'

'Lay so much as a finger more on me this evening, your Grace, and I assure you, I will scream until all the household comes running!' Ellie warned him with icy pride; she might have allowed herself to be seduced by her feelings for this man, but that did not mean he would ever know of them.

He straightened, eyes glittering. 'This is far from over, Eleanor.'

'Oh, but it is,' she insisted. 'There will be no more "lessons" for me from you tonight. Or, indeed, any other night! Now please leave my bedchamber.' She turned her face away to indicate an end to the conversation, her heart pounding in her chest as she waited to see if Justin would do as she asked. Having no idea what she would do if he did not!

There was deathly silence for several minutes, then Ellie heard the opening of the door, before it was gently closed again seconds later.

At which time she allowed the tears to fall as she began to cry as if her heart were breaking.

Which it was.

Chapter Eleven

'Is this a bad time, Royston…?'

Justin arched a brow as he looked up at the man standing in front of him, stirring himself to sit up from his slouched position in his chair beside one of the unlit fireplaces at White's, as he recognised Lord Adam Hawthorne, the grandson of one of his grandmother's dearest friends.

And there had not been so much as a single 'good time' for anyone to approach and speak to Justin over the past three days, not since the evening he had made love with Eleanor and she had then so soundly routed him from her bedchamber.

Three days when he and Eleanor had, as agreed, maintained a perfectly civil, if stilted, front whenever they were in the company of his grandmother. Away from the old lady's curious, shrewd gaze it was a different matter entirely; Eleanor avoided his company whenever she could, spending hours in another part of the house from him when she was at home, and other times out visiting, accompanied by her maid or the dowager. And, without Eleanor being aware of it, one of the footmen from Royston House, as extra protection from the threat Justin now considered Litchfield to be.

Not that Justin could blame Eleanor for that avoidance. No, despite that bump on his head from the blow of the saucer, and the headache that had followed, she was not the one to blame for the strain which now existed between them. The blame for that clearly lay entirely on Justin's own shoulders. He had fully deserved her anger, her physical retribution, had seriously overstepped a line with her. One Justin, even with his nine more years of maturity and experience, had absolutely no idea how to cross back over. Eleanor's frosty demeanour towards him certainly gave him the clear impression she had no wish for him to even try healing the breach between them!

Justin had spent the same three days trying to ascertain more about the events of twenty years ago, where Muriel Rosewood had gone to live once she returned to England, and what had become of her. Something which, without the help of Muriel herself, was not proving as easy as Justin had hoped it might. Many of the soldiers who had been in India at the same time as Litchfield, but later also returned to England, had died during the battles against Napoleon, and their widows, or the soldiers who had survived, were scattered all over England.

The Rosewood family had proved most unhelpful, too, the note of query Justin had delivered to their London home having only returned the information that they knew absolutely nothing about Henry's widow, none of the family having so much as set eyes on her again after Henry's death. And the widow's allowance, paid to her by the family lawyer on behalf of the estate, had ceased the day she had married Frederick, severing all ties with that family.

Except for Eleanor…whom the Rosewoods seemed to have no knowledge of whatsoever. As further proof that she was definitely not Henry's child?

The only other way of finding an answer as to where Muriel had settled on her return to England from India, would have been to question Eleanor about her childhood before her mother had married his cousin Frederick.

There were two very good reasons why Justin had not done so; for one, Eleanor was barely speaking to him any more, and secondly, he was trying to avoid telling her about any of this for as long as possible. There was, after all, still the possibility that Richmond could be completely wrong about this whole situation.

And yet, he mused, the coincidence of the earl's concerns, coming so quickly on the heels of his grandmother's request for Justin to try to discover who Eleanor's real father was, as well as the Rosewood family's lack of knowledge of Eleanor's very existence, made that highly unlikely.

'It would appear that it is,' Hawthorne commented ruefully at Justin's lack of reply to his query. 'Sorry to have disturbed your reverie, Royston.' He turned to leave.

'No! No, really, Thorne,' Justin repeated wearily as the other man turned to arch one dark, questioning brow. 'Please, do excuse my rudeness and join me, by all means.' He indicated the chair on the opposite side of the fireplace.

The same age as Justin, Adam Hawthorne had never been a particular friend of his until recently, despite their grandmothers' lifelong friendship. But the two men had been involved together in a matter personal to Hawthorne just weeks ago. One, which, thankfully, had been resolved in a manner most satisfactory to Hawthorne and the woman to whom he was now betrothed.

Justin waited until the other man was seated before speaking again. 'Was there something in particular you wished to discuss with me?'

'As it happens, yes.' Hawthorne, known in the past for his taciturn and prickly nature, hence the reasoning for that shortened version of his surname, now gave a boyish grin. 'You are aware, no doubt, of my upcoming nuptials…?'

'Oh, yes.' Justin rolled his eyes. It was the announcement of Hawthorne's betrothal, and forthcoming marriage, which had caused Edith to renew even more strongly her urgings that it was past time he chose a bride for himself.

Hawthorne gave a sympathetic smile. 'The dowager still proving difficult?'

'Well, your betrothal has certainly not helped my own desire not to marry as yet!' Justin admitted.

'I would imagine not.' Hawthorne laughed. 'I hear that you have once again taken up residence at Royston House.'

'Yes.' No need for Justin to ask from whom the other man had heard that snippet of information; the dowager duchess and Lady Cicely, along with Lady Jocelyn Ambrose, were, and always had been, as thick as thieves!

'My grandmother mentioned how happy it has made the dowager duchess,' Hawthorne confirmed Justin's surmise.

Happy did not even begin to describe Edith's jubilation in having Justin living with her at Royston House. Indeed, the dowager was so contented with the arrangement that her health seemed to have improved exponentially, to a degree that there had been no need for any further calls to Dr Franklyn.

A fact which relieved Justin tremendously. Although he couldn't help being a touch suspicious of this rapid improvement in her health…

Cynical of him, perhaps even egotistical, but Justin found he could not help but wonder if the dowager's recent ill health had been yet another ruse on her part, one that had succeeded in his agreement to reside at Royston House, at least, and as such put him another step closer to the idea of matrimony?

It would please him, of course, to know that his grandmother's health was not as precarious as she had given him the impression it was, but it would irritate him immensely if he were to learn that he had fallen victim to her wily machinations.

Except Justin knew he wasn't living with her solely out of concern for her health, that it was also concern for Eleanor—which she would likely not appreciate if she knew of it—that had been the main factor in his decision. He was only too well aware now of Litchfield's viciousness of nature, which in turn made Eleanor, and Justin's grandmother, both prime targets if the earl should decide to act upon that viciousness.

'Royston…?'

Justin gave himself a mental shake as he returned his attention to Hawthorne. 'You mentioned your upcoming nuptials…?'

The other man nodded. 'You have made quite an impression on my darling Magdelena, you know.'

'Indeed?' He eyed the other man warily; Miss Matthews was a beautiful and charming young woman, and he had been pleased to assist Hawthorne in freeing her of the devil who had been so determined to ruin her life, but other than that he had no personal interest in her, and if Hawthorne thought otherwise—

'So much so,' Hawthorne continued, 'that she will hear

of nothing less than that you stand as one of the witnesses at our wedding.'

'Me?' Justin could not have been more shocked if Hawthorne had invited him to dance naked at Almack's!

Hawthorne's eyes gleamed with devilish laughter. 'I realise how unpleasant that task must be to one as opposed to matrimony as you are, but Magdelena is set upon the idea.' And he was obviously a man so much in love with his future bride that he would allow nothing and no one to deny her smallest desire.

Ordinarily Justin would have found it repugnant to witness such a change in character as he had seen in Hawthorne since he had fallen in love with Miss Matthews. But, for some inexplicable reason, Justin now found his main emotion to be curiosity.

An unhappy first marriage had soured Hawthorne to repeating the experience. Until he had met and fallen in love with Magdelena Matthews, an occurrence which Hawthorne did not at all seem to regret. Indeed, the very opposite was true; Justin had never seen the other man look happier than he had these past few weeks.

Where were Hawthorne's feelings of resentment at the thought of conceding his freedom? Of being led about by his nose and his manhood for the next forty years? Of the possibility, unless he took a mistress, of sharing his bed with the same woman for decades? Also, Hawthorne had a young daughter from his first marriage—had he thought of her welfare in all of this—?

'Magdelena and your ward, Miss Rosewood, have become such fast friends these past few days.'

Justin straightened abruptly as he realised he had once again allowed himself to become so distracted by his own thoughts, he had not been paying attention to Hawthorne's conversation. 'Did you say Miss Matthews and Eleanor are now friends?'

The other man nodded. 'They have become inseparable since the night of the Royston Ball.'

Which explained why Eleanor had been accompanying the dowager on her visits to Lady Cicely's home recently, as Miss Matthews was residing with Lady Cicely until after the wedding.

'Indeed,' Hawthorne continued, 'the two of them are out together now, in the company of our mutual grandmothers, deciding upon material for Magdelena's wedding gown.'

Damn it, it appeared that Hawthorne knew more about Eleanor's movements than he did! Which, given the circumstances of her complete aversion to his own company, was not so surprising…but was incredibly galling.

'My young daughter, Amanda, who is to be a bridesmaid, is also with them,' Hawthorne relaxed back in his chair. 'A great concession on her part, believe me, as she would much rather be in the stable with her pony than shopping for dresses. I believe it was her deep affection for Magdelena and Magdelena's for her—and, of course, the bribe of calling at Gunter's for ice-cream, once the unpleasant task has been completed—which went a long way towards convincing Amanda otherwise!'

So it seemed that Hawthorne's daughter from his first marriage had not been in the least excluded from her father's happiness in his forthcoming marriage. Or, quite obviously, the time and affections of her future stepmother.

Hawthorne quirked a questioning brow. 'Why are you looking at me so strangely?'

Justin's jaw tightened; he had not realised he was being

so obvious. 'You appear—' He stopped, gave a wave of his hand and then tried again. 'You actually seem to be happily anticipating remarrying, Hawthorne.'

The other man grinned. 'Incredible, is it not, considering our conversation on the subject just weeks prior to the announcement of my betrothal?'

A conversation in which both men had voiced their aversion to entering into the married state—Hawthorne ever again, Justin until some distant time when he could no longer avoid his duty of providing the heir—both men bemoaning their grandmothers' machinations in trying to bring that unhappy event about for them.

'Perhaps we are all to receive news of another betrothal quite soon…?' Hawthorne suggested.

Justin stiffened warily. 'What on earth do you mean?' Close as Eleanor's friendship with Miss Matthews was purported to be, he could not imagine Eleanor confiding their lovemaking to the other woman. And even if she had, Eleanor's aversion to his company did not in the least give him the impression that she hoped there would be more of the same, or that it would eventually lead to a proposal of marriage. The opposite, in fact! It was—

'I am referring to Endicott and Miss Rosewood, of course.' Hawthorne eyed him curiously.

Lord Charles Endicott and Eleanor?

That young pup Charles Endicott and *Eleanor!*

What the devil was going on? He almost couldn't think straight as lights seemed to explode behind his eyes.

'It would be considered a good match for your young ward,' Hawthorne continued conversationally, seemingly unaware of Justin's sudden turmoil of emotions. 'Endicott is both wealthy and second in line to a dukedom.'

Admittedly, Endicott was indeed as Hawthorne described, and at two and twenty, he was also considered charming and handsome by those society mamas looking for a suitable and wealthy son-in-law. But as far as Justin was aware Eleanor had only met the other man once, on the evening of the Royston Ball, when she stood up to dance a single set with him. Of course, he had noted that one of those dozens of bouquets of flowers, delivered the day after the ball, could have been sent from Endicott, but even so...

Justin gave a decisive shake of his head. 'I have no idea how you have hit upon such a misconception, Hawthorne, but I assure you that Eleanor does not have any such ambitions where Endicott is concerned.'

'Oh?' Hawthorne looked surprised. 'In that case, perhaps it might be kinder if she were to discourage his attentions, rather than appearing as if she enjoyed them.'

Justin looked confused. 'I have absolutely no idea what the devil you are talking about!'

The other man gave him a speculative glance before replying slowly, 'No, apparently you do not...'

'What do you think, Ellie?' Miss Magdelena Matthews prompted as their party stood outside Gunter's confectioner's shop in Berkeley Square. 'Was that not the most delicious ice-cream you have ever tasted?'

Ellie returned the smile. 'Most certainly.' It was also the only ice-cream she had ever eaten; there had been no money for such extravagance as this during her childhood and she had never been to London during her years as Lord Frederick's stepdaughter, nor had there been the time, or the money, to indulge in such things since she had become companion to Edith St Just.

But Ellie had hoped—willed herself—to give every appearance of enjoying herself, as she conversed and smiled and ate her ice-cream with the others in their party, the enchanting Miss Amanda Hawthorne having most especially enjoyed the latter treat.

Yes, outwardly, Ellie felt sure she gave the impression of happiness and contentment. Inwardly, it was another matter, however...

This past three days, since the evening of her error in allowing Justin to make love to her in her bedchamber, and realising she was in totally and futilely in love with him, despite his behaviour, had been nothing short of hellish, made more so by the fact that the duke now also lived with her.

As arranged, he had duly arrived at ten o'clock the following morning, his entourage of valet and private secretary in tow, the former arranging for the excess of luggage to be placed in the ducal chambers situated at the front of the house—well away, thank goodness, from Ellie and the dowager duchess' apartments at the back of the house—whilst the latter took over the study and library for the duke's personal use.

Edith St Just, as predicted, had been beside herself with joy at this turn of events. Indeed, the dowager had been flushed with excitement ever since, thankfully showing no sign of the illness or fatigue that had previously plagued her, as she happily reorganised the household to fit around the duke's daily schedule.

Ellie had been far from joyous. In fact, she had hoped, once Justin had time to consider the matter following the incident in her bedchamber, that he would have sensitivity enough to find a way in which to delay—indefinitely!—his plans to move in.

She should have realised that would be expecting too much from a man who obviously cared for nothing and no one, other than his grandmother's comfort and, of course, his own!

Ellie was therefore left with no choice but to absent herself from Royston House as much as possible. Something that had proved only too easy to do when the invitations, to theatre parties, dances and assemblies, and alfresco dining, had flooded in following her success at the Royston Ball. And, too, she had developed a deep friendship with Magdelena Matthews, the two of them finding they had much in common as they talked together whilst the dowager was visiting with her dear friend Lady Cicely.

Indeed, if not for Justin's depressingly broody presence at Royston House, and her unrequited love for him, Ellie knew she would have enjoyed her change in circumstances immensely.

Indeed, she was determined she *would* enjoy herself, in spite of the brooding, distracting Duke of Royston!

She turned to smile at the young, handsome gentleman standing beside her. 'How fortuitous that we should meet you here today, my lord.'

Lord Charles Endicott gave a boyish grin. 'Not so much, when you consider that I overheard you and Miss Matthews discussing the outing when I chanced upon you during your walk in the park yesterday.'

'That was very naughty of you!' She laughed merrily.

His eyes warmed with admiration for her appearance in a gown of pale green with matching bonnet. 'A man has no shame when he is in pursuit of a woman!'

She raised auburn brows. 'And are you pursuing me, my lord?'

'Doing my damnedest, yes.' He nodded, a gentleman aged in his early twenties, with fashionably styled dark hair and flirtatious brown eyes set in that boyishly handsome face. 'Excuse my language, if you please,' he added awkwardly.

'I find your remark too flattering to be in the least offended,' Ellie assured with another chuckle; Lord Endicott was perhaps a little too much of a dandy in his dress for her tastes, but otherwise she found his company to be both pleasant and uncomplicated. Unlike another certain gentleman she could name!

'Will you be attending Lady Littleton's musical soirée this evening?' he enquired eagerly. 'If so, might I be permitted to—?'

'My ward plans to spend this evening at home, Endicott,' a cold voice cut repressively across their conversation.

A voice Ellie recognised only too easily.

As indeed did the others in her group as they all turned in unison to look at him, the dowager with some surprise, Lady Cecil and Miss Matthews with some considerable curiosity.

Ellie took a moment to straighten her spine—and her resolve—before she also turned to look at him, instantly aware that neither her straightened spine or her resolve were sufficient for her to withstand the icy blast of his glittering blue gaze as it swept over her before alighting on the hapless Lord Charles Endicott, as that young gentleman bowed to the older man.

Lord Endicott was a picture of dandified elegance in his superfine of pale blue and waistcoat of pastel pink, the collar of his shirt uncomfortably high, neckcloth intricately tied at his throat, and giving him all the appearance of a posturing peacock when placed next to Justin's sartorial elegance, in grey superfine, charcoal-coloured waistcoat and snowy white linen.

Although possibly only half a dozen years separated the two men, they were as different as day and night, the one so bright and colourful, the other a study of dark shadows.

Ellie bristled defensively as she saw the contemptuous curl of the duke's top lip, and the scathing amusement in his gaze, as he also took in the other man's foppish appearance. 'I believe you are mistaken in that, your Grace.' She refused to so much as blink or lower her gaze as he raised one haughty brow in question. 'I am certain her Grace will concur that we have accepted Lady Littleton's invitation for her soirée this evening.'

'Then you, at least, will have to unaccept it,' Justin informed her implacably.

Her eyes widened. 'And why should I wish to do that?'

He looked down the length of his arrogant nose at her. 'You are looking tired, no doubt from all the gadding about you have indulged in recently, and an evening at home will be far more beneficial to you than another evening out.'

Telling Ellie more succinctly, than if he had spoken the words aloud, that—despite the deliberate brightness of her gown and her efforts to give the appearance of being both contented and happy—he did not consider her to be looking her best!

As if she was not already aware of that. As if she was not also aware at whose highly polished, booted feet the blame for that lay!

Her last few days had been filled with a flurry of engagements, in an effort to keep busy and at the same time absent herself from Royston House. Her nights had been… restless and sleepless, to say the least, caught as she was in the puzzling dichotomy of deeply regretting that the intimacies she had shared with Justin had ever happened, and the quivers of pleasure, the love for him, which still coursed through her each and every time she thought of what they had done together!

Nevertheless, she did not welcome him bringing attention to her fatigue, or even in mentioning it at all! 'I have no intentions of cancelling attending Lady Littleton's soirée this evening.'

'Oh, I believe that you will,' the duke answered softly, dangerously, as their gazes remained locked, his challenging, Eleanor's defiant.

'No.'

'Yes!'

'Royston?' the dowager duchess prompted sharply at this public battle of wills.

It had not been Justin's intention to leave the carriage when he had instructed his driver to return to Royston House by way of Berkeley Square, but a single glance towards the establishment known as Gunter's had revealed Eleanor and his grandmother to be standing outside, in the company of the female members of Hawthorne's family.

And that blasted Endicott fellow!

Justin had not given himself time to think as he instructed his driver to stop, barely allowing his carriage to come to a halt before jumping out on to the cobbled road and marching towards where the happy group lingered in conversation.

Just in time, it would seem, to prevent Eleanor from making yet another assignation with Endicott, for later this evening!

Chapter Twelve

'I trust you will forgive me for intruding on your outing, ladies.' Justin chose to ignore Eleanor's furious glare for the moment as he turned to bestow a charming smile upon the other ladies gathered outside Gunter's.

His grandmother was predictably frowning her disapproval of his behaviour, Lady Cicely and Miss Matthews gazed at him with polite curiosity and Miss Amanda Hawthorne, a beautiful little angel with golden-blonde curls, still bore evidence of her recently eaten ice-cream about her little rosebud of a happily smiling mouth.

'I happened to be passing by in my carriage,' Justin continued lightly, 'and could not help but notice you all standing here in conversation. It would have been rude of me to just drive past without stopping to pay my respects.' He made a polite bow.

A gesture of politeness that was immediately answered by his grandmother's loud and disgusted 'humph'! 'That is all very well, Royston,' she snapped. 'But what is your reason for denying Elli—Eleanor the pleasure of going to Lady Littleton's soirée this evening?'

It had been Justin's experience that such evenings were both tedious and tiresome, rather than a pleasure! 'As I have already stated, Grandmama—' he maintained a pleasant, reasoning tone '—Eleanor looks somewhat fatigued and I simply feel that an evening at home resting would be more beneficial to her health than another night out.'

'I—'

'You must forgive me, Eleanor, I had not noticed before now,' the dowager duchess spoke over Eleanor's angry protest, 'but Royston is right; you are indeed looking slightly pale and fatigued this afternoon.'

'There.' Justin turned to Eleanor, triumph glittering in his eyes. 'I do not believe the dowager and I can both be wrong?'

Ellie narrowed her eyes on her tormentor's gaze, dearly wishing that the two of them were alone at this moment— so that she might launch another cup and saucer at his arrogant head! Or a heavy tome. Or perhaps something even deadlier than that! For she did not believe a word of what he had just said, from his 'having just been passing by' in his carriage to his obviously fake concern about her supposed 'fatigue'.

Considering the size of the city, and the numerous other pursuits the duke could have been enjoying today, it seemed far too coincidental that he should have been 'driving past' Gunter's at this precise moment. Nor did Ellie believe the duke had ever given a single thought about the state of her health, this day or any other.

No, Ellie was utterly convinced that Justin was merely determined to once again exercise his steely will upon her. As determined as she was that he would not succeed in that endeavour!

She smiled up at him now with sugary and insincere sweetness, a smile that instantly caused him to narrow his own eyes in suspicion. 'I agree the dowager is never wrong, your Grace,' she conceded lightly—at the same time implying that he, on the other hand, did not have that same distinction. 'But in this instance she is misinformed. I feel perfectly well and am greatly looking forward to attending Lady Littleton's soirée with her this evening.'

His mouth thinned. 'And I would rather you did not.'

'I have noted your objection, your Grace.' She nodded.

'But choose to ignore it?'

'Yes.' It was as if they were the only two present, so intense was their current battle of wills.

Something Justin was also aware of as his mouth tightened. 'Perhaps we should leave these dear ladies to their shopping and continue this conversation in my carriage?' he suggested through gritted teeth.

Her chin rose. 'I believe we had finished shopping, your Grace, and are now returning to have tea with Lady Cicely.'

Nostrils flared on that aquiline nose. '*We* are leaving now, Eleanor.'

'Oh, I say—'

'Did you have something you wished to add to this conversation, Endicott?' Cold blue eyes focused with deadly intent on the younger man at his interruption.

Ellie could not help but feel sorry for Charles Endicott at that moment, his face first suffusing with embarrassed colour, and then as quickly paling, as Justin continued to glower down at him, appearing every inch the powerful and haughty Duke of Royston; it was like watching a fluffy little lapdog being confronted by a ferocious wolfhound. Indeed, Ellie would not have been in the least surprised if the duke's top lip had not curled back in a snarl to bare a long and pointed incisor at the younger man!

'Perhaps it would be as well if you were to return with Royston, Eleanor.' The dowager duchess, ever sensitive to not causing a scene in public—unlike her arrogant grandson!—agreed smoothly. 'I am perfectly happy to go alone to Lady Cicely's.'

Ellie was bursting with indignation at Justin's high-handedness, longing to tell him exactly what he could do with his offer to drive her home in his carriage—which had not been an offer at all but an instruction! At the same time she knew she could not, would not, do or say anything which might upset the dowager duchess; she owed that dear lady too much to ever wish to cause her embarrassment—the very clothes she stood up in, in fact!

'Then we are all agreed.' The duke took a firm hold of Ellie's arm. 'Ladies.' He bowed to them politely. 'Endicott.' His voice had cooled noticeably, eyes once again icy blue as he scowled at the younger man.

Charles Endicott was the first to lower his gaze. 'Your Grace,' he mumbled indistinctly before his expression brightened as he turned to Ellie. 'If you are not to be at Lady Littleton's this evening, perhaps I might call upon you tomorrow—'

'My ward is otherwise engaged tomorrow, Endicott.' To Ellie's ever-increasing annoyance, it was once again Justin who answered the other man glacially. 'And the day following that one, too,' he added for good measure.

The younger man frowned. 'But surely—'

'Come along, Eleanor.' The duke did not wait for her to agree or disagree, allowing her time only to sketch a brief curtsy as her own goodbye before turning on one booted heel and walking in the direction of his waiting carriage, Ellie pulled along in his wake.

She had never felt so humiliated, so—so manhandled and managed in her life before, as she did at this moment. And by Justin St Just, of all people.

But who else would dare to treat someone—anyone!—with such overriding arrogance *but* the arrogantly insufferable Duke of Royston!

He—

'You may give vent to your feelings now, Eleanor, for we are quite alone.'

The haze of red anger shifted from in front of Ellie's eyes at this mockingly drawled comment, enabling her to realise that she had been so consumed with that fury she had allowed herself to be put into his carriage, the door having already been closed to shut them inside.

It was the first time Ellie had been completely alone with him since—well, since 'that night', as she had taken to referring to it in her mind. And to her chagrin she was instantly, achingly aware, of everything about him. The golden sweep of his hair, the glitter of deep-blue eyes set in that hard and chiselled face, the way the superb cut of his superfine emphasised the width of his shoulders and tapered waist, his legs long and powerful in pale grey pantaloons and black Hessians.

Her feelings for him also made her aware of the tingle of sensations which now coursed through her own body, her breasts feeling achingly sensitive, that now familiar warmth between her thighs.

A reaction which only increased her growing anger towards him…

* * *

Justin did not need to look at Eleanor's face to know that she was furious with him; he could feel the heat of that anger as her eyes shot daggers across the short distance of the carriage that separated them.

Justifiably so, perhaps. He had behaved badly just now. Very badly. Towards both Eleanor and Endicott. A fact his grandmother would no doubt bring him to task over at her earliest opportunity.

And yet Justin did not regret his actions. Not for a moment. He had been incensed from the first moment he had seen that young dandy Endicott made up one of his grandmother's party. To add insult to injury, his first glimpse of Eleanor, as bright as a butterfly in her gown of pale green, had been as she was laughing at something that young popinjay had just said to her.

Justin's mouth tightened as he thought of the scowls or blank looks *he* had received from her over the past few days! 'If you have something you wish to say, then for God's sake say it now and get it over with!'

'*If* I have something to say?' she repeated incredulously. 'I—it—you, sir, have the manners of a guttersnipe!'

'It would seem that today I have, yes.' His mouth twisted into a humourless and unapologetic smile. 'And if you intend to insult me, Eleanor, then you will have to do better than that.'

'You are the most insufferable, obnoxious *bully* it has ever been my misfortune to meet!' she hissed angrily, obviously warming to the subject, her cheeks also heating, those green eyes glittering across at him like twin emeralds.

His lips thinned. 'Because I prevented you from embarrassing yourself?'

She gasped. 'I do not believe I was the one causing any embarrassment!'

'I disagree.'

'I—you—in what way was I embarrassing myself?' she finally managed to gasp through her indignation.

'By your flirtation with Endicott.'

'What?'

'But of course.' Justin flicked an imaginary piece of lint from the cuff of his superfine. 'And, as I will never give my permission for you to marry that young peacock, you might just as well give it up now and cease your encouragement of him.'

'I was *not* encouraging him—'

'I beg to differ,' he cut in harshly. 'And it is not only I who appears to think so,' he continued as she would have made another protest. 'Indeed, the society gossips have it that there will be an announcement made before the end of the Season!'

Her eyes widened. 'I beg your pardon?'

Justin shrugged. 'The two of you are currently the talk of the *ton*.'

She gave another gasp. 'But I have only spoken to Lord Endicott on three occasions, once at the Royston Ball, again at a dinner party the evening before last, and then again at the park yesterday in the company of Miss Matthews.'

'And again just now,' he reminded her. 'That would appear to be four occasions in four days.'

'Well. Yes. But—I had no idea we would even be seeing Lord Endicott today!'

That was something, at least; Justin had been sure the two of them must have prearranged this latest meeting. 'I doubt Endicott's presence at Gunter's was as innocent as your own.'

A blush coloured her cheeks. 'He did mention something about having overheard Magdelena and I discussing the outing yesterday. Do *you* believe that Lord Endicott has serious intentions towards me?' she asked.

'Yes.'

She looked nonplussed by the starkness of his statement. 'Oh…'

Justin's mouth compressed. 'Indeed.'

She swallowed. 'But even so—surely the *ton* cannot seriously have made such an assumption on but a few days' acquaintance?'

Justin felt a stab of remorse for the bewildered expression on Eleanor's face; her eyes were wide green pools of disbelief, her cheeks having paled, her lips slightly parted and unsmiling.

All come about, he now realised with horror, because he had taken exception to being described as a bully. Even if, in this particular case, he had most certainly behaved as one. But only for her own good, he reassured himself determinedly. If Hawthorne, a man who cared nought for the gossip of the *ton,* for society itself, had been led to believe Eleanor was seriously interested in Endicott, then the rest of society must believe it too.

Justin sat forwards on the seat to reach across and take one of Eleanor's tightly clenched hands into both of his. 'The *ton* has made such assumptions on far less, I assure you, my dear,' he murmured in a more placating tone of voice.

She looked up at him curiously. 'You sound as if you speak from personal experience.'

His mouth tightened. 'It is your own reputation that is

currently in jeopardy; I accepted long ago, and you confirmed it three days ago, that my own reputation is considered beyond redemption!'

Ellie looked thoughtful. The gentlemen in society appeared to either admire or fear the Duke of Royston. The ladies, married or otherwise, to desire him. The young débutantes considered him as being the catch of the Season—any Season this past ten years or so! The mothers of those débutantes appeared to either covet or avoid coming to his attention, aware as they were that the Duke of Royston had successfully avoided the parson's mousetrap for a long time; it would be a feather in any society matron's bonnet to acquire the Duke of Royston as her son-in-law, but equally it could be the social ruin of her daughter if he were to offer that young lady a liaison rather than marriage.

As such, Ellie had no idea who would have dared to make remarks about her to him. About herself and *Lord Endicott,* of all people. Why, she considered that young man as being nothing more than an amusing and playful puppy. Oh, he was handsome in a boyish way, and pleasant enough—if one ignored his atrocious taste in clothes—but her feelings for Royston meant she did not, and never would, consider Lord Endicott as being anything more than a friend. That anyone should ever imagine she might seriously consider *marrying* the foppish boy, was utterly ludicrous!

That Justin should believe such nonsense she found hurtful beyond belief. How could she possibly be interested in any other man, when Justin himself had ruined her for all others?

And Eleanor did not mean her reputation.

No, her ruination was much more fundamental than that, in that she simply could not imagine ever wishing to share such intimacies with any other man but the one she had finally accepted she was in love with.

She had done everything she could to keep herself busy since that evening, and as such give herself little time for thought. And she had endeavoured to see as little of the duke as possible, considering they now shared the same residence. But there had been no denying the barrage of memories that plagued and tortured her once she was alone in her bed at night. No way then of ignoring how her nipples pebbled into aroused hardness and between her thighs dampened, swelled, just remembering the way Justin had kissed her and touched her there.

With those memories to haunt her, how could anyone, least of all Justin himself, ever believe she had serious intentions in regard to a dandy like Charles Endicott?

Her lashes lowered again as she looked down to where Justin's hands now held one of hers in his grasp. Those same hands had touched her so intimately, caressed and stroked her to a peak of such physical pleasure it still made her toes curl to even think of it.

A reaction she did not wish him to ever become aware of, let alone find out that she was in love with him. That would be a humiliation beyond bearing.

Ellie drew in a steadying breath as she raised her head, smiling slightly as she deftly removed her hand from his. 'It is all nonsense, of course, but how exciting to think that I might soon receive my first proposal of marriage!'

Arrogant brows arched. 'Your *first* proposal…?'

'But of course.' Her smile widened deliberately at his obvious astonishment. 'The dowager has informed me that a young lady can only really consider herself a complete success in society once she has broken at least half-a-dozen hearts and received and refused her third proposal!'

The duke's back straightened, his expression suddenly grim. 'I sincerely trust, just because of our recent interlude, you are not considering counting my own heart as among the ones which you have broken?'

Ellie forced an incredulous laugh to cover the jolt she felt at hearing Justin refer so dismissively to their lovemaking. 'I believe the only thing broken on that particular evening was a cup and saucer, your Grace. Besides,' she continued evenly, 'surely one has to be in possession of a heart for it to be broken?'

'So you do not believe I have one?'

She raised auburn brows. 'Are you not the one who once stated he has no intention of ever falling in love?'

His nostrils flared. 'I believe what I actually said was that I have no intention of being in love with my wife. But,' he continued drily as she would have spoken, 'you are actually correct. The truth is, I have no intention of falling in love with any woman.'

'Why not?' Ellie could have bitten out her tongue the moment she allowed her curiosity to get the better of her. And yet a single glance at his closed expression stopped her from instantly retracting the question.

But it *was* a curiosity that a man such as he, a man who could have any woman he wished for, had decided—no, refused, to fall in love with any of them. 'Well?' she prompted as he made no reply.

His lips quirked. 'Perhaps it is that I have observed too many of my friends succumb to the emotion, and prefer not to behave in the same ridiculous manner? It surely makes a man far too vulnerable.'

It was both a glib and insulting answer, but at the same time it somehow did not ring true to Ellie's ears. She wondered anew if his aversion did not have something to do with what he had once referred to as his own parents 'exclusive marriage'. 'Is the object of that love not showing the same vulnerability by allowing her own emotions to be hurt?'

'Then why take the risk at all?' the duke argued.

Ellie shrugged. 'Possibly because it is the natural instinct of human beings to need the love and affection of others?'

'The implication being, therefore, that my own feelings on the matter must be unnatural?' he rasped.

She looked at him for a minute, the blue of his eyes glittering—with anger or something else? 'You are avoiding answering my original question...' she finally murmured.

He gave another humourless smile. 'How very astute of you.'

'And you are still avoiding it.'

'That being the case, would it not be a prudent move on your part to move on to something else?' he suggested.

Ellie's cheeks warmed as she lowered her gaze and turned to look out of the window beside her. 'I do not believe I may claim to have been particularly "prudent" in our...relationship, to date, your Grace.'

Justin could certainly vouch for that!

Indeed, Eleanor had been anything but prudent in her dealings with him this past week, to a degree that he now knew her body almost as intimately as he did his own: the satiny smoothness of her skin, the taste of her breasts, the warm touch of her lips and the expression on her face as she climaxed against his fingers.

Just as he could not help but notice the perfection of the calm profile she now turned away from him: the creamy intelligent brow, long lashes surrounding those emerald-green eyes, her cheek a perfect curve, freckle-covered nose small and straight, her lips full above her stubbornly determined chin.

Eleanor had grown in elegance as well as self-confidence this past week, her pale-green bonnet, the same shade as her gown, fastened about the pale oval of her face, with enticing auburn curls at her temples and nape, her spine perfectly straight, shoulders back, which only succeeding in pushing the fullness of her breasts up against the low bodice of her gown, knees primly together, dainty slippers of green satin peeping out from beneath the hem of her gown.

Yes, Eleanor was certainly the picture of an elegant and beautiful young lady, and Justin realised that her air of self-confidence was due to the admiration and attentions of fawning young dandies, of which Endicott was no doubt only one.

In sharp contrast to those eager young fops, he knew himself to be both cynical and aloof, and not at all what might appeal to a young woman who was so widely admired and fêted. Indeed, her remarks about his cynicism towards the emotion of love would seem to confirm that lack of appeal. A realisation which irritated Justin immensely.

So much so that he felt a sudden urge to shatter her air of confidence and calm. 'I assure you, dear Eleanor, I have absolutely no complaints at your lack of inhibitions in the bedchamber. Nor would you hear any objections from me if you were to decide to behave that imprudently again!'

'Justin!' She gasped as she whipped round to face him, a fiery blush colouring her cheeks.

Perhaps, if in her shocked surprise Eleanor had not addressed him by his first name, Justin might have decided not to pursue this any further.

Perhaps…

Chapter Thirteen

Justin rose and crossed to the other side of the carriage and sat down next to Eleanor, his thigh pressed against the warmth of hers. He reached out and pulled the curtains across each of the windows, throwing the interior of the carriage into shadow, but not dark enough for them not to be able to see each other and know what he was doing, as he untied the ribbon on Eleanor's bonnet before removing it completely.

'We will reach Royston House shortly…' she protested breathlessly.

Justin reached up and tapped on the roof of the carriage.

'Your Grace?' his groom responded.

'Continue to drive until I instruct you otherwise, Bilsbury.' Justin raised his voice so that he might be heard above the noise of the horses' hooves on the cobbled street.

'Yes, your Grace.'

Eleanor seemed frozen in place, unable to move or look away as Justin deftly removed the pins from those fiery red-gold curls, before releasing them on to her shoulders and down the length of her spine, reaching almost to the slenderness of her waist.

Justin groaned low in his throat, closing his eyes briefly, as he imagined how sensuous those long curls would feel against the bareness of his own flesh, his shaft now hardening, thickening, just at imagining it. 'Dear Lord...!' He opened his eyes and raised his hands up to cup either side of her face before lowering his head to claim her parted lips with his own.

Desire, hot and strong, erupted between them, leaving no room for tentative exploration and seduction as Justin felt the instant and powerful surge of his own desire as his arousal curved up strong and pulsing against his stomach, his arms sliding about Eleanor's waist as he drew her firmly against him, breast to chest, the flatness of her abdomen pressing against the heat of his shaft.

She clung to him, her face raised as he deepened the kiss, sweeping his tongue over the softness of her lips before entering, then plundering the beckoning, enticing heat beneath.

For Ellie it was as if the last three agonising days of avoiding Justin had never happened, the instant heat of their desire making it seem as if this was a continuation of their previous lovemaking. Her love for him made it impossible to resist being crushed against him, his reaction to her telling her more surely than anything else that he was just as aroused as she was.

She became totally lost in the barrage of emotions as he continued to kiss her. Then he lifted her above him, the length of her gown rising up her legs as she straddled his muscular thighs, allowing him to pull her in tightly against him, her knees resting on the seat either side of him.

Her drawers had parted, allowing the fullness of his arousal to press up against the swollen heart of her, only the material of his pantaloons now separating them.

Ellie gave a breathless gasp as the rocking of the carriage rubbed his firm length against the sensitive nubbin between her own thighs, totally lost to sensation as Justin unfastened the buttons at the back of her gown. He broke the kiss to ease her slightly away from him to allow her gown to drop away, revealing her breasts covered only by the thin material of her chemise, his eyes becoming hot and glittering as he raised his hands to cup the twin orbs.

Ellie looked down, her cheeks flaming as she saw what Justin had done; her breasts were fuller, the nipples swollen and hard at their tips as they pouted up and forwards invitingly.

'You are so beautiful…!' he murmured huskily, gently pushing her chemise aside before his head lowered to draw one of those swollen berries into his mouth.

Ellie's whole body now felt suffused with heat as she thrust her fingers into his hair, every caress of that moist tongue a torture that coursed hot and molten through her veins.

She loved this man, needed—Lord help her, she needed—

She gave a low moan, throat arching, head thrown back, as Justin responded to that need, his fingers caressing unerringly that heat between her thighs, stroking in the same rhythm as his tongue now rasped against her other nipple, taking her higher, driving her insane with mindless desire.

'Unfasten my pantaloons, Eleanor…!' His breath was hot against her aching breast as he bit gently on her nipple. 'Let me feel your hands on me,' he pleaded gruffly.

Her cheeks burned as she sat back slightly, her fingers

fumbling with the buttons of Justin's pantaloons in her haste to see and touch the hardness that had pressed against her so insistently, barely able to breathe as he leant back against the seat, lids half-closed, as she finally allowed that long, pulsing length to burst free, as if it had a will of its own.

Even as she gazed down in fascination a bead of liquid escaped the tip before sliding slowly downwards. Ellie looked at him uncertainly. 'May I…?'

'Please…' he encouraged hoarsely.

She quickly removed her gloves before touching that hardness tentatively, her fingers barely able to meet about its thickness. She was surprised, as she began to run her fingers slowly up and down it, at how silky the skin felt. She ran the soft pad of her thumb across the tip to capture a second bead of escaping moisture, looking up quickly as he gave a low groan. 'Am I hurting you?'

He gave a brief laugh. 'Only with kindness!'

Ellie gave a relieved smile, capturing her tongue between her teeth in concentration as she unbuttoned his waistcoat and pulled up his shirt to bare his chest before allowing her gaze to become fixed once again on the hard, silken length of his shaft. She continued to caress him instinctively, fingers tightening around his arousal, responding to his groans of pleasure as she began to lightly pump up and down. Justin's thighs began to thrust up into the circle of her fingers and she tightened her grip as she heard his loud gasp, the expression on his face now almost one of pain, despite his earlier assurances.

Ellie stilled. 'I am sure I must be hurting you—'

'No!' He lifted his hand, fingers curling about hers as he encouraged her to continue that rhythmic pumping. 'Do not stop, Eleanor, please do not stop…!' His head dropped back against the upholstered seat, lids completely closed, long golden lashes dark shadows against the harsh planes of his sculptured cheeks.

Ellie had never seen anything as beautiful, as intensely wildly beautiful, as the fierceness of his pleasure in her caresses. It was somehow empowering, so fiercely primal, to know that she could give such pleasure to the man she loved.

'Harder,' he encouraged achingly. 'Oh lord, faster…!'

Ellie's fingers tightened further about him as she followed his instructions, eyes widening as his shaft seemed to grow even longer, thicker, with each downward stroke, the head more swollen, and glistening with moisture.

Justin groaned harshly, the pleasure so intense, so all consuming as he thrust up into Eleanor's encircling fingers, every particle of him concentrated on that intense, mindless desire as he felt his release threatening to overtake his control.

It took tremendous effort of will not to give in to the need to spill himself, as he instead opened his eyes before capturing her wrist and putting a stop to her caresses. 'Together this time, Eleanor. We will come together.'

She blinked, her eyes a dark emerald in her own arousal.

'Like this,' Justin urged as he placed his hands on her waist to once again pull her thighs in tight either side of him, his breath leaving him in a pained hiss as he felt the burning heat of her against him, causing him to harden still further.

'Justin…?'

'Do not be afraid, Eleanor,' he soothed as he stroked gentle fingers down the length of one of her rosy cheeks. 'I swear I will not take your innocence. Or hurt you in any way. I only want to give you pleasure. To give us both pleasure. Do you trust me to do that?'

Did Ellie trust Justin? To give her pleasure? Oh, yes, she already knew how capable he was of sending her to the heights. But did she trust him not to break her heart?

Ellie feared it was already too late for that!

What other explanation could there be, she mused, other than that she had fallen in love with him, for the way in which she responded so willingly, so wantonly, to his every caress?

'Eleanor, *please?*' he begged at her continued silence.

It was unacceptable that this proud, powerful man should plead with her. That he should plead with anyone for anything!

Nor did she wish to continue to waste this precious time together lingering on her own emotions. 'Yes, I trust you, Justin,' she said, her hands clinging to the width of his shoulders as he sat up to edge forwards on the seat, his gaze once again holding hers captive as he began to move, the hardness of his shaft stroking against the swollen nubbin between her dampened thighs, the wetness there allowing his silken hardness to glide up and between her swollen folds rather than entering, breaching, the sheath beneath.

Ellie moaned in ecstasy as the nubbin between her thighs throbbed and pulsed in response to each stroke, her cheeks aflame with her arousal, her breathing ragged as she felt the pressure building inside her, taking her higher and ever higher, her breasts tingling almost painfully, as that heated pleasure between her thighs became almost too much to bear.

'Now, Eleanor!' Justin gasped between gritted teeth. 'I am going to—come for me now, Eleanor!'

His words meant nothing to Ellie, it was the tightening of his hands about her waist as he held her firmly in place, and the intensified throbbing and bucking of his shaft against her, that threw her totally over the edge and out into a maelstrom of almost unbearably erotic sensations.

Wave after wave of pleasure claimed her, as Justin's shaft continued to stroke to that same rhythm, before he also lost control, and a fiery liquid pulsed hotly on to her nubbin, sending her into a second, even more intense climax than the first.

Justin trembled and shook in the aftermath of the most intense release he had ever experienced, his ejaculation so fierce, so powerful, and lasting for so long he felt as if he had been ripped apart and was still in pieces, only the sound of their ragged breathing breaking the silence inside the carriage. Eleanor had fallen forwards weakly as her second climax faded, her head now resting on his shoulder as her body still shuddered and quivered with the aftershocks of that dual release.

It was incredible, beyond belief, that Justin should have responded so wildly, so intensely, to just the touch of her hands upon him and the heat of her between her thighs. He enjoyed sex as much as the next man, had bedded more than his share of women the past ten years or so, but he could never remember experiencing such a depth of pleasure before, such a fierce release. It had seemed never ending, until he had felt as if it had started in his toes and been drawn up from his very boots.

His boots…

Damn it, not only were the two of them still fully dressed, but they were also sitting in his moving carriage—a carriage that now reeked of the smell of sex! What on earth had he been *thinking?*

* * *

Ellie was so weakened, so lost in wonder, that it took her several minutes to realise that Justin's shoulder had tensed beneath her brow. His chest was steadily rising and falling against her breasts, while his hands had fallen away from her waist.

She raised her head warily and looked at his harshly etched features; there was a frown between his eyes, his cheekbones appeared like blades beneath the tautness of his skin, and his jaw was tightly clenched.

So clearly not the face of an indulgent and satiated lover.

She moistened her lips with the tip of her tongue before speaking. 'Are you angry with me?'

'With myself,' he corrected harshly.

Her eyes widened. 'Why?'

'You can ask me that?' He gave a self-disgusted shake of his head as he placed his hands on her waist once again in order to lift her off him and sit her on the seat beside him. He briskly pulled up the bodice of her gown and refastened the buttons at the back before straightening his own clothing.

Ellie's legs felt decidedly shaky as she pressed her knees tightly together, gasping as she felt another wave of pleasure emanate from that still-swollen nubbin nestled in the auburn curls between her thighs. Her cheeks suddenly blazed again as she became aware that the uncomfortable dampness of her drawers was not entirely her own.

Could this be any more embarrassing? Not only had she once again lost complete control in Justin's arms, but the proof of his own uninhibited display was impossible to ignore. How could she have allowed this to happened again? It was utterly mortifying—

'This should not have happened again!' the duke echoed

at least some of her thoughts, his voice a growl in the silence. 'And it would not have done so if not for—' He broke off abruptly, eyes glittering darkly as he glared fiercely at nothing in particular.

'If not for what?' Ellie prompted.

'We have delayed long enough; I suggest you now tidy your hair and replace your bonnet,' he instructed as he pulled back the curtains and allowed in the sunshine before reaching up to once again tap on the roof of the carriage. 'Royston House, if you please, Bilsbury.'

Ellie continued to regard him for several seconds before turning away to look sightlessly out of the window, unwilling to allow him to see the tears which now stung her eyes as she did as he instructed and tidied herself.

The way Justin now spoke to her, and the harshness of his expression, could not have made it any more obvious that he deeply regretted what had just happened.

As she must now regret it, though for a completely different reason.

While technically she might still be an innocent, she was certain he had ruined her for any other man. She would only ever want him. Only ever love him. It was a total disaster.

Justin could not think of a single thing to say or do that would erase the expression of hurt bewilderment from Eleanor's face; that his behaviour had been reprehensible, totally beyond the pale, was beyond denial, as well as being a betrayal of his role as her guardian.

She still looked utterly dishevelled, delicate wisps of her hair having escaped her ministrations, her cheeks pale, her lips slightly swollen from the force of their kisses, her gown crushed and slightly soiled—and he winced just to think of the state of her underclothes.

Damn it, he had told himself after the first time that such a depth of intimacy must never happen between the two of them again. Nor did he believe it would have done so now, if he had not been so infuriated by her obvious enjoyment of Endicott's attentions, when recently she could barely spare him the time of day.

Which begged the question—why had Eleanor's obvious liking for Endicott so infuriated him, when the sooner she received a proposal of marriage from someone of Endicott's ilk, and accepted it, then the quicker Justin's own onerous responsibility as her guardian would come to an end? Just as her possible problematic connection to Litchfield would then become her husband's business rather than his own.

Which was exactly what Justin wanted, was it not? To be free of her so that he might return to his uncomplicated life before her come-out in society had caused him such inconvenience and irritation?

His uncomplicated life before Miss Eleanor Rosewood...

As Justin recalled, he had been lamenting the boredom of that life on the evening his grandmother had voiced her concerns regarding Eleanor's future, with the request that he provide her with a dowry and his protection. An emotion Justin could not recall experiencing even once since that evening.

True—except the very reason he had not found himself overcome with boredom this past week was because he had not had a minute to call his own in all that time!

His whole life had been tumbled into disarray since she entered it. He had not even found the time for his usual pursuits, such as his thrice-weekly visits to Jackson's Boxing

Saloon. An oversight he intended to rectify at the earliest opportunity, if only in an attempt to prevent himself from once again falling victim to her physical charms.

That decision settled in his mind, Justin now turned his attention to the difficult task of diffusing the awkwardness that had been created by this latest lapse. 'There is never a teacup and saucer available when one so sorely needs one—'

'Do not try to make a joke out of this!' she turned on him fiercely.

He gave a pained wince. 'Once again I offer my apologies—Eleanor, are you crying?' He was appalled as he saw the silvery tracks of those tears falling down the paleness of her cheeks. 'Eleanor—'

'Or touch me again!' she warned even as she flinched away from the hands he had lifted with the intention of lightly grasping her arms. 'Or be mistaken into thinking these tears are caused by anything other than anger, and a recognition of my own stupidity, in having once again having allowed myself to fall prey to your experienced seduction!'

Justin's jaw tightened grimly at the insult as he continued to look at her for several long seconds, aware of the challenge in her own gaze, before he drew in a deep breath and rose agilely to his feet to move and sit on the other side of the carriage. 'Better?'

Her chin rose as she replied just as tersely, 'Much.'

He let out a ragged sigh. 'Eleanor—'

'I really would prefer it if you did not speak to me again.' Her voice shook, whether with anger, or some other emotion, Justin was unsure. 'I have—I am in no fit state to talk about this now.' She gave a shake of her head, her gloved hands tightly clasped together in her lap.

Justin was surprised that either of them could speak at all after the intensity of their lovemaking! Indeed, his own body was currently filled with such lethargy, so physically satiated and drained, that he dearly longed for a hot bath in which he might ease away some of those aches and strains.

'Very well, Eleanor,' he acquiesced. 'But when you are feeling better—'

'I am not ill, your Grace,' she assured him with a humourless laugh. 'Merely full of self-disgust and recriminations,' she added honestly.

The fact that she was once again addressing him as 'your Grace' was enough to inform him of her state of mind, of her need to put as much distance between them, metaphorically, as she possibly could. 'Nevertheless,' he pointed out as gently as he could, 'we cannot just ignore what has happened in the same way that we did the last time.' Just the thought of a repeat of the three days that had just passed, when Eleanor had avoided his company as much as was possible, and spoke to him even less, was totally unacceptable. 'My grandmother, as you have already remarked, is a highly astute woman and a continuation of the recent tension between us is sure to alert her to the fact that there is something seriously amiss.'

Eleanor's eyes flashed a deep-emerald green and angry colour returned to her cheeks. 'Should you not have thought of that sooner, your Grace?'

Justin should have thought of a lot of things sooner! The fact that he had not was testament to his own state of mind. What little mind he seemed to have left about him whenever he was alone with her!

'Perhaps we will be lucky enough to have my grandmother attribute your obvious displeasure with me as the result of my earlier high-handedness in forbidding you from attending Lady Littleton's soirée this evening?' Justin suggested heavily.

'No doubt,' she agreed stiltedly.

Whatever his grandmother might choose to think or say was really unimportant, it was the antagonism Eleanor now showed towards him that concerned him the most…

Ellie heaved a sigh of relief as she saw they were approaching Royston House at last, barely waiting for the carriage to come to a halt and the groom—Bilsbury, no doubt!—to open the door, before stepping quickly outside, in desperate need to put some distance between herself and Justin.

She would need to bathe and change her clothing, too, before Edith St Just arrived home; as Justin had already remarked, his grandmother was indeed a very astute lady, and the dowager would only need to take one look at Ellie's dishevelled appearance to realise exactly what must have taken place between them in Justin's carriage on their drive back to Royston House!

It was to be hoped that the dowager had not arrived home ahead of them…

Ellie had no idea how much time had passed while she and Justin made love in his carriage, but it would not have taken the dowager so very long to take tea with Lady Cicely. It would be too humiliating if she had arrived home ahead of them—

'We will go inside together, Eleanor.' The duke put his hand lightly beneath her elbow to fall into step beside her as she hurried up the wide steps fronting the house.

Ellie shot Justin a fuming glance, especially as she saw

that he looked just as fashionably elegant as he always did, with not a hair showing out of place beneath the tall hat he took off and handed to Stanhope once they had entered the grand entrance hall. 'I shall take my bonnet and gloves upstairs with me, thank you, Stanhope,' she refused with a strained smile as he offered to take them from her. 'If you could arrange for hot water for a bath to be brought up to me as soon as is possible?'

'I would like the same brought to my own rooms, if you please, Stanhope,' Justin requested.

'Certainly, your Grace, Miss Rosewood, I will see to it immediately.' The butler hesitated, his expression one of slight perturbation. 'I should inform you… A visitor arrived whilst you were out, your Grace.'

The duke raised his brows. 'And who might that be?'

Ellie was curious to know the answer to that question too; she had been acquainted with Stanhope for the past year, knew him to be unflappable, whatever the situation. And at the moment he was most certainly disconcerted, to say the least.

'Good afternoon, Justin.'

Ellie was aware of Justin drawing in a hissing breath beside her, even as she turned in search of the owner of that husky feminine voice. Her heart beat wildly in her chest as she found herself looking at an elegant and beautiful, blonde-haired woman, as she stood framed in the doorway of the Blue Salon.

A beautiful woman whom Justin undoubtedly recognised—but so obviously wished he did not!

Chapter Fourteen

It was a belief that was instantly born out by Justin's next accusing comment. 'What are *you* doing here?'

Ellie flinched at the angry displeasure she could hear in his voice, knowing she would shrivel and die a little inside if he should ever speak to her in so disparaging a tone.

But the elegantly lovely woman standing across the hallway did not so much as blink in response to that harshness as she turned to smile at the discreetly departing Stanhope before answering Justin chidingly, 'Really, darling, is that any way to address me when we have not seen each other for so many months?'

'And whose fault is that?'

She smiled sadly. 'On this particular occasion I believe it to be your own.'

Ellie felt as if this entire day had turned into a nightmare she could not wake up from. Firstly, the fierceness of their lovemaking in Justin's carriage, which had once again ended so disastrously. And now, it appeared, she was to meet a woman whom Justin had obviously once been—or perhaps was still?—involved with. A woman, moreover, who was so much more beautiful and sophisticated than Ellie could ever be.

Justin had not believed this day could get any worse, but the proof that it actually could was standing directly across the cavernous hallway. The last thing, the very last thing he had expected today was to find this particular woman waiting for him when he returned to Royston House.

'Are you not going to introduce us, Justin?' she now prompted as she looked pointedly at Eleanor. 'Or perhaps I can guess who you might be, without Justin's help,' she added ruefully when no introduction was forthcoming from him. 'You are no doubt Miss Eleanor Rosewood, the lovely young lady who was the stepdaughter of Frederick St Just, and whom Edith has kindly taken under her wing?'

'I am Eleanor Rosewood, yes.' She sketched a curtsy, still looking confused.

A puzzlement Justin had absolutely no wish to satisfy, yet he knew he had no choice but to do so. 'Eleanor, may I present to you her Grace, Rachel St Just, the Duchess of Royston. My mother,' he added curtly as Eleanor continued to look at him blankly.

'Your *mother*...?' Eleanor gave a gasp, her expression one of wide-eyed disbelief as she stared at the woman who did not look old enough to be the mother of a boy of eight, let alone a grown man of eight and twenty.

She never had, Justin acknowledged begrudgingly, having always considered his mother to be one of the loveliest women he had ever set eyes upon. As a child he had thought her as beautiful as any angel. And she continued to be, despite now being in her late forties.

Her fashionably styled hair was as golden and abundant as it had ever been, her blue eyes as bright, her face and throat as creamily smooth, her figure still as resplendently curvaceous in the blue gown she wore—

The blue gown she wore…?

To Justin's knowledge his mother had not worn anything but black since the death of his father three years ago. And yet today, here and now, she was wearing a fashionable silk gown the same colour blue as her eyes, satin slippers of the same shade peeping out from beneath the hem of that gown.

Did this mean that his mother had finally—finally!—decided to end her years of solitary mourning for his father?

Ellie could only stare at the woman Justin had just introduced as his mother.

Was it any wonder she had assumed her to be something else entirely? This tall, beautiful woman definitely did not look old enough to be Justin's mother. Did not look old enough to be Ellie's own mother!

'I am sorry we did not meet when your mother and Frederick were alive, but so pleased that we are doing so now.' Rachel St Just smiled warmly as she seemed to glide across the hallway to where Ellie stood, the older woman hugging her briefly before then holding her at arm's length, her perfume light and floral—and hopefully masking the musky smell of Eleanor's own clothing! 'You are every bit as lovely as Edith wrote and told me that you were.'

'Grandmama wrote and told you about Eleanor?' Justin repeated slowly.

Ellie glanced at him, frowning slightly as she saw the incredulity in his expression, quickly followed by the narrowing of his eyes as he continued to look at his mother guardedly. Ellie noted that there was no attempt on the duchess's part to greet her son with the same physical warmth of the hug she had just received.

Perhaps the relationship between mother and son was so obviously strained that she knew Justin would reject such a gesture from her out of hand?

Ellie saw the sadness that appeared briefly on Rachel's lovely face in acceptance of that truth, before she smiled and asked, 'Is there some reason why Edith and I should not regularly correspond with each other?'

'None at all,' Justin replied tersely. 'I am merely surprised that one such missive, apparently about Eleanor, seems to have brought you back to town after all this time.'

'Oh, it was not just one letter, Justin,' his mother revealed. 'Edith has talked of nothing else but Eleanor for months now, until I decided I must come and meet this beautiful paragon for myself.'

Ellie now looked for any sign of the cynicism and mockery that were such a part of her son's nature, knowing herself to be neither 'beautiful' nor a 'paragon'—especially now, when her appearance was so bedraggled! But she could discern only kindness in the duchess's face as she continued to smile at her warmly.

Another glance at Justin showed that cynicism and mockery to be all too visible on *his* too handsome face! 'The dowager duchess is too kind,' Ellie answered his mother quietly.

'My mother-in-law is indeed kind,' Rachel agreed. 'But, I assure you, in this instance she was being truthful as well as kind.'

'Are you seriously telling me that you have decided to give up your years of solitary mourning in the country—'

Justin eyed his mother derisively '—to come up to town out of a mere curiosity to meet Eleanor?'

The duchess raised golden brows. 'Why, what other reason can there have been?'

His jaw tightened. 'Grandmama did not write and tell you she has recently been…indisposed?'

Ellie saw now where Justin was going with this conversation. He was concerned that Edith might have confided more fully as to the seriousness, or otherwise, of her illness with her daughter-in-law than she had him, and it was that very confidence which was now the reason for his mother's unexpected, and for Justin obviously surprising, return to town.

'I believe I will leave the two of you now and go to my room to bathe,' Ellie spoke softly into the tenseness of the silence that had now befallen them all.

Justin shot her a bleak glance, knowing their own conversation was far from over, but also accepting that the conversation he needed to have with his mother now took priority over any awkwardness that had once again arisen between Eleanor and himself. If, indeed, it had ever ceased!

Quite what he was going to do about Eleanor, and the habit he was rapidly falling into of making love with her at every available opportunity, was beyond his reasoning at this moment. The force of their lovemaking such a short time ago, and the unexpected appearance of his mother, had succeeded in completely destroying his ability for logic.

He also accepted that Eleanor, despite his mother's compliments, was looking less than her best—her hair so obviously in disarray beneath her bonnet, her gown appearing crushed, that she was no doubt feeling less than comfortable in the duchess's presence.

Justin gave an abrupt nod. 'We will talk again before dinner.'

Dark-green eyes looked away from his. 'I have a slight headache, your Grace, and believe I will take your advice after all and spend the evening at home in my bedchamber.'

His mouth twisted grimly at Eleanor's use of the word 'advice'—they both knew only too well that he had issued an order earlier rather than well-intentioned advice! 'Then I will call upon you in your room after dinner.'

That brought her gaze swiftly back to him, those green eyes flashing her displeasure. 'That will not be necessary, your Grace, when I have every intention of going to bed and then to sleep shortly afterwards.'

And she was no doubt hoping—perhaps even praying?— that when she awoke, this afternoon would turn out to be nothing but a nightmare!

Justin's own life was also becoming increasingly unbearable. Not only did he still have his grandmother's illness to worry about, and now his mother's unexpected arrival at Royston House to ponder over, but Dryden Litchfield, and his possible connection to Eleanor, still lurked threateningly in the background of these other, more immediate, concerns.

Boredom? Hah! Once again Justin acknowledged that he no longer had the time in which to suffer that emotion!

'Very well.' He thrust a hand through his hair. 'But if your headache worsens I wish for you to ring for Stanhope immediately, so that Dr Franklyn can be sent for.'

'I am not a child, Justin, to be told by you what I should or should not do!' Eleanor's cheeks instantly coloured a vivid red as she remembered they had an interested audience listening to their conversation. Her tone had been scathing to say the least, her use of his first name implying a familiarity between them which had certainly not been apparent until now. 'I apologise, your Grace,' she made that apology pointedly to his mother rather than Justin—obviously implying she did not feel she owed him an apology! 'I am afraid I am feeling less than well today myself.'

'You poor dear.' His mother's expression was wholly sympathetic. 'Would it be acceptable to you if I were to come up to your bedchamber and check on you later this evening?'

Justin turned back to Eleanor, derisive brows raised over challenging blue eyes.

Ellie had avoided looking at Justin following her irritated outburst, although she sensed his mocking gaze was now fixed upon her. Deservedly so; in her annoyance with him, she had forgotten all sense of propriety. In front of his mother, of all people.

'Perfectly acceptable,' she warmly accepted the duchess's suggestion.

'I will take care not to disturb you if you are sleeping.' Rachel continued to smile reassuringly, as if she had not noticed Ellie's familiarity towards her arrogant son.

'Your Grace.' Ellie bobbed a curtsy to the older woman. 'Your Grace.' Her voice had cooled noticeably as she gave Justin only the barest hint of a departing nod, not even waiting for his acknowledgement of that less-than-polite gesture before turning to hurry across the hallway, lifting the skirts of her gown to quickly ascend the wide staircase.

Even so, she could not help but overhear the duchess's next comment.

'Is there something relating to your young ward, which you feel the need to discuss with either Edith or myself, Justin?'

Justin continued to watch Eleanor for several more seconds as she hurriedly ascended the curved staircase, only turning his attention back to his mother once she had reached the top of those stairs and disappeared rapidly down the hallway he knew led to her bedchamber. 'Such as?' He eyed his mother coolly.

She sighed. 'I see that you are still angry with me.'

'Not at all.' His mouth twisted. 'Anger would imply a depth of emotion which simply does not exist between us.'

His mother gave a pained frown. 'That is simply not true! I have always loved you dearly, Justin—'

'Oh, please!'

'But—'

'I have no intention of continuing this conversation out here in the hallway, where anyone might overhear us.' He turned to stride in the direction of the Blue Salon, waiting until his mother, having hesitated briefly, now entered the room ahead of him, before following her and closing the door firmly behind her. 'Why are you really here, Mother?'

'I told you—'

'Some nonsense about meeting Eleanor.' Justin waved away his impatience with that explanation as he stood with his back towards one of the bay windows that looked out over the front of the house. 'To my knowledge, Eleanor has resided at Royston House with Grandmama for this past year, so why the sudden and urgent interest in her now?'

His mother sank down gracefully on to one of the sofas before answering him. 'Edith mentioned that, with your help, she intended bringing Eleanor out into society.'

Justin's hands were clasped tightly together behind his back. 'And have you come to offer your own assistance in that endeavour?'

She gave a sad shake of her head. 'I wish that you would not take that scathing tone when you address me.'

He drew in a deeply controlling breath, aware that he was being less than polite to the woman who had, after all, given birth to him.

'I apologise if I sounded rude.'

'That is at least something, I suppose—Justin, are you aware that your neckcloth is looking…less than its usual pristine self?' She eyed him with questioning calm.

Considering the depth, the wildness, of the desire which had seized him in his carriage just minutes ago, when Eleanor had unfastened his waistcoat and then pushed his shirt up his chest so that she might touch and caress him there, Justin was surprised only his neckcloth was askew as evidence of their passionate encounter!

'I believe we were discussing the suddenness of your decision to come up to town, not my neckcloth?' He refused to so much as raise a hand and attempt to straighten the disarray of that scrap of material, and to hell with what deductions his mother might care to make in that regard.

Eyes so like his own dropped from meeting his as his mother instead ran a fingernail along the piping at the edge of the cushion upon which she sat. 'It is not so sudden, Justin. I have known for some time that one of us must attempt to heal the breach which exists between us. And when you failed to visit me on my birthday this week, I realised it must be me.'

Justin had completely forgotten that it *was* his mother's birthday just four days ago. Indeed, he had been so preoccupied, with both his grandmother's illness, and this unaccountable passion he had developed for Eleanor Rosewood, that he was no longer sure what day of the week it was, let alone that he had missed altogether his mother's forty-ninth birthday!

He winced. 'Once again I apologise.'

She gave a teasing tilt of her head. 'Enough to give me the kiss you failed to give me earlier?'

'Of course.' Justin crossed the room to briefly press his lips against the smoothness of her cheek; it was a small price to pay, after all, for such negligence.

His mother nodded. 'And will you now sit here beside me and tell me all about Miss Rosewood?' She patted the sofa cushion beside her own.

A gesture Justin ignored as he instead walked over to one of the armchairs placed either side of the unlit fireplace. He folded his long length down into it in a deliberately relaxed pose, his elbows resting on the arms of the chair as he steepled his fingers together in front of him, all the time avoiding acknowledging the disappointed look he knew would be on his mother's face. 'Would Grandmother not be a more reliable source of information on Eleanor than I?'

'I do not believe so, no…'

His gaze sharpened as he looked across the room at his mother through those steepled fingers. 'Would you care to explain that remark?'

'Not really, no.'

Justin knew that he and Eleanor had both looked decidedly dishevelled when they entered the house together just now, but he was sincerely hoping his mother hadn't realised the cause. 'Then perhaps you would care to tell me your real reason for coming up to town?'

She looked pained. 'Could it not be that I wished to see my only son?'

His mouth thinned. 'Somehow I doubt that very much!'

'Oh, Justin.' His mother sighed heavily. 'Why do we always have to fight whenever we meet?'

He raised blond brows. 'Perhaps because we do not like each other?'

'Justin!' Tears filled his mother eyes as she sprang restlessly to her feet, her cheeks having blanched to a deathly white. 'That is just so—so cruel of you! I love you. I have always loved you!'

And Justin had always loved his mother, too. Even when he had been angry with her, hurt by her, resentful of her negligence, he had still loved her. He loved her still.

But those years, when he had very often not seen his mother or his father for months at a time, had created a gulf between them which he truly believed to be insurmountable.

'It is not my intention to be cruel to you, Mother. I just—why can you not just accept that there is too much between us, too many years spent apart, for us to be able to reach any common ground now?'

There was a strained look beside those tear-wet eyes and lines beside her unsmiling mouth. 'There are things—' she broke off, as if seeking the right words to say to him. 'You asked why I have come up to town. The truth is, when you forgot even to acknowledge my birthday, I decided—'

'Damn it, I have already apologised for my oversight!'

She shook her head. 'It is still a symptom of the way our relationship now stands. And there are things you should know, things I have not told you before now, which I think you have a right to know.'

Justin frowned. 'There is nothing you can say to me now that could ever take away all those years of neglect, when you chose to travel about the world with your husband—'

'My husband was your father, don't forget that! And we

did not spend our lives simply enjoying ourselves, as you seem to be implying we were!' Her expression was anguished, her gloved hands clenched tightly together in her agitation. 'Nor was my decision to accompany him an easy one to make. But I made sure you were away at school before I decided to do so, and you had Edith and George if we had not managed to return for the holidays.'

'Yet my grandparents, dear as they both were and still are, were no substitute for my own parents!' This subject was too painful, too close to Justin's own heart, for him to remain his usual icily controlled self.

'Justin, I remained behind, stayed at home with you, until you went away to school at the age of ten,' she reasoned anxiously. 'Do you not remember those years before then, Justin? The wonderful years we spent together in Hampshire, swimming or fishing together in the summer months, sledging and ice-skating on the pond in the winters? And the excitement we always felt when we knew your father was to return from—from his business abroad?'

His eyes narrowed to icy slits. 'I remember the years that followed far more clearly.'

Her shoulders drooped in defeated. 'You have become a hard and unforgiving man, Justin.'

He shrugged. 'I am what my life has made me.'

'Then I am sorry for it.' His mother gave a sad smile. 'You are an intelligent man. Can you not think of any reason why your father travelled abroad for almost the whole of your life, first to India, then to the Continent? Other than enjoying himself, of course,' she added with uncharacteristic tartness.

Justin glanced at her curiously, having absolutely no idea

where this conversation was leading. 'I was always told that he went away on business...'

'And he was.'

'Then I do not see—'

'That business was not his own!'

'Then whose was it?' Justin made no attempt to hide his growing impatience with this conversation.

She looked rather irritated now. 'Can you really not guess, Justin?'

He stared at her, a critical gaze that his mother continued to meet unflinchingly, unwaveringly, as if willing him to find the answer for himself.

Justin tensed suddenly as an answer presented itself, sitting forwards in his chair suddenly. 'Can it be—?' He paused, shaking his head slightly in denial. 'All those years—did my father work secretly as an agent for the crown?'

He knew the answer he had found was the correct one, as a look of relief now flooded his mother's beautiful face, making it radiant.

Chapter Fifteen

'I know you are not asleep, Eleanor, so you might just as well give up all pretence that you are!'

Ellie was indeed awake, and she had heard the door to her bedchamber being slowly opened just seconds ago before closing again. But she had hoped, whoever her visitor might be, that they were now on the other side of that closed door.

She remained unmoving and silent now beneath the bed-covers, not wanting another confrontation with Justin. If she refused to answer him, surely he would simply go away?

Ellie's bath earlier had been very welcome and Rachel St Just, as promised, had visited Ellie in her bedchamber before the family dined downstairs, that sweet lady arranging for Stanhope to bring Ellie some supper on a tray after she had confessed to still having a slight headache.

Shortly after that Ellie had heard one of the carriages being brought around to the front of the house, and then the departure of the St Justs to Lady Littleton's soirée. Several hours later, she still hadn't heard that carriage return.

She had assumed—wrongly, she now realised—that Justin, despite his reluctance to attend such social occasions, would have accompanied his newly arrived mother, and grandmother, to Lady Littleton's for the evening.

'Eleanor...?'

Her lids remained stubbornly closed, despite the fact that she could now discern the glow of candlelight through their delicate membranes. Justin had obviously moved closer to where she lay in bed.

'Damn it, are there not already enough women in this household who prefer to avoid my company this evening!' he muttered truculently.

It was that very truculence, a cross little-boy emotion, and so at odds with his usual arrogant self-confidence, that caused her lids to finally open, in spite of her previous decision to ignore him and hope that he would just go away.

'Ah ha!' Justin looked down at her triumphantly as he stood beside the bed, lit candle held aloft.

Ellie turned to lie on her back and rest up against the pillows, the sheet pulled up over her breasts as she looked up at Justin guardedly in the candlelight. She quickly realised he seemed to be leaning against the bed for support, his appearance also less than presentable; he had removed his jacket and neckcloth completely some time during the evening, several buttons of his shirt were unfastened at the throat and his waistcoat was also unbuttoned.

Another wary glance at his face also revealed that there was a brightness to his eyes and a slight flush to the hardness of his cheeks. 'Justin, are you inebriated?'

He blinked, before pausing to give the matter exaggerated thought. 'I believe I may have drunk a bottle of brandy, or possibly two, since dinner...'

This was just too delicious for Ellie not to enjoy to the

full. It was certainly impossible to ignore the fact that the haughty Duke of Royston, was so foxed he could barely stand! 'Perhaps you should sit down before you fall down— I did not mean there!' Ellie gave an indignant squeak as he immediately sat down on the side of her bed, causing her to scoot over to the other side if she did not wish to be crushed. 'Justin, you should not be in my bedchamber at all, let alone sitting on my bed!'

'Why not—?' He swayed slightly as he leaned forwards to place the candle and its holder on the bedside table. 'Uh oh…' He straightened again with effort, sitting still for several seconds before swinging his booted feet up on to the bed and lying back against the pillows beside her. 'Am I imagining things or is the ceiling spinning?'

'Justin!' Ellie sat up to frown down at him impatiently, her earlier amusement at his expense having completely disappeared as he lay back against the pillows with his eyes closed, golden lashes fanning across those flushed cheeks. 'Justin?'

His lids remained closed as he gave a wide smile of satisfaction. 'You have the hang of saying my name now, I see.'

'Justin!' she repeated with considerable exasperation as she took a grasp of his arm and shook it, with no apparent result as he simply settled more comfortably on to the pillows. 'You must get up now and leave immediately!'

'Why must I?'

'Your mother and grandmother will be returning soon—'

'They will not be back for hours yet.' He raised a hand to cover a yawn. 'And it was dashed lonely downstairs in the library on my own, whereas it is warm and cosy up here with you.'

Ellie stilled at this unexpected admission from a gentleman who gave the clear impression that he had never needed anyone's company but his own. 'Why is it that you think your mother and the dowager are avoiding your company?'

'Do they need a reason?' He gave a shrug.

To Ellie's mind, yes, they most certainly did; Rachel St Just had been so emotional earlier at seeing her son again, after what seemed to have been a lengthy separation, and the dowager was prepared to forgive her grandson anything since he had returned to live at Royston House. 'Why did you not accompany them to Lady Littleton's?'

He prised one lid open to look up at her. 'I may be in the mood for company, Eleanor, but I am not so desperate I would resort to that particular torture!'

She gave a rueful grimace at his obvious disgust. 'I was thinking of it more in terms of doing something which might please your mother and the dowager, and in doing so, perhaps regain favour with them?'

He gave a shudder as he closed that lid. 'I am not as anxious as that to regain their approval!'

'Obviously not.' Ellie sighed at this obvious display of his usual arrogance. 'Nevertheless, you really cannot remain here with me, Justin.'

'Why not, when your bedchamber is so much more comfortable than my own?'

Ellie did not see how that could possibly be true. The dowager had shown her about the main parts of the house when Ellie first came to live here a year ago and she seemed to remember the ducal suite as being opulent, to say the least, with its huge four-poster bed and deep-blue brocade curtains, Georgian furniture and luxurious blue-and-gold Aubusson carpets; her own bedchamber was nice enough, but only a quarter of that size, the bed barely big enough for the two of them to lie down upon together.

An observation which she should not even have been able to make! 'I cannot believe that. Nor do I think it wise for you to remain here any longer—Justin?' She eyed him uncertainly as he turned on the bed to face her, and in doing so making her self-consciously aware of the fact that she wore only her nightrail beneath the bedcovers, the bareness of her shoulders currently visible above the sheet, which was now trapped beneath his heavier weight.

'Did you know you have the most beautiful hair I ever beheld…?' Justin reached out to take a long red strand between his thumb and fingers. 'So soft and silky to the touch and like living flame to gaze upon.' He allowed the silkiness of her hair to fall through his fingers.

'I do not think this the time or the place for you to remark upon the beauty of my hair.'

'When else should I remark upon it when it is normally kept confined or hidden away beneath your bonnet?'

'Not always…' A blush brightened her cheeks.

No, not always…for had Justin not wound these silken tresses about his partially naked body just hours earlier?

He moved up on one elbow the better to observe how smooth and creamy her skin now appeared against that living flame. 'I could not see you properly in the carriage this afternoon.' He smoothed his hand across the bare expanse of her shoulder now clearly visible to him. 'You are very beautiful, Eleanor. Your skin is so soft…'

She held herself stiffly, but even so could not hide the quiver caused by the touch of his caressing fingers. 'Unless you have forgotten, Justin, I, too, am currently avoiding your company…'

He gave a wicked smile. 'I have forgotten none of what took place between us this afternoon, Eleanor.'

The colour deepened in her cheeks. 'Nor, unfortunately, have I. Which is why—'

'Unfortunately?' Justin's fingers curled about her shoulder to hold her in place. 'That is not particularly flattering, referring to our lovemaking like that, Eleanor.'

'Lovemaking which should never have taken place!' She wrenched out of his grasp, quickly moving to the side of the bed and throwing back the covers to stand up, before retrieving her robe from the bedside chair and hastily pulling it on over her nightrail.

Justin lay back, taking unashamed advantage of being able to gaze upon the nakedness of the body he glimpsed briefly through the sheer material of that nightgown before Eleanor fastened her robe: firm, uptilting, berry-tipped breasts, slender waist, curvaceous hips and thighs above long and slender legs.

A pity, then, that the copious amount of brandy he had consumed earlier this evening appeared to have robbed him of all ability to do anything about it!

He gave a self-disgusted groan as he lay back on the pillows before lifting his arm to place it across his eyes. 'Does it seem overbright to you in here?'

'You, sir, are seriously foxed!'

He gave a grunt of acknowledgement, having no need to look at Eleanor to know that she would be glaring down at him disapprovingly. 'Not at all a surprising state of affairs after the things I have learnt this evening. And not only that,' he added gruffly, 'but it seems I am to be bedevilled by desire for a young woman totally unsuited to the role of becoming my mistress!'

Could *she* be the young woman he meant?

If so, then he was perfectly correct; for she had no intention of ever becoming his mistress or any other man's, 'bedevilled by desire', or otherwise!

She drew in a sharp breath. 'You will leave my bedchamber right now, sir!'

'Can't,' he mumbled.

'What do you mean, you can't?' She continued to glower down at Justin as she stood beside the bed upon which he still lounged so elegantly, inwardly decrying the fact that he still managed to look so impossibly handsome, despite his less-than-pristine appearance. Or perhaps because of it...

Justin looked far more of a fallen angel in his current state of dishevelment, the gold of his overlong hair having fallen rakishly across his brow, with similar gold curls visible at the open throat of his shirt.

He cracked open that single eyelid once again as he answered her. 'I mean, dear Eleanor, that if my cock is incapable of rising to the occasion after I have gazed upon your delicious near-nakedness, then you may rest assured the rest of me is incapable of rising too!'

Ellie felt the embarrassed colour burning her cheeks. 'You are both behaving and talking outrageously! And likely you will seriously regret it come morning. Indeed, I believe you will wholeheartedly deserve the debilitating headache that will no doubt strike you down—Justin!' She gave a protesting hiss as he reached out to grasp her wrist before tugging determinedly, causing her to tumble back down on to the bed beside him. 'Stop this immediately.' She fought against the arm and leg he now threw across her breasts and thighs in order to keep her beside him.

He scowled at her impatiently. 'Damn it, woman, cease

your struggling and try to be of some assistance to me for a change!'

She stilled as she realised he was not attempting to be intimate with her, but was merely using the restraint of his arm and leg as a means of stopping her from struggling any further. That she was not quite as immune as she'd like, to his close proximity and rakish good looks, was no one's fault but her own. 'In what way could I possibly be of assistance to you?'

He frowned. 'You are a woman, are you not?'

'I believe you are as aware of that as I.' She raised pointed brows.

'Exactly.' He nodded his satisfaction with that fact. 'And, as such, you understand the way a woman's mind works.'

'I understand how my own mind works, I am not so sure about other ladies.'

'In the light of there being no other lady available, with whom I might discuss this, you will have to do.' Justin blew out an irritated breath as he once again lay down beside her on the bed to stare up at the ceiling of her bedchamber. 'Explain to me, if you can, why it is a woman, who has lied to her only child for over half his lifetime, now expects that child to fall at her feet and ask *her* forgiveness for not understanding sooner, once she has finally—finally!—explained the reason for that lie.'

Ellie at him closely, seeing the evidence of his pain in the way his eyes had darkened and those grim lines had become etched beside his mouth. 'And would this woman, this mother, happen to be your own?'

He nodded. 'For years I have believed my mother and father to have been so engrossed in their love for each other, in their need to be exclusively with each other, that they had no room or love to spare in their lives for me, their only child,' he rasped. 'And now this evening my mother has told me—I can trust you not to discuss this with anyone else…?'

'Of course.' She bristled slightly at his need to ask.

He nodded distracted. 'This evening I have learnt what my mother and grandparents have always known, that my father was a hero and worked secretly for the crown for many years. That he risked his own life again and again. And latterly my mother chose to put herself in that same danger, when she insisted on travelling with him after I had gone away to boarding school. The two of them succeeded in collecting information which has saved many hundreds of lives over the years.'

And it was obvious, from the mixture of pain and pride Ellie now detected in Justin's voice, that he had not decided as yet how he felt about that…

Not surprising, really, when he had so obviously become the cynical man that he now was because for so many years he had held a quite different opinion about his parents.

It also confirmed Ellie's previous belief that this might also be the reason Justin had repeatedly declared he had no intention of being in love with his own wife, when the time came for him to marry and provide an heir. For what man, who had believed himself to have been excluded from his parents' lives because of their all-consuming love for each other, would ever want to inflict that same neglect upon his own children?

Ellie moistened her lips with the tip of her tongue as she chose her next words carefully. 'I am sure that both your mother, and the dowager, understand your feelings enough to realise you will need time in which to completely absorb and adjust your thinking concerning the things you have been told this evening.'

Justin glanced at her. 'How would you feel if you were to learn that your own father had not been who you thought all these years?'

Ellie shrugged. 'I hope that I would eventually find a way to come to terms with that truth.'

Justin's eyes glittered. 'That would surely depend upon who your father is!'

'Was,' she corrected softly.

'Well…yes,' he conceded awkwardly.

'It appears your own father was something of a hero.' Ellie said, sensing that they were now talking slightly at odds with each other, as if Justin's conversation was about something entirely different to her own. 'And I have every reason to believe, despite never having met him, that my father was an honourable man, at least.'

'Yes.'

'Unless…' she eyed him warily '…you have heard otherwise?'

Too late Justin realised that he had allowed his mother's revelations, and an overindulgence of brandy after not eating enough at dinner, to loosen his tongue in a way he would not otherwise have done and had now appeared to have cast doubts in Ellie's mind about her own father.

How much worse would those doubts be if she were ever to discover that both Justin and the Earl of Richmond, suspected Dryden Litchfield of being her real father, as a result of his having raped her mother!

Damn it, here he was, wallowing in self-pity—probably exacerbated by that overindulgence of brandy, the effects of which seemed to have dissipated entirely during the course of this current conversation—when the truth was his own father had been a hero of major proportions, his mother, too, when they had both decided to travel to places that were often highly dangerous.

What an idiot he had been. How utterly bloody selfish. Instead of getting blind drunk, what he should have done earlier this evening was get down on his knees and thank his mother for all that she and his father had sacrificed for their king and country.

His mother had been right, of course, in that he *had* forgotten those years before he went away to boarding school. Happy and contented years when Justin had his mother's almost undivided attention, interspersed with weeks or months when his father would return to them and the three of them would then do those things together.

Eleanor, on the other hand, had no memories whatsoever of any father, either in her childhood, or now. Frederick would have been less than useless, he thought acerbically. And the one Justin might give her, if Litchfield should indeed prove to be her father, was nothing short of a nightmare.

'I have not heard anything detrimental about Henry Rosewood, no,' he answered carefully.

'You seemed to imply otherwise a moment ago...?'

'If that is so, then I apologise. I assure you, they are nothing more than the ramblings of an inebriated man.' He swung his booted feet to the floor before sitting up on the side of the bed. 'I apologise for having disturbed your rest, Eleanor. I believe I shall now go to my own bedchamber and endeavour to sleep off the effects of my over-indulgence.'

There was no denying that he had been inebriated when he'd first entered Ellie's bedchamber, but she did not believe that to be the case now. Nor did she care for the way in which the conversation had turned to the subject of her own father just a few minutes ago, then just as quickly been deflected by Justin. As if he were privy to some information which he did not intend to share with her...

His next comment in no way alleviated that suspicion. 'Good lord, look at the time!' He glanced down at the watch he had taken from the pocket of his waistcoat. 'You are right, my mother and grandmother will be returning at any moment and they must not find me here in your bedchamber when they do.' He replaced his pocket watch before straightening in preparation for departing.

Ellie now sat up against the headboard of the bed, her legs curled up beneath her. 'Justin, you would...share the information with me, if you were to learn anything of my father which might damage the dowager duchess in society?'

He turned to look at her sharply. 'And what of your own reputation?'

She shrugged. 'I came from obscurity and will quite happily return there, but I could not bear to think that I had caused the dowager, or indeed yourself or your mother, any social embarrassment before I did so.'

Justin's expression softened. 'And would you not regret or miss anyone or any part of that society on your own account?'

Having been reluctant at first, Ellie knew she would now miss many things. The warmth and kindness of Edith St Just, and now her daughter-in-law, for one. The friendship of Magdelena Matthews, which, never having had a close female friend before now, had become so very dear to Ellie these past few days. And lastly, she would miss Justin himself.

She had not spent all of her time earlier this evening in bathing and eating a light supper, but had found more than enough time in which to dwell on what she truly felt for Justin. To come to the realisation, that much as she might wish it otherwise, she was indeed in love with him to the extent that, if she ever *were* to be rejected from society, from *his* society, that she might, out of a need to be with the man she loved, even go so far as to accept his offer, if he were ever to make it, of becoming his mistress.

'I should miss the St Just family,' she now answered him honestly. 'You have all been extremely kind to me—'

'I have not been in the least kind to you, Eleanor!' he contradicted harshly.

'But of course you have.' Her expression softened as she looked across at him. 'Your…methods of doing so may have been slightly unorthodox,' she allowed ruefully. 'But, nevertheless, you have done much to make it possible for me to be accepted into society.'

That might be so, Justin acknowledged with inner frustration, but he also held the knowledge that would allow that same society to completely shun her!

Damn it, something would have to be done about this situation with Litchfield, and sooner rather than later.

Chapter Sixteen

'Something must be done about Litchfield, Richmond!' Justin voiced that same sentiment the following afternoon, scowling across the distance that separated the two men as they sparred together at Jackson's Boxing Saloon.

'I agree—if only so that you no longer feel the need to try to beat me into the canvas!' Lord Bryan Anderson drawled ruefully after Justin had landed a particularly vicious jab to his jaw. Both men were stripped to the waist, the perspiration from their efforts obvious upon their sweat-slicked bodies.

Justin drew back. 'Damn it! I apologise, Richmond.' He straightened before bowing to the other man, as an indication that he considered their bout to be a draw and now over.

The Earl of Richmond eyed him curiously as they strolled across to where they had left their clothes earlier, his muscled physique appearing that of a much younger man, the hair on his chest reddish-gold rather than the premature white upon his head. 'Your concern for your young ward is…admirable.'

Justin paused in towelling himself in order to give the earl a sideways glance. 'Your implication being...?'

Richmond chuckled softly. 'She is a beautiful young lady.'

'And possibly in possession of a father who is considered as being anything but a gentleman!'

The older man appeared thoughtful as he sat down to towel off the worst of the evidence of his own physical excess. 'And does that fact affect your own regard for her?'

'Do not be stupid, man!' He scowled.

'Some men might feel—'

'Then some men do not know how to appreciate a diamond when it is placed in front of them.' Justin's scowl darkened as his face emerged from pulling his shirt over his head.

'But you do?'

His mouth twisted. 'So much so that I am giving serious thought to—' He halted, realising he was being indiscreet.

'Yes?'

Justin changed his tack. 'Eleanor cannot be held responsible for who her sire may be.'

'Even if it should indeed turn out to be Litchfield?'

'Even then,' he said grimly, having realised the previous evening, after he had chosen to go to Eleanor's bedchamber to confide in her, that his 'regard' for her was of a more serious nature than he had previously allowed for.

His mother's revelations about his father seemed to have somehow stripped away all of his defences, to such a degree that he could no longer hide the truth, even from himself.

He had been so determined to maintain his lack of emotional involvement where women were concerned, that he had not fully understood until after he had returned to his own bedchamber the previous night, completely sober but unable to sleep, the difference she had already made in his life.

The main change had been that he had moved back into Royston House, after years of refusing to do so. He might have excused that move to Eleanor as the need for him to be close at hand if his grandmother should become ill again, but inwardly he had always acknowledged that it was really Eleanor, and the need he felt to protect *her,* most especially from men such as Litchfield, that had been his primary reason for returning home.

A need to protect her which had just resulted in a deeper, even more startling, realisation…

'It is curious, is it not,' Richmond continued slowly, 'considering Litchfield's licentiousness, and obvious disregard for whether a woman consents or not, that there are not more of his bastards roaming the English countryside.'

Justin shrugged. 'We do not know that there are not.'

'Then perhaps we should make every effort to prove that?'

'For what purpose?' Justin asked curiously.

Richmond avoided meeting his gaze as he buttoned his waistcoat. 'I have my reasons.'

'Which are…?'

'I would prefer not to discuss them at this point in time.'

'Damn it, Richmond!' Justin exploded. 'If you have any knowledge whatsoever that might indicate Litchfield is not Eleanor's father, after all, then for God's sake have a little pity and share it with me!'

'Why is it so important to you?' the earl asked.

Justin glanced away. 'My grandmother is very fond of Eleanor—'

'And you are not?' Richmond derided.

Justin's jaw tightened. 'Mind your own damned business!'

'I trust you will forgive me for saying so, but my impression is that you have become more than a little "fond" of Miss Rosewood yourself.'

Justin's eyes narrowed to steely slits. 'You go too far, Richmond!'

'It is to be hoped, as Miss Rosewood is a young lady unprotected in the world by any but your own family, that you have not gone too far with her yourself,' the older man warned.

Justin drew himself up to his full, impressive height. 'I have appreciated your assistance this past week, Richmond, and have always regarded you as more than just an acquaintance, but that does not give you licence to question me about my relationship with Eleanor.' Especially when Justin was unsure himself, as yet, as to exactly how to proceed with her!

The two men's gazes clashed in a silent battle of wills, Richmond the one to finally back down as he sighed. 'I apologise if I have given offence, Royston.' He gave a stiff bow.

'Your apology is accepted.' Justin smiled. 'In fact, if it is not too short notice, then why not join us for dinner this evening at Royston House, and then you may see for yourself how ill-treated Eleanor is!' he teased.

'I would never accuse you, or any member of your family, of ill treatment towards anyone,' Richmond protested.

'I trust you will allow me to make Litchfield the exception, if it becomes necessary?' Justin drawled, cracking his knuckles meaningfully.

'Let us hope that it does not.' Richmond grimaced. 'I have heard tell that your mother has recently returned to town.'

'All the more reason for you to rescue me from yet another evening of dining in an all-female household!'

The earl gave a rueful smile. 'In that case, I believe I should very much enjoy dining with you and your family this evening, thank you.'

'It is settled then.' Justin, now fully dressed and ready to depart, nodded his satisfaction with the arrangement. 'As it happens, I am expecting another report on Litchfield to be delivered later today, which we might discuss once the ladies have left us to our brandy and cigars.' But, considering the pounding in his head when he had finally woken up at lunchtime today, and which had still not completely gone away, Justin very much doubted he himself would be imbibing!

'I had no idea that you were so well acquainted with Richmond!' The dowager duchess eyed her grandson curiously as the family gathered in the Blue Salon that evening to await the arrival of their dinner guest.

It was the first time that Ellie had seen Justin since he had left her bedchamber so late the previous evening. She had left the house that morning before he had appeared, hopefully suffering with that severe headache she had predicted the night before when he did!

Although he did not appear to be suffering too badly this evening…

Just to look at him in his black evening clothes and snowy white linen, the last of the sun's rays shining in through the windows giving his hair the appearance of molten gold, the severity of his features thrown into light and shadow, those piercing blue eyes sharp with intelligence, was enough to make Ellie's heart beat faster, much to her own annoyance.

She had been unable to fall sleep the previous night once he had left, as she thought over all he had told her, and realised how those things must have affected his views about marriage.

It was easy to see how, as a child, Justin would have made the assumptions he had concerning his parents long and frequent absences, and what he had believed to be their almost obsessive love for each other that they would abandon their only child in order to be together.

Just as she now believed it was the reason he had decided that such a love in his own marriage was not for him.

Unfortunately, that understanding made absolutely no difference to how she felt about him.

It was no longer the girlish infatuation she had felt for his rakish good looks and arrogant self-confidence just a few short weeks ago, but a deep and abiding love that would surely cause her heart to break when she had to leave him. As she surely must. Loving him as passionately as she did, marriage to another man had become an impossibility for her. But she also had to accept that one day Justin had to marry, if only to provide his heir—and she could not remain at Royston House as witness to such a cold and calculated alliance.

Except he was not married as yet, or even betrothed.

'Can you possibly be referring to Lord Bryan Anderson?'

Justin had been surreptitiously watching Eleanor until that moment, as he admired the creamy swell of her breasts visible above the low neckline of the deep-emerald silk gown she wore, a perfect match in colour for her eyes and lending a deep richness to the red of her hair as she sat demurely in the armchair beside the unlit fireplace.

It took some effort on his part to turn his gaze away from her beauty in order to concentrate on answering his mother's query. 'He is recently returned to society himself following the death of his wife last year.'

'I had no idea the countess had died!' A frown now marred his mother's brow.

'Possibly that is because you have hidden yourself away in the country these past three years?' the dowager reminded her.

'Yes.' Rachel nodded distractedly.

Justin was at a loss as to what significance the death of Richmond's poor wife—surely a blessing to all concerned, after so many years of suffering?—could possibly have to any of them personally.

'Justin looks quite bemused, Rachel!' His grandmother gave a chuckle.

Humour at his expense, obviously, although he failed to see the reason why. 'Mother?' he queried cautiously as he saw the becoming blush that now coloured her cheeks.

'My dear boy, it has been such a time of revelations for you!' His grandmother looked amused as she continued, 'My dear, if Rachel and Robert had not met and instantly fallen in love with each other, then Richmond might now be your father in his stead…' she explained gently.

Although not a part of this conversation, Ellie had nevertheless been following it with great interest. An interest which now turned to concern for Justin as he looked suitably stunned by the dowager's comment.

Ellie reacted purely on instinct as she rose quickly to her feet to move to Justin's side—surely this latest disclosure would prove too much, even for him, on top of all he had been told about his father the previous day? Indeed, the hand he placed briefly in front of his eyes, as he shook his head, would seem to indicate as much.

Until he lowered that hand to reveal a teasing grin. 'Perhaps it is not too late, Mama? After all, you are now both widowed.'

'Justin!' his mother gasped, the blush deepening in her cheeks.

His grin widened. 'You could do far worse than Richmond, Mama. Did you meet him at the Royston Ball, Eleanor? And if so, what is your opinion of the man?' He turned to her, that mischief gleaming in the warm blue depths of his eyes.

Ellie returned Justin's smile as she gratefully responded to the warmth in his eyes. 'I danced a quadrille with him, I believe, and found him to be a very charming and handsome gentleman.'

Justin quirked a mocking brow. 'Not too charming or handsome, it is to be hoped?'

Now it was Ellie's turn to blush. 'In a fatherly sort of way,' she finished quickly.

Justin continued to study her admiringly for several long seconds. They had not had the chance to talk alone together as yet today and he had felt slightly wary about trying to do so, uncertain of his welcome after his reprehensible behaviour the night before in such an inebriated state. But he had felt slightly reassured a few moments ago when she had come to stand beside him as he learnt of the friendship that had once existed between his mother and Richmond. Almost as if Eleanor felt a need to protect him…

An irony in itself, when Justin knew that he was the one who needed to protect her, even from himself on occasion!

'There you have it then, Mama.' He turned back to his

mother. 'You have both Eleanor's and my own blessing if you should decide to—'

'Really, Justin, this is not at all a suitable conversation, let alone an amusing one, when the earl is due to arrive here at any moment.' His mother gave him an admonishing glance.

He smiled unapologetically. 'I was merely assuring you that you have my wholehearted approval if you should decide to…renew your acquaintance with Richmond.'

His mother looked more flustered than ever. 'And I am telling you that I have no need of such approval, when I have no intention of being anything more to the Earl of Richmond than the middle-aged mother of his friend!'

'You are still a very beautiful woman, Rachel,' the dowager put in.

Her daughter-in-law threw up her hands in exasperation. 'You are all gone mad!'

'Ah, but what a wonderful madness it is, Mama.' Justin was no longer able to resist the desire he felt to touch Eleanor in some way, so he placed his hand lightly beneath her elbow.

She looked uncertain. 'I believe that must be the earl I hear arriving now,' she murmured.

Justin was not so sure as he heard the sound of a raised voice outside in the hallway, followed by Stanhope's quieter, more reasoning tone, and then another shout.

'Justin, can you see what that is all about?' The dowager looked concerned.

He nodded, releasing Eleanor's elbow. 'Stay here,' he advised the women before crossing the room in long determined strides. He had barely reached the door before it was flung open to reveal an obviously furious Dryden Litchfield standing on the other side of it and an uncharacteristically ruffled Stanhope just behind him.

Litchfield's face was mottled with temper as he glared at Justin contemptuously. 'Just who the hell do you think you are, Royston?' he snarled.

'There are ladies present, Litchfield,' Justin reminded with cold menace.

'I don't give a damn if there is royalty present!' The other man's voice rose angrily. 'You have a bloody nerve, poking and prying about in my private affairs—'

'I remind you once again that there are ladies present!' Justin held on to his own temper with difficulty, inwardly wishing to do nothing more than to punch Litchfield on his pugnacious jaw, an action as unacceptable, in front of the ladies, as was the other man's swearing.

Litchfield snorted. 'I am sure they are all well aware of what an interfering bastard you are—'

'You, sir, will remove yourself, and your foul tongue, from my hallway immediately!' The dowager duchess, obviously having heard more than enough, now stood up to glare imperiously at their uninvited visitor.

Litchfield gave her a sneer. 'You all think yourselves so damned superior—'

'Perhaps that is because they are superior?' Eleanor interjected. 'Certainly to you. In every way.'

Justin turned slowly to look at her, his chest swelling with pride as she stared at Litchfield down the length of her tiny freckle-covered nose.

Her chin was tilted at a determined angle as she stepped forwards. 'It is entirely unacceptable for you to burst in here, uninvited, and then insult the dowager and her family.'

'Don't get hoity-toity with me, missy, when I know your own mother to have been no better than a who—'

'That is quite enough, Litchfield!' a third male voice thundered across the entrance hall.

Ellie's startled glance moved past Lord Litchfield to see the Earl of Richmond moving swiftly across the hallway, his evening cloak billowing out behind him, his handsome face dark with anger.

'You will excuse my interruption, ladies.' He gave them an abrupt bow before turning his attention back to Dryden Litchfield. 'We will take this conversation elsewhere,' he ground out.

'And why would I do that?' the other man challenged insolently.

The earl narrowed hazel-coloured eyes. 'Because if you do not do as I suggest, then I will have no choice but to have you arrested forthwith.'

'Arrested?' Litchfield scorned. 'For what, pray?'

'I believe there are any number of charges which might be brought against you.'

'By whom? You?' he sneered.

'If necessary, yes,' the earl bit out grimly.

Litchfield gave a contemptuous shake of his head. 'I believe all your years of being married to a madwoman must have addled your own brain, Richmond—' His words came to an abrupt halt as the earl's fist landed squarely on his jaw, his eyes rolling back in his head even as he toppled backwards.

Stanhope, in a position to catch him as he fell, instead stepped aside and allowed the other man to drop to the marble floor of the grand entrance hall, his top lip turned back contemptuously. 'Shall I have one of the footmen assist me in ridding us of this…person, your Grace?' He looked enquiringly at a grim-faced Justin.

'Yes—'

'No,' Richmond put in firmly before turning to bow to all the St Just family. 'I apologise for my impertinence.' He looked at the duke, his expression stern. 'But information has come into my keeping this evening which I believe dictates we must settle this matter with Litchfield once and for all right now, Royston.'

Ellie was still bewildered by Lord Litchfield's insulting remark about her mother. Shocked that this obnoxious man should have even known the sweet and gentle Muriel! Nor did she completely understand his comment concerning the Earl of Richmond's deceased countess, although there was no mistaking his intended insult—and the earl's swift retribution for it!

The duke scowled at the unconscious man. 'Have him carried to the library, Stanhope.'

'Justin, would it not be better if we were to all hear what the earl has to say?' the dowager asked, quite pointedly, it seemed to Ellie.

The duke met his grandmother's gaze, a silent message seeming to pass between the two of them before he turned back to the earl. 'Richmond?' he said finally. 'My grandmother, at least, is already conversant with…some of the events of the past.'

The earl winced. 'The truth of that is…not as we thought it might be, Royston.' He glanced uncomfortably at Ellie as he spoke.

Which only served to further increase her alarm, following so quickly on the heels of Lord Litchfield's earlier remark about her mother. 'Justin, what's going on?'

* * *

Justin could tell Eleanor was deeply disturbed by recent events.

He was also troubled by Richmond's implication that Litchfield was not Eleanor's father, after all.

For if not Litchfield, then who…?

Surely not someone Muriel Rosewood had met after returning from India; the timing of Eleanor's birth was all wrong for that to be the case.

Then perhaps some other gentleman Muriel had been close to in India?

Chapter Seventeen

'You will ask chef to delay dinner for half an hour,' Rachel St Just instructed Stanhope once the butler and a footman had deposited Litchfield on the rug in front of the unlit fireplace, the dowager having refused to allow him to soil any of the Georgian furniture with his less-than-clean appearance. 'After which, you may come back and remove him from our presence,' she added with a disdainful curl of her top lip.

Justin had never admired his mother more than he did at that moment, the truths she had told him yesterday at last allowing him to see her for the redoubtable woman that she was, rather than the mother he had believed to have abandoned him for so many years.

Richmond, he noted abstractly, was also regarding her with similar admiration.

'Justin…?'

He drew his breath in sharply, knowing he had been avoiding looking at Eleanor for the past few minutes as he saw to the removal of Litchfield, knowing he could delay no longer. A lump formed in his throat as he turned to see that she looked more lost and vulnerable than ever.

He stepped forwards with the intention of taking her in his arms.

'Lord Anderson,' the dowager made what was undoubtedly a timely interruption at the same time as she shot Justin a warning glance, 'would you care to tell us what you meant when you threatened to have this obnoxious creature arrested?'

'I fear the reasons for that are not for the delicate ears of ladies.' The earl's voice contained an edge of restrained anger. 'Suffice it to say, the man is completely beyond redemption.'

'What did he mean by his remark about my mother?' Eleanor asked.

'Royston!' the dowager protested as Justin moved determinedly to Eleanor's side.

He chose to ignore that second warning and instead placed an arm protectively about her waist. 'I believe it would be beneficial if you were to sit down,' he suggested kindly.

Ellie was stunned by the compassion and gentleness of his expression as he guided her to an armchair, both of them emotions she was unaccustomed to seeing on the face of the man she loved. There had been concern for his grandmother's health, yes. Also that inborn arrogance that was so much a part of him. Passion and desire, most certainly. But she had never seen the endearing combination of more tender emotions in him before now.

'You are keeping something from me,' she spoke with certainty as she refused to sit down.

He straightened tensely, a shutter falling over those deep-blue eyes. 'Eleanor—'

'Royston is not the one responsible for keeping something from you,' the Earl of Richmond interrupted firmly.

'Then who is?' she wanted to know.

'I am.' The earl looked uncharacteristically nervous as he crossed the room to take one of Ellie's hands in his both of his. 'And it is my sincerest wish—'

'What the hell are you doing, Richmond?' Justin exploded, immediately filled with a possessive fury that the handsome man was touching her so familiarly. He still wasn't sure Richmond didn't have a *tendre* for her.

'Justin, please…!' His mother sounded distraught at his aggression.

His glittering blue gaze remained fixed on Bryan Anderson, his jaw clenched. 'Take your hands off her!'

Ellie blanched. 'I do not believe Lord Anderson means to give offence, Justin,' she murmured.

'He is offending me by touching you!' Justin continued to glower at the older man. 'I told you to let her go!'

'Really, Justin, do try to remember the earl is a guest in our home,' his mother reproved. 'Your own invited guest, in fact.'

Lord Anderson gave Ellie's fingers a reassuring squeeze before releasing her to turn and bow to the two St Just ladies. 'Do not be alarmed, ladies. As Eleanor's guardian, Royston's objection to what he thinks is my familiarity with Miss Rosewood is perfectly in order.'

'I don't just think anything—you *were* damned familiar!' the duke bit out tautly.

Ellie reached out to place a hand lightly on his tense forearm, unsure why he was reacting so strongly. 'Please allow Lord Anderson to continue.'

Justin drew in a deep controlling breath, before nodding in reluctant acquiescence. 'Just keep your hands to yourself,' he warned the earl.

At any other time it would have been thrilling for Ellie to imagine that Justin's behaviour might mean that he truly cared for her, that he actually disliked seeing another man's hands upon her. Except she already knew that he did not, that he had stated quite clearly, on several occasions, that he would never fall in love with any woman. His protectiveness towards her now was, as Lord Anderson had already stated, merely part of his role as her guardian. 'Lord Anderson?' she asked.

'It is my sincere wish that you will try to understand and forgive what I am about to tell you, El—Miss Rosewood,' he swiftly amended as Justin gave a low, warning growl. 'To believe me when I say that if I had known at the time, I would have behaved otherwise—' He broke off, obviously finding this difficult. 'There is no easy way to say this. No way that I can soften the blow for you—'

'Then why say it at all?' Justin said darkly. 'Surely there is no need, when you have already stated that Litchfield was not the one responsible?'

'He is not.' Richmond's face appeared very pale against his white shock of hair and black evening clothes. His gaze returned to Eleanor. 'May I first say how like your mother you are, my dear.'

She blinked. 'You knew my mother?'

He nodded. 'Many years ago, in India.'

Her throat moved as she swallowed before speaking. 'Then you must have known my father, too?'

'I was Henry Rosewood's commanding officer.' Richmond told her. 'He was a well-liked and heroic officer.'

A tinge of pleased colour warmed Eleanor's cheeks. 'I never knew him, and—my mother talked of him so rarely.'

'Perhaps because it was too painful for her to do so,' the earl suggested gruffly.

'Perhaps.' Eleanor smiled sadly.

'The likeness between you and your mother is—startling. I had no difficulty in instantly recognising you as Muriel's daughter when I first saw you the evening of the Royston Ball,' Richmond continued emotionally. 'A fact I noted to the duke shortly afterwards.'

'He did not mention you had done so.' Eleanor gave Justin a brief puzzled glance.

'Perhaps because I did not see it as being of particular importance at the time.' He shrugged.

'But it is now?'

Justin had admired Eleanor for her intelligence more than once, but at this moment he might have wished her a trifle less perceptive.

'Justin, is it possible this business has something to do with that private matter I requested you look into?' his grandmother asked sharply.

God save him, he was surrounded by intelligent women! 'Yes,' he sighed.

The dowager looked down in horror at the man still prostrate upon her Aubusson rug. 'Surely not…?'

'Richmond seems to think not, no,' Justin confirmed drily.

'That is something, at least!' His grandmother raised a relieved hand to her ample bosom.

Justin agreed wholeheartedly with that sentiment. Although he could not help questioning Richmond's certainty on the matter.

Ellie looked dazed, having no idea what the dowager was referring to. But then, most of this past few minutes' conversation was a complete mystery to her. 'I still fail to see why Lord Litchfield forced his way in here uninvited this evening. What on earth was the matter?'

Justin's mouth twisted contemptuously. 'He obviously took severe exception to learning I had employed someone to investigate into his private affairs.'

She blinked. 'Why would you do such a thing?'

The dowager stood up. 'I am afraid I am partly to blame for this, Ellie.' She ignored her grandson's glower at her use of the shortened name. 'I asked Justin to…to look into a certain matter for me and it would seem that this is the unfortunate result.'

Ellie was none the wiser for this explanation. 'But surely this can have nothing to do with me?'

'I am afraid it has everything to do with you, my dear.' The dowager raised her hands in apology. 'But I had no idea, when I made my request to Justin, that the matter would become so complicated.'

Again, Ellie was no nearer to understanding this conversation than she had been a few minutes ago. 'And what request did you make of Just—the duke?'

'I merely—I had realised—' The dowager appeared uncharacteristically flustered as she quickly crossed the room to take both Ellie's hands in her own. 'There is no easy way to say this, my dear, so I shall simply state that Henry Rosewood was killed in battle exactly a year before you were born.'

Ellie literally felt all the colour drain from her cheeks as she absorbed the full import of this statement. Henry Rose-wood could not have been her father.

She stumbled slightly as she pulled her hands free of the dowager's to drop down into the armchair she had earlier refused. Tears blurred her vision as she looked up at Justin accusingly. 'You knew about this.' It was a statement, not a question.

A nerve pulsed in his tightly clenched jaw. 'Yes.'

'How long have you known?'

'A week, no more. Eleanor—'

'No! Don't!' She lifted a restraining hand as Justin would have moved to her side, grateful when he halted in his tracks. She needed to—had to somehow try to assimilate exactly what this all meant to her.

Obviously she was Muriel's daughter. But not Henry's. And if not Henry's daughter, then whose—?

Her horrified gaze moved to Litchfield, who still lay unconscious upon the rug in front of the fire. No! She could not bear to be the daughter of such a dreadful man! It would be worse, even, than learning that she was illegitimate—

'I am your father, Eleanor.'

Ellie was barely aware of the combined gasps of all the St Just family as she raised her stunned gaze to look at Lord Bryan Anderson, the Earl of Richmond.

'I am your father, Eleanor,' he repeated as he came down on his haunches beside her, his hazel gaze unwavering upon her face as he took the limpness of her chilled hands in his. 'I swear to you I did not know it until a few hours ago, but I know now, beyond a shadow of a doubt, that I am your father. And you can have no idea how very much it pleases me that I have a daughter,' he added emotionally, tears glistening in his eyes.

Ellie continued to stare at him for several long breath-less seconds, looking for—hoping to see—some likeness to herself in his face. His eyes were a mixture of blue, green and brown, his features both strong and handsome, his hair that premature shock of white, his form both fit and mus-cled for a man his age.

But she saw nothing, no likeness to herself, to confirm that he was, indeed, her real father.

'My hair was once as auburn as your own,' the earl sup-plied, as if he knew her thoughts. 'I received a severe shock in my mid-twenties, which turned my hair completely white. You see, my wife of only a few months was involved in a hunting accident, from which she never fully recovered, physically or mentally. We never had a true marriage again.'

'So you were married when you and my mother—when the two of you—'

'I was,' he confirmed grimly.

Darkness started to blur the edges of her vision as the shock of it all suddenly hit her with the force of a blow, that darkness growing bigger, becoming deeper, as she felt her-self begin to slip away.

'Out of my way, Richmond!' she heard Justin shout, be-fore strong arms encircled her just as the darkness com-pletely engulfed her and she collapsed into unconsciousness.

'For goodness' sake, stop your infernal pacing, Justin, and go up to the girl if that is what you wish to do!'

Justin made no effort to cease his 'infernal pacing' as he shot his grandmother a narrow-eyed glare. 'I am the last person Eleanor wishes to see just now.'

'Nonsense!' the dowager dismissed briskly. 'Once she

is over the shock she will be gratified to know she is the daughter of an earl—'

'The illegitimate daughter of an earl!'

'I am sure Richmond will wish to acknowledge her as his own.'

'Whether he does or he does not, I very much doubt that Eleanor will thank any of us for our part in this,' Justin muttered dully. 'In just a few short minutes she has gone from believing her father to be Henry Rosewood, to that reprobate Dryden Litchfield, only to finally learn that her father is actually the Earl of Richmond.'

Doctor Franklyn had been called to attend to Eleanor, first giving a minute of his time to declare that Litchfield was only suffering from a badly bruised jaw from Richmond's blow. After which Justin and Richmond had both very much enjoyed telling that obnoxious gentleman exactly why it was he would not be talking of this evening's events, or those of the past, to anyone. The information they had both gathered, on Litchfield's behaviour this past twenty years or more, was more than enough to put him behind bars if charges were levelled against him, several other reputable ladies having also suffered at his brutal treatment. Knowledge they would prefer did not become known to the public, but which they would quite happily testify to in private, if necessary.

As for Eleanor, this last few minutes was too much for any young woman to accept with equanimity. Damn it, he was having trouble coming to terms with Richmond as her father, so how could she possibly be expected to do so!

Nor, knowing her as he did, would she easily forgive his own part in keeping such knowledge from her.

Justin had carried Eleanor upstairs after she had fainted,

and she was upstairs in her bedchamber even now, being attended to by Dr Franklyn and watched over like a protective hawk with its newly hatched chick by Bryan Anderson.

By her real father…who had a lot more authority to be there than Justin did.

The earl had spared only enough time, as they waited in Eleanor's bedchamber for the doctor to arrive, to tell them all briefly how it had come about.

Richmond's own enquiries into the events in India twenty years ago had resulted in more than just the damning information he had gathered on Dryden Litchfield. He had received a letter earlier this evening, from the wife of a fellow officer who had also been a particular friend of Muriel Rosewood, in which she had stated that Muriel had given birth to a baby girl exactly nine months after leaving India. Exactly nine months after Bryan Anderson had spent a single night with Muriel before she sailed back to England.

'Do not judge him too harshly, Justin,' his mother now advised as she placed her hand gently on his arm. 'He had already lived five years of hell with his deranged wife when this occurred. It is all too easy, during wars and hardship, for such things as this to occur. And let us not forget that Lord Anderson offered Muriel refuge in his own home following Litchfield's attack upon her.'

'Before then bedding her himself!'

'Eventually, yes,' she allowed. 'But you know him well enough to realise it would not have been without her consent. And, as a woman, I can tell you exactly why Muriel would have welcomed the attentions of a gentleman such as Bryan Anderson. She needed his physical reassurance, that pleasanter memory, to take home with her to England after suffering Litchfield's brutality.'

'It would seem that she took far more than a pleasant memory back to England with her!' Justin's hands were clenched into fists at his sides.

His mother nodded. 'And decided, quite admirably, that it was not fair to tell Richmond of the child she was expecting. Think, Justin, of the dilemma it would have placed him in if he had known, how he would then be torn between loyalty to his deranged wife and the woman who was now the mother of his daughter. I am sorry I did not know Muriel better when she was married to Frederick, as she is to be commended for her unselfish actions twenty years ago. She and Richmond were not in love, after all, had merely been thrown together in adverse circumstances, which then led to the birth of a daughter.'

Justin sighed. 'I am not the one who will need convincing of the rightness or otherwise of that, Mama.' Eleanor was his only concern in this matter. A tenderness of feeling he knew was not returned—indeed, he had every reason to think that she now wished him to Hades for his part in keeping the truth of the past from her!

Certainly he had not been the first person she had asked for once she had recovered from her faint. No, Richmond had that honour.

'As this seems to be an evening of confessions…'

Justin's lids narrowed as he glanced sharply at his grandmother. 'What other deep dark secrets are we to be made privy to now?'

The dowager pursed her lips. 'I am afraid I was not completely truthful with you last week regarding my own health, my boy.'

He rolled his eyes. 'It was all a ruse, was it not, Grandmama? Another effort on your part to persuade me into residing at Royston House once more? To eventually get used to the idea of matrimony?'

The dowager's eyes widened. 'You knew all the time?'

'I was certain that was the case, yes,' he allowed with a wry smile. 'You hadn't allowed anyone else to be present in the room, even Eleanor, during Dr Franklyn's visits. Nor am I so lacking in intelligence that I did not see the vast improvement in your health within hours of my having moved back here. Tell me, Grandmama, how did you achieve the effect of the whitened cheeks that night you sent for me?'

The dowager gave a sniff of satisfaction. 'A little extra face powder was most convincing, I thought.'

'Oh, most,' Justin conceded drily. 'No doubt your letters to my mother these past months, informing her of Eleanor's introduction into society, and my own presence back at Royston House, were also part of your machinations?'

'You are being impolite, Justin!' The dowager looked suitably affronted.

'But truthful?'

'Perhaps,' she allowed airily.

He grinned. 'Well I am sorry to disappoint you, Grandmama, but my own reasons for moving back to Royston House had absolutely nothing to do with your pretence of ill health.'

'I am well aware of it.' She gave an imperious nod of her head.

He raised his brows. 'You are?'

'Oh, yes.' She smiled smugly.

'Grandmama—' He broke off as Dr Franklyn appeared in the doorway of the Blue Salon where they all waited for news of Eleanor. 'Well, man, do not just stand there, tell us how she is!' Justin barked.

'Miss Rosewood is quite recovered now,' the doctor assured. 'And she shows no signs of suffering any lasting effects from her faint.'

'And?' Justin scowled darkly.

'And what, your Grace?' the doctor replied.

'Did she not ask for—for anyone?' he pressed urgently.

The doctor's brow cleared. 'Ah, yes, I believe she did ask if she might speak with—' Justin had already left the room, taking the stairs two steps at a time, before the doctor had finished his statement '—the dowager.'

Chapter Eighteen

Ellie was quite unprepared for the way Justin burst into her bedchamber, only seconds after the doctor had departed.

'What do you mean by entering Ellie's bedchamber un-invited, Royston?' Richmond frowned his disapproval of the younger man's actions.

To say this past hour had been…life-changing for her would be to severely understate the matter. To learn that Henry Rosewood, a man she had never known, was not her father after all and that Lord Bryan Anderson, the Earl of Richmond, was, had come as a complete shock to her.

But once she had got used to the idea, it was actually a pleasant one.

She should perhaps continue to be shocked, distraught, and take weeks, if not months, to acclimatise herself to the things she had learnt this evening, to all that Lord Anderson had gently explained had befallen her poor mother in India twenty years ago.

Except Ellie found she could not summon any of those emotions…

It had always been difficult for her to feel anything more than respect and affection for the man who had died before she was even born, and Frederick St Just had never been more to her than her mother's second husband, a man with whom Muriel was so obviously not happy. For Ellie to now learn that she had a father, after all, and such a well-liked and respected man as the Earl of Richmond, was, she now realised, more wonderful than she could have imagined.

It had also given her hope that perhaps her changed circumstances, despite her illegitimacy, meant that she and Justin were not so socially far apart as she had always believed them to be. The earl had already told her he was going to publicly acknowledge her as his daughter and he was influential enough to carry off the scandal with aplomb.

Although the fact that Justin had just walked into her bedchamber, as if he had a perfect right to do so, obviously did not sit well with her brand-new father!

Justin ignored the older man's disapproval, having eyes only for Eleanor as she sat on the stool in front of the dressing-table; her face was still very pale, her eyes dark-green smudges and the freckles on her nose very noticeable against that pallor. 'Should you not be in bed?' he demanded as he quickly crossed the room to stand in front of her.

'I only fainted—'

'You have received a severe shock.'

'But a pleasant one.' She turned to reach up and clasp her father's hand, the earl returning the shyness of her smile with one of warm affection. 'Justin, may I present my father, Lord Bryan Anderson, the Earl of Richmond. Father, Justin St Just, the Duke of Royston.'

Justin's admiration for this young woman grew to chest-bursting proportions at the gracious elegance and ease with which she made the introductions. Most females in Eleanor's present situation would be having fits of hysterical vapours by now, crying and carrying on to an unpleasant degree. But she was made of much sterner stuff than that, had so obviously absorbed, and then swiftly accepted her change in circumstances.

'Richmond.' He nodded stiffly to the older man.

'Royston.' The earl's nod was just as terse.

Eleanor gave a puzzled smile. 'I thought the two of you were friends?'

'We were,' the two men said together.

She looked taken aback. 'What has happened to change that?'

Richmond gave a humourless smile. 'Will you tell her, Royston, or shall I?'

Justin's frustration was evident as he glared at the earl; this was not the way he had wanted to approach this. 'I am afraid, Eleanor, that your father seems to be aware of the closeness that exists between us and he is feeling protective and disapproving, to say the least.'

'Oh,' she gasped, her cheeks flushing a becoming rose.

'It would be impossible not to know,' Richmond rasped, 'when the very air seems to quiver and shift whenever the two of you are in the same room together!'

'Oh,' Eleanor breathed again.

'The question is, what are you going to do about it, Royston?' Richmond said bullishly.

'Oh, but—'

'I,' Justin cut in firmly over Eleanor's protest, 'am going to do what any gentleman should in these circumstances, and ask for the honour of your daughter's hand in marriage.'

Ellie stared up at Justin, sure that he had gone mad; her

circumstances might have changed, but her heartfelt desire, her determination to marry a man who loved her as deeply as she loved him, had not changed in the slightest!

In truth, she loved Justin, more than anything else in the world, just as she was certain she would continue to do so for the rest of her life. Nor could she deny that she had felt a brief thrill just now—a very brief thrill—at the thought of becoming his wife. Until good sense had prevailed and Ellie accepted that Justin had made the offer only because honour dictated he do so and not because he loved her, too.

She stood up. 'I would like to answer that request for myself, your Grace,' she said stiffly, her chin raised proudly high. 'And my answer in no. Thank you. Nor is there any reason why you need make such an offer.' She looked at her father. 'There may be a detectable *frisson* in the air whenever we are together, Father, but I assure you, nothing has happened that the duke should ever feel he must propose marriage for.'

'If you would allow us a few minutes alone, Richmond?' Justin quirked a questioning brow at her father.

'My answer will not change—'

'Richmond?' Justin spoke ruthlessly over Ellie's objection.

'I believe, Eleanor, that it is in your own best interest to listen to what Royston wishes to say to you,' the earl encouraged, satisfied that Justin wanted to do the honourable thing by his daughter.

Her lips pressed stubbornly together. 'My answer will not change, no matter what he has to say. And Justi—his Grace is well aware of the reasons why it will not.'

'It is always a bad sign when she resorts to calling me that,' Justin confided, smiling ruefully.

Richmond did not return the smile. 'You understand that I will fully accept whatever decision Eleanor makes?'

He sobered. 'I do.'

'Very well,' the earl said briskly. 'I will rejoin the two ladies downstairs. I am sure I must still have some explaining to do in that quarter.' He grimaced.

Eleanor looked distraught. 'There is no need for you to leave—'

'There is every need, damn it!' Justin's temper was not as even as he wished and he made a visible effort to suppress it.

'I will not leave the house until I have spoken to you again,' Richmond reassured Eleanor gruffly as he bent to kiss her lightly on the cheek. He gave Justin a warning frown before crossing over to the door and closing it quietly behind him as he left.

Leaving a tense and awkward silence behind him.

A silence Justin knew, as Eleanor glared at him so mutinously, that it was his responsibility to fill. 'Will you at least agree to hear what I have to say?'

Her eyes flashed deeply green. 'I do not see the point in it, when you are already aware that I refuse to marry any man whom I do not love and who does not love me.'

Justin continued to meet that stormy gaze as he answered her huskily. 'Yes, I am.'

She grimaced. 'There is your answer then.'

'What if I were to say I am already in love with you, and was willing to wait, in the hope that you would eventually fall in love with me too?'

Her face paled as she shook her head. 'You do not love me.'

Justin had spent years hiding his emotions behind a barrier of arrogance and cynicism, out of a desire, he now knew, not to be hurt and rejected again. There was no place between them for that barrier now.

Nor did he attempt to prevent that barrier from falling away from his emotions, as he moved down on one knee in front of her. 'I love you more than life itself, Eleanor Rosewood-Anderson,' he stated clearly. 'More than anything or anyone. If you feel anything for me at all, desire or even only liking, then would you please marry me and allow me the opportunity to show you my love, prove it to you, and perhaps one day persuade you into loving me in return?'

Ellie felt numb as she stared down at him, sure that this usually proud man could not just have declared on bended knee that he was in love with her and that he wished to make her his duchess.

'There will never be anyone else for me, Eleanor,' he continued fervently at her continued silence. 'Much as I did not want to ever fall in love with any woman, I know that I love you beyond life itself. I think I've been in love with you since the night of my grandmother's illness when you summoned me here—which was not a true illness, by the way, but a wilful machination on her part to persuade me into moving back here—and then you brought me to task for my tardiness.'

'The dowager was not really ill?' Ellie found it safer to focus on that part of his statement rather than those other wonderful—unbelievable!—things he was saying to her.

'Not in the least,' Justin said with a twinkle. 'Nor was it my true reason for moving back to Royston House.'

'What was your true reason?' Ellie's heart was now beating so loudly in her chest she felt sure he must be able to hear it. Justin had said that he loved her. More than anyone and anything. Beyond life itself!

'To protect you,' he revealed grimly. 'From Litchfield and other men like him.' He sighed deeply before admitting, 'Also I know now that I was beside myself with jealously of the attentions being shown to you by so many younger men. It was my intention to thwart those attentions as often as possible.'

Justin had been jealous? The proud, the haughty, the arrogant, the self-assured Duke of Royston, the man who gave the impression of needing no one, had been *jealous* of the attentions shown to her by dandified young boys like Lord Charles Endicott? Did Justin not know—could he not *see* that no other man existed for her but him? That they never had, and never would?

'Oh, Justin…!' Eleanor sank gracefully to her knees in front of him before raising her hands to cup either side of his dearly beloved face. 'I have *loved* you for months now. Have fallen even more deeply *in love* with you this past week or more. I will always love you, Justin. I could not have responded to you as I do, have made love with you in the way we have, if I was not already in love with you!'

Such an expression of joy lit up his face at her declaration, a glow in the deep blue of his eyes, his cheeks flushing, the wideness of his smile making him appear almost boyish. 'How much I love you, Eleanor!' He swept her into his arms, cradling her against him as if she were the most precious being upon the earth. 'Please marry me and be my duchess,' he pleaded as he moved back slightly to look at her with all of that love shining in his eyes. 'I promise you will never ever have cause to regret it.'

'Yes! Oh, yes, Justin, I will marry you!' Eleanor's expression was as joyous as his as she launched herself into his arms and the two of them became lost in the wonder of their love for each other.

* * *

One floor below them, in the Blue Salon, Edith St Just smiled with a quiet inner satisfaction at the knowledge that, on the morrow, she would be able to show her two closest friends the name of the young lady, written on a piece of paper to be held in safekeeping by Lady Jocelyn's butler, in which she had predicted who would become Royston's duchess.

That name was Miss Eleanor Rosewood...

* * * * *

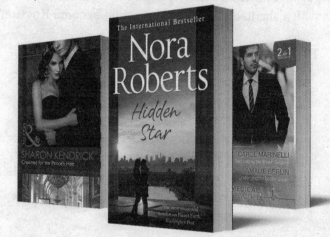